NOAH'S BOY

Sarah A. Hoyt

NOAH'S BOY

This is a work of fiction. All the characters and events portrayed in this book are fictional, and any resemblance to real people or incidents is purely coincidental.

A Baen Books Original

Baen Publishing Enterprises
P.O. Box 1403
Riverdale, NY 10471
www.baen.com

ISBN: 978-1-4516-3904-9

Cover art by Tom Kidd

First printing, July 2013

Distributed by Simon & Schuster
1230 Avenue of the Americas
New York, NY 10020

Library of Congress Cataloging-in-Publication Data

Hoyt, Sarah A.
  Noah's boy / Sarah A. Hoyt.
      pages cm
  ISBN 978-1-4516-3904-9 (trade pb)
1. Friendship—Fiction. 2. Dragons—Fiction. I. Title.
  PS3608.O96N83 2013
  813'.6—dc23
                                                      2013005978

10 9 8 7 6 5 4 3 2 1

Pages by Joy Freeman (www.pagesbyjoy.com)
Printed in the United States of America

NOAH'S BOY

⇥ CHAPTER 1 ⇤

The sun was setting in a splendor of red and gold over the Rocky Mountains, glistening like a fire over the remaining snow on the mountain tops when the young woman drove into Goldport in a brand new red pickup truck.

No one watching would have been particularly struck by her or by the pickup truck.

Nestled against the peaks of the Rockies, Goldport had once been a settlement of miners and frontiersmen and it was now a city of students and computer technicians, with a Victorian core forming the center of a town that was gentrifying and growing, acquiring a few spectacular glass-fronted high-rises and a vibrant art and tourism scene.

In that environment, a college-age woman driving a four-wheel vehicle was the most common of sights. That she was Asian or partly Asian would startle no one since Goldport was host to a vibrant Asian community. And no one would have thought anything was particularly strange when she parked outside a low slung building atop of which a neon sign blinked the words THREE LUCK DRAGON.

Someone might have thought it a little odd, though, when she entered the shiny red lacquered door and a hand reached out to the window and turned the OPEN sign to CLOSED, right at the beginning of the dinner hour.

Beatrice Bao Ryu, better known to her friends as Bea Ryu, didn't find it funny, when they closed the restaurant as she came in. She found it distinctly unsettling. But she managed a small smile, striking a pose of nonchalance as she said, "I don't actually intend to shift and start a battle with Himself in here, you know?" Her warm Georgia accent drawled out onto what seemed for a moment to be the uncomprehending server—a skinny young man with Asian features. But he bowed to her, looking scared. "No," he said, his accent less obvious but no more Asian. But he didn't flip the sign to OPEN again. Instead, he led her to a door next to the one marked RESTROOMS and knocked politely, then said something in rapid-fire Chinese.

Bea didn't understand it. Her maternal grandmother was Chinese, but her maternal grandfather was tall, blond and of Germanic ancestry. As for Bea's father, he was the great-grandson of Japanese immigrants to the United States. Bea's parents spoke English and their daughter had never learned either Chinese or Japanese till college, where she'd taken two years of Japanese. All of which meant she could catch the occasional word and say almost nothing.

A curt Chinese-accented voice answered from inside the mysterious door. The server opened the door and remained bowed while Bea walked into the room.

If she'd thought about it, although she'd never done so specifically, she'd have expected the place to be a sort of throne room, perhaps with some ancient gilded chair in the center.

That would have fit with what she'd read in the letters in her father's desk drawer.

Whatever this criminal organization was, it dressed its leader in very pretty words: "Himself," "Revered One," "Ancient One." It seemed to denote silk and gold and the sort of culture that required both.

Instead, the room she entered was small—only big enough to contain a desklike table and two chairs, one on either side. It might have been an interrogation cell, except that the person on the other side of the table had a vast metal bowl in front of him into which he was shelling peas. With a pile of unshelled peas to the right of the bowl, and a pile of shells to the left, the sleeves of his white button-down rolled up to his elbows, and his hands working busily at the homely task, the man could have been any of a hundred middle-aged Chinese employees at a hundred different Chinese restaurants.

Bea cleared her throat. "I'm sorry," she said. "I think I've come to the wrong room. You see, I came to talk to the Ancient—"

The man looked up and Bea took a step back and caught her breath, not scared exactly but startled, because his eyes were older than the middle-aged face. They were older than any face. Looking out of barely creased features, they appeared old as time and twice as deep, as though he'd existed through the uncounted ages of mankind and kept track of every slip, every error humans had made on the way to civilization.

"Oh," Bea said.

The man said three brief words in Chinese and then his eyes widened, as though in shock. He closed his eyes a moment. "You don't speak Chinese." It wasn't a question. He raised an eyebrow. "Japanese, then?"

She cleared her throat. "I— No. You see, I took two years in college, but—"

He shrugged, dismissing the matter. "It's of little importance," he said. "Our people have spoken many tongues throughout the centuries. What we speak doesn't matter, except for comfort and a sense of heritage." His own English was almost unaccented, save for a faint hint of something British and very highbred. "What I need from you requires no great linguistic competency."

Bea swallowed hard. She'd rehearsed this, all the long drive from Atlanta, and the nights in motel rooms, but somehow, suddenly it seemed very hard to say the words she'd planned. It was the look of immense age in the man's eyes, she thought. But she swallowed again and said, her voice sounding strangely wavering in her own ears, "I don't care what you require from me. I came to tell you to leave my parents alone—to leave Dad's business alone."

The man looked up and frowned a little. His hands resumed his work of shelling peas. "Your parents," he said at last, "finally saw the light and sent you over. Now they have nothing more to fear from my people."

She shook her head. "My parents did not send me over. Not

that it matters. I have no intention of doing whatever you want me to do. And why you think—"

"Sit down," the man said, gently.

Bea shook her head. Those soft words had sounded like an order, but she had no intention of obeying. In fact, despite all her best intentions and everything she'd decided to tell this creature about himself and his criminal organization, face to face with him, she found the best she could do was disobey. Just—disobey and hold on to her rebellion with every fiber of her being, even as she felt him trying to bend her to his will.

He raised his eyebrows at her. "Surely," he said, "your parents have told you what you owe me."

"No," she said. "Owe you? I don't even know who you are except someone who has been messing with Dad's business."

"Truly? Then you don't know we're an organization of dragon shapeshifters?"

"Sure," she said. "I know that. But the only reason I even knew you existed and that you wanted something from me was that I overheard Mom and Dad talking. I found out you were the reason Dad's office got vandalized and about the calls to his clients. The reason Dad has had so much trouble keeping afloat as a veterinarian. And that to make it stop you wanted me to come and...and do something. I wasn't sure what."

"I see. Well, you came. That's what matters."

"I came to tell you it must stop."

The man looked up at her and smiled. "Ah. Spirit will serve you well, but do sit down. I have a long explanation to make, and I despise having to look up to do it."

She hesitated, but the truth was she wanted to know why anyone, even a criminal organization of shifters would require her presence urgently enough to interfere with her father's business to get it.

She knew she was attractive. She had a mirror. She knew that the combination of her varied heritage had resulted in an oval face, large green eyes, and a pleasant combination of other features, all of which became even more striking with her long, glossy black hair. Since about the age of sixteen, she'd become used to looks of admiration from the male half of the species.

But she had no illusions about the full extent of her beauty. She was pretty and striking, but not so out of the normal leagues in attractiveness that dreams of modeling had ever occurred to her. The campus of the college where she studied art could count at least a hundred women more beautiful than her.

None of her other characteristics were any further out of the ordinary. She was smart and talented, but was not going to set the world on fire with either her intellect or even with her art talent. She hoped, someday, to make a good living in commercial art and design, but that was about it. So why would this criminal organization want her that badly?

She knew it had something to do with her turning into a dragon, but it was just now and then. Occasionally. Truly, hardly ever, since she'd turned twenty and learned to control herself.

"So?" Bea asked. "Why is it so important that I come here? And why do you think I should obey you? Or that I owe you anything?"

The man smiled. It was a surprisingly engaging smile. It seemed to her as he narrowed his eyes that a sense of amusement touched them too. "I think," he said, softly, "that I'm about to shock you very much. However, I trust you'll let me explain my motives before dismissing them."

She swallowed, wondering what he meant by that.

"Forget what I said about owing me. That was . . . You see, where I come from, it is assumed you owe your ancestors unusual respect, and I'm the ancestor of most of the dragon shifters alive today."

"That is hardly likely," she said. "I know all my grandparents, and I—"

"I am not your grandfather. Not even your great-grandfather. It's much . . . older than that. Thousands of years. How many, I'm afraid I've lost track."

"But that's imposs—"

"Please, Miss Ryu." He paused, his hands holding a pea pod over the bowl, looking at her. Then he said, "Hear me out."

It wasn't a command—or it shouldn't have been, spoken in that voice as soft as crackling flame. But she stopped and listened.

His nail ripped the pea pod apart and his finger swept down the green envelope, trickling glistening little globes into the bowl. "I have . . . that is . . . I don't suppose your parents told you that I am your ancestor on"—he seemed to be counting in his head—"your mother's mother's side and your father's mother's side."

"I don't understand," she said. "My father is Japanese and you—"

"Oh." He dropped another spent pea pod on the growing pile and made a gesture, either dismissing that restaurant or the entire world. "This is an identity of convenience," he said. "I told you my people predate most such things. Dragons—dragons belong to the whole world, even if our type is mostly of Asia. There are other types—"

He resumed shelling peas, now very fast and adroitly, as he spoke. "It is the immutable rule of our people that the Great Sky Dragon must be a descendant of the previous Great Sky Dragon in the male line. Unbroken male line. And that he must be a dragon shifter. We don't know why but that's how…that's how it works." Peas tinkled into the metal bowl like falling rain. A green smell filled the room. "That was me, the many times grandson of the Great Sky Dragon, growing up on the banks of the Yalu River at a time when—" He shrugged. "It doesn't matter, except to say that in my very long life, and sometimes I forget how many thousands of years it is exactly, I've had wives, concubines and lovers, but—" He looked up and smiled at her. "There is no reason to blush. In a life as long as mine, well, there will be friendship and love, and, occasionally, less honorable associations. But what I meant to say is that of all my connections with human and shifter, many daughters were born. My line is threaded through dragonkind, Ryus and Lungs and many other family names are honorably descended from me. But in that time, only one son was ever born to me." He looked up again, and amusement pulled at the corner of his mouth. "He was not born of a normal marriage. It was more…a treaty and a ritual pairing. Years ago, there was a…another dragon tribe. Near the frozen…ah…I believe what is now called Scandinavia. Their ruler was a female. She was called the Queen of the West, as I was the King of the East. We made a treaty, to keep our people from fighting each other. There was a symbolic marriage. This resulted in a son, who was not a shifter. I thought our blood didn't work together, that we'd never have children who were shifters from that line, so I ignored it.

"Until someone stole the Pearl of Heaven and I found that while I could touch his mind, I could not control him as I could other dragon shifters. And it wasn't just because he had dragon blood from the tribe of the west, for I could sense he had my blood too. I had people trace back through his ancestry and found that he was descended from that long-ago forgotten son. And he is my only male descendant on the unbroken male line, the only one with a power close to my own. The only one who can carry my burden. The one who *will* carry my burden."

A fleeting *poor bastard* crossed Bea's mind, but she did her best to look attentive and blank.

"His name is Tom Ormson and he is..." The man she was now sure was the Great Sky Dragon shrugged. "Very young. I think in his early twenties. He lives here in town and owns a diner, The George."

"Yes?" Bea said.

"I'd like you to marry him."

For a while, Bea was speechless. She'd heard of arranged marriages, of course, particularly in Asia, but her parents were American and thoroughly modern, and they would no more think of contracting a marriage for her than they would think of binding her feet. When she found her voice, she said, "And he's agreed to this?"

"Oh, no. He doesn't even know about it." A frown pulled at the old dragon's mouth. "In fact, I think he has plans of marrying a panther shifter. He's living with her. Completely unsuitable, of course. Her people are not our people."

"But you think he'll agree?" Bea asked.

"I think he'll tell me to go to hell," the old dragon said, and looked up with a faint smile. "And so will his girlfriend. She's feisty enough, and she has no fear of me."

"But... you want me to marry him? You said you can't make him do what you wish, so..."

"No. You'll have to find how to make him do what I wish."

Bea stood up. Her legs were trembling. She couldn't let her father lose the business he'd worked for all his life, but neither could she agree to this. The elderly man-dragon wanted her to seduce a total stranger who was in a serious relationship. No. There were limits to what she was willing to do, even for her beloved father. They'd get tired of trying to force his hand eventually. They'd leave them alone. Bea couldn't sell herself for life for the sake of her father. That was prostitution and slavery, combined.

Standing, she glared down at the Great Sky Dragon. She could feel power rolling off him, though she could not have explained what type of power or how she felt it.

"I'm sorry," she said. "You've got the wrong person. I'm sure there's someone else you can call on, who will be willing to do it. I don't want to trick a man who is in love with someone else into marrying me. I don't want an arranged marriage."

There was a long silence. "I'll let myself out," Bea said.

"Stay!" It wasn't so much an order as a sudden plea. She'd turned to leave the room and now turned again. The Great Sky Dragon was looking up at her, and his eyes held an expression she'd have thought impossible: raw, undiluted fear.

"Don't you understand?" the Great Sky Dragon said, his voice low. "Do you think this is something I'd want, throwing an untrained girl at a stubborn boy and hoping for the best? Compared to me you're nothing but babies. I thought he could have his panther girl and be happy, and when it dissolved in a century or two, then I could guide him towards a marriage that will produce dragons.

"But there is a trial coming and I'm not sure I can— If I'm not here, he'll need to be married to one of our own, recognizably our own. He doesn't look like our kind. My people will rebel at his orders. And it will need to be known that he will have dragon children, to rule after him. In the battle ahead, there might not be thousands of years to spawn."

Bea didn't realize she'd sat down, but her trembling legs were about to not let her stand up anymore. "Why would he be giving orders?"

"My grandfather told me of the dragons-beyond-the-stars who could—who would one day attack the Earth." The Great Sky Dragon shrugged. "I always thought it was a legend, nothing more. But—lately I've had signs that it is not. There is a great power out there, encircling, trying to remove me, trying to..." He frowned. "I think trying to attack my people. I've lived very long, and death doesn't scare me, but—"

"But?"

"But when I go, all my power—and the destiny of my people— will fall on the head of Tom Ormson, a stranger, raised outside our traditions." He held up a hand to keep her from interrupting. "Oh, I know, you also have not been taught our traditions, but everyone knows your parents, both of them, are descended from my firstborn daughter. They will fall in line. And you can help your husband through the trial to come by winning for him the respect of our people."

⊰ CHAPTER 2 ⊱

Riverside Park, at the edge of Goldport, was a thrill whose time had passed. Competing with the various flags, gardens and other franchised, national attractions which specialized in rides based on the latest technology, its main advantage was being cheap and therefore it appealed mostly to the young, the recent immigrants and the impecunious.

Slumbering quietly at the edge of a small lake—the river in the name being one of those mysteries no one could explain—it displayed a flashy entrance tower that dated from the orientalist period of the nineteenth century when pseudo arabesques had been in vogue. It appeared quite nice at night, when bright little lights outlined its contours making it look like something out of a fairy tale and when no one could see its flaking paint and the parts that were boarded up.

Its vast central pavilion, which once had hosted shows by all the big bands and dancing by all the fashionable local couples, now housed bumper cars. The hippodrome that had seen horse races back in the middle of the twentieth century had long since closed. Its sun-bleached carcass, encircled in a tall wall that stood, as incongruous and forlorn as the bones of a long-dead dinosaur, was posted all over with signs warning visitors off exploring its dark interior.

Not that many visitors were interested. Most came for the corny spider rides, the colorful dragon roller coaster, and the not very horrible house of horrors. A few aficionados and romantic souls came for the wooden roller coaster or the turn-of-the—twentieth—century merry-go-round.

But right then, early May, the only people in the park were there to work. Teams of men fanned out up the slope and down the path, cutting down the knee-high grass and calling to each other in Spanish.

Jason Cordova straightened up, as the mower he'd been pushing choked on the knee-high weeds. *Man, the least they could do is get some riding mowers. Rent them or something. And if not, then with grass like this, we should be using scythes.*

Despite the relatively mild weather, sweat glued his T-shirt to his body and his jeans felt like they had insects climbing up inside them. He knew it was probably his imagination, but he still had to suppress an urge to scratch and an even stronger urge to take off his jeans and shake them.

He listened to the chatter around him and frowned. *It's like they went to the day labor office and picked everyone with a Spanish name.* Which was probably exactly what they'd done. And it wasn't that Jason didn't speak Spanish. He did. He'd studied it in college. For all the good it was doing him in the current economy.

A shout that he couldn't quite understand but that seemed to mean he should be getting back to work made him say, "Yeah, yeah," as he started pulling the cord to restart the mower. But the motor only sputtered, and then he realized the shout hadn't been at him.

Instead, his coworkers were shouting to each other and running towards an area where tall grass remained. *Oh, what the hell,* Jason thought, as he ambled in that direction, wondering exactly what they'd found there. A credit card? Someone's illegal weed patch? Or, judging by the trend of the conversations he'd heard before, and what seemed to really interest all his coworkers, perhaps there was a girl there who'd somehow lost all her clothes?

Before he got to the center of the excitement, he saw two of the guys running away, their faces more green than olive, and another one throwing up into a recently mowed patch.

Jason jogged forward the next few steps. And froze. Laying on the trampled tall grass was one his coworkers. He was small, probably Mexican. What remained of his white T-shirt was torn and covered in red-black blood. The lower half of his body was unrecognizable—his stomach torn open, the guts spilling. It looked like something had eaten a good portion of the man's insides.

Jason would never know quite how it happened, but he found himself throwing up, too, right beside the tall grass. But as he straightened, wiping his mouth on the back of his leather gloves, he realized there were a lot fewer men around. Like . . . none. Though he could see one or two in the distance, jumping the fence, and another desperately swimming across the lake.

Oh, good God, he thought, as he called aloud, "Stay, don't go. We must report this to the police." Which he realized was exactly the wrong thing to say, as they ran even faster.

A trail of moving grass near at hand called his attention, and he rushed there, determined not to face the police alone. "Stop," he said. But then realized it wasn't one of his coworkers he was looking at. It wasn't any human. It had to be the largest feral dog he'd ever seen. Well . . . feral something. Immense, beastly, its maw stained with blood, it looked like what happens to big bad wolves who die and don't go to heaven.

Jason felt his body clench and twist. His mouth contorting, he made an effort to speak, as he managed to pull off his jeans and T-shirt before they got shredded. "Nice doggie," he said.

Rafiel felt like he was going stark, raving mad.

Okay, so no murder investigation—or in this case, what seemed to be the investigation of death by misadventure—was ever a good thing. Ever.

Goldport wasn't exactly a crime capital, but as one of four senior investigators in its serious crimes unit, Rafiel saw his share of the seamy underside: thefts, break-ins, the occasional drunken Saturday night mutual shoot-out, and the share of drug traffic that couldn't be avoided anywhere these days. They even had murders—quite a few recently.

But on this particular Friday afternoon, he'd been finishing his paperwork, and giving some thought to the girl his parents had arranged for him to go out with that night. His parents—heck, his entire family—were anxious to see him matched up. Nearing thirty and living in your parents' house was not how the story should go. Particularly not when you were a successful police officer. But Rafiel's parents should know better.

They knew that their son shifted into a lion at the drop of a hat, or sometimes even without any hats dropping. They knew he lived in fear of hurting someone while shifted, and also that normal people, who didn't change shapes, wouldn't understand that he remained throughout more than half human: that in either form he tried to do the best he could and serve justice.

What did they think would happen if a woman came home to find her husband—or fiancé—had changed into a giant jungle cat? Did they think she would take it as an inconvenient but endearing thing? *Oh, well, he's a lion shifter, but at least he makes good coffee?*

He could only imagine his parents' desire for grandchildren had overwhelmed their common sense, leaving him with the task of taking this "daughter of old friends" on a first date, being polite and nice but cold, so she wouldn't feel too disappointed when he never called again.

Some days he wished he didn't know there were female shifters in the world, people with whom, theoretically, he could share both sides of his nature. He also wished he were unaware that Kyrie Smith, one of his two best friends, shifted into a panther. Some days he wished he could help thinking that he and Kyrie could have made a go of it, if the other one of his best friends hadn't been around. But Tom Ormson was around. And though he was quite unsuitable for Kyrie as a shifter—shifting into a dragon—he was very compatible with Kyrie as a human.

Rafiel had had doubts about that, in the beginning, but once those two had gotten together, they'd stopped being individuals and become a whole that was bigger than the sum of its parts: they'd become Tomandkyrie, a composite creature more competent than either of them was separately, and so inseparable that he might as well try to come between Siamese twins.

What made things worse, was that Rafiel wasn't even sure he would have a chance with Kyrie if something happened to Tom. He had a feeling that a Rafielandkyrie creature would not be nearly as good as Tomandkyrie, and might in fact fail to gel at all. And besides, he liked Tom—the scruffy, scaly bastard that he was—and, if needed, he'd die ensuring nothing bad happened to Tom. The two of them had fought together enough, been through enough danger to develop a brother-in-arms camaraderie, stronger than any romance.

No. What Rafiel really needed to do was find a girl he could love and who wouldn't mind his shifting. And the last requirement cut down the population of eligibles to a negligible number, most of whom would live too far away for him to ever meet.

He'd been contemplating that when his afternoon got worse, with the phone call about the man found mauled. At Riverside Amusement Park—where, even at the height of the season, if one dropped a virus that selected for nonnative Spanish speakers, no one would catch it—a man had had some sort of death by misadventure and the police were called to investigate.

It had been hard to understand what the heck was going on, because the person calling it in kept lapsing into something that Rafiel suspected was Greek. But Rafiel had caught stuff about a mountain lion and Mexicans and—this was emphatic—definitely not the owner's fault.

Now he stood in the middle of Riverside, while a medic, who'd accompanied the police, patched up one of the workers: the only one remaining. Well, the only *live* one remaining.

Not far from them, in the long grass, a forensic team went over the victim: Hispanic, late twenties and dead. Very dead. According to the forensic team, several feet of intestine—and various other internal organs—were missing.

They hadn't found the mountain lion yet. But that wasn't the worst news. The guy who'd been mauled and was being patched up said it wasn't a mountain lion but more like a dog, but even that he wasn't sure of. He said it was a weird animal.

And Rafiel could smell shifter. It was a smell he'd decided only shifters could smell, metallic, with a salty tang, and unmistakable once you first smelled it. And it was all over the place.

"So, it was a dog?" he asked the guy who sat on the chipped cement bench by the closed spider ride—the big black apparatus with its cuplike seats frozen and vaguely threatening in the afternoon light.

The guy's name was Jason Cordova, notwithstanding which, he spoke English perfectly and without the slightest hint of an accent. His only Spanish words came flying out as the emergency medic bandaged his arm and shoulder, which had been mauled by something. Something with sharp teeth. His white T-shirt, smeared in blood, lay on the bench by his side.

Jason was dark enough to be some variety of Hispanic, though most of it, Rafiel thought, would be due to his working outside in the sun. He wore his hair short, with the tips dyed white-blond, and he looked at Rafiel, shook his head, then tried to shrug, which brought about another outbreak of Spanish, in which the word "Madre" featured prominently. "Thing looked like a dog," he said, at last, looking at Rafiel out of narrowed eyes, though they seemed to be narrowed more in pain than in suspicion. "But it didn't fight like any dog. And it didn't bite like any dog." He shook his head. "I was lucky I had my hunting knife, because the day labor office is in a bad area and— Anyway, I must have cut it halfway to pieces before it let me go. And its jaws were like . . . steel clamps."

"I've never seen a bite like this," said the medic who'd come with the ambulance Rafiel had called. He blinked grey eyes behind coke-bottle glasses. "I've treated all sorts of injuries, even people mauled by mountain lions." He looked at Jason. "You're very lucky to be alive."

"Yeah, I feel lucky," he said, in the tone that implied he didn't. "I'm unemployed, divorced, crashing on a friend's sofa and, in good months, making enough to pay for my own food and fuel, and now I'm going to have to pay for the ambulance someone called. It's not like the park has insurance."

The medic grinned, and started to put his stuff away in a little bag. "Nah, the park will pay. They don't want you to go to a hospital and have to show papers. I've sent the ambulance back anyway, so it's just my time." He stopped. "And I suppose you do have papers."

"Sure I have them. I was born in California, so I have a birth certificate," Jason said, sounding vaguely amused. "I suspect I was the only one. I mean of the workers. But I didn't tell the owners. They can't pay minimum wage or do all the paperwork stuff, and if I'd told them I wanted that, they'd never have hired me."

"Yeah, I won't tell them. You keep a watch on that. I disinfected as much as I could, but there might be something left in there. It's a deep wound. If you notice a ring of red form and start to expand, get yourself to emergency and fast. Oh, and . . ."

But Rafiel was no longer listening. Instead, he was smelling the air around him. It didn't much matter to him—or not exactly—whether the creature was a dog or a mountain lion, or some mutant, undefined creature.

What mattered—and this was very important—was that he could smell shifter in the area, all around, in fact. There was a sweet-metallic tangy scent that he knew all too well. He smelled it every day in his own clothes, rising from his own body. And he smelled it from Kyrie and Tom and the dozen or so shifters who frequented The George—the diner Kyrie and Tom owned together.

The thing was that the scent lingered in areas where shifters had been. Sometimes for hours. It had been so strong around the dead man, that Rafiel was sure the man had been a shifter. But was the killer a shifter or not?

It made all the difference. As Rafiel stood here, away from the scene, he could hear the forensic team discussing their findings in the blood-spattered area with long grass, where the body lay.

If the killer was just a wild animal on the loose, then Rafiel could let the team figure it out in their own way. There would be the routine police investigation, the normal adding up of evidence till they could take the case to trial and corner whoever was responsible for the animal being loose: police, park or perhaps the owner of the animal. Then whoever was responsible would be fined or given community service, or something similar.

In that case, Rafiel would function just as Officer Trall, a professional and well-trained police officer.

But if the killer had been a shifter *in* his shifted form, it all changed. Because a shifter who killed once, rarely stopped killing unless he were caught. And it wasn't as though Rafiel could bring the apparatus of the law to bear on him. You couldn't really tell a judge, "This isn't a dog, it's a werewolf."

Well, you could. But then they put you in a nice resting place, medicated to the eyeballs. And, given that Rafiel himself was a shifter lion, heaven only knew how the meds would affect his shifting. He might become a lion and eat a few nurses not-in-a-good-way. He took a long whiff of the air. There was the smell from the dead body, the smell around it, and another smell.

"Hey, something wrong? You allergic to something?" the medic asked.

And Rafiel became aware that he'd been sniffing for all he was worth, as though he expected to find his way with his nose. Which he probably could. In fact, he would swear the smell came from the path to the parking lot, past the closed-up hippodrome.

"Ragweed," he said automatically. It had the advantage of being true, not that it mattered. "So, could you write me an informal report on the wounds? In case I have to take this to trial."

"You can't take an animal to trial," the medic said. Then he grinned sheepishly. "Though I suppose you could take his owner. And maybe you should. But I bet you it doesn't have one. I bet you it's one of those wild animals that seem to show up further and further into town every year. Like that Komodo dragon that went around eating people—what was it? two years ago?—and did you hear about the bear who went through the trash dumpster behind the alcohol and tobacco kiosk on Fifteenth? He then ran through bar row, looking in dumpsters. When they tried to catch him, he ran through ten backyards and across five streets before being struck by a car as he ambled across the road in front of Conifer Park. And I bet you that they treated him and freed him, too, probably not too far from town. Ready to do the same again next year. A miracle he didn't kill someone."

Rafiel made a perfunctory nod and said, "Nothing we can do, eh? It's the way it is. But I still need that report."

"Right. I'll write up something. It won't be Shakespeare."

"No problem. Shakespeare didn't really report on medical conditions and it wouldn't do us any good to be told the wound is not as wide as a church door," Rafiel said. The intensity of the smell was driving him insane. It was separating itself into strands, too: the dead body, or the area around it, and a trail leading to the hippodrome and another...

He should—to follow proper procedure—go over to where the forensic team was working and see if there was anything else they needed. Instead, Rafiel frowned as Jason put his blood-spattered but intact T-shirt over his badly mauled body. At that moment, the shifter-smell hit Rafiel full in the face, and he stared, his mouth half open.

The medic was walking away, far enough along the path that he wouldn't hear anything that Rafiel or Jason said. Jason turned a puzzled and slightly weary face to Rafiel.

"Lucky you had your hunting knife, huh?" Rafiel said. "I don't suppose you want to show it to me?"

Jason blinked. A dark tide of red flooded behind his tanned skin. "I must have dropped it," he said. "Somewhere in the grass, I guess." And with a shrug, he continued, "Maybe your team will find it."

Rafiel sighed. He sat in the clear space of bench beside Jason. "I'd think *you* were the killer, you know, and that those wounds were received from whatever that poor bastard"—a head inclination towards the crime scene—"turned into, except that they say he's been dead since probably really early morning, before you came to work. They think he was one of the guys they hired yesterday, and he decided to bunk here for the night. And your wounds are fresh. So it's clear there's yet a third shifter around—or maybe merely a second, if that's only his smell around the corpse—but he's still around and you got those wounds in a shifted fight with him. Don't go telling me about a hunting knife. You might have cut the other shifter up pretty bad, but it was all teeth and claws, wasn't it?"

Silence went on so long, that if Rafiel couldn't smell the scent of shifter coming from Cordova—a scent made stronger by exertion, and mixed with that of his blood—he would have thought he was imagining it.

But then Cordova spoke, his voice very tired. "I see. The police know."

"Eh. This policeman knows," Rafiel said, inhaling for all he was worth, intent to detect a shift in adrenaline that would signal that the man was about to attack. Or shift and attack. It never came. The man had been taken by surprise. Isolated shifters often didn't realize a certain smell meant "shifter"; they just thought it was their own smell. But the surprise didn't necessarily translate to anger. Good. Rafiel extended his legs in front of him, doing his best to appear at ease.

Turning, he found that Cordova was staring at him, studying him. "What . . . do *you* change into?" the man asked at last.

"Lion. You?"

"Bear." And to what must have been sudden comprehension in Rafiel's face, "Hey, I'm broke, and I guess I like liquor? I don't know. I don't remember much when I'm already tipsy and then become . . . you know . . . That hike from the forest preserve about killed me too. Just happy we heal fast. And that the person who found me thought I'd got drunk and undressed while drunk, and got me clothes and food."

"I have a cell phone," Rafiel said, "strapped to my thigh with one of those plastic coil things. Stays in place even when I shift. That way, if I end up too far from where my clothes are, I can always call friends."

"Smart, that," Cordova said, and looked down at his feet. "Only you have to have friends who know, and I don't have those. Even my wife didn't know. She thought I kept disappearing and was having an affair, and when I didn't want to talk to her about it, she said I was emotionally unavailable." He shrugged.

They sat side by side a little while, then Cordova said, "But that guy, the dead one, I don't think he was shifter. I think the shifter-smell is from the killer. It's really strong around all that area, and it goes that way." He pointed the same way Rafiel had been smelling it.

"Could it be one of the other workers?" Rafiel asked. "Where did they go?"

A grin answered him. "It's as I told you before," he said. "They ran so fast, they're probably halfway to Mexico by now."

"Yeah, but what path did they take out of the park, do you remember?"

This got him a very odd look, as it should have, because Jason was not stupid. Clearly, from his diction, his vocabulary, the man was smart and well-educated. He stood up on visibly shaky legs. "Three of them went that way. And a bunch ran that way. And then a few ran that way."

He pointed in three directions, in which the park ended in a fence, bordering a little used road. Which made sense if you were an illegal worker trying to run away.

"Not that way?" Rafiel asked, pointing in the direction of the path to the parking lot.

Jason shook his head. "Nah. None of them had cars, you know? The owners picked us up in a truck." He hesitated a moment. "Say, you're not going to try to catch them or...?"

"I'm not INS," he said. "And if I caught them, there would only be a mess and they'd end up on the streets again."

"It's just," Jason said, gesturing with his head towards the ticket house where a motley group of people clustered, "that I don't think they have much choice." The people in the ticket house looked Greek and seemed to be the extended family of the owner of the park. They were arguing—or perhaps just talking—in very loud voices.

"The workers?" Rafiel asked.

"Any of them. The workers come because they're hired, and

these people hire them because they couldn't afford minimum wage much less all the deductions and things." He frowned. "The minimum wage law and the benefits and things, it's all very pretty on paper, but it's like legislating the weather, man; it does no good. All it does is make you think everything is fine until reality bites you some place or other."

Rafiel nodded and said, "So none of them went where the smell goes," he said. "Which means . . . Shit. There is definitely another shifter at large, isn't there?"

Cordova hesitated. He lifted his hand, then let it fall. He looked over his shoulder and all around, to make sure he was suitably isolated and that no one could hear him. Then he sighed. "Man, I don't want to tell you this. You look like you have troubles enough."

"What?"

"After . . . in the fight, you know . . . I had a pretty good grip on this dude, and I was biting and then . . ."

"And then?"

"He shifted and slipped out of my grasp," Jason said. "He just became this skinny, young dude, maybe fourteen or fifteen . . ." He hesitated while Rafiel gave vent to a string of profanity.

Jason Cordova just nodded, as though Rafiel had made an observation worth noting, then said, "Yeah, but . . . that's not the worst of it. I grant you I was shifted myself, and I don't remember what happened really clearly, but from the way he looked and how . . . well . . . I don't think he's all there. And I'm almost sure he's not, you know . . . normal. His eyes, you know. They were more feral as human than in animal form."

⚞ CHAPTER 3 ⚟

Tom turned in bed, almost but not quite fully awake. He felt Kyrie stir, waking up.

Being in the same bed with someone was still an odd feeling. For so many years, Tom had been afraid of sleeping near any other human—scared of changing shapes in his sleep and killing his companion by morning.

But he and Kyrie had shared this house for over a year, and this bed for five months now, and even Kyrie had started to talk about it as "our bed" instead of "my bed." So the feeling was odd, but good. Married feeling, Tom thought. Not that marriage was for the likes of them. Not really. They couldn't have kids. Kids might inherit their shape-shifting. And if one of them did something horrible, it was better not to have a spouse who would have to live it down.

He sighed and let go of what couldn't be, and instead opened his eyes just a little: enough to see that Kyrie had thrown off the covers and was asleep on her stomach, in a tiny T-shirt and tinier shorts, her exposed arms and legs long and golden in the sunlight.

While negotiating a loan for the new fryer, the bank officer had demanded to know what Kyrie's race or background was. He'd thrown out in succession, as guesses, Greek, Italian, Spanish and Native American. The man, a precisely speaking worker at some city bureaucracy or other, had seemed personally offended that Kyrie had refused to admit to one or another background. He'd pointed out all the benefits that the diner Kyrie co-owned with Tom could get from being minority owned. Loans and other benefits were apparently theirs for the taking with much easier terms than the bank could otherwise offer.

But even if Kyrie had wanted to claim the benefits—she didn't, suspecting the too-easy gift—she would have been hard-pressed to guess at her origins. Her personal history, what she knew of it, started on a Christmas night twenty-two years ago, when the churchgoers coming out of midnight mass at a Catholic church in Charlotte, North Carolina, had found a baby girl asleep in a bassinet. After that there had been a never-ending train of foster families, one of whom had been named Smith, which surname had been joined to the given names she'd got from the person who'd discovered her that Christmas Eve: Kyrie Grace Smith.

God's Grace. To Tom she'd been all that and more, the one person to whom his actions and his well-being mattered. Sometimes he thought she kept him sane and strong and, in the end, human . . . even when he shape-shifted into a dragon.

His hand reached out, as though of its own accord, and ran along her smooth, golden thigh.

Kyrie mumbled something against the pillow, then turned her head, throwing back the curtain of her brown hair—the fringe dyed to resemble a tapestry in Earth tones—and blinked foggily at him.

"Hello, sunshine," he said half ironically. He knew that she, like him, was not a morning person. Or maybe not an afternoon person, because they usually went to bed around seven in the morning, and woke up around four or five to start work at the diner they co-owned in time to take the later part of the dinner shift at six.

She growled at him, and gave him a dirty look, in mock exasperation. Then she reached out a hand and patted at his shoulder, as if not sure it was really there. Reassured, she mumbled between clenched teeth, "Time?"

He turned his head to look at the alarm clock on his bedside table, in reality a little bookshelf they'd bought at the thrift shop to serve the duty. "Four," he said.

She sighed a deep sigh and turned on her side to face him. "I suppose," she said, "we have to get up." And leaned towards him for a kiss, he didn't at all begrudge. He never understood complaints of morning breath.

"We could take a few minutes," he said hopefully.

She kissed him again, and he tried to turn on his side. Tried to, because as he started to turn, several sharp points inserted themselves into his calves and something gave a good impression of a demonic scream. "Ah," he yelled. "Not Dinner." The utterance would have seemed cryptic to anyone who didn't know them, but not to any of the clients of their diner, or even their neighbors, who were used to the unusual name of their orange tabby tomcat.

More out of habit than thought, Tom returned his legs to the position they'd been in, and after a while the pain of claws on his calves waned. "I don't think Not Dinner approves of the program," he said.

"So?" Kyrie said. "Let him not approve. I will—"

She had just started to rise, when one of their cell phones rang. Kyrie's. Had to be because the tune, playing muffled and distant from somewhere in the house, was "She Only Comes Out at Night."

"Shit," Kyrie said, slipping out of bed and opening the door of the bedroom before dashing off into the house in search of the phone.

Fortunately, Tom thought, the house wasn't very big, so it wasn't like she could look in a lot of places. He sat up, leaned down and, carefully, removed Not Dinner from his legs. The cat bristled and yowled, but let him do it.

Just as Tom set his feet on the floor, Kyrie's phone switched off, and his own—"I Need a Hero"—started ringing.

It was somewhere in the room. He was almost sure of it. He stumbled to the armchair in the corner, which was in fact never used as a chair, but as a repository of clothes worn once but not dirty enough to wash yet. He picked up the jeans he'd worn the night before and patted at both pockets, then found his black leather jacket and patted those pockets, before he woke enough to realize the sound was in fact coming from behind the chair.

He'd bent over the back of the chair and was trying to reach his phone on the floor, aware that Kyrie had come back and stood at the door to the room, when his phone stopped ringing and the house phone started.

There was only one house phone, and it was attached to the wall in the kitchen. The house was small enough that the coiled cord could extend to almost the whole place.

Tom straightened and turned and ran out of the room, across the living room and down the hall to the kitchen, two steps behind Kyrie.

Someone was desperately trying to reach them. He and Kyrie owned a greasy spoon together, The George, on Fairfax. The fryer had probably exploded, killing their cook and splattering several employees and diners. The damage charges alone would put them out of business and—

But his nightmarish scenario was interrupted by Kyrie, who'd picked up the phone and listened attentively for a few seconds, then covered the mouthpiece, and looked up—her eyes solemn. "It's Rafiel," she said, naming their best friend, one of Goldport's finest. "He says there's been a death at the amusement park."

"And?"

"He thinks it's a shifter. From the look of the things, wild shifter."

"Wild?"

"You know, feral? One who has no clue he shouldn't kill or eat humans."

Tom rubbed his hand down his face and groaned. In some ways a lawsuit and being put out of business was a less scary scenario.

"What does he mean by feral, I wonder" Tom said, as he got behind the wheel. They'd showered very fast and at the same time, which was a triumph of love over solid geometry, since the shower in the house they rented was maybe comfortable for one skinny person, and okay for two people if they were both very slim and close friends. Kyrie and Tom were, for those purposes, very good friends. But it was a trial to get out of the shower without wasting time in anything but showering.

Now, they were in the car, their hair still wet, Kyrie giving directions from the text message that Rafiel had left her. "He couldn't believe we don't know where Riverside is," she said.

"He grew up here. And besides, I hear he has a life that includes days off and vacations," Tom said, not resentfully. "He doesn't work at a diner. But what does he mean, feral? Did he tell you?"

"He thought there might be some impairment," Kyrie said. "Some form of mental issue, in addition to the shifting."

"How would he know that?"

"He said the witness thought the human form looked more . . . feral and desperate than the shifted form."

"Oh," Tom said. As he headed towards the highway, he added, "Witness?"

"Apparently. To both the animal and the shift to human. I didn't ask, because Rafiel was in a flap, but that's what I gathered."

"Joyous," Tom said, and tried not to think too much about what that might mean. Sooner or later shifters would be outed, but perhaps they could avoid making it today? Or not. And asking Kyrie for more details would only cause her to worry more, which wasn't fair. Her entire conversation with Rafiel had lasted maybe two minutes. She didn't know any more.

They'd have to wait till they got to the amusement park, and then they'd know.

Tom resisted the impulse to close his eyes and pray, mostly because he couldn't really drive with his eyes closed, but also because he'd never been very good at the praying thing. Once, in the worst possible circumstances, he was fairly sure his prayers had been answered. He didn't have the nerve to bother whoever was up there again just now. It didn't seem right. He should be able to deal with most things without bothering God about it.

They left the highway in the least fashionable end of town and wound their way amid narrow streets with houses as small as theirs, but less well kept. Kids played in some yards, and sullen teenagers stood around street corners.

The park was at the end of that neighborhood, where a larger street bordered it. There was a bodega, and then, with surprising suddenness, a six-foot-tall dilapidated white wall, in desperate need of a good paint job, with the letters Riverside Amusement Park, stencilled on it in reddish brown.

At one end, a tower of vaguely oriental design presided over what was clearly an entrance, and a sign painted on splintered wood said PARKING LOT with an arrow pointing west.

It was a parking lot, if you wanted to call it that, or really more a large expanse of sandy beaten dirt, hard as concrete, with no lines or demarcations.

Not that lines were needed at the moment, since the only cars there were three police vehicles, Rafiel's SUV and another white SUV. Tom applied the parking brake and got out after Kyrie.

She stood in the middle of the parking lot, sniffing.

He got out after her and took a deep breath. "Shifter," he said. It wasn't a question.

"Like the whole area has been drenched in it," she said. "Makes me wonder if the owner is a shifter."

"Could be. In which case we've probably seen him at The George for coffee and eggs." He tried for a smile, but missed in his attempt. Their diner, The George, had been drenched in shifter pheromones before the two of them had bought it. The pheromones—they had been designed to bring shifters to it, in service of a rather deranged shifter's mating needs—apparently could influence shifters as far as a hundred or more miles away, without the person influenced ever being aware of it. But of course, once it brought them there, it didn't make them go in, and it certainly couldn't make them become a regular of the diner, even if lots of shifters did. He pointed. "The smell gets stronger this way."

She nodded, but her face pinched. "There's blood," she said.

He wondered if he could really see behind her very human eyes the shadow of the panther—the animal she became when she shifted. He wasn't sure. After all, Kyrie wasn't starting to shift, nor making any efforts towards shifting. Yet there was in the expression of her eyes something that reminded Tom of the panther. The interested look of the animal scenting blood.

He reached out a hand for her, grabbed at her hand, which felt cold and dry in his. She gave a little laugh. "I wasn't going to shift," she said.

"No," he said, and it was as much reassurance to her as to him. For years, neither of them had had much control over when and how they shifted. In his case, his past was full of stupid attempts to control the shifting, that often had made things worse. There had been his addiction to heroine, because heroine was a central nervous system depressant. And there had been his stealing of the artifact known as the Pearl of Heaven from a triad of Chinese dragon shifters.

That episode had left Goldport strewn with bodies that Rafiel had worked very hard to attribute to an escaped Komodo dragon. And it had almost left Tom dead, too.

But strangely the thing that seemed to work best for control was his relationship with Kyrie. The same could be said for her.

Tom couldn't remember the last time they'd accidentally shifted. Well, not after the thing six months ago when the association of really bad shifters who called themselves the Old Ones had come to town. But that, he thought, was hardly accidental. They'd had to shift. And fight for their lives.

As they followed the smells, her hand in his, up a small path towar the hippodrome, they could see wood had been stripped ror e boarded-up entrance, and they noted splats of blood on end of the path. Broad stripes, as though something had ofusely while running.

stopped a few feet from the entrance, hesitating, and n wondered how to ask Kyrie to wait while he went in the creature that had left the blood drops might be, out of the ruined door. Which was good, because ly as not to insist on going in, too.

e?" Kyrie asked, before Rafiel could speak.

led, someone else came up behind him, and Tom ready to go into a defensive crouch, or even if because the person was a complete stranger: ilt, with olive skin and short-cut hair with ond.

's look and said, "Oh, this is Jason. Jason ness I was talking about."

rward, his hand extended. "Hi." A small

m, stepping forward and shaking Jason's h. I'm a panther."

gaze on him, extended his own hand.

up. "You— What? Dragons don't exist." "He does. As do some serious bad er the Komodo dragon thing? Yeah." ou not in the affairs of dragons for with ketchup and all that. Though me fancy sauce." It was a mark of didn't even smile at his own joke, eyes looking haunted. "It's bad," is, I think it's been living in the ll my team, there are other ... foxes, but people, too."

"People?" Kyrie said, and her voice squeaked. "Wouldn't someone have reported it?"

"Lady," Jason said, "from the clothes and stuff, they were homeless and possibly illegals. No one would know."

⇥ CHAPTER 4 ⇤

"So this is what I suggest we do," Rafiel said. "I suggest we go in, two by two, and look around and see if we can find this creature."

"Okay," Tom said. He was frowning at Rafiel, his blue eyes hard. He hadn't tied his waist-long black hair as he normally did, and it was drying and being blown into a mess by the wind. He'd also forgotten to shave. The combination of the unkempt long hair, and the shadow of beard against Tom's naturally pale skin made Tom look like a seriously dangerous man out on a spree. At least he wasn't wearing the black leather jacket, Rafiel thought. If he were, some of the rookie officers who didn't know him might arrest him on sight.

Tom frowned more intently. "I'll bite," he said. "We're going to go in and look for this guy who has already killed two people, and who is a shifter. And what do we do when we find him? Go *argh* and die?"

"He didn't kill me," Jason Cordova said, "though he messed up my shoulder something awful. I think he's some sort of pre-historic dog."

"Prehistoric," Tom said, and in his tone Rafiel could hear the unspoken question, *Is this another of the ancient shifters come to town to mess with us?*

29

Rafiel shrugged his ignorance in the matter. "My idea," he said, enunciating carefully and trying to make himself sound official and in control, "is that there would be two of us and maybe he will be too scared to shift."

"Yeah, because being scared never causes anyone to shift," Tom said, while at the same time Kyrie put in, "But fear normally makes you shift."

Rafiel sighed. "We have to do something, okay? We can't leave a bad shifter on the loose. I mean, if it really were just some dog or something, we could hope maybe it would generallly be afraid of people and not come out, or not, you know, confront more humans. But if it's a shifter . . . and if it is a feral shifter, who can tell what it will do?"

Tom didn't answer, just pulled back his hair with both hands and gave a huff of exasperation. Kyrie bit her lip.

"Look," Jason said, then seemed to realize he'd spoken up in front of a bunch of people who'd clearly dealt with this sort of thing before, and visibly hesitated, then sighed. "Look, guys, maybe if we approach it together. I mean, there's only so much it can do, right? What is it going to do against four?"

"Sometime," Tom said, "remind me to tell you about this creature who was a dire wolf and who—"

"Yeah, but this is not quite that bad," Rafiel said. "I don't think Dante Dire would have been living in an abandoned hippodrome, okay? I don't think this guy is that smart." He cleared his throat. He could feel sweat run down his back, under the Hawaiian shirt, and he wondered if he was already late enough to get out of his date with the excuse of police work. He had to look for all the silver linings he could.

Tom put his arm around Kyrie's waist, as Rafiel seemed to hesitate before saying, "I should go call my people before I show it to you, but there were rustlings and things, and I'm afraid . . ." He bit at his lip. "I'm afraid that it is still around there somewhere. So I'll have to risk contaminating the crime scene."

"Crime scene?" Jason said, and snorted. "The newest of those human remains must be at least a month old, maybe more."

"Still a crime scene," Rafiel said. His inner struggle was visible in his tense face, the frown that pulled his eyebrows together. Tom was accustomed to it by now. He was aware that Rafiel must forever fight between his duty as a police officer and his attempts at keeping shifters and their kind secure. He understood it, too. He didn't like it. He didn't have to like it. It was as much a part of Rafiel as the policeman's mane of blond hair, consistent in both human and lion form.

He waited until Rafiel—who looked almost terminally relaxed in his surfer T-shirt and khaki pants if you didn't look at his face—finished the interior debate that Tom knew wound him more tightly than a year-long clock, and said, "The thing is, well . . . as long as you guys don't touch anything. After all, you could have been with us when we first went in there to explore." And when they didn't protest, he seemed to Tom to give up on being saved from himself, and adhering religiously to his policeman's duty, he said, "Well, come then."

They went into the boarded-up hippodrome, squeezing past the broken boards at the entrance.

There is no way to be an honest copper and a shifter, Rafiel thought, not for the first time. Back when he'd first found out he could shift, while in college for law enforcement, he'd almost given up on the idea of going into the force.

But then he'd solved his girlfriend's murder, a crime that involved shifters, which would have gone unsolved without his intervention. And he'd found his vocation for law enforcement again, because, if not him, who would enforce law to shifters? And who would protect them—both from detection and from each other?

He'd been walking that narrow, knife's edge path ever since. But he didn't have to like it.

He heard Jason's boots crunch behind him, and Tom and Kyrie walk behind that, as he led them past the collapsed seats, among waist-high grass. His nose kept track of the three shifters behind him, and traced the other scent present here, as its trail wound through the grass. He tried to be aware if a new, fresher shifter-scent joined it, giving away the location of the killer.

Cordova was another problem. Well, not a problem. The poor bastard couldn't help turning into a bear, any more than Rafiel or Kyrie or Tom could help their shape changes. But they'd have to figure out something for him. What he'd said, about not knowing anyone else who knew he could shift . . . Rafiel had never been that alone. His parents had figured out his secret early on, and had not been scared or repulsed by it. Rafiel knew, though, that Tom and Kyrie had each spent many years alone with that secret, trying to survive in a world that would kill them or worse should it find out. And he had enough empathy to figure out how terrible that must be.

The thing was, every shifter, by the nature of shifting, was, after a while, less than sane. What kind of crazy was Cordova?

His own particular form of insanity, just now, seemed to be to behave about as sane as a brick and twice as unconcerned. He gave Kyrie and Tom a running narration as he walked around patches of high grass and carefully avoided stepping on needles and human waste, "We came this way, you know, following the scent. And just here, it's going to get really bad."

It did, and Rafiel was ready for it this time. It wasn't bad in the sense of really intense shifter-scent, but of the shifter-scent being overpowered by the sweet, sickly smell of decay.

Tom put his arm around Kyrie and they advanced behind Rafiel into the ruined place. If he were forced to admit the truth, though he hoped he wouldn't be, Tom would have said it was as much for his comfort as hers. He didn't know if Kyrie was in need of comfort, but he was.

Coming here, and looking at human remains killed by a shifter, reminded him of his own days of living wild, of his own fears of what he might have done in the nearly blank hours when he surrendered to the animal. Even now, there were portions of that time that were a blankness and a forgetting, and that he hoped remained so, at least if any revelation involved dead people.

They crossed a musty passageway, composed of rotting boards and the remains of what looked like a ticket booth, and then across a short gravel path and into chaos.

It looked like the ruins of Pompeii, only not nearly so neat. If the place had been encased in lava, there wouldn't be a riotous growth of vegetation. People wouldn't have dumped trash everywere. And teens wouldn't have got in there, who knew *how*, to do who knew *what*. Though some of the *what* was answered easily enough by the discarded condoms and the syringes and needles embedded in the grass.

Tom pulled Kyrie back before she stepped on an exposed needle. He pointed it out to her, hoping it would make her more careful, but neither of them spoke. They could smell it now, more intensely than before. They shouldn't startle whatever was there.

Past a pile of broken wood and rusted metal, which must once have been bleachers or seats, around a pile of sand that looked like someone had dumped it there so they didn't have to cart it back after a construction project. Then into the tall grass and . . .

The smell changed, and enveloped Tom. It wasn't shifter-smell, anymore, but the smell of decay. It was so strong and so offensive that he thought they'd stumbled on another body. But what lay in the tall grass were the remains of several rabbits and what might have been a fox. The fox looked the most recent. It was partially eaten, partly rotting in the warmth of the Colorado spring.

The smell of decay was so strong it caused them to lose the scent. Tom hesitated, but then as Rafiel started to follow a path of beaten-down grass, Tom followed, still holding Kyrie around the waist as though he could protect her from all evil that way. After all, Rafiel was trained. They weren't. And Kyrie shouldn't have to face horrors.

He saw the teenager before he knew what he was seeing. For a short moment, he didn't seem so much like a human being, but like a Rorschach stain against the grass—a collection of dried grass and stones and blood-stained sand. But then Tom blinked, and saw that it was human, and a teen. A young man on the verge of manhood, with overlong, lank, and probably very dirty blond hair, completely naked, his body stained and battered in a way that indicated naked was his normal state.

There were slashes across his middle: the blood they'd been following. And then the smell of shifter hit Tom's nose.

Rafiel had stopped between them and the boy. "A victim?" Tom asked, in a whisper.

Rafiel shook his head. "The victim cut at him. Bear claws."

"The—"

Tom didn't know if the boy understood them or if something else triggered his alarm. His eyes widened, his barely human face lengthened. He coughed once, then writhed.

"He's shifting," Kyrie said and sprang forward, but Tom grabbed her, pulled her back. "We don't know into what. This is not the time to—"

And then he realized that Rafiel too was writhing and twisting violently.

As the boy changed into...something low-slung and heavy-jawed, and took off running, past them, out of the hippodrome, Rafiel was only seconds behind—a slick, golden lion, leaving a pile of tattered cloth behind him.

Kyrie and Tom followed, running, but by the time they got to the parking lot, the two animal-shapeshifters had jumped the fence at the back and were running along the little access dirt road.

Kyrie started to pull her T-shirt up, and Tom realized she meant to shift. "No, Kyrie. We can't have a parade of felines and a dragon run around Goldport in daylight."

She hesitated for a minute, pushed her lip out and looked like she'd argue, then pulled her shirt back down, opened the car and slid into the passenger side. He slid into the driver's side, amazed she'd chosen to let him take the wheel. As though knowing what he was thinking, she said, "You're better for crazy driving."

He grinned, but didn't say anything. In his long distant past, before he'd even been legal for driving, he had made his upper-class parents insane by stealing cars to go joyriding in. He knew Kyrie disapproved of his past, but her mentioning it indicated she was coming to terms with it. Perhaps...perhaps this relationship would last, after all.

He turned the ignition on, shifted, pushed the gas down and took off, out of the parking lot in a squeal of tires, and turned sharply right onto the little country road. He saw the doglike creature and the lion run around a curve and accelerated after them.

But by the time he got there, they'd turned and were running among the high grass on the roadside. He couldn't follow them in Kyrie's compact. If they had an SUV...

"There are neighborhoods that way," Kyrie said. "Past the fields."

"Yeah," Tom said.

"I hope no one will see them."

"I hope *they* won't attack anyone." And in Tom's mind was some innocent kid, or even someone's pet, coming out of his home...to be devoured. He remembered the half-eaten rabbits and foxes. They weren't dealing with a civilized shifter. Nor with a sane one.

Tom coughed, then coughed again, and felt his body trying to writhe, to twist to expand into the dragon shape. He coughed again, and reached for the hem of his T-shirt, from long habit, to pull it off before he ripped it in shifting.

Kyrie's hand grabbed at a wrist that ached with that bone-deep pain of a body part trying to elongate and change shape.

"No," her voice penetrated through the fog in his senses, the whistling blood in his ears, the drumlike thudding of his heart, and the rush of need to do something, to help. "Rafiel," he said, and the sound came out oddly sibilant.

"Yes, but no," Kyrie said. "What you told me holds, and—it won't do you any good. Truly. When people like me are seen or photographed, they can explain intrusions of the wild into the world of humans by mutual encroachment. But a dragon? What would that be? Encroachment from a fairy tale?"

She was right. Tom knew she was right. He blinked eyes already endowed with nictitating eyelids, and took a deep, deep breath, which sbrought back a semblance of rationality. As it was, he should be grateful that Kyrie hadn't taken off. She'd obeyed him. She'd controlled herself, and now he needed to control himself too. This relationship thing involved mutual control and accepting . . . accepting someone else's opinions as to what he should do. Tom took deep breaths and imagined the air as a cooling force, pouring in on his heated temper, his sense of urgency. He forced his half-shifted body back to normal, and as his mind cleared, he realized no worse damage had been done than popping the button of his jeans.

"If he doesn't call or come back by nightfall I'll need to shift and fly a patrol over the area," he said. "If he gets in trouble, maybe I can pull him out of it."

"Rafiel is a big boy," Kyrie said. "I'm sure he can figure out how to beat a skinny, famished homeless shifter and get back home in time for dinner. I just wonder where that kid came from. And why he attacked a human."

⊱ CHAPTER 5 ⊰

"My fear..." Tom said, and paused. "For years, I've been afraid I might have killed and eaten a human my first night out from my parents' house," Tom said ruefully, in a half whisper, and Kyrie looked at him startled.

She loved Tom. No. That wasn't even it, though it was true of course. She was attracted to Tom physically, had been even back when she thought she hated him. She joked to customers and employees and to Rafiel—which might be cruel—that she was dating the hottest man in the entire tri-state area. Tom was a couple of inches shorter than her five-seven height, but he didn't look short. In fact people often talked about him as though he were at least six feet tall. Part of it was the arms and chest. While his legs were muscular enough—how not, when his entire job consisted of standing by the grill or walking around the diner all night—his arms and chest displayed the kind of slick musculature that normally took a personal trainer and all sorts of expensive equipment to manage. Or the ability to grow a pair of wings and take to the sky several times a week. The muscles, from supporting the dragon's weight in the air, translated into a sculpted male chest that would make a body builder cry with envy.

Above it was a face not quite pretty enough to be a pretty girl's, though if it had been a girl's, she wouldn't have been all that ugly, either. From that face, a pair of enamel-blue eyes stared, bright and—right then—anguished.

"The first night you were—? What do you mean? The first night you shifted or—"

"No," Tom said. "The night I was kicked out by Dad."

Tom had been forced out of his apartment at sixteen, at night, in the middle of New York City, barefoot and in a robe. His father, a noted criminal lawyer with ties to a triad of dragon shifters had thought, mistakenly, that Tom had caught the shifting from his clients, and had been afraid that if Tom stuck around he, too, might start shifting.

In retrospect, Kyrie understood both of them—to an extent. She knew Edward Ormson had been terrified. Since reestablishing contact with his son two years ago, Tom's father had tried to explain himself, and he'd bought them the diner and moved to Denver to be within driving distance and, in his self-absorbed, blinkered way, did his best possible to—belatedly—be a good father. Growing up, Tom had been a difficult child and a difficult teenager, had a string of minor offenses on his record, and had viewed his ability to shift as a superhero thing. Getting pushed out into the street had been the shattering of his comfortable upper-middle-class world and, probably, had saved him from becoming an insufferable adult.

He'd learned to survive. If asked, he never gave details. He'd say that New York City had services aplenty for runaways, which he could pass as. Besides, at seventeen he'd claimed to be older and signed up for day labor.

He would say—had said it often—that were it not for his shifting, he would have settled down long before now. He would have become what he was now: a young man of moderate means, with a fixed residence and a comfortable place in the world. But the shifting, and being afraid to shift, and being unable to fully control the shifting had ruled his life until he had met Kyrie at twenty-one and they'd made a pact against the world. Rafiel helped too, as did the other people who came to The George for food, and who changed into various kinds of animals.

But at this moment Kyrie saw in Tom's eyes the sort of blank worry, the odd detachment she'd seen in them when she'd first met him, when he'd been drug addicted—another effort at controlling his shifting—and just barely not-homeless.

"I have a vague memory," he said. "In those days I could never remember clearly what happened, when I changed. I mean, I had a fuzzy idea, flashes. I remember this guy running after me. I have no idea what he wanted. I couldn't have looked like I had enough money to rob. He had a knife. I ran, until he cornered me, and then..." He blinked. Then shrugged. "I shifted. I have a memory of blood, of..." He shook his head. "Then there was this gentleman. When I shifted back to human, there was this old man I knew. He sold chestnuts down the block." He rubbed the back of his hand under his nose in a gesture that seemed to Kyrie must have come from a much younger Tom. "Turned out he was an orangutan shifter but...but his own family didn't know about it. He had"—wave of the hand—"ten children and a wife, and they were all very kind to me. Took me in for the next day. Gave me clothes. But he wouldn't tell me what happened to the man confronting me. Always said I didn't want to know. I've wondered if...if I ate the man with the knife."

"Well, you probably didn't eat the knife," Kyrie said, then regretted her words and sighed. "Look, why *would* you eat him? Kill him, maybe, if you were really upset. Though I'll point out *you don't want to know* could have meant *anything*. Like, he was a shifter too. Why torture yourself? You haven't eaten anyone since; you probably didn't eat that guy either."

Tom gave her a sideways glance. "I might have."

"Yeah, well. I was about to say you might also have flown around, but in fact you probably did." She reached out and touched his cold wrist. "Let it go, Tom. Nothing you can do about it. It's not much use telling you that a full-grown man with a knife chasing around a half-naked teen probably deserved to get eaten—but it's still true."

He managed a wan smile. "I— It's just my seeing that kid. It's like he doesn't know he shouldn't eat people."

"And he might not, but Tom, you can't fix everyone and everything. One day one of your...strays is going to hurt you badly."

He took a deep breath. "I know. I know." A glance at the clock on the dashboard and he started the car. "And we're now all out of time and should get to The George as soon as possible, or Anthony will be late again, and his wife will be upset."

Kyrie managed a smile in return, as soon as Tom edged out of the parking lot, kicking up gravel as he went. She cast a worried glance in the direction in which Rafiel had disappeared, pursuing the creature. "When it's dark," she said, "and dinner traffic calms down a little, you can go look for Rafiel. If he hasn't called yet."

⊰ CHAPTER 6 ⊱

They heard the sirens as soon as they turned onto Fairfax Avenue, where The George sat. Definitely fire engine sirens. A scent of smoke came into the car's air circulation.

Tom clenched his jaw and told himself that Goldport was a large city. Okay, not massively large, but large enough, particularly during the school year, when students from CUG—Colorado University at Goldport—swelled the numbers of residents to triple its population. Large enough to support several restaurants and a few dozen skyscrapers' worth of office buildings. Large enough to have its own newspaper and three hotels. Large enough to have a symphony orchestra.

Large enough for the fire raging somewhere along Fairfax Avenue to be, in fact, anything but a raging inferno in his own diner. But Tom's jaw clenched and his cheek muscle worked, and in his mind he knew very well where all that screaming of sirens came from. As he got closer, it was obvious they were going in the same direction as the sirens, and he clenched his teeth even harder—so hard it hurt.

And when, within five blocks of the diner, he saw that the billowing clouds of smoke were coming from about where the diner was, he let out his long-held breath and along with it a wordless curse.

To Kyrie's startled glance, he said, still through clenched teeth, "It was the damn fryer. I bet you Anthony forgot the timer again. His wife probably called and he stayed on the phone and . . . Let's hope at least it didn't kill anyone."

As they got to the diner, he found the parking lot was so cluttered with fire engines, he had trouble pulling in behind the restaurant. Tom wedged the car on the side of the building, where no official parking place existed, and jumped out, ready to ask the nearest firefighter if anyone had died, when he realized that the smoke came from behind him, and that the only thing wrong with the back door to the diner was that two employees and a lot of customers were pressed against it, gawking out, and would see him as well.

At his glare, Anthony, the day manager, looked like he'd suddenly remembered something important and ran in, and Tom, a bit calmer, turned around to look at the fire.

The back parking lot of The George—it didn't really have a front parking lot, except for a couple of spots on the street, reserved for take-out customers to dart in and out—was a square of asphalt bordered on the west by Pride Street, on the east by a narrow, dark alley that looked onto the backside of a bunch of warehouses and apartment houses. On the north side, there was a huge building. Tom gathered it had once been a rooming house of early twentieth-century vintage.

Though Tom had only had occasion to use the bed-and-breakfast for a stretch of a few days, and the owner, of course, rarely came to The George, the two establishments maintained the sort of friendly interaction of good neighbors, sharing snow removal expenses and parking lot lighting and a few other expenses that benefitted both of them.

The woman who owned the bed-and-breakfast, a motherly middle-aged woman, stood between two fire engines, wringing her hands. Not far away, a group of firemen were gathered near the tower, one man talking on a cell phone.

Tom frowned at the towering structure. There was fire halfway up it, but the top seemed to be untouched, and on a dormer window at the very top, there was a shadow that looked like someone looking out. "Is there someone up there?" he asked Louise Carlson, the owner of the bed-and-breakfast.

Louise turned around and said, "Oh, it's you, Tom. Yes, a nice

Asian girl. Ms. Ryu. Checked in this morning. I— Oh, damn it, I'm sure Elmer set this fire. He keeps saying people confuse us with his hotel, which is nonsense, but...damn it." She ran her hand back through her greying hair. "This is going to take forever to rebuild."

Tom ran his eyes over the body of the building, where the fire was almost completely out, extinguished by high pressure water. The tower was proving more difficult. He wondered where the fire had started, but the alley was too narrow to admit the fire trucks parking there, and the water jet was hitting only the brick wall. Considering this, he said, "You have insurance." It wasn't a question.

"Of course. Whether it covers acts of dragons—"

"Dragons?"

"Nonsense, isn't it? But whoever called in this fire said they saw two *dragons* flying away north and flaming the tower." Louise gave a nervous giggle. "At least they were right about the fire, even if they were completely drunk." She twisted her hands together. "The problem is the time it will take to rebuild will wipe me out financially anyway."

But Tom was thinking of that girl in the tower. "Why don't the firefighters climb up and get her out?" he asked.

"The ladder won't reach, and she won't jump. Not that I blame her."

Tom didn't either. The tower was six stories high, sticking up above the neighborhood. The rooms there were more expensive because of the view.

A group of firefighters came back, stained with soot and looking like they were ready to drop. "We can't go around," they said. "Some of the floor on the way to the tower is unstable, and it looks like the tower stairs are gone anyway."

Tom started edging away. The thing was that he could save the woman. He didn't want to do what he would have to to get her, but on the other hand he couldn't stand the thought of her burning up in there. He edged behind the group of firefighters gathered around the cell phone, and he overheard, "You don't understand, if we send to Denver for a tall enough ladder, she'll be dead long before we—"

Tom slipped into the alley. After looking around to make sure there were no windows overlooking his spot, and seeing that no one was paying any attention here, he stripped with the speed born of habit, folded his clothes and hid them behind a dumpster.

Then he willed the shift upon him, coughing and writhing and spasming, as daggers of pain pushed into his bone and muscles as they changed shape.

His face and his arms elongated. From his arms a pair of wings grew as his body became long, serpentine and familiar to those who might recognize the carved prows of Viking ships.

The dragon took to the sky, retaining enough of the human mind to fly behind the bed-and-breakfast tower, to a spot where no one was likely to see him land.

⊰ CHAPTER 7 ⊱

Asphalt under paw pad changed to dirt. A road lined by houses turned to no road, just rock and scrub and dirt. The lion had no idea where he was running or, frankly, *why*. In his mind it was all dirt and stone, scrub oak and barren expanses, scent and hunt. Around him night fell.

The thing ahead of him looked like a dog but smelled feline. It also smelled young, undernourished and scared. The lion snarled softly, confident of his victory once he caught the creature. It wasn't even good sport.

Rafiel, somewhere within the lion's mind, was relieved when they left behind populated areas and the road—along with the possibility of a passing car seeing them and reporting them to the police or animal control. Instead, they ran into the border of a national forest, and then out of the trees, onto a slope that must have been torched in the last wildfire and which was now barren, save for a sparse growth of scrub oak. His paws hurt, as did his legs. He'd been at the chase a long time.

He closed the distance with the young creature fleeing ahead of him. The creature turned around and let out a high cry of distress, the complaint of a hopeless victim. The lion reared triumphant, as the . . . shifter? animal? . . . cowered and skittered sideways and whined, a frightfully high, odd whine.

And then it happened. It was all too fast for the lion brain to follow, even as the lion's eyes saw it. Out of the shadows, something came, yellow-tawny. It was huge, twice the size of the lion. Its paws hit the ground with so much force that clods of baked-dry earth flew in all directions. It snarled, its lips pulled back from long glimmering fangs.

Rafiel-the-lion turned away from the cub to face this new menace. With raised hackles, he growled into the snarling face and the tawny yellow eyes.

Then Rafiel smelled it. The smell rolled over him, like a wave, submerging the lion's brain and confusing Rafiel.

She stood growling in front of Rafiel.

She. No doubt about that. He could smell her, a sweet-spicy tang that indicated a female in heat.

His brain stopped. Parts of the lion body long ignored came to life and urgency. Rafiel stood smelling her, while at the back of his mind a primeval jungle, a primeval need beckoned.

She snarled and leapt. Her paw caught him on the side of the face, putting out his eye, taking most of his cheek, sending him flying, then sprawling in an unnatural position. He felt as though his spine had snapped and agony dulled his thoughts while the creature stood over him and growled.

One snap from those jaws and he'd be dead, his head separated from his body. Such a death blow would mean no coming back.

Kyrie saw Tom edging around to the alley and knew what he was going to do.

She closed her eyes, took a deep breath. It smelled of fries and gyros, which had come to mean "home" to her since she and Tom had owned the diner. The smell calmed her a little. She said a general prayer that Tom wouldn't get caught by a cell phone camera or worse. You'd think he would know better than to shift where there were bound to be people with cameras. But you might as well try to keep Tom from rescuing people as keep him from breathing. She decided at least to minimize the damage to the diner.

She would make sure fewer people were watching who could talk about mysterious flying dragons. And she'd make sure Anthony didn't get so carried away he forgot the fryer.

✧   ✧   ✧

Bea woke up in a smoke-filled room. For a moment, blinking upward at the black-blue cloud between her and ceiling, she wondered if she were flying. Then she smelled burning. Not just burning wood, as in a fireplace, but the particularly unclean smell of a burning house, and then—

She ran to the window, which was closed, and looked down at firemen far, far below, holding up one of their jumping rigs. Jumping from here to there would be kind of like jumping from the top of a giant diving board into a washtub like in all those cartoons she'd watched when she was a kid.

She opened the window, took a lungful of air and yelled down, "No." Because she couldn't jump. She just *couldn't*. They yelled back, but she couldn't hear them.

The worst part of all this was that her mind felt foggy and slow and she couldn't figure out why she was here, in what appeared to be the prototypical tower for a fairy princess—a tower that was on fire below her. No. Not the prototypical tower. A look around disclosed that she was in a well-appointed room with a canopy bed, a nice armchair, and what looked like an antique desk. There was a bathroom opening off her right. The usual little cards on how to call the concierge gave away this was a hotel room. But where?

Instructions for what to do in a fire came back from her elementary school days. She ran to the door to the room, and felt it. Burning hot. Well, she wasn't going to open that door. Instead, she went into the bathroom, soaked one of the towels, and stuffed it under the door.

This cut down the smoke, and her head cleared a little.

It still felt too painfully slow, as though she had a cold or were recovering from illness.

As she pushed the towel under the door with the tip of her toe, she remembered what she'd seen out the back window, across the parking lot. There was a diner there. There was something to do with a diner . . .

All of a sudden the voice of the Great Sky Dragon came back to her, telling her that she must meet and marry Tom Ormson, the co-owner of a diner.

She'd told him in no uncertain terms that she had no intention of marrying a total stranger—and more, a stranger who was in love with someone else—just because some many-times ancestor of hers decreed it. And she'd withstood his barrage of protest, telling him she wanted nothing to do with this, and she couldn't understand why it would be more likely that the dragon shifters would obey Tom because he was married to her since she was also not Chinese.

He'd yelled at her. He'd lapsed into Chinese, or perhaps some even more ancient Asian language. And then she'd turned to leave.

Her head felt sore, and fingers run gingerly across her scalp disclosed a bump over her left ear.

Oh, no, he didn't she thought. But it was clear that the Great Sky Dragon had in fact done something to her. Her head hurt. She was probably concussed. And the idiots had put her here and set the house on fire. Why? Was it dearest many-times great-grand's attempt at punishing her for not obeying? How nice of him.

Though to do him justice, perhaps he hadn't set the house on fire. She went to the window again and saw that few people were watching the window. So, all she needed to do was shift, and then she could fly away from this, and—

And absolutely nothing. She tried to induce the shifting. Normally the problem was trying *not* to shift when she was panicked. Now, nothing would happen. Could the Great Sky Dragon take her shifting away? Surely not. He wasn't magical. She didn't know what the shifting was, but it wasn't magic. Not the wave-a-wand type of magic at least.

She squeezed her hands so tight that she thought she was going to put holes into her palms, but nothing happened.

Why wasn't the shift working?

Had the Great Sky Dragon done something that meant she couldn't shift? But why? And why put her in this room, behind the diner? What in heaven's name could he mean by this? And by setting the building on fire? Bea realized she was absolutely sure that he'd done just that, though she couldn't say why. If only her head didn't hurt so badly.

Smoke was now coming in from outside too, a thick pillar of it obscuring the parking lot. She coughed and for a moment thought she was going to shift, but the burn up her nose and at the back of her throat told her it was only the smoke.

There was a *thud* on the roof ledge outside her window, and she ran toward the sound. Through the smoke, she had a brief glimpse of glistening green scales, a set of silver claws, and a rolling golden eye, and then—

A young man was there. He was dark-haired, blue-eyed, and completely naked. His black hair was curly and much too long, making him appear a wild man. But she remembered the scales, the claws, the eye. A dragon shifter. She wondered if he were one of the Great Sky Dragon's. She wondered what excuse he meant to use for being naked. But none of it mattered. He knocked at the window. She opened it. And then—

And then he was reaching in and saying, "I'm sorry, this is going to sound very odd—"

He stopped and sniffed, and for a moment she wondered what he was smelling, besides the obvious smoke in the air, but his voice was subtly different as he said, "Or perhaps not so very odd. Listen, I shift into a dragon and I'm going to shift. And then I'm going to fly you down to an area behind the dumpsters where I can shift and change. Do you think you can climb on my back?" he asked, even as his face seemed to already be elongating for the shift. "And hold on while I fly you down?"

She wanted to make a joke about wanting to be introduced first, but instead she nodded once and watched as he coughed and writhed in the change from human to dragon. The hand grasping madly at the windowsill changed to a giant clawed paw.

The dragon facing her looked nothing like her own dragon form. He was sturdier, more massive and looked less like the serpentine dragon of Chinese myth. Bea didn't look like Chinese dragons in tapestries and parades either. For one, she had wings. But this man's dragon looked more like something that might have been carved into the front of a Viking ship: barrel-chested and heavy-jawed.

His mouth worked, and he said something that sounded like "now."

She scrambled hand over hand, grabbing at his neck, surprised by the feeling of warm scales, wondering if hers felt like that too; then she stepped onto the narrow ledge of shingles, trying to throw a leg over the massive ill-balanced body, and mentally cursing the Great Sky Dragon.

She lost her footing and held her breath, seeing the fire trucks so far below. He grabbed her with his spare paw and threw her over his back, barely giving her time to hold onto his neck before flying down, carefully keeping behind the smoke, to land with a jar in the alley, behind the dumpsters. He began contorting almost immediately and Bea jumped off.

She stood, shaking, not believing she was on solid ground, and it was all she could do to keep herself from kissing the compacted dirt of the alley.

Moments later, he was saying, through a coughing fit, "I'm sorry. I had to hurry you. If the breeze shifted, they would have seen us."

"No, that's fine," she said and averted her eyes, as he dove for a bundle of fabric behind the dumpster. "Thank you for saving me." She wasn't sure if she should fake astonishment at his being a shapeshifter, but in the next second she was glad she hadn't, because he came from behind the dumpster, fully dressed, grinning, tying back his hair with a rubber band.

"So," he said, "I guess you don't shift into something that flies."

"I—" She started, then hesitated. "I . . ." And blushed. "Dragon actually. But . . . how did you know?"

"You smell shifter. You know?" His eyes widened. "No. You don't know. I see. Dragon?" His eyes went up to the tower. "But then—"

"I . . ." She took a deep breath. "I don't know. There was . . . there was . . . I woke up in there. It was on fire. And I couldn't shift."

"Oh?" Tom Ormson said, but didn't press it. Instead, he said, "We'd best go around and you tell them you came down . . . the drainpipe or something. Dang. We should have tied some sheets together to make it seem more likely . . ."

"That we didn't *fly* down?" she asked with a shaky smile, unexpectedly liking this man more than she'd expected to when she figured out he was the Great Sky Dragon's candidate for her hand. "I don't think it will matter. The way my door felt, the fire was just behind it—"

A loud *crash-bang* from the tower, and Bea looked up to see the roof cave in. A scream went up from the parking lot. Tom took a deep breath. "Well, that's that," he said.

He walked her around to the parking lot, where the firefighters were looking up at the tower with a look of the sheerest horror. That was when a matronly woman suddenly yelled, "Ms. Ryu!"

Bea was puzzled. She had no idea how this woman knew her name.

"You poor thing," the woman said. "You're confused and no wonder. Of course, when you checked in, you didn't really spend much time talking to me. I'm Louise Carlson, the owner of the Spurs and Lace, of course."

"Oh?" Bea said. "I checked in?" Zombie drugs. They must have given her zombie drugs.

"Oh dear. Well, of course you'll be confused. You know, you were wearing those dark glasses, and I never realized how unusual your eyes are. I was thinking about you up there on the tower. I'm just glad you got out. How—"

"I ... climbed down sheets," she said. "Until I could get to the shed roof."

Louise blinked, "I didn't think we had *that* many sheets."

"Er ... closet. Ten."

"Well, very glad to see you," the nearest firefighter said. "We have a paramedic who—"

"No, I'm quite well," Bea said.

"I'm just going to take her into the diner and get her some coffee," Tom said, with a tone of quiet authority. His absolute calm—his absolute certainty—seemed to carry its own weight. One of the firefighters made a sound, but Louise pointed out that Ms. Ryu couldn't be involved with starting the fire, after all, nor could she know anything about it, since it had started several floors below her, and then Tom Ormson was leading her to the back door of the diner.

As they entered, Bea was impressed by the fact that with the tragedy playing itself out back there in the parking lot, there was no one watching at the back door of the diner, or through the window that faced the fire. In fact, it seemed almost as if she'd just entered a classroom where kids had been very naughty and then became models of good behavior when the teacher came back. There was a strained "I'm being good, Ma" quality to the groups sitting around the tables, and even to the two employees behind the counter, one a young man manning a grill and fryer and the other a woman doing something to vegetables that included a lot of very fast chopping. Neither of them gave off the vibe of being the "teacher" figure.

And then Bea saw her. She was tall—taller than Tom Ormson—and, Bea thought dispassionately, she was also very beautiful with golden skin and long brown hair, the edge of it dyed in a way Bea wouldn't mind imitating if she could figure out how.

Bea knew two things at once. One was that this was Tom Ormson's girlfriend. And the other was that if she tried to steal this woman's boyfriend she would be in for a hard, hard fall.

Not that she had any intention of stealing Ormson. Even if he was nice and good-looking. The world was full of nice, good-looking men, and trouble like this she didn't need.

The woman turned from giving coffee warm-ups to the table she'd been attending, and as she looked toward Ormson, Bea could sense some form of communication pass between them. Bea felt Ormson touch her arm very lightly and he pointed at the corner booth in obvious invitation, but she dug in her heels, turned around and said, "I— I'm sorry, Mr. Ormson, I—"

"Sit down," he said, very quietly, "and tell me who sent you."

She realized she'd called him by name and he'd never introduced himself. She could explain it. She could say that she'd heard it somewhere. But as she slid into the booth and saw those blue eyes watching her with an odd mixture of interest, amusement and wariness, she realized that perhaps it would be best if she avoided any unneeded complication and told him everything. He was a dragon shifter—the only one she knew other than the Great Sky Dragon. And unlike the Great Sky Dragon, *he* seemed to be sane.

Sitting quietly, she folded her hands on the table. Tom Ormson got two cups of coffee, slid one in front of her, took one for himself, sat down. "Now, suppose you start talking. In itty-bitty words, because it's already been a long day. Tell me who sent you." He gave her a look. "You don't look quite like one of the Great Sky Dragon's people, but you look close to it."

⊶ CHAPTER 8 ⊷

For a moment Tom thought she was going to bluff him. He could see the thought passing behind her jade-green eyes. Unusual eyes in an Asian face, but Asian was only the predominant cast to her features. Beneath it, she looked as exotic and unplaceable as Kyrie.

Then she sighed. "My name is Beatrice Bao Ryu. Bea to my friends. I am..." Deep breath. "I was an art student at the University of Georgia, but—"

"You shift into a dragon."

"Oh, yeah, since I was about fourteen. But it seems, because they don't— It took them a while to find out what I was and that I was..."

"Them?"

"My parents and...and whoever it is, who works...the Great Sky Dragon's people. My parents aren't shifters. They only found out I shifted over Christmas. And I think...there started to be trouble at Dad's business. Dad is a vet. Veterinarian. Clients would get anonymous calls saying that he was mistreating the animals when he boarded them and that he...well...other bad stuff. And the animal hospital was broken into twice, and everything...what wasn't stolen was smashed. I didn't know why, though I knew Dad was worried and, well...that we were having money trouble."

She looked up and saw Tom's blank look. "I know, it sounds unrelated, but it isn't. I heard my parents talk, and I found out that—you see...my dad was being blackmailed. He had to send me...send me here. Send me to the Great Sky Dragon, or they were going to bankrupt Dad. I didn't like the sound of that"—she made an airy gesture—"so I came out to see who this Great Sky Dragon, Ancient One person was, and to tell him what I thought of what his triads were doing to Daddy."

"Oh, I'd have paid to see that," Tom said, and grinned. "I think I was the only one to ever defy him before."

She shrugged nonchalantly. "I went to see him where his letters to my dad said to meet." She waved her hand again. "At the Three Luck Dragon."

"Yeah, he likes that place," Tom said. He had his own memories of the restaurant, his own reasons to stay away from it. For one, he'd been eviscerated in its parking lot. Fortunately dragons weren't that easily killed. In fact, short of cutting the body into two or more pieces or separating head from body, they would come back from about anything.

Still, Tom remembered dying and, knowing the Great Sky Dragon had considered that a gentle spanking, it made him very careful about the creature. He took a sip of his coffee. "So, what did he want with you? And did you say no? Is that why two dragons tried to roast you?"

She covered her face. When she looked up her cheeks were glowing red. "No. Yes. I mean...I said no. But then...but then I don't remember anything. I woke up in that room, and...and I couldn't shift." Her last words came out in a near whine.

As Kyrie approached, Tom extended a hand to touch her. He needed the reassurance of her proximity, the comfort of knowing that whatever madness was about to engulf them—from feral shifters to whatever it was the Great Sky Dragon's people were cooking up now—they would face it together.

"I think they knocked me out," the girl said. "I have a lump over my ear. I think they knocked me out and..."

Kyrie looked at Tom and he looked back at her. Feeling married extended beyond sharing the same bed and kissing without worrying about morning breath. Kyrie's glance said as clearly as possible, *You have to tell her the truth. She has to know what she's up against.*

Tom didn't know how much of Bea's story Kyrie had heard, but he knew she was right. He took a deep breath. "No. I think he killed you."

The girl blinked, looked startled. "I-I beg your—pardon?"

Tom took another deep breath, feeling like he was diving into freezing waters. Kyrie kissed him and patted his shoulder as though to give him courage, before going off. "Sorry. I don't know how else to say it. The Great Sky Dragon doesn't think it's a very bad punishment...He..." He paused and took another deep breath.

"I'm not dead," Beatrice said, her voice just a little too loud.

"No. Of course not. The only way to kill a dragon is to separate the head from the body or cut the body in two. And even that I'm not sure about, if the two halves are brought together immediately. I'm also fairly sure you can't come back from being burned to cinders, but I might be wrong. You're not dead, but my guess is that the Great Sky Dragon gave you a killing blow and did it on purpose, so you were temporarily dead. The telltale is that you can't shift. You usually can't shift for about a day after you recover...come back to life. Whatever. And he probably had someone else check in in your place, because Louise sounded all confused about your checking in, and you don't remember it. You must have been dead some days...Usual is three days, of course."

"Dead? I...what day is it?"

"Wednesday."

"It was Sunday." She put her head in her hands.

"Yeah," Tom said, as gently as he knew how. "That would... well...Usually it takes a few days to come back, and I'm going to guess he knew exactly where to put you and...I have bad news—I heard two dragons were seen setting fire to the bed-and-breakfast."

"He—He wanted me to burn?" She looked almost wooden, her face unnaturally immobile, but she'd gone very pale. And before Tom could answer, she added, "I'm sorry. Where is the—"

He pointed her to the restroom and she went. She came back minutes later, looking composed, but still faintly green.

⇥ CHAPTER 9 ⇤

Bea couldn't understand why the idea that she'd been dead and was alive again would have made her throw up. Perhaps it was the shock. And she couldn't say she felt better afterwards. She wasn't sure "better" was the word, except that the physical distress and then rinsing her mouth and washing her face and hands had made her feel like some time had elapsed. Like she'd had time to catch her breath.

Ormson was sitting at the table eating, but his girlfriend was hovering at the end of the hallway, waiting. She led Bea to the booth, and Ormson got up, tied on a bandana to confine his hair, and went off to the restroom.

There was a steaming pot of tea and two cups on the table, and the woman poured the tea and pushed a cup toward Bea, "I thought tea was better for you just now," she said. Then she pushed a container of sugar packets at Bea. "And sugar is good for shock."

Bea rarely sweetened her tea, but she did it now.

The woman waited till Bea took a mouthful, then said, "My name is Kyric, by the way."

"I . . . my friends call me Bea." She paused. "How— Why did Mr. Ormson say that about . . . about the Great . . . about my being killed?"

Kyrie looked serious. "Because you can't shift afterwards, for about a day or so. Just getting hit on the head doesn't stop your shifting, but being dead and coming back does."

Bea was going to ask how they knew that, then stopped. She didn't even want to know which of them it was who had been killed before. Instead, she inclined her head and drank a mouthful of sweet tea. And swallowed. And looked up—to meet sympathy in the young woman's eyes.

"If it makes you feel better, he once gutted Tom from neck to groin and left him for dead. I thought he was dead. The morgue here still talks about it as one of the oddest cases of shock. But... I thought he was dead." Her eyes were dark with pain.

"But why?" Bea asked. "What was the point of roasting me alive? Or... undead or something?"

The woman smiled. "I think," she said, "that this is the Great Sky Dragon's idea of introducing you to Tom in a romantic fashion."

"What?" Bea swallowed hard. "I want to tell you that I—"

"Don't have the slightest interest in my boyfriend?" Kyrie said, and smiled. "Yeah. I kind of figured. You don't look like an arranged marriage sort of girl, but you know, the... Himself is very old, and—"

"And has read way too many comic books?"

"Oh, more than likely," Kyrie said dryly.

At that moment *She Only Comes Out at Night* sounded in the tinny tone of a cell phone, and Kyrie dug into her pocket to bring it out. She listened for a moment, then said, "Shit," not as though it was a swear word, but as though it was a statement of fact. "Shit."

Rafiel woke up. It was... cold, very cold, and it was hard and prickly under him, as if he were lying on a bed of thorns.

So this is what hell feels like, he thought. His mouth was parched, his body hurt as though someone had worked him over with sandpaper, and his eyes appeared to be glued shut. His skin was icy cold, but covered in sweat. At least he hadn't lost a whole day.... Had he lost a whole day?

Working against what seemed to be heavy weights sitting on each of his eyelids, he opened his eyes and looked up at a red-tinged sky. Only one eye worked. His left eye appeared to be obstructed—blackness was all he saw. Memory came back to him, of pursuing the feral shifters, of the strange female feline, of... her paw penetrating his left eye.

Had she killed him? He had no idea if, like dragon shifters, lion shifters also came back from the dead, but he had a feeling that the same rules applied, that they were, somehow, all parts of a whole.

He managed to raise himself onto his elbows. No, this was not something he could wait and heal from. For one, he was starving for protein—so hungry that if a rabbit crossed his path, he'd eat it raw, fur and all. For another, he was scratched, scraped and bitten over most of his body, and his left thigh appeared to have been torn open by a massive claw.

For a moment he was afraid to look at his right thigh. Then he did, and the phone was still there, secured by its orange coil.

It took him forever to get the phone off his thigh and even longer to dial Kyrie's number, even though both she and Tom were on his contacts' list. He kept hitting the wrong buttons. When he dialed it, he put the phone to his ear and then almost fell asleep, listening to the phone *meep* against his ear.

Suddenly there was Kyrie's voice. "Hello?"

He had to swallow twice before he could talk, "Kyrie. I'm... hurt."

"Where?"

"Out I-25," he said, then thought. "Goldminers Road? I think." He swallowed, trying to gather what was left of his saliva. "Field... Tom? Aerial?"

"Shit," Kyrie said. "Shit."

"Sorry. Risk. Hate to have him shift, but I—"

"Don't mention it," Kyrie said. "It's just... we don't have anyone to man... Wait while I see if Anthony will stay on a little longer."

"I—" Rafiel had to take a deep breath and was still shaky as he said. "It's just I'm afraid whatever it was will come back and kill me."

Kyrie didn't remember what she'd told Bea. In fact, she had started to get up from the table and leave without saying anything at all, until it occurred to her that the poor woman was likely to wonder. Then she turned back and said, "Beg your pardon. A friend of ours is in trouble and needs us."

Anthony was taking off his apron when Kyrie opened the pass-through and entered the area behind the counter, where the grill and Tom's new fryer and all the food preparation machinery was. Something in her face must have alerted Anthony to trouble, because he turned around and said, "No. Don't even think about it. My wife is already—"

"You have to, Anthony," Kyrie said. "You just have to. We have to go and help Rafiel. It's a matter of life or death."

"Rafiel?" Tom said, turning around and catching Kyrie's expression, which warned him that there would be absolutely no discussion of the trouble Rafiel had got himself into. "Oh . . . that . . . thing?"

Kyrie nodded.

Anthony looked fit to be tied. "You know, I thought the police force had teams and intervention and, you know, *stuff* for this kind of thing. Why does Officer Trall always need you guys to pull his fat out of the fire?"

⟜ CHAPTER 10 ⟞

It was a good question, and Tom wished he had an answer to it. But he didn't. After all, it was impossible to tell Anthony, whose closest-held secret was that he danced bolero with a local troupe, that his bosses and their best friend shifted into animal shapes, an affliction that often landed them in trouble and caused them to have to get each other out of said trouble.

Kyrie cleared her throat, and Tom knew he had to come up with something as his employee stood there, holding the folded dark red apron with The George emblazoned on the chest, and looking from one to the other for some explanation.

"It's a secret thing," Tom said. "You know, he does things . . . that is, you know, there is trouble with . . . with drug dealing, and Rafiel is undercover and if he's picked up by other police officers, his identity will be blown."

"This is Goldport," Anthony said, almost yelling. "There are only—what? Half a dozen senior officers? I bet half the city knows him. Certainly the half of the city that is likely to have run-ins with the police. They'll figure out who he is, even if it's you two picking him up!"

"They haven't. He has a really good undercover disguise," Tom said.

"Really good," Kyrie said, full of fervor.

It must have been her tone of voice that convinced Anthony. He rolled his eyes towards the ceiling, which had been newly degreased and painted just two months ago, and seemed to be contemplating the meaning of life, or perhaps the meaning of his bosses' madness. "Fine," he said, at last, as he put his apron back on. "Fine, fine, fine, fine. You're lucky that I'm kind of fond of you, though you're both complete lunatics. But I'm warning you right now, if my wife divorces me, I'm going to come gunning for you."

Never having figured out if Anthony was Greek or Hispanic or some other culture with a very close-knit family, but knowing for a fact that Anthony knew everyone in the neighborhood, and that everyone was likely to know Anthony, and that half the neighborhood were perhaps not as...clean-cut as they could be, Tom took the warning seriously. "She won't. We'll pay you double time."

Anthony glared at Tom. "You're a nut. Go on, hurry up, but don't leave me here all alone with Conan's thing tonight."

"Conan's thing?" Kyrie asked. She had turned to get out of the space behind the counter, but now she turned back. The words had an ominous ring, if she could just remember what they referred to.

The thing was, she suspected there had been a lot of talking, or perhaps pleading from Conan, who often seemed to mistake Tom for an indulgent father. The relationship was weird, given that Conan had started out by trying to kill Tom at the orders of the Great Sky Dragon, back when Tom had stolen the Pearl of Heaven, and the Great Sky Dragon had been trying to capture him and—from the looks of it—kill him.

But then there had been...something. Kyrie wasn't sure what and neither was Tom, who refused to have more to do with the boss of the Chinese dragons than was absolutely necessary. But suddenly, just when an ancient shifter called Dante Dire had come to town bent on punishing Kyrie and Tom, the Great Sky Dragon had sent Conan to guard Tom. In the ensuing battle and for good enough reason, Tom had claimed Conan's fealty from the Great Sky Dragon.

And it seemed that no matter how many times Tom told Conan he was free, the Chinese dragon shifter couldn't quite believe it and, instead of merely treating Tom as a boss, treated him somewhere between a father and his liege lord. And Kyrie was sure that was what had happened here. She was as sure as she was of standing here that Conan had decided to ask Tom for something—probably something absolutely stupid, and that Tom had given it to him out of kindness and a desire not to be pestered.

Her suspicions were confirmed when Tom put his hand on her arm and said, "I'll explain on the way out."

I'll explain on the way out from Tom usually meant *You are less likely to bite my head off if we're moving.* Which meant whatever he'd agreed to relating to Conan must be a spectacularly bad idea.

But they couldn't argue in front of Anthony. Besides, Rafiel was waiting. The thought of Rafiel made her look back over her shoulder, "Tom, we should take meat. He hasn't eaten in—"

"Of course," Tom said. "You start up the van. I'll be right there."

Kyrie nodded, got under the pass-through, and headed to the curving corridor that led to the restrooms and the back door.

"You know I really can't deal with this alone," Anthony said. "Laura is doing the prep work, but I have no one to tend to tables, or for that matter to arrange tables and chairs for Conan's thing."

Tom looked up from the meat he was cutting. "You can't call one of the part-timers?"

"Not many of them around just now, with the end of the college year and finals and all that."

"Um." Tom ran an eye over the patrons, looking for friends he could recruit. Over the last year, many of the patrons had become friends—particularly those who were shifters and who knew that Kyrie and Tom were also shifters. But now, though the tables were full—and Laura had to keep interrupting her real work to go attend tables—he was having trouble finding a familiar face.

Until he heard a voice from the counter, "Hey," the voice said. "Hey."

Tom focused on the man standing between two of the stools at the counter. He was stocky, olive-skinned, wore a black T-shirt, had short-short hair with the tips frosted white, and looked anxious. "Hey, did you hear about the police officer? I mean, how is—"

"Jason, right?" Tom said. "Jason Bear."

A smile. "No, Jason Cordova," the man said. "But yeah. Did you hear from Officer Trall?"

"Yeah. In fact, we have to go and...help him. Uh. Have you ever waited tables?"

"What?" Nod. "Yeah. Couple of times. Pizza Hut and stuff."

"Would you do it, at least for tonight? To help us out?"

"What? You mean, like a job?" Was that an anxious light in the man's eyes?

"Like a job, if you need it. We're always short-staffed, and now with students leaving we will be very short-staffed all summer. Here." Tom grabbed an apron from under the counter and shoved it at the man.

"Minimum wage?" the man asked lifting an eyebrow.

"We pay ten fifty-five an hour, double time for overtime, and you get all the meals you're here for."

"Suits me," Cordova said putting on the apron.

"Good. Anthony. Jason here will be doing the tables. Teach him the ropes as he goes, will you?"

Anthony rolled his eyes. "What I like about this job," he said, "is the variety. Every day is a new experience. And the teaching opportunities—I really like that."

"Good," Tom said. "Then you have it covered." He grabbed the carryout container and ran out the door.

Kyrie had completely forgotten about Bea, and she nearly jumped out of her skin as Bea surged out of the booth and grabbed her arm. "Let me come with you," she said. "Let me help."

Kyrie hesitated. On the one hand Bea was a shifter, which meant she wasn't likely to turn in shifterkind. On the other hand, though what she'd heard of the girl's story sounded good, they hadn't questioned her, and it was possible she belonged to one of those shifters organizations who thought it was their duty to keep every shifter in line.

Bea looked anxiously at Kyrie's face, then said, "I know you have no reason to trust me, and I don't even know what is happening here, but think about it from my perspective. I was almost roasted alive, and I don't know why, nor whether the Grea— Himself is not likely to do the same thing again."

Her terror was either real or the girl was the most gifted actress alive. Kyrie nodded. "Okay. Come on."

✧   ✧   ✧

Tom was surprised that Kyrie and Bea were both in the van. Almost as surprised as he was that they'd left the driver's seat to him. He hadn't expected the not-exactly-Chinese girl. And he never expected Kyrie to let him drive. "I couldn't leave her alone," Kyrie told him in an undertone, understandable only to a lip reader. "She was attacked and almost killed, after all."

Tom tried not to smirk but must not have managed it, because Kyrie sighed. "It is not in the least like your taking in all sorts of strays."

"No?" Tom said, and left it at that, because Bea was, after all, in the back seat.

"No. Not in the least. Now tell me what it is about Conan's thing."

"No," Tom said, starting the van, the large vehicle they normally took to farmers' markets in summer. "First you tell me what it is about Rafiel and where we're going, and why."

"Oh. He was attacked by something. He couldn't describe it, because . . . he sounded pretty weak. But he was attacked by something, and he's very hurt. Somewhere out 25, near Goldminers Road. He said he's in a field, so when we get near, we'll need aerial recognizance, which is why we needed you."

"I see. So, I'll drive out to Goldminers, then you can follow me while I fly. That way I minimize the time I spend in the air, during which someone might get a picture of me."

"And what is Conan's thing?"

"You're not going to forget that, are you?" Tom said, turning out of the parking lot and into the bumper-to-bumper traffic on Fairfax Avenue, the street that crossed Goldport from one end to the other. He headed west on it, and traffic cleared after the warehouse district.

"No. It's something with the diner. And you're not supposed to do anything to the diner without telling me. Is he having a party or something?"

Tom shook his head. "No. You know Wednesday is our slow night, right? So I thought there would be no problem at all with letting him sing."

"What? Tom!"

Tom sighed. He'd known for the last few months that while Conan was a decent waiter and could hold down the fort when they were needed elsewhere, Conan had ambitions beyond food service. Having grown up in Nashville, Tennessee, where his parents owned a Chinese restaurant, he wanted to be a country-western singer. "He can't be that bad," he mumbled.

"How do you know?" Kyrie asked. "We have never heard him sing. And he couldn't have practiced the guitar in the time he's spent regrowing the arm he had ripped off. He could be absolutely horrible."

"Well, Wednesday is our slow night," Tom said. "If he's absolutely horrible, we only let him do one song. But he wanted to sing in front of an audience, never having done that before, and he asked, and—"

"And you have no ability to say no?"

"I don't see what it can hurt. Remember, the coffee shop down the street has really bad poetry readings? They still bring people in."

"Yes, but . . . if you have really bad singing, that makes people go out."

A sound like a snuffle from behind them made Tom look in the rearview mirror, to see Bea hiding her mouth, her eyes filled with amusement. "You find us funny?" he said.

"It's just that . . . are all shifters like this?" she asked. "Do you live in communities that behave like families?"

"No," Kyrie said. "I suspect most shifters in the world are all alone, and don't know anyone like them. We have two things that make us different. One of them is that at some point someone—we'll tell you the story another time, if you must hear it—someone sprayed the entire area around The George with pheromones that attract shifters from hundred of miles round. The other is that—"

"The Great Sky Dragon has at least temporary headquarters in town," Tom said.

"No," Kyrie said. "I don't know why he has that, but I know—"

"Because you're his heir," Bea said.

"What?" Tom said. He couldn't have heard the words right. She'd said it so naturally, it was as though it were something obvious.

In the rearview mirror, he saw Bea's eyebrows arch over the bright green eyes. "You didn't know that?" she asked. "That's why he wanted me to marry you." In a hurried voice she told a fantastic story of the successor of the Great Sky Dragon having to be a male, who could shift—apparently it wasn't a given all of his descendants could—and who was descended on the male line unbroken. Tom was actually descended from the Great Sky Dragon's son on both sides, Bea told them, shrugging, the male line broken of course by his mother on one side.

"It sounds... inbred," Tom said. "And neither of my parents is even slightly Chinese. Dad is of Swedish ancestry, and I think most of Mom's ancestors were French, though I'm not sure now why I think that." He added, as explanation, "She left when I was a kid."

"Oh," Bea said. "But this would be thousands and thousands of years ago. I gather the Great Sky Dragon is near immortal."

"Which brings up the question of why he needs an heir."

"Because he says something is coming that might kill him."

"Irrelevant, since I don't intend to lead a triad, even if they obeyed me, which I doubt. But... so that's why he's taken an interest in me." Tom was now driving out of town and into the country expanses of I-25, with unlit fields on either side. "Would you watch out for the turn to Goldminers Road, Kyrie? Otherwise I might miss it in the dark."

"Yes. But what you said about the Great Sky Dragon has nothing to do with the community of shifters around the diner. What makes it... well... a coherent group, instead of just a bunch of unrelated people—what makes us work together and cover for each other, and... care for each other is Tom."

Kyrie said it so convincingly it was no use Tom laughing. Instead, he said, "I'm not some kind of saint."

"No. You're just a natural leader—and you care about people. It's one of those natural things. You either have it or you don't."

"Maybe that's why the Great Sky Dragon thinks—" Bea said. "I mean—"

"Irrelevant. As I said, I have no intention of leading a triad any more than you have any intention of marrying me."

"No. Of course not. It's just... look at what he did to me," Bea said.

"Oh. Yeah. I expect he'll be trouble," Tom said. "And that's nothing new."

"Goldminers on the right, Tom. Exit."

Bea sat quietly. She was starting to get, if not a clear idea of what was happening, a suspicion that she might comprehend it sometime. There was... a shape of events forming in her mind, and she wasn't sure what they were. But there was a sense of a pattern.

Tom took the exit off the highway onto a narrow street flanked by trees. The street became a dirt road and ran through an expanse of rocky ground covered in what appeared to be low, thorny bushes.

Tom pulled over to the side and parked the van. He got out, stepping into the circle of the headlights. When he then moved out of the light, for a moment Bea wondered why, then realized that it was so he could undress—presumably in respect for her modesty. Meanwhile Kyrie moved over to the driver's seat. A few minutes later, Tom emerged into the headlights. No. Tom's dragon.

His scales glistened blue-green in the light, and it was impossible to believe that this was the same young man who'd been talking to them and driving moments before. Impossible, that is, until he turned to look at them and she got a good look at the dragon's blue eyes, which were, very reassuringly, Tom Ormson's.

She wondered how much knowledge of their human self other people retained while in shifted form. She'd never known anyone else who shifted, never had a chance to ask. She just knew that her control over where the dragon went had improved over the years. When she'd first shifted at fourteen, she'd hardly known what she did when she was the dragon. Later, there had come memories of her actions—as if in a dream—and by the time she was sixteen, she could control the dragon to some extent. Now she could control what the dragon did, and she could even—most of the time—avoid shifting when she didn't wish to shift.

But she wondered if everyone else was like that. Clearly Tom Ormson was. But was that normal or just part of being a descendent of the Great Sky Dragon?

"Okay, here we go," Kyrie said, as Tom took to the skies, unbelievable in his look of archaic fantasy, flying over a land crisscrossed by highways and lighted by electricity.

Bea shivered a little. "I've always wondered," she said, "why none of us is photographed. I mean . . . when I had little control, I was flying over this Atlanta suburb."

Kyrie shrugged. "My form? I change into a panther. I've often wondered if we're responsible for all the sightings of great black cats. And if other shifters account for all the out-of-place animals seen here and there. But with dragons and other . . . less normal forms, I suspect the thing is partly that no one believes it. People don't fully believe what they're seeing. Other people look at pictures and think what a clever Photoshop job. I've told Tom we could make a great deal of money on the side by taking pictures of him and Conan flying over the city and making a calendar. Everyone would think it was made up."

Bea turned the idea in her mind. "Except that over time it might give people the idea that . . . well, that it exists."

"That's what Tom says, though you know, dragons shifters are not just a genetic impossibility. They're a physical impossibility. Those wings of yours shouldn't be able to hold you up."

The road bumped under them, and Bea held onto the seat with both hands, despite the seat belt across her middle. Kyrie turned willy-nilly onto something that couldn't possibly be a road, only a bumpy sort of track amid a burned landscape. Ahead, Tom descended towards a field where Bea's eyes couldn't discern much more than thorns and rocks.

"Are you saying we don't exist?" Bea said.

"How can I?" Kyrie turned off the ignition. "I'm saying that you are impossible, but, hey. I live with Tom. He very much exists. Come on."

They got out of the van and closed it. Bea looked for the huge form of the dragon ahead but couldn't see it. It took her a moment to realize that Tom had shifted and in fact stood nearby, putting his shoes on. She wondered if he'd carried his clothes. That was control she'd never quite managed.

Then she realized there was someone at Tom's feet and stopped suddenly with a gasp.

⊱ CHAPTER 11 ⊰

Her first thought was that the man was dead. He lay on the ground, naked, covered in blood. There was blood on the ground around him too—Bea could sort of see it, but more importantly, she could smell it. Something that she was more sensitive to than normal humans, no matter what her form, was the smell of blood. It made the dragon stir within her and get hungry.

Then she realized the pale, blood-smeared chest was rising and falling, and that Kyrie had brought something else out of the van. Kyrie squatted by the man, and told him, "Come on, Rafiel, drink." From the unholy blue fluorescence of it, the drink she was tilting towards the man's lips was one of those sports drinks sold to exercise fanatics that were supposed to replace electrolytes.

From the man's slight movement and the sounds of his drinking, he had to be alive or at least trying to be. As Kyrie withdrew the drink, he said in a raspy voice, "There was a mama. I mean, the creature...I think it's a juvenile. It has a mother. It—"

"Don't talk about that now." This was Tom who had come back and stood at the man's other side. "Can you sit up? I have no intention of hand-feeding you."

Something like a chuckle from the man, and then he dragged himself to a sitting position. A trick of moonlight gave Bea a full

71

view of his face. It ought to have horrified her. To an extent it did horrify her.

His left eye was a congealed mass of blood, and there were deep-cut claw marks from his nose to his temple, perhaps all the way to his scalp, because the blond hair on that side was matted with dried blood.

He turned his right eye to her, though, and it was dark brown and filled with unholy amusement. "Hello," he said. "Tom? Kyrie?"

"Oh, this is Bea. We'll explain later. Don't worry. She's a dragon. One of us," Tom said.

The man's mouth twitched and it should have looked horrible, but it felt friendly and relaxed. "Oh, sure. You always introduce the pretty girls to me when I'm just back from the dead." He accepted the box of takeout meat and a plastic fork from Tom and started eating with manners that, Bea suspected, were due to her presence. Tom wasn't making that much of an effort. He was shoveling food into his face from the other takeout box. Kyrie got up and went back to the van.

"Did you . . . did you die?" Bea asked, afraid that she would sound like an idiot.

"I don't think so," the man said. "I might have though. It felt like she snapped my spine, but that must have been wrong, or I wouldn't be able to sit up. My eye hasn't healed yet, so I assume—"

"It will heal?"

"Probably," Rafiel said. "We seem to have a regenerative capacity that evades other humans." The single brown eye was still laughing at her. And the meat, as he ate, seemed to visibly make him feel better. "Coming back from the dead usually takes days, anyway. Not that I've ever done it, but Tom has, and from what we understand from . . . ah, our older shifter friends, that's a shifter thing, not a dragon thing. If we can trust our sources, at least."

"Which is a stretch, considering that our sources most of the time are elderly, addled, often homeless, and occasionally aligatorish," Tom said. "But at least the explanation makes sense."

"So, I don't think I was dead, no, ma'am . . . Bea. But yes, I think my eye will come back and . . . the wounds will heal, probably by tomorrow."

Kyrie came back, and handed the man, who had finished his takeout container, a folded bundle.

In the end, Tom had to help Rafiel dress—in jogging pants

and a shirt, and had to more carry him to the van than help him walk, though Bea noticed Tom was careful to preserve the appearance that he was only assisting.

They strapped Rafiel in the back, in the seat next to hers, though there was a space in between. He looked groggy, half awake, except when that bright right eye turned in her direction. It should have discomfited her, given what a wreck he looked, but it didn't. There was humor in his glance, and he smiled a little.

"So, why is Bea along?"

Tom explained.

"Ah, I sensed we had a lot in common. You died. I almost died."

"More importantly," Kyrie said gravely, "it brings us to ask—where are you two going to go? You might not be safe in town, either of you."

"Go?" Bea asked.

"Well," Kyrie said. "Someone might try to kill you again, Bea—particularly if the Great Sky Dragon knows you have no intention of obeying, and as for Rafiel... he can't heal like this in public. You have to see that. Too many explanations. We heal really fast. People will wonder. He can't hide his face."

Rafiel seemed immersed in thought for a long time. "My parents' cabin," he said at last. "My car is at Riverside, but... Perhaps it's best if you lend me a van. One of your vans? Less likely to be tracked." He took a deep breath. "My parents have a cabin in the mountains, south of here. Middle of nowhere. I have the keys on my key ring. Strapped to me, with the phone. I can go there while I recover and while we find out how to keep Miss Ryu safe."

Bea should have been offended at his presumption or perhaps suspicious of this plan to throw her into a cabin all alone with a guy she barely knew. Instead, she felt perfectly safe and oddly relaxed about it.

True, she hardly knew Rafiel, and yet she felt that she'd known him for a long, long time. It wasn't so much that she liked him, but she felt she belonged around him—like they'd known each other such a long time she needn't worry about what impression she was making or how he felt. He just was and she just was. If it weren't such a comfortable feeling, it would be downright scary.

✧　　✧　　✧

"You know," Tom said. "If you'd told me I would send a young and innocent girl off with Rafiel like that, just a day ago, I'd have told you that you were insane."

"We have no proof that she's innocent," Kyrie said.

Tom smiled at her. "Probably too innocent for love-them-and-leave-them Rafiel."

"Who by his own admission is more *leave* them and less love them. I'm more worried about Rafiel than her," Kyrie said. They were driving back from seeing Rafiel out of town, just in case, and were starting to hit the heavy traffic on Fairfax. "Notice she already made sure she got to drive, not him."

"Um," Tom said, as he avoided a large heating-and-plumbing service truck hell bent on changing lanes on top of him. "Considering for now at least Rafiel has only one working eye, I'm glad she did. Sensible of her."

A sly, sideways look from Kyrie, and she said, "You like her."

"Oh yes. Unless she's a very carefully contrived plant, that girl has—what did they use to call it? Moxie. Almost as much as you." He reached and squeezed her hand. "And you must admit this whole thing has to be fairly bewildering for someone like her, born and raised American—you know..."

"Yeah, unlike Conan Lung whose parents more or less told him he now belonged to the Great Sky Dragon the very first time he shifted and whose parents at least have the full expectation of belonging to someone in a feudal sense, Bea grew up thinking of herself as free," Kyrie said. "So knowing a many-times ancestor has decided her marriage had to come as a shock. And speaking of Conan—"

"For all you shift into a panther, you're rather like a bulldog, aren't you? Once you get hold of something, you just won't let go."

"Well... Tom, what if it damages the reputation of the diner? What if people stop coming?"

"No one will be there to hear it. Note we didn't even put a poster up. No one knows. And I set it for eight p.m., so the dinner rush will be done. It will just be a dozen regulars, and they won't hold it against us if Conan sounds like the unfortunate encounter between a tin cutter and a cat in heat. And if he's that terrible, I won't let him do it again."

"Okay," Kyrie said, seemingly appeased. "As long as there aren't too many people in attendance."

✧   ✧   ✧

There were way too many people there, Kyrie thought. The parking lot was so full they had to drive up the cross street that ran along the side of The George. And even Pride Street was parked almost bumper to bumper, so it was some blocks before they found a place to park.

They hurried back in silence, except for Tom's saying, in a plaintive tone, "But there weren't even any posters."

Only there was now a banner stretched across the front of the diner, announcing, TONIGHT, THE DEBUT OF CONAN LUNG. SIX-STRING DRAGON! YOU AIN'T HEARD NOTHING YET.

"Tom!" Kyrie said, in a strangled voice. How had this happened? How had one of Tom's projects gotten so out of hand?

"Well...it's...er...I mean, at least he said 'heard,' right, so people can't think he's a stripper."

"Tom!"

"Right. What do you expect me to do? I mean, all these people are here for it, clearly. Look, we'll sell some souvlaki or...or whatever...and if it's terrible, we'll promise not to let him sing again, and then it will be all right."

Kyrie just shook her head, but her mouth was twitching upwards. Tom was...irrepressible, she decided. It had been a long, long time since she had been able to get mad at him. This was stupid, but it was such a Tom stupidity that she couldn't help smiling. "Idiot," she said.

"Come on," he said. "How bad can he be?"

"Six-string dragon!" she said, and broke into giggles.

"Okay...bad. But let's give him a chance, shall we?"

The diner was packed as they came in. Kyrie noted with approval that beyond the normal tables, which had been packed into as small a space as possible, there had been rows of fold-able chairs set up.

"We got them from my church," Anthony said. "I called and sent Jason over."

"But how did all these people know?" Tom asked, from behind Kyrie.

"Well, seems like Conan put up a video of himself singing on Facebook, and it went viral."

Kyrie swallowed hard, feeling as though her heart had dropped somewhere around her knees. "Oh, no. They're here to mock him, right? It's like that guy on that show whose audition tape was so bad."

"I don't know," Anthony said. "He might think that though. He's gone and locked himself in the storage room in the back."

"Uh..." Kyrie said. Great. The only thing worse than having Conan sing and be absolutely terrible at it, was, of course, not to have Conan sing at all. That would get them eaten alive—metaphorically—by the patrons of The George. With all her heart she hoped it was metaphorically. Scanning the crowd she could see enough faces that turned into something fanged or carnivorous not to be absolutely sure. "Has Rya—"

Rya, a fox shifter attending CUG was Conan's...well, maybe not precisely girlfriend. Kyrie didn't think Conan had enough confidence to ask anyone out, but they were known to hang out together and, occasionally, go out for coffee or to shows.

"She was here, yeah. She's still here somewhere, I think. She pounded on the door to the storage room and asked to be let in, but he wouldn't."

"Oh, lord," Tom said. "I'll handle it." He already had his apron and bandana on, and he looked hesitatingly at Kyrie. "Can you take care of it here, while I go and get Conan out of the storage room."

"His master's voice?" Kyrie asked, and regretted it immediately as Tom gave her an injured look back.

Tom didn't like the implication that he had some sort of power over Conan. Oh, he knew it was true, to an extent. When you've been browbeaten into becoming a slave, it's easier to become the slave of yet someone else than to spring free and be your own person. He'd freed Conan, but he was aware that was one-sided. Conan still looked to him for guidance...to put it mildly.

He walked down the hallway and knocked at the door to the back storage room, because he couldn't imagine even Conan in a snit locking himself in the freezer room. Also, from inside this storage room came forlorn plucking at the guitar strings.

Tom knocked again. For a moment, only more forlorn plucking answered him, then Conan's voice, wavering and thin, "Yeah?"

"It's Tom. Open up."

"I can't. I have laryngitis. I can't sing."

"Oh, for the love— Conan. Open this damn door or I kick it in, and then I make you pay for the new one."

There was a *shuffle-shuffle* sound from the other side and then the sound of the lock sliding. Tom opened the door, while telling himself that they really needed to get rid of the deadbolt on the inside of the storage room. And they would have, by now, if it weren't for the fact that the storage room was where he and Kyrie and other shifters in their confidence retreated to change clothes, or to put clothes on, when their clothes had been lost to an unfortunate shifting episode. It was also where they retreated when they absolutely must discuss something the nonshifting employees couldn't know.

The room looked as usual: vast metal shelves held up supplies of paper products, barrels of flour were stacked against one wall, and vats of condiments against another. Despite the irregular use to which it was put, the room was kept scrupulously clean. It was the rule around here that if you used the room you must make it perfectly clean afterwards.

In the middle of the shiny linoleum, Conan stood irresolutely. He was, Tom thought, preposterously attired. Not that Conan was ever much for clothes. Normally he made do with jeans and T-shirt. But now ... but now he'd got himself wearing what— probably in his own mind—a country-western star should wear.

That is, he had probably gone to that stupid touristy store downtown, the one that had the huge plastic cow on the roof, and he'd bought everything that was thrust at him. Which meant he was wearing a shirt in giant blue-and-white checks with big, bejeweled mother-of-pearl buttons, jeans with rivets so large they probably hurt, a vest with fringe on the pockets, a bolo tie—a bolo tie, for heaven's sake—and the biggest cowboy hat that Tom had ever had the misfortune of seeing.

In his everyday persona, Conan was not a bad-looking man. He was small, thin, Asian, with hair that insisted on falling in front of his eyes. But his thinness was wiry rather than under-nourished, and his eyes tended to crinkle at the corners when he smiled. He had certainly made an impression with Rya, and there were probably several other young women in the diner who would have given him a chance.

But now he disappeared inside those preposterous clothes, and had to tilt his hat up for Tom to see his face. That face was so pale that Conan looked like he was made of wax. His wide eyes were fixed in terror that Tom couldn't remember seeing, even when he and Conan had fought side by side against overwhelming odds.

"What is this now?" Tom said, more softly than he'd meant to. "People are out there to hear you, Conan."

Conan backed up to sit on one of the flour barrels. His guitar was propped up against it. "I know," he said softly. "I was such an idiot. I thought if I put it on my Facebook page, a few of my friends might come."

"I'd say—"

"No, you don't understand. I was all excited, and I made the banner and everything—"

"Six-string dragon, Conan?"

A pallid smile. "Well, seemed like a good idea, okay?"

"Yeah? And why is it not now?"

"Anthony said..." Conan swallowed audibly. "Anthony said that people probably made it go viral because they thought it was funny, because it was so bad."

"Anthony said that?" Tom asked, shocked, because Anthony was many things but cruel wasn't one of them.

"Uh...not...he didn't *exactly* say that, but he said that people shared all sorts of crap they found funny, and I remembered all those videos people share, people from Hong Kong singing 'I'm sexy' and stuff...and I thought..."

"And you thought crazy stuff. Did anyone make fun of it on your page?"

"No. But they wouldn't, right? Can...can you tell them, please..." Conan looked up at Tom, his eyes immense and fearful. "That you, you know, that you found that...that it's against regs, or something?"

Tom pulled himself up on the plastic flour barrel next to Conan's. "I can do that, Conan, if you want me to, but you need to think this through very carefully."

The blank look in Conan's face indicated that Conan's brain was rather like a skittering rabbit, incapable of focusing on anything. Tom tried anyway. "Look, it's always scary to take a big step to realize our dreams. Do you think I wasn't scared when my dad said he'd get Kyrie and me this diner? Do you think I wasn't afraid of screwing it up?"

"That's different. People weren't making fun of a video of you running a diner."

"You don't know if they are," Tom said. And paused, not because of hesitating about what to say to Conan, but because of a weird feeling he couldn't quite pinpoint. It was, he thought, as though something cold and strange had touched his mind for just a minute. "You don't know," he started again, "that they're even making fun of your video. They could very well be enjoying it, and that's why they told all their friends. Look, Conan, if they were making fun of you, someone would have told you. Rya or someone."

"I told Rya to go away," Conan said, as though confessing a crime. "She's going to be so mad at me."

"Unlikely. You know, she knows you're nervous." The feeling was there, again, stronger this time. Something was touching Tom's mind, something cold, ice cold. Something alien. He had once had the Great Sky Dragon in his mind, and it hadn't felt that alien or that cold.

"Look," he said, ignoring the weird sensation and concentrating on the problem at hand. "You have stage fright. It's completely natural. You should go out there and face your fears. If you shrink from it now, you'll never—" There it was again, and now with a stab of near-physical pain. "You'll never be able to try again. You must go out there *now*, Conan. You must."

"Are you okay?" Conan asked, concerned.

"Yeah, I'm fine. I guess I just shifted once too many times tonight and—" and at that moment, the Great Sky Dragon was in Tom's head, or at least his voice was, loud, unavoidable, *I DIDN'T INTEND IT THIS WAY,* it said, *BUT YOU MUST CARRY MY BURDEN NOW. PROTECT MY PEOPLE.*

There was a scream, and Tom wasn't sure if it came from the Great Sky Dragon or from himself, but it was loud, high-pitched, blotting out all thought, and then ... and then unbearable pressure and light, from within.

Damn, I'm going to shift, Tom thought, and his last conscious act was to try to get Conan out of there, before he found himself locked in with a larger dragon out of control. "Go out there, Conan. Go out there and sing. That's an order."

His voice seemed to reverberate unnaturally off the walls. He registered that Conan's terrified face managed to look even more terrified, and then Conan bowed and ran from the room, closing the door behind him.

Tom let himself fall to his knees, under the weight of pain and pressure he could not understand.

And then blackness blotted it all out.

⇥ CHAPTER 12 ⇤

Bea liked the cabin. She'd been expecting something bare, perhaps with bathroom facilities outside. She'd never seen much point in that sort of thing. As far as she was concerned, humans had spent thousands of years getting away from the icky and stinky parts of nature, and it would be an insult to their efforts for her to go back and live like a savage. She liked indoor bathrooms and heated showers.

But she hadn't been counting on getting them this time, and she was half ready to rough it. After all, it might be a matter of life and death, both for herself and for Rafiel.

And she still couldn't understand why she felt so comfortable driving through the night next to this heavily mangled man. He'd given her some instructions and then let her drive while he slept. He hadn't been joking about the healing capacities of shifters.

She knew that she, herself, had always healed fast from the scrapes and hurts of childhood, but she'd never been as injured as Rafiel was. And she could see him healing before her eyes as he slept. She saw the scrapes shrink, grow pink, disappear.

Twice, she had to wake him to ask the way at unmarked intersections. City gave way to countryside with startling suddenness, and they were soon driving a little road up a mountainside, with the only lights distant glimmers.

And she was sure they were going to be in a bare log cabin, with only wood for heat, and only water they could pull up from some well.

But when they approached the end of the directions, and Rafiel woke up, he said, "Down this driveway, there. Yeah. I know it looks like a goat track. Don't worry. It's large enough for the car. I often come here when I have to get away because...when I have to get away."

The driveway wound and wound, and was more than a mile long, but at the end of it, they came to a little clearing in the midst of the tall trees. In the clearing, stood...It was, in fact a log cabin, and not very big. When they approached, the light over the door went on, and it was undeniably electric and brilliant.

"It's on a sensor," Rafiel explained. He opened the door and got out, and, as Bea turned off the engine, walked around to open her door. "I'm sorry you didn't have a chance to get your clothes."

"No. They were in my pickup, and that was in the parking lot of the Three Luck Dragon—"

He held the door open for her, and extended a hand to help her get out. "My mom probably has some stuff in there. Don't look so outraged. She mostly wears dresses and stuff when she's out here, so you can probably borrow something. And if not, I have T-shirts. Though I'm afraid my jeans won't fit you."

"Your T-shirts would probably be dresses," she said. Although she was by no means small, certainly not by the standards of most Asian women, as she got out, she felt tiny beside Rafiel, who had to be well over six feet.

He grinned. "Well, there. Problem solved."

He led her to the door, which he opened. Surprise. The walls were made of logs, just like any log cabin's, but the floor was modern wood, sealed, probably presealed in the factory. The little hallway they entered had a coat rack and a table.

She followed Rafiel into a central room with a massive fireplace. But it was obvious even to her inexperienced eyes that the fireplace was wired for gas. The walls were covered in bookcases filled with books. Not the pretty-pretty leather-bound books that people bought to look important, but paperback books with colorful covers. This was a place inhabited by serious readers. And they did their reading in spacious brown leather sofas.

Rafiel looked back over his shoulder with a deprecating smile. "I'm afraid," he said, "that my family has a thing for mysteries. That's why my mom named me what she did."

"Raphael?" Bea asked, desperately trying to understand the significance.

"No. Rafiel. After Agatha Christie's character in *Sleeping Murder and*—"

"*Nemesis*," she completed, smiling.

"I see you read mysteries too."

"Doesn't everyone?" she asked. "My dad is a big Christie fan. He read me to sleep with her work."

"So did my parents. So much so, I almost forgive them for giving me a name that forced me to correct my teachers all through school. Okay, let me show you around."

The cabin consisted of two bedrooms in addition to the living room and a sleeping loft which, Rafiel said, "Is where I normally sleep, but you can have it if you want to. It has a skylight and you can look up and see the stars." When Bea had expressed her admiration for the room, with its broad, quilt-covered bed and its view of the evening sky, Rafiel had insisted she take it. "No," he said. "Really. We changed the sheets the last time we were here. Mom drilled it into my head it's always the last thing we do before we leave." He patted her on the shoulder. "Let me show you something."

He pressed a button on the wall near the skylight, and it slid open. "Normally I keep it closed," he said. "But sometimes in the summer, when it's really warm, it's worth it to sleep, you know, with the smell of the trees all around. It's like being in nature, but still having a real bed with clean sheets."

The other creature comforts of the cabin included not one but two fully equipped, modern bathrooms, and a hot tub out on the balcony that jutted off the loft. "I don't know if Mom left a bathing suit," Rafiel said, "but if not, you can try it out next time."

The weird thing was not that he was talking as though absolutely sure that there would be another time of her coming out here with him, but that she felt as though he was perfectly justified. There would be another time, or possibly many times. They would come out here, together, and spend time even when they weren't running from anything.

The rational Bea scolded her. There was no way she could know that. Perhaps he always brought girls out here. Perhaps he didn't like her. And even if he liked her, with the trouble they were in, it would be a miracle if they survived, much less if they got to play house together.

She was being stupid and reverting to middle school. There would be time enough for a game of "he loves me, he loves me not" if they survived this. And if he loved her not, she really hadn't lost anything.

"I'm going to take a shower," Rafiel said. "The kitchen is that way." As though realizing what he'd said, he added, "In case you're hungry. Why don't you see if there's anything you want to eat, and I cook when I come out?"

She grinned. "Good," she said. "Because I've been known to burn water. I'll go look."

Kyrie heard Tom shout, but didn't have time to give it much thought, because Conan came running out of the storage room, banging the door behind him. She guessed, as she turned to take orders for coffee and sandwiches from the people seated on folding chairs, that Tom had finally lost patience with Conan and shouted at him.

Well, good. It seemed to have worked.

No one laughed, as Conan scurried to the open space in front of the tables, close to the corner booth with the picture of St. George slaying the dragon over it. Jason put a stool up there, at the last minute, and of course they didn't have microphones, and so Kyrie hoped that Conan could make himself heard over the low murmur of noise around the diner.

The murmur changed to approval as Conan climbed onto the stool, which was one from the bar, and a little too tall, so his feet didn't quite touch the floor. He looked like a kid wearing western wear for some play, but no one laughed, which must be a good thing.

She thought he was hiding his face behind his hat, but that was okay, provided he didn't sing too badly. On the other hand, perhaps his voice, rather soft in normal everyday interaction, wouldn't carry enough to be heard. Which could be a plus. People would applaud politely, then leave.

This suspicion of what was about to happen was confirmed when Conan said, "My name is Conan Lung, and I'm going to sing my cover of 'Home.'"

He could barely be heard and only the front row of tables clapped.

Well, okay, Kyrie thought. *It won't be great, but it won't be a disaster.* She sought out Tom in the crowd, and when she failed to find him, assumed he was in the addition, perhaps, taking orders. As busy as they were, it would be all hands on deck.

And then Conan started playing. Kyrie was not an expert, but it clearly was good guitar playing, so that was something.

Then he sang. It was a shock. The voice that came out of the little Asian man in funny clothes was at least three times as large as his speaking voice, large enough to fill the entire diner. He was a tenor, but his range was . . . magnificent. Kyrie stepped backwards, as the rich voice enveloped her, singing of going home, of the longing for home. The song was of course familiar, but the voice—that voice. It wrapped around the diner, it echoed with emotion, it reached in and touched something in the mind and the heart.

The diner had gone absolutely quiet, so quiet it was as though people had stopped breathing. The only sound other than the singing was the hiss of frying oil behind the counter, and it took all of Kyrie's presence of mind to realize that if the song had affected Anthony as it had affected her, then he'd be in danger of burning something. It took willpower too, to move behind the counter and remove the fries from the oil and into the draining vat, then put another batch in.

As though her movement had awakened him, Anthony lurched to life, and started taking care of things, asking her in a whisper, "Where is Tom?"

"I don't know. He must be waiting tables."

"I don't think so. He hasn't brought me any orders."

"Well, he must—"

The song finished and talking became impossible over the storm of applause. In the center of it, Conan tilted his hat back and looked in shocked surprise at the crowd. Slowly, a dark red color suffused his cheeks. "Uh . . . You . . . You think . . ." He cleared his throat. He took his guitar up properly again and played a few chords. The crowd quieted immediately.

Conan smiled at them. "The next song is one I wrote, and it's dedicated to a really special woman, Rya. Rya, if you're out there, I was a jerk, and I wrote this for you."

For a moment, Kyrie was afraid. Just because the man had a voice like golden syrup pouring on the perfect stack of pancakes, it didn't mean he could write songs.

But the chords he played were slow and sad, and coherent, and when he started singing... Well, her first impulse was to dart up front, hit him on the head, make him stop singing.

Not that it was a bad song. On the contrary. It was a beautiful poem about wishing one could fly away from all one's cares and mistakes. It was called "If I Could Fly to You."

The problem was exactly that. Kyrie thought anyone would know this was about the experience of being a dragon shifter. And it took all her not inconsiderable self-control to hold back and allow herself to realize that while the lyrics were plain to *her*, they wouldn't be to anyone else. She needed to shut up and let the man play.

She'd been accustomed to thinking of Conan as a boy, perhaps because of how he behaved with Tom, but it was obvious he was a man. His voice made him so, and she could see the shyness and the deference drop away from him as he sang, the people in the crowd clearly drinking in his voice and his words.

As he started a third song, after a storm of applause, Anthony said in a whisper in the sudden silence, "I'm fairly sure Tom is still in the storage room, Kyrie. And that's just not normal. He knows we'd need him out here and besides, you know... he's not... he's not that trusting, and he wouldn't trust me with this load of frying if he were all right. He would be out here to check on me by now."

Kyrie wished she could say otherwise. But Anthony had a point.

Except... except maybe Tom had gone into the storage room to avoid making Conan nervous? No. That made no sense. Tom had gone into the storage room *because* Conan was nervous.

"You're right," she said. "I'll go." She stepped out to the pass-through, and down the hallway to the door to the storage room.

From within she could hear someone groaning, but it didn't at all sound like Tom. She called out "Tom?" And then she pushed the door open.

✧   ✧   ✧

He had too many legs. That was the first thing Tom thought, followed shortly by the unavoidable fact that he had too many arms. In fact, he also had too many eyes. The eyes were everywhere, looking at everything from full daylight to darkest night. The arms and legs were here and there, picking things, moving things, walking, running.

Some of his bodies appeared to be fighting. Others were sleeping. But he was all of them. He was everywhere.

No. Nonsense. I am Tom Ormson. I am in Goldport, Colorado, in the storage room of a diner called The George.

This was absolutely and undeniably true. But it wasn't the whole truth. He was also Johnny Li, a teenager in New Jersey, involved in a street fight, and trying very hard not to shift into a dragon. He had only shifted twice before, and he didn't have a lot of self-control. He didn't know how to avoid it.

Tom sent a firming thought Johnny's way, with the admonition not to shift, but the moment of clarity, of identifying that as one of his bodies, had already passed. In its place was the feeling of being everywhere and everyone at once.

He knelt on the floor of the storage room, and pressed his fists to his forehead, trying to calm a myriad of sensory impressions that he knew were not coming from *his* body, but which were, nonetheless, as real and immediate as though they were.

Eternity seemed to pass, and all he could manage was maintaining the certainty that his principal part, his principal and most important body, was Tom, here, in the storage room, kneeling on the floor.

But with this self-possession came a call—a need in many voices. All those people, all those bodies he was and yet wasn't, were calling him. He must be the dragon. He must be seen. He must let the most important of them come and pay him homage. He must let the nearer ones assemble and recognize that the tribe of dragons had a new head, that the slain Great Sky Dragon lived again.

He understood enough of the call, of the need, of the mess in his head, to know what had happened, and what he was in for. He staggered to his feet, and stood, shaking, "I don't want it," he said to the clear air around him. "Someone else should take it. I'm not even Asian, let alone Chinese. And I'm not the head of any triad."

From the other side of the door—seemingly from another world away—Kyrie's voice said, "Tom."

And then the door opened, and let in the strains of a strong and smooth male voice singing "You are Not Alone." And the sight of Kyrie's shocked face staring into his.

⊰ CHAPTER 13 ⊱

Her first thought was that Tom had had a stroke. That was the only explanation she could summon for the manner in which he stood there, barely moving, his face looking like he was concentrating for all he was worth. But concentrating on what?

"Tom?" she said hesitantly, then again, more strongly, "Tom!"

He didn't move. He didn't look up. A tremor passed through his hand, upwards, then passed downwards again. It was not a movement she'd ever seen in Tom, even when he shifted. She took a deep breath and tried to think of what to do.

She knew what she would have done if this were anyone else, anyone but one of the people she knew who shifted shapes. If Tom had been an anonymous person off the street, one who didn't smell like a shifter; if someone in the diner had started behaving like this, shaking a little from position to position, but neither reacting to voice nor looking up, nor . . . moving normally, she would have called an ambulance immediately.

But for shifters medical services must always be a risk, a careful balance between pain and control. If you were in pain or scared, you were likely to change shapes and then where would you be?

Tom's dragon wouldn't even fit in an ambulance. Being squeezed inside a small space would only make him crazier and more unable to shift back to human—she knew this from when he'd accidentally shifted in their tiny bathroom once before.

And then there were all sorts of other considerations. They hadn't fully determined, yet, what certain medications did to them. They were okay with aspirin, and Tom's drug use seemed to have left him addicted only in a way that could be kicked rather quickly: after all with a shifter's healing capacity, this might be expected.

But who knew what stronger sedatives would do? They might knock out the upper brain, while leaving the animal shifter to rampage happily through the hospital wards.

In Kyrie's mind, headlines proclaiming that a dragon shifter had decimated the patients and medical personnel of Memorial Hospital ran in stark black on white. Only let that happen once, particularly with an animal that no one could imagine had simply wandered in from outside, and next thing you knew the authorities would be hunting shifters. Given all the legends of shifters throughout the centuries, the hunt wouldn't end well for either party.

No. She had to figure out how to deal with this without the hospital. Tom had come back from the dead once. Surely even recovering from a stroke wouldn't be impossible. She had to keep him stable and quiet till then.

She walked into the room, closing the door behind her, cutting off the sound of applause as Conan finished his song. She moved in a measured and slow way because even she truly had no interest in facing an upset dragon. "Tom," she said. She put a hand on his shoulder, shocked to find it burning hot, as though he were running a fever. "I know that you're not feeling well, but I don't know what's wrong. I want to help."

He moved his other hand fast—too fast. It looked to her like the sudden movement of a lizard when aroused. But all his hand did was clasp over hers, squeezing it a little. It felt like her hand was caught between two hot plates, but she didn't protest.

Tom raised his head slowly and looked at her.

She heard herself make a strangled sound of protest, even as her heart sped up in an explosion of panic. She would have stepped back if she could, but she couldn't with her hand caught between his hand and shoulder.

His eyes looked . . . like Tom's eyes and perfectly normal. And also *not*. They were the same shape and color they usually were, the enamel blue that made such a contrast with his dark hair. But there was something that made them different—so different that it was like looking into the eyes of a stranger.

The eyes looked old. It was as though gazing into them could lead one to see into the vanishing centuries, into millennia without end.

They weren't really Tom's eyes, unless they were Tom's eyes in a couple thousand years after he had, several times, outlived the world he was born into and the friends of his youth.

He nodded slightly at her, almost formally, as if to tell her he understood her fear. He removed his hand from atop hers. She didn't move, because she didn't want to run away from Tom, And if she took a step back, she would flee.

His mouth opened. His tongue licked at his lips as though they were too dry, which they probably were, considering how hot he was. And then he spoke.

The words that came out . . . if they were words, if he was not just croaking . . . sounded alien. They didn't have the sound of any western language, or the sound of any Asian language she'd ever heard.

Perhaps the stroke, or whatever it was had affected his speech center, but those sounds felt like words, though words she couldn't possibly know.

"Tom, I don't understand," Kyrie said.

It was Kyrie's touch that woke Tom. Though perhaps waking was not the right word. He knew he'd been awake, aware the whole time. Perhaps more aware than he'd ever been before.

But at Kyrie's touch, the infinity of awareness, the broad vistas of being everywhere and everywhen at once changed. He was Tom Ormson, and he was in the storage room of The George.

It felt as though he'd been spread, amoebalike, over the entire world, a nebulous cloud of Tom permeating everything and not at all present in the body to which Tom should belong.

At Kyrie's touch, at her cool hand on his shoulder, the nearness of her, her presence, the cloud of Tom's consciousness pulled in, concentrated, occupied once more the contours of his familiar body, and he was Tom Ormson, in his own head, staring out of his own eyes.

A nagging feeling informed him that he was also something else. There was some*one* else at the back of his head, some sort of entity. Not the Great Sky Dragon, but... but the essence of everything the Great Sky Dragon was supposed to be.

"I—" He looked at Kyrie and managed a smile, though it took so much effort he wondered how natural it looked. "I'm all right, Kyrie."

She raised her eyebrows. He could smell her fear, but she remained standing right by him, her hand on his shoulder, her eyes showing only concern for him. "Are you sure?"

He patted her hand now, gently. "I think so. I...Something happened to me—"

"A stroke?"

He frowned. Was that what it was? He'd heard of people who had strokes that made them think half of their body wasn't even theirs. But he'd never heard of anyone who had a stroke and suddenly thought he had more than one body, or that his being occupied the space of several bodies, all over the world. "No," he said, speaking slowly. "I don't think that's what it is." He probed tentatively at whatever was in his mind, that other entity residing...behind his skull, looking out through his eyes. Was this how multiple personality disorder felt? But no. He looked at it, tried to make sense of it. This wasn't like another person or another personality. This was more like...He frowned. How odd. "It's like a file catalogue," he told Kyrie. "Sorry. I know that doesn't make any sense, but it's like someone downloaded a lot of compressed files onto the back of my mind."

"Compressed?" she asked.

"Yes. I can't...I have to think of each of them in turn to see what is inside, and I suspect it would take an effort of will to open one fully. One of them seems to have pictures...very old pictures and...information about dragons. I—"

"A human being is not a computer!" Kyrie protested. "People can't get stuff downloaded into them."

"Yes, but are we people?"

"Of course we're people. What else would we be?"

Tom had thought he knew, now he wasn't so sure. There was an unsteadiness beneath his certainty about the world. He felt as though if he moved a foot wrong, he'd find there was nothing beneath it, and—what he thought of as himself—would fall through the solid contours of what he thought of as the world, and be lost in a formless limbo beyond retrieving. "Yes. And if you're going to say that if you cut us we bleed, I'll agree we're human so long as humans are considered to be sentient beings with at least theoretical control of their own actions. But that's not what I'm asking, Kyrie. Not philosophy, but physics, biology... what we are, the things we are. As beings we can turn into other forms, and people—at least normal people—can't. So perhaps we can get things downloaded into us too. How would I know?"

She was searching his face with anxious eyes. "What if all the... the files open? Will you be someone else?"

Tom probed the vast mass of information hiding somewhere in the recesses of his mind. "Kyrie, I don't think I have enough space for all of them to open. I don't think it would be possible. It feels like just one file has... as much... as much in it as the rest of me: a lifetime, a full personality."

Kyrie let go of his shoulder now and went to the shelves that were stacked with mustard pots. She started turning them so they all faced the same way, and spoke as though to the mustard pots. "I don't like this," she said. "I don't like the idea that there's... other... that there are other people in there."

"They're not people. More like... the information in people," he said slowly, more sure as he went along and touched each file, without opening it, and yet getting from it a listing of contents. "Like, what they learned."

"Don't care. Where did this came from? Who downloaded it?"

"I think," Tom said slowly. "I feel it was the Great Sky Dragon, only that's not quite right."

"Damn him. First Bea, now this."

"Well—"

"Are you going to be all right?"

"Yeah," Tom said, making tentative movements, and taking a step towards Kyrie. It all worked fine. "I just... I think I was momentarily overloaded. It was very hard not to shift. I was afraid I'd eat Conan. How is *he* doing, by the way?"

"What?"

"How is his *show* going? I remember hearing clapping."

"Oh, yes. He can sing, Tom. He really can. They're... people love it, and he's lapping it up, even if he has the world's worst taste in clothes."

"We should go out there, Kyrie," Tom said, feeling he had to do something normal, to act normal in some way or he was going to implode. Inside him, the locked information was like a sore tooth that one tries to avoid touching with one's tongue, but which one is always aware of. "We should be selling stuff, and making sure the serving staff isn't overloaded. I suppose Laura has left now, and she was never supposed to serve, anyway, which leaves Jason serving and Anthony manning the fryer. He might forget to keep a close eye. What if the fryer explodes?"

"You have a weird relationship with that fryer," Kyrie said.

Tom grinned at her, and this time he didn't feel like he had to force it. "I don't like things that can destroy the diner if they blow up."

"Like half the customers?"

"Well, that too, but then so can I. I meant..."

"I know what you meant." Kyrie touched his arm tentatively. "On the good side, you're no longer burning."

"No, I think that too was a function of the...download," he said. He opened the door and waited for her to step through.

She started to, but then turned around. Through the open door came the strains of "You are Not Alone," in a powerful voice no one could believe might come from Conan's unimpressive frame. "Tom? What was that you said? When I touched you first? Was it...what language was it?"

Tom had no idea what she was talking about, at first, but then remembered pronouncing words, words that made his throat hurt saying them. He remembered their coming out of his mouth, though he didn't remember forming them in his brain, and as he thought of them, his mind automatically zoomed in on one of the more deeply-buried files, the ones that his brain told him were oldest.

A touch brought up memories of a similar language, though he needed to make an effort to open the subfile for all the words he'd heard. Words in a language whose sounds made his throat hurt with remembered injury poured out, their meaning *felt* rather than known.

He squinted against the stronger light coming from the hallway, against the sound of clapping out there. He tried to concentrate on English, as the other language blurred and blended with it, the edges indistinct.

"It was..." he said. "I am not...gone...no. I am not dead. I'm... covered? Hidden? No. Buried. I am buried...beneath...the dragon."

He cleans up nice, Bea thought. And on the heels of that thought was shock at herself for letting her guard down.

There was something faintly scandalous about the whole situation. She was in a cabin in the woods, isolated, with a man she had never met until a few hours ago, and he'd just come out of the shower, smelling of soap and shampoo.

He was wearing what looked like running shorts, very short and loose, and a tan T-shirt that had a picture of a big lion with "The Lion Sleeps IN Tonight." Her eyes widened a little at the words, remembering he shifted into a lion, and he followed her eyes, and had the grace to blush. "My mom gave it to me," he said. "When I was twenty or so, because, you know, it's what I wear on weekends, when I do sleep in."

She nodded, but still felt uncomfortable. Not because she felt they were too intimate, but because she didn't feel shocked at their being so intimate. There should be...more embarrassment, she thought, rather than just embarrassment at not being embarrassed.

With a shrug at her own foolishness, she said, "I found some steaks but they're all frozen."

"We can defrost them," he said. "We have the technology!" He opened a sliding door to display a wall-mounted microwave discreetly hidden behind it. "Mom just doesn't like to give the impression that this is in the twenty-first century, you know—but it doesn't mean she wants to cook over an open fire. Though we do that too, at times. There's a grill out back."

"Yeah," Bea said, blushing a little, and not sure why. "Only, you know, I think steak is better if it is allowed to defrost properly, right?"

"Right, and marinate," Rafiel said. "What else do we have?"

"Well, you have a bunch of frozen veggies."

"Yeah, Mom buys them in the summer, then deep-freezes them for when we come up in winter, but the last winter was so bad we didn't come up much." He opened the freezer drawer at the bottom, and looked up at her. "Do you eat chicken?"

"Sure. I mean...doesn't everyone?"

He shrugged. "I'll cook up a couple of chicken breasts, make a sherry sauce to disguise the defrosted-in-haste taste, and I think we have rice somewhere up there—would you look?" He pointed at a cabinet and she looked, bringing out a package of brown rice. He nodded. "I'll make us some stir-fried veggies to go with it. Tomorrow we'll go to the local market and grab fresh veggies. It's kind of a small market, for the communities up here, but it does have veggies, or it should by now, even if the selection will be more limited than in the city."

While he talked, he stood up and started the chicken defrosting, then got out the still-frozen vegetables: carrots and mushrooms and green beans. He made a face. "It won't be the best thing I've ever cooked." His hair was damp from the shower and rather than standing up like a mane, curled around his ears and the back of his neck. For some reason this made him look young. It was very endearing. He concentrated wholly on the cooking.

The spacious kitchen had a central isle, with the stove on it, and that was where he moved to work. She pulled one of the barstools to it, and sat there, watching him.

He looked up at one point, half-smiling. "So, you don't cook at all."

She waggled a hand at him. "Ramen. I'm in college, remember?"

"Ah, yes. So ... your parents ... do they have any idea where you are?"

She hesitated. "I think they believe I'm back in college. I tried to make sure ... I didn't expect to be gone this long." She hesitated again. "But if I call them ..."

"The Great Sky Bastard will track you down? Likely. He doesn't seem to ever forget a grudge, does he?"

"No." She hesitated. The whole idea of what had happened to her, the idea that she had in fact been dead for some unspecified period of time was unbearable. She sighed. "No."

Rafiel dumped the vegetables from the cutting board into the oil. Then he grabbed a wooden spatula and started working the spattering, still-frozen veggies around. "I could call them. My cell phone, I mean. Whatever— I mean, I don't think whatever it was ... whoever it was who attacked me has the type of capabilities of the Great Sky Dragon. I could call your parents and tell them you're fine, and will get back in touch when—"

"No," the word practically screamed itself. She sighed. "I'm sorry, but really, *no*. You know, the thing is ... I mean ... You're a man."

He laughed lightly as he turned the fire down. "Noted. And

yeah, I can sort of see your point." He bit his lip. "Tell you what . . . I have to call my mom anyway, or they'll worry." He blushed a little, again looking much younger than his late twenties. "I know it's silly when I'm a grown man, but really, they will worry, so I tell you what—I'll call them and ask them to call your parents. Would that work?"

"It might," she said. "The Great Sky Dragon might suspect I'm in Goldport, but he knows that anyway. Yeah. That might work."

"All right," Rafiel said. "It's a deal." But something in his eyes looked worried.

⊹⊱ CHAPTER 14 ⊰⊹

When they returned to the diner's dining room, Conan was standing up in the little circle they had cleared for his performance. Somehow it had gotten much smaller, with various people crowding around, all trying to talk to him.

He had his guitar in one hand and was bowing, seemingly in response to everything addressed to him. Tom patted Kyrie on the shoulder. "I'll go rescue the poor man; you make sure people have food, if they linger, and that no one leaves without paying."

It was easier said than done, but on the other hand, the diner seemed to have acquired several volunteer servers. "They said they're regulars," Jason said. He was red-faced and looked beat, but was grinning. "And Anthony confirmed it. Some guy called James Stephens who said he's half a horse, and a big man who goes by Professor Squeak."

"Oh, Professor Roberts."

"Is he really?" Jason asked, as he and Kyrie crossed back and forth giving warm-ups and bussing tables.

"A professor? Yeah. Pharmacology. CUG School of Medicine."

"Oh, wow. I thought he was just nuts. He started telling me how he had all these names, including Speaker to Lab Animals and Professor Squeak."

Kyrie hesitated, but in the press of people it wasn't a good time to mention shape-shifting, so she just said, "He's eccentric, but a very nice man."

"Yeah, well, he was taking orders and didn't know what to do with the tips."

"Well, no," Kyrie said, when their paths crossed again.

Their desultory conversation wound down as the diner returned to normal activity for that time of night—almost empty with only three tables still occupied by large groups. Three or four people remained near Conan too, one of them the fiercely protective Rya who was standing between him and a large, well-dressed man, who was trying to talk to Conan about something.

Kyrie looked over at Tom, who leaned over one of the tables, talking to regulars, a smile on his face as he traded jokes with the man they'd long known as the Poet, who turned out to be Rya Simmons' father, Mike.

Tom looked . . . natural, Kyrie thought. Or at least, if she hadn't known that something was very wrong, she would have thought that he looked perfectly natural. He seemed tired and moved in a slightly forced way, like someone valiantly dragging himself past his last ounce of strength and willpower. But there was nothing unusual, no odd movements, as he picked up the tray with the used plates, and laid down the accounting for the table of seven people.

"So, do you think he'll make enough to marry my daughter?" Rya's father asked Tom with a wink, as Kyrie approached them.

"He has asked?" Tom said. "Braver than I thought."

"She's probably asked him," Mike conceded with a smile. A retired TV weatherman, he was writing a novel in his sleepless nights, to stay conscious and not turn into a were-fox. He'd left his daughter at five, trying to avoid tainting his family with his weirdness. But when his daughter had started shifting herself, she had found him.

"Well! I'd be happy about Conan and Rya," Tom said, and for just a moment his voice reverberated oddly, seeming to echo off the walls of the diner and to be imbued with authority and knowledge that had never been Tom's. He must have noticed it too, and the people at the table all stared up at him, but then Tom cleared his throat, "Anyway, at least he didn't completely tank and chase our customers away. I'm not sure how much we made, but it was a lot."

"Well, then, maybe you should give my future son-in-law a cut?" Mike said, only half joking.

Tom assured him he intended to do just that, then went back to the counter, with Kyrie trailing him anxiously.

Behind the counter, Anthony was removing his apron, with an air of grim determination, "I have to go now, Tom, really. My wife is threatening to change the locks."

Tom nodded as he set down the tray loaded with dirty dishes, and put them in a holding area, waiting for the washing machine to finish its cycle. "We'll see how much we made and make sure you get a cut, too," Tom said.

"Well, that might help. We need to move to a bigger apartment."

"You do?"

"Yeah, you know. There will be a kid, any minute now."

Was Tom's smile a little forced as he said "Congratulations"? And even Kyrie couldn't avoid a pang as Anthony beamed at them, saying, "About time you two had some, but you got to get married first! And think about it. Our kids could play together."

"Our kid would totally beat up your kid," Tom said, but it was automatic.

From the other side of the counter, leaning on it, Rya said, "Mr. Ormson!" She'd been introduced to Tom as Tom, and to Kyrie as Kyrie, but she insisted on calling them Mr. Ormson and Ms. Smith. Which was funny, since she was probably only two years or so younger than Kyrie. "Mr. Ormson. You'll let Conan sing on Wednesdays, right? Here?" Conan, standing behind her, looked hopeful. Behind him were two men, also looking hopeful.

Tom turned around. There were dark circles under his eyes, but his gaze had a strange brilliance. "I'd rather he sings Saturdays, though we might need to come up with some new table arrangement to get more people in. Why?"

Rya gestured to the two men nearby. "They want to hire Conan to sing at their bars, and I was saying he shouldn't do that, when he has worked for you all this time, and you're friends and—"

The two men started up with a babble of explanations from which the word "nonexclusive" emerged. Tom nodded. "I don't see why he can't sing for them other nights. I'll take the night he can give us. It's a small venue here anyway, but, Conan, don't sign anything without getting it looked at by a lawyer." And with those words, the reverberation, the sound of authority was back.

Conan raised his eyes, staring at Tom with wide-open eyes, as Tom went on, "My dad will help you out, when he comes to visit. Just don't sign anything till he tells you it's okay."

Conan didn't answer. He was still staring at Tom. He pushed Rya gently aside. He tried to get under the pass-through, but the hat caught. He looked as if he would speak, but then realized there were nonshifters nearby. He swallowed hard.

"Tom," he said, "I must talk to you."

"No, Mother," Rafiel said. "No, I'm not lying to you. Yes, I'm quite sure I'm all right. Well, I wasn't for a while. No. It was a fight that...well, it doesn't matter. Yes, a fight with a creature. You could say that. Yes, very much like the sabertooth last winter, but this one is female. No, not that type of female."

There was a pause. Bea watched his face, attentive, patient and more than a little bit embarrassed.

"Well," he said. "No. I hope not. She almost killed me. No. I'm fine now. You know how quickly I heal.

"Beg your pardon? No, I'm fairly sure I didn't break Stephanie's heart! I never even met her. Mother! When I was five doesn't count. And I'm sure she's forgiven me for breaking her doll by now. No, I don't think I need to marry her to repair that particular sin."

There was a long interval in which he answered her questions, and slowly, Bea started to realize what they had in common and why he had felt so familiar to her.

He finished hesitantly with, "Mom, could you call this number?" He took the number Bea had earlier scrawled on a paper napkin. "Tell them their daughter is all right, that you don't have any details, but she's safe and will come home as soon as possible. I...don't mention any names, certainly not my name."

There was a silence, and red climbed up his cheeks. "No. I... no. It's related to that attack. Besides, the dragon triad is after her. Uh? No. Not involved." And suddenly he was looking up at Bea, and she realized for the first time that while the eye that had been injured looked somewhat bloodshot, it wasn't missing anymore—no longer a mass of dried, black blood. Instead, it was a normal eye which, like the other eye, was the color of dark, aged brandy. And both of them twinkled with amusement. "She's very nice. No. Well, we'll see. Maybe you'll get to meet her."

Rafiel hung up, and Bea had time to control her blush. She said, slowly, "Your parents...are very protective."

And now he turned around, and now his own cheeks were red, and he was trying to explain, stammering, "No, this is the thing, see, they found out I could shift when I was thirteen, and Kyrie and Tom think I'm some sort of wimp because I still live at home, but the thing is, it's not that I'm afraid of going out, it's—"

"I know," she said, very quietly, interrupting him. "I know. It's not so much that you are afraid of going out. You aren't. I'm not. It's that you're concerned for how worried they are for you, and you want to make sure that nothing—nothing—ever happens to you that can hurt them. You...you're very protective of them, not the other way around."

He looked at her, speechless, for a moment, then a small smile formed on his lips. "Yeah. You get it. If they'd treated me badly when they found out—if they'd been like Tom's father when he kicked him out—then I would have been free to grow up, go away and...be on my own. But they are the kindest people in the world, and they do everything they can to protect me. They feel so guilty that they somehow passed this genetic doom to me. The only thing I can do, the only thing I can think is how not to hurt them. They were very worried when I was at college in Denver, you know. They used to come up for dinner twice a week, and I ended up driving home most weekends, and everyone said I was a mama's boy, but that wasn't it, you know? That wasn't it at all. I didn't want them to worry."

"I understand. I do the same thing with my parents," Bea said. "Which is why I was so worried that they might...you know... worry themselves sick, or think the evil dragons had got me, or something."

"Yeah," he said. His hand was on the kitchen isle. "Yeah."

She touched his hand briefly with her fingertips, then she said, lightly, casually, trying to make little of that touch, "We should eat. Is the chicken ready?"

Tom looked at Conan, and it seemed to him he was looking at his friend as though from a long, long distance away. Which was weird. Objectively, he knew that Conan was just out of reach of Tom's outstretched arm, if that far away. He was just standing there, looking up at Tom, his eyes as wide as he could make them. He'd removed his hat, revealing a wealth of very black, glossy hair. In what remained of his performance outfit, clutching the guitar neck, he looked like a Chinese elementary school kid masquerading as a cowboy. The impression was increased by his look of bewilderment. "Tom, I must talk to you."

In Tom's ears, the words sounded like something said a long way off, through a membrane, echoing as weirdly as Tom's own voice had sounded inside his skull for the longest time. And Conan looked tiny, as did Rya and even Kyrie. He could turn around and look at them, in turn, but while he knew they were all crowded right there around the counter, the feeling was that he was very alone in the middle of a vast circle of emptiness with all his friends looking on from a great distance.

He swallowed hard. *Maybe this isn't just the obtaining of some files. Maybe there is more to this than just my receiving knowledge from the Great Sky Dragon.* A bad thought of how the Great Sky Dragon had spoken through his lips was dismissed. Instead he swallowed hard again and heard his own voice vibrating oddly, trembling. "Kyrie," he said, probably louder than he intended, and full of the urgency of someone who feels his control falling away. "Kyrie, please take over. I . . . I need to talk to Conan for a moment. It's"—swallow to try to keep his voice clear—"important."

Kyrie, looking up at his face, seemed like she'd argue, then decided not to. She nodded.

Tom ducked under the pass-through and rushed down the hallway, not quite sure where he was going, but aware that Conan was following him, wherever that was.

They stepped outside the back door, and there was an alligator by the trash dumpster. This was neither strange nor unexpected. Old Joe, an alligator shifter, often hung out near the dumpster. Rescuing a kitten from Old Joe's happy-snapping jaws had saddled Tom and Kyrie with a pet cat.

But Old Joe didn't even slow down Conan, which was odd, because Conan never trusted the alligator.

And as the warm air hit Tom, he felt something odd. He felt like he was going to shift. But it was like no shift he'd been through before.

"Be careful," Conan was saying. "You can't do that here. Not unless you want to give the whole thing away."

"What?" Tom asked, still feeling as though he were dizzy and nothing made much sense at all.

Now Conan was grasping his arm, squeezing, "Listen, Tom, before you shift. You must pay attention. The dragons are coming. All the dragons. All who can get here in time. You are now the Great Sky Dragon, aren't you?"

Tom tried to make some protest, but he couldn't quite speak, and then Conan said, "You are. I knew it when I looked at you in the diner. It was all I could do not to— I knew you would be someday, but not...this soon. Tom. You must not shift here, or if you do, you must fly away soon. Where are you going? Where are you going that the dragons can come?

"They're coming, Tom. You can't stop it. They're coming to pay you homage, to see with their own eyes that we still have a leader. And you must be where they can all land, and not be seen by everyone."

The parking lot of the Three Luck Dragon, Tom thought. And the idea was obvious, as was, in retrospect, the advantage of that place. It explained why dragon gatherings took place there so often. Set against the cup of a hillside, its near neighbors—a jewelry store with a prominent sign that it bought used gold, and a little hole-in-the-wall laundromat—were closed at night. Which left the parking lot—far more vast than necessary for three such establishments—free for gatherings of large-bodied, flying, secretive creatures.

"The parking lot," Tom said. "Restaurant." And saw Conan nod, which was good, because Tom was already shifting. And that was bad in itself, because they were in the parking lot, where customers of The George might see it.

Half-running, feeling as though he were already losing control of his body, Tom rushed into the alley and behind the dumpster. Barely in time. He'd just managed to hide when the pain of shifting hit him, and he managed—just—to discard his clothes before they tore. He was aware that Conan was doing the same, but it didn't matter. Shifting was a private hell, a nerve-ending searing experience that preempted all rational thought and made it impossible to see clearly.

When it was done, Tom realized Conan was indeed nearby, a red dragon, Chinese style, with the funny catlike face of Chinese dragons and unusually long red whiskers. Conan's look at Tom was the first time Tom realized something was wrong.

Oh, not wrong, exactly. But something was strange. He'd been shifting into a dragon for over seven years. By now he should know what his dragon felt like. Only this felt different—bigger.

It was, he thought, like when he had a growth spurt as a young boy, and would for a few days feel as though his outlines, his sense of where his body was, had gotten horribly distorted.

Now, when he spread his wings their span was huge, and as he flapped them to get to the sky, he flew much faster. He could sense Conan flying behind him, too, and he had a sudden, odd impression of himself as having grown ... what? Two times as large as he'd been. *Note to self, shifting in a small powder room could kill you.*

His size changed everything, including his perception of where he was going—or how long it would take to fly there. But he managed, feeling as awkward and strange as a male adolescent in a suddenly large body. Which, he thought, in the human mind at the back of the dragon's thoughts, might very well be what he was.

The parking lot of the Three Luck Dragon seemed to rush up at him far too quickly, and he landed awkwardly near the closed doors, aware that even as he landed, they opened, and two men already in the process of changing rushed out to stand behind him.

He had no time to wonder who they were or where they'd come from. It was as though his landing had been a signal, but more than likely his landing had been just in time. Because this would have happened wherever he was: as soon as he landed, he was aware of the sound of wings all around, a flapping noise, like sheets in the wind, like exceptionally large flags being whipped around.

He turned around, barely able to take in the sight.

From every direction, dragons were flying in: dragons in all colors and sizes. All of them that he could see had the faces of Chinese dragons, and many had the sinuous bodies that appeared in Chinese representations, as well. They came in all sorts of tones, from light pastel to deep-jewel red and blue and green: sometimes all in one individual. They came flying in so fast that Tom thought half of them wouldn't be able to land. They came in so massed that sometimes it seemed two and three were flying almost one on top of the other, and it was amazing none of them collided, or entangled wings.

They landed, so close that it was like a crowd of people standing with no room to move their arms. They stood, wing jostling wing, a moving mass of shining scales, large and small, bright and pale.

Tom understood, suddenly, a fact delivered by those sealed files at the back of his mind, that size was a function of age for dragons, as well as a function of natural heredity. None of which explained his own size change. He was almost sure that he hadn't aged a hundred years in minutes.

And he wished he knew what to say to them. As he thought this, he knew immediately that he'd be able to speak clearly because he'd be using dragon language, delivered up by yet another of his files. And yet he balked at it. He was not who they thought he was.

But there was no point arguing with the instinctive knowledge of what to do. He had a sense of how many times this ritual had been repeated—and only twice in error—throughout the millennia uncountable that dragons had been on Earth. And that twice had been...best for the ritual to take place anyway. Without the ritual, dragons wouldn't have a head. And it would be a bad, bad thing to have giant lizards, many of them only theoretically controlled, fanning out over the world and doing what they pleased to the nonshifting mass of humanity.

He felt his dragon mouth adjust into unfamiliar shapes, as sounds came out of it, "I am the Great Sky Dragon," he said, knowing he lied, but not caring just then. "He is not dead. He lives."

As though in a ceremony in the church Tom had attended as a child, the audience seemed to have an instinctive reaction to this.

One by one, the shining bodies that made the parking lot look as though it were covered in a patchwork of shining, bejeweled cloth, dipped, as each dragon knelt his front legs and lowered his powerful neck and massive head towards the asphalt in a sign of respect.

Almost every dragon. At the back, two—dark blue and huge—stood defiant, staring Tom in the eye.

Bea had gone to bed in the little loft bedroom which she privately thought of as "eagle's nest." There was no reason to think of it that way and, on the face of it, it was a stupid designation, since she understood eagle nests were made of the usual twigs and sticks, and this space was as neat or neater than the rest of the house.

It was also, she understood, peculiarly Rafiel's.

Over dinner, he'd told her that—as fond as he was of the house where he and his parents lived in Goldport—all his favorite memories of childhood were bound up in this cabin, because when they were here, his often-busy father wasn't distracted with police work or anything else, but was free to spend time with Rafiel. And his mother who, in town, worked as a librarian and rarely had time for home cooking, much less baking, would bake endless batches of cookies and treats. And Rafiel would be free to roam around the surrounding forest, after having been instructed on how to avoid dangers.

They'd come here, he told Bea, a lot of weekends, but also two solid weeks every summer, as well as at Christmas. And because they were usually here on weekends when he was growing up— unless his father was working over the weekend—most of Rafiel's hobbies and leisure activities from when he was a kid were here.

It seemed to be true. She noted a telescope in a corner, which would have been fun—would probably still be fun—if one opened the skylight and pointed the telescope at it. She noted, too, an assembled Lego robot of some sort in a corner. And there were walkie-talkies tucked in the same corner.

Not that there were many toys. It was clear what remained must have had special significance to Rafiel and had stayed behind while the rest was discarded or put in storage. What there was now in the room seemed to make it a comfortable retreat for a busy man. One of the walls, short, at the end of the sloping ceiling, was covered with bookcases made of polished pine and double-stacked with colorful mystery paperbacks.

Agatha Christie, Carolyn Hart, and a lot of other names she recognized on scanning. She would have to look at them more carefully during the day, she decided, but she felt oddly tired— perhaps from the drive, and the night air of the forest.

Or perhaps, she thought ruefully, it was that she had died and come back to life. Seemed like an activity that would tire anyone out.

She shook her head. No. This was no time to think about it. But it was no time to read either. She felt relaxed as she hadn't been in a long time. Perhaps—of course—it was the very excellent bottle of chianti that Rafiel had unearthed and opened for them after dinner. That could be the reason, since she rarely drank and usually not half a bottle.

But now, her job was to get in a nightgown and in bed. Rafiel had brought her a nightgown, still in plastic packaging, explaining, "No, it's not my mom's. Mom and Dad keep nightgowns, pajamas and T-shirts out here in about every size for when they have parties, so that if people drink too much, Mom can persuade them to stay overnight."

The nightgown was actually a large-size T-shirt emblazoned with "GOLDPORT, COLORADO, THE GOLDEN CITY."

"I think Mom bought them bulk when the city was changing designs or something," he said. "Anyway, there's new toothbrushes in the drawer in your bathroom, and there should be toiletries in the cabinet under the sink."

There was all that, and Bea laid out the nightgown, brushed her teeth and took a long and reassuringly warm shower, before crawling into bed beneath a homey quilt.

Drifting to sleep, she hoped that Rafiel's mom would get through to her parents. And in the next moment, she was stark awake, with a message—no, a need—running through her head.

There were no words in it, or at least no words she recognized, but it was an imperative order. She must get out of bed. She must shift. She must fly in the direction the need pulled her.

If the feelings in her had words, the words would be: *The Great Sky Dragon has died. The Great Sky Dragon lives forever. Every dragon within wing-reach of him must pay homage.*

She had a fleeting thought that she couldn't shift. It was less than twenty-four hours since she'd been dead. And yet...and yet, she must shift, the imperative was *that* serious.

The pangs of shifting twisted her muscles, as her bones tried to change shape. If she didn't obey the need, her body would do it anyway, and she would shift here, and be wedged in this room, possibly breaking half the furniture.

With all her willpower, she held off the shift, as her hand found the button that Rafiel had shown her, the one that opened the skylight above. The colder night air hit her on the face, as she stripped off the nightgown.

Even standing on the bed, the skylight was impossibly above Bea's reach. She grabbed Rafiel's desk chair and, with an apology to the sheets, set it on top of the bed. At least she wasn't setting the chair on top of the quilt and risking tearing it.

Climbing on the chair, unsteady upon the mattress, she managed to grasp the edges of the skylight. Pushing with her feet to get a better grip made the chair fall from under her, crashing sideways onto the floor.

It left her suspended from the skylight. Fortunately, she was not a normal woman.

If there's one thing growing wings does, Bea thought, *it gives you a set of arm muscles that would give Olympic lifters a case of envy.*

She pulled up her feet in a graceful gesture that would have made gymnasts cry. And then, planting her bare feet against the side of the skylight, she pulled herself out, until she was stark naked, standing on the roof of the log cabin beside the skylight.

For a moment, she wondered what she would say if Rafiel appeared in the room, or down in front of the cabin and asked what she was doing.

Fortunately the question didn't arise. Almost immediately her body started hurting for real, as breath was knocked out of her body by her muscles and bones twisting and changing, and by wings extending, strong as silk, translucent as clouds from her shoulders.

She had barely transformed when, the drive in her demanding it, she took to the sky, wings outspread.

Rafiel had been asleep. At least, he was almost sure he'd been asleep. He didn't quite know how to describe the state he'd been in.

His mother would have been deeply gratified had she known that Bea had, in fact, made such an impression on him that he was considering a relationship.

He couldn't have explained why to himself, much less to his mom. Or to Bea. Which was why he intended on saying exactly nothing until he found a coherent way to explain how he felt.

But the truth was, deep inside, and in a way that made no sense to him and probably would make no sense to anyone else either, he was already sure that Bea was the woman he wanted to spend the rest of his life with. Which was loony, right? After all, she was a dragon. If he was going to settle with another shifter, shouldn't it be a nice lion girl?

The idea made him smile sleepily as he lay there, between sleep and wakefulness, between reality and dream.

So, Bea was still in college. Art. Well, the advantage of art was that she could practice her profession anywhere, right? He hadn't asked what year she was in, but she'd said she was twenty-one, so it should be either her junior or senior year.

It would be hard of course, Georgia was a ways distant, and Bea hadn't flown here, and he wasn't sure how long it would take her to fly as a dragon—but probably too long. It took Tom an hour just to get to Denver, though to be honest the only time he flew to Denver was when it was such bad weather that he couldn't drive, and his father had some sort of emergency.

Anyway, so flying was a third of driving, and that was still too long. Over a weekend, she'd be able to do little more than fly here and fly back.

But there were airplanes, after all, and though he was suspicious of airplanes, as he was suspicious of all forms of transportation or lodging requiring him to be compressed in next to someone else, he could manage that. He could fly up and visit every other weekend. Expensive, but doable.

Doable for a year. And then they could get married, and she could move here.

In his mind's eye he could already see them married, with a few kids, bringing the kids up to the cabin on weekends, with grandma and granddad. They would buy a place of their own. Even his parents had to understand that. They would settle down in a routine and take the kids for the Tuesday-children-eat-free special at The George, and having Tom go all goofy as he usually did around kids, and make his special dragon-shaped fries and rocket-ship jelly doughnuts for the little ones.

In the middle of this pleasant revelry, imagining a slightly more plump Bea sitting across from him at the diner table, smiling at their kids' antics, he heard a big crash.

It wasn't quite enough to wake him, but it was enough to startle him. He was aware it came from above. But he didn't hear Bea cry out or any other sound of distress, and he assumed she'd just tripped and knocked something over. For him to go running to see what it was would only make her feel uncomfortable and out of place, which was not something he wanted to do.

So, instead, he stayed very still. But as he was starting to drift into dream again, he heard the sound of dragon wings.

It was unmistakable to anyone who had heard it even once.

That *flap-flap-flap* might sound somewhat like sheets waving in the wind, but only if the sheets were massive and more substantial than any sheet ever was, and if the wind whipping them around was gale-force.

No. It was a dragon.

Rafiel sat up in bed listening, as the sound of wings circled the cabin. His heart was beating very fast, near his throat.

Was it Bea? It might be, even though they'd thought she wouldn't be able to shift for a day. But why would she be shifting like this, without telling him? Was she really, secretly, an agent of the Great Sky Dragon or some other shifter organization? Had she shifted in order to take word to someone else? Or was something else at work? Was she uncomfortable? Had *he* made her uncomfortable? Had he come on too strongly? He'd tried to be good about it, but what if he'd hinted at his certainty that they'd end up together? That was enough to spook many a young woman, dragon or not.

And what if it wasn't Bea at all, but one of the dragons of the Great Sky Dragon? He had to know.

Half awake, he rushed into a robe, then across the hallway and the kitchen to the back door of the cabin. It opened onto a covered porch, set with rocking chairs, on which his parents sat on Saturday afternoons and read while watching the wildlife around.

Rafiel ran down the back steps, barefoot, thinking belatedly that he was going to get the mother of all wood splinters, and trying to ignore it.

He ran a little while down the back path, trying to look up, but there was no dragon in sight.

"Umph," he said, standing on the beaten-dirt path as a raccoon ran out of the forest, took one look at Rafiel and disappeared running into another part of the forest.

"Right," he said. He'd imagined the wing sound, and probably the big crash too, for all he knew. He would go back upstairs and . . .

At that moment it hit him. It was a smell, but it was a smell such as he'd never smelled as a human before. It was . . . louder than words, a symphony of feelings, of offers, of seduction.

It was, he realized, the smell of a female feline in heat. As the thought crossed his mind, he had already changed, and was running, headlong, into the forest, lion paws striking the soil so hard they brought up dirt clods. His nose followed the divine scent.

✧　　　✧　　　✧

Kyrie finished counting out the drawer and tallying everything. It wasn't as difficult as it had once been, because while buying the expensive fryer, they'd chosen to go into deeper debt for a computerized cash register. So she had an accurate account of all the credit card purchases as well as a clear figure of what she should have in cash—which she had and a little more. For a moment, she was confused, then remembered that Jason had told her Speaker had insisted on not taking tips. She sighed. It just made things difficult, but she imagined his intentions had been good, and it would be churlish to be upset.

The take was still staggering, particularly the profit part of it. Partly because most of what people had ordered had been relatively low-overhead items like coffee and iced tea. And they'd ordered a lot of drinks.

She looked up to see a disconsolate Rya hanging around. "I think they went on, er . . . flying business," she told Kyrie.

Kyrie nodded. "I thought so," she said, as she wrote down figures to verify later.

Rya blinked owlishly at her. "How do you put up with it? The"—she lowered her voice, though the diner was almost empty no—"the dragon thing? It seems more complicated than all the shape-shifting is."

You have no idea how complicated it can get, Kyrie thought, but didn't say it. Instead, she said, "Oh, it's . . . well . . . You cope with it. Everyone has weird stuff, right?"

Rya nodded, but looked doubtful. "It's all the ancestral loyalty and stuff . . . though I think you don't get that from Tom."

"You'd be amazed," Kyrie said, then took a deep breath. She felt just as out of step as Rya looked. She'd guessed Tom and Conan had gone, as Rya put it, on "flying business" but what the business might be, she had no idea. She did have a good idea that something had happened to Tom, something relating to the Great Sky Dragon, something she hesitated to think about too much, because every time the Great Sky Dragon came into their lives it was bad news. Oh, sure, the last time, he had prevented Tom from being killed—probably several times over—but . . . That was barely enough to forgive him for what he had done to Tom before. And besides, it seemed whenever the Great Sky Dragon became involved, things were about to get complicated.

Either it was some problem with the dragon triad or . . . or one of the other older shifter organizations. It seemed to Kyrie—though, admittedly, her actual experience of this was limited—that all the older shifters went crazy in a peculiar way, becoming paranoid and trying to enforce shifter law, whatever that was, with a like-minded group of other shifters, who were the only ones in the world they would trust. There were the triad and the Ancient Ones; Old Joe, the alligator shifter who often hung out around the dumpster of the diner, had hinted there were others.

Thinking of Old Joe made her stand straighter. Yes, Old Joe was probably nuts in many ways. But then, from things he'd said about being alive before the domestication of horses... she was fairly sure that no human brain—no shifter brain either—was designed to store that much information. Though he wasn't addled as such. It was more that he'd decided that following human rules, or shifter rules, or any rules at all was no longer in his interest.

In his human form, he lived the life of a vagrant, hitting all the soup kitchens and the clothing giveaways in the city—and the diner too, half the time—and sleeping in parks and under underpasses. In alligator form... well... He roamed all over town, and seemed to enjoy himself immensely, judging from reports of people finding an alligator in all sorts of unusual places, including but not limited to the archeological dig at the edge of town, which he haunted for reasons that he'd never been willing to explain to Kyrie. *Probably like old people hanging out at the cemetery,* Kyrie thought. *They're digging up dinosaur bones, after all. He's probably looking up old friends.* The idea was very silly. Old Joe had never given any indication of being on Earth before human occupation, which might not have been possible anyway.

But one thing was sure. Old Joe was one of the older shifters still alive, and if something weird was happening with Tom and the dragons, he would probably be able to explain it to her. That is, supposing she could get him to tune in to the present and pay attention to her for a change.

His memory might or might not be erratic, but Old Joe often gave the impression that his perception—the part of him that was aware of his surroundings—wandered through the millennia in which he'd been alive. His responses were random and nonsensical most of the time.

Unless Tom was around, of course. For reasons not immediately clear—unless it was gratitude to Tom for looking after him—Old Joe seemed very fond of Tom, or perhaps amused by him.

Kyrie finished her notes on the accounting for the night, and caught Jason's eye, right after he set down a load of dirty dishes. There was only one table occupied in the diner right now, though there would be the usual burst of activity at about half-past midnight, as people came in from late movies and late art shows, or just having finished a study session. But Jason had been tried by fire in one of the most demanding nights the diner had ever seen. "Jason, do you think you could hold down the fort for an hour or so?" she asked.

"Uh." He looked behind the counter dubiously. "I don't know how to operate anything. I suppose I could manage the dishwasher and the grill, but..."

"Well, that's fine. Just tell them we're out of fries. It's actually true; I think we went through all the potatoes, certainly all the peeled ones we had reserved. It will be an hour or a little more."

Rya cleared her throat. "Are you going to... find out where the guys went?"

"Sort of. I'm trying to figure out what made them go. What... this is all about."

"Um," Rya said. "Sometimes I help out. When Conan works on Saturday afternoons. I think I can manage the grill and stuff, if Jason will do the serving, and I will do some potato peeling too."

"The fryer? You can manage the fryer?"

Rya looked up at the sky. "I've given a hand now and then when... you know... dragon business."

"Don't tell Tom. Whatever happens, don't tell Tom," Kyrie said. "He'd go insane thinking of the insurance costs. But," she said, more calmly, as she took off her apron and passed it to Rya, "if you can man... er... woman the cooking now, we won't say anything more about it. I'll go and see an alligator about some dragons."

Tom looked at the dragons standing at the back, and though he didn't say anything, and though none of the other dragons moved, he had the sense that every one there was aware of the dragons at the back and of their standing in... defiance? challenge?... of him.

He looked at them a long time, while the back of his mind

ruffled through files. He had an impression he should know their names, should know who they were and what they wanted. "Li Liu," he said at last as the names came to him, as well as the explanation that these two were brothers. "And Sun Liu. Do you believe you're bigger than the Great Sky Dragon?"

"We are collaterals of the Great Sky Dragon," the taller of the two dragons said, hissing his language like a pro. "We are the many-time sons of the Great Sky Dragon's brother, and we say our claim is greater than yours."

Tom hesitated. Of course, rationally, he wanted to say, "Fine, you be the Great Sky Bastard, then," but he suspected that like most things involving the triad this was not a gentleman's dispute, involving his stepping down and their receiving the honor. In fact, he wondered if they could receive the honor at all, even were he dead. He didn't think so. He remembered the Great Sky Dragon's gambit with Bea, and he very much doubted so. There was something else going on here that he could not fully comprehend, at least not yet.

He felt, as if a touch in his mind, a thought from Conan. It was both friendly and diffident, not so much an intrusion in his mind, as there had been when the Great Sky Dragon had sent him warnings before, but rather a hesitant touch, as though of a friend knocking at a room's door. He received the touch with relief, and Conan's voice said in his mind, weirdly still in his Southern drawl, "I don't think they understand how it works. I mean, no one does. Everyone thinks it's being the son's son of the Great Sky Dragon, but I think...it's more than that."

Tom gave him a mental indication that it was indeed more than that. But meanwhile, he suspected the blue gentlemen dragons would not be fobbed off with that. He tried to reach into their minds, but he could not. Wasn't the Great Sky Dragon supposed to be able to reach into the mind of every member of the triad?

"See, you are not him," Sun Liu said. "We can keep you out."

A pull through Tom's mental files brought up the idea that the Pearl of Heaven, which Tom had had in his possession far too briefly, would solve that, but the process seemed complicated, and Tom wasn't at all sure he understood it. What he was sure of was that this was not the time for a philosophical discussion.

He sighed. The file also informed him the only way to solve this was to kill his challengers, and it gave him a deep knowledge in his blood and bones of the sense of how to do it. It was as though he'd grown up in the culture and fought a hundred such battles—which the Liu brothers very well might have. He didn't want to kill anyone. Then a thought intruded. Fortunately, in the dragon world, death could be painful and, in fact, horrible, but it need not be permanent.

Tom reared on his hind dragon legs, and flapped his wings to the sky. "We fly," he said. "We fly."

Old Joe wasn't by the dumpster, and Kyrie walked some way down the alley, whistling his peculiar whistle, which had become Tom's way of calling him.

She was about to give up, when something moved inside the ruin of the burned-out, water-soaked bed-and-breakfast across the parking lot from the diner. At first she thought it was a cat or a dog. That part of the ruin, where the tower collapsed, was open to the world, but when she blinked, she realized it was an old man, white-haired, soot-smeared, coming towards her, with a smile that exposed broken and missing teeth.

She recognized Old Joe at the same time she realized he was wearing a trench coat and was barefoot. He also looked like he'd been sleeping in a coal pile.

His smile enlarged, and he squeezed his eyes in amusement. "I was getting some clothes," he said, "so I could come into the diner. I thought there might be some clothes in there, no? And there was." He gestured, proudly, towards his trench coat.

It was something Kyrie appreciated in Tom, that he could have heard a declaration like this and smiled and said, "How nice." But Kyrie was not Tom and their minds didn't work in the same way. Throughout her upbringing, she'd often found herself being the oldest foster child in seriously inadequate households, and having to look after all the young ones, as a means of keeping them from being neglected. This had bred a personality into her that was somewhere between mommy and educator. The mommy was willing to concede that Old Joe putting on... anything before sauntering into the diner was an improvement. It wouldn't be the first time he crouched outside the side windows, popping up now and then like an insane jack-o-lantern, his hair all on end, and his wrinkled, naked body flashing up and down, trying to catch Tom's eye, so Tom would bring him clothes or food. The educator, on the other hand, felt forced to say, "Well, yes, but it's filthy. Come into the back, I'll get you clothes, and you can wash and put them on."

Old Joe looked dubious, but followed her into the hallway of the diner and waited while she got clothes from the pile they kept for him in the storage room. They bought them at the thrift store on any-piece-of-clothing-for-a-dollar day, and blew a couple of hundred dollars twice a year. As far as Old Joe's mind went, clothes were consumables. He'd wear them when he had to, but he wouldn't bother to take them off, or hide them so he might wear them again. Instead, he would shift and either tear them to shreds in the process or soon afterwards, while he walked around.

Kyrie had often read reports of an alligator wearing a tattered T-shirt, and it was only the fact that she had some willpower and could control her more whimsical moods that had saved her from giving Old Joe a bowler hat.

When she came out with the bundle of clothes, he took them, but looked at her sheepishly. "I got to wash?" he asked.

"We don't want people in the diner to be all disgusted at your being filthy," she said.

Old Joe looked very sad and said something she couldn't quite understand, but which she suspected was his version of "When in Rome," though considering this was Old Joe, it might very well be "When in Atlantis" or "When in Mu."

He disappeared into the women's restroom, because it was the more spacious one, and also because Kyrie, frankly, didn't trust him not to try to wash in the urinals. So, whenever Old Joe washed, he washed in the ladies' room. Kyrie stood at the door, waiting, preventing any woman from trying to get in. Not that any did. There were still few people in the diner, and none got the urge just then.

When he was clean, Joe knocked from the inside, and Kyrie opened the door.

He still looked like a derelict. To make Old Joe look like something other than a derelict would take... well, probably plastic surgery. The truth was that his wrinkles had wrinkles, and that the wrinkles on his wrinkles had got so much ground-in dirt in them that they might as well be tattoos. Or maybe they were tattoos. Whenever Old Joe had grown up, it was now almost unimaginably long ago, and it was almost certainly a preliterate society that had left no trace. Maybe facial tattoos had been a manhood ritual or something.

So, he still looked dirty, and his remaining white hair looked as wild as Einstein's but less clean. And he...It wasn't so much that he stooped or shambled. Oh, you could say he did both, but the words were, to an extent, inadequate. Yes, he stooped. Yes, he shambled. But his posture was more reminiscent of someone who had collapsed into place over centuries, becoming not so much aged as...petrified, stratified. Like a little mountain in human form.

Still, the eyes that looked at her weren't tired or stony at all. Instead, they were full of the merriment he seemed to find in anything unusual or unsettling.

And Kyrie realized there was something very unusual indeed, as she realized he was still clutching the filthy trench coat in his—presumably just-washed—hand.

Old Joe had dressed in that trench coat without Tom or herself making him. And that was kind of like hearing the sun had risen in the west, or that soup had fallen from the sky. It was impossible. Absolutely and completely impossible.

But he'd done it.

She looked into the twinkling eyes and asked carefully, with slow suspicion dawning that she wasn't going to like the answer at all, "Why were you going to come into the diner?"

He grinned. "I hear dragon boy got dragon egg. I wanted to know how he's doing with it, because..." He looked suddenly embarrassed. "I like dragon boy. He's nice people."

Uh-oh. He knew what had happened to Tom. It should have been a relief, Kyrie thought, because if Old Joe knew, it meant that Old Joe could tell her what had happened, and maybe even why and how to get around the problem. But it didn't feel like a relief. This whole *dragon egg* thing didn't sound pleasant. She had a vision of a juvenile dragon bursting from Tom's chest and bit her lower lip.

"Go into the corner booth," she said, "and wait. I'll bring you food."

And she was left to torture herself with scary suppositions while she wiped off the soot marks from wall and sink and dried the water splashes on the floor. They really should install a shower in the storage room the next time they had some spare cash.

Having people wash in the ladies' room was messy and probably violated all sorts of rules and regulations.

Of course, next time they had some spare cash was assuming things would return to normal. And Kyrie wasn't sure of that at all.

Was it really Tom up there, in front of the restaurant? Bea had trouble believing it. She'd met his dragon, after all, on the ledge of that bed-and-breakfast tower, but the truth was that if Tom perched on that ledge now, he would have taken it down in a crashing heap.

He was...enormous. How did a dragon *grow*? And then she heard his voice in her mind. Standing at the edge of the crowd, she saw the two idiots stand and challenge him. Not that she was sure they were idiots. But then, they had to be. No sane person would challenge something the size Tom was now. And no sane person would challenge anyone, dragon or human, whose eyes showed as much bewildered fear as Tom's did at that moment.

Tom didn't want to be where he was. That didn't surprise her. She'd gathered he had no intention of being a leader of the triad. But he was there and—as he issued the challenge, because it was very obvious what he meant by "We fly"—she realized he would fight for the position he didn't want.

She wondered why.

Then she stopped wondering. She'd met Tom only this day, and she couldn't say she was his lifetime friend. But Tom was...The Tom she'd met had seemed to be polite, caring, nice—in outdated but probably accurate terms, a good man.

Nothing could have prepared her for seeing his dragon take to the air, flanked by the two blue dragons.

It should have come as no surprise that both blue dragons went up at once. Or perhaps it shouldn't have. She didn't know. What were the rules of sportsmanship for dragons? And did it matter if two went up at the same time against another dragon that was so massively larger than either of them?

Like every other dragon present in the parking lot, she sat back and turned her face up to watch.

Tom flew straight up, green-blue underside flashing bright. He looked bigger, more substantial than the other two. But the other two weren't daunted. The larger one tried to fly to the side of Tom and bite him on the neck. Tom evaded it, almost skewering himself on the other dragon's claw—out and trying to disembowel him.

And then it seemed to her that Tom lost patience. He reached out with arm claws, and grabbed the other dragon's arm and twisted viciously and pulled. Clearly he had more strength than the others, because the arm tore off the dragon's body. A fine rain of blood fell on the upturned faces of dragons.

Tom kicked away the larger blue dragon trying to attack him, almost eviscerating the dragon in the process, and turned his fury on the smaller blue dragon. Methodically, like a psychopathic little boy with a fly, he ripped off the dragon's other arm, then the nearest leg.

And then he flamed, burning off the dragon's wings as the dragon, in shock, tried to run away. And as the dragon's brother tried to attack Tom by burning at Tom's side, presumably to pull him off the other, Tom turned without hesitation and burned him, full in the face.

The smaller blue dragon had fallen like a stone onto the parking lot, his blood spattering those who'd hastily moved away from his falling path. The bigger one now fell too, hitting the pavement with force, close to Bea who'd scuttled back onto the little side street to give him room to fall. She had a chance to see him hit, blood splattering up from the impact, and then shift, almost immediately, into a small Chinese man with a burned face and shoulders. He was dead. Very, very dead. She felt queasy and looked again as Tom returned to stand in his spot in front of the restaurant.

Was this really the same civilized, kindly man she'd met earlier? She couldn't believe it.

Neither could she believe the way the other dragons closed in around the fallen, not stepping on them but surrounding them completely, not wary of being near corpses or paying them any more mind than if they'd been a discarded candy bar wrapper.

He reared up on his hind legs, stretching his body to the sky, "The Great Sky Dragon is dead. The Great Sky Dragon lives forever." And, as though on cue, every dragon prostrated themselves, and Bea did, too. But she wondered how bad this would get.

← CHAPTER 15 →

"What do you mean by the dragon egg?" Kyrie asked, sliding into the booth across from Old Joe. She'd put a bowl of clam chowder in front of him, and slid a plate of souvlaki and gyro meat in beside it. She had put silverware down, too, but Old Joe was always whimsical about silverware, using it when he very well felt like it, and ignoring it or treating it as jewelry the rest of the time.

This was one of the times he'd chosen to ignore it—which was just as well, because the sight of Old Joe with fork and knife twisted into what remained of his hair always made people turn and stare, and Kyrie would much rather they didn't attract attention just now.

So she tried not to act offended or put off as he drank the clam chowder from the bowl and stuffed meat in his mouth with his fingers. He must have been aware of her disapproval, nonetheless, because he used the napkin on his fingers and lips before answering her. "It's the knowledge of all the dragons. It always passes to Great Sky Dragon when Great Sky Dragon dies."

"Uh? What do you mean it passes to him when he dies? Do you mean in the spirit world or something?"

Old Joe shook his head, then resumed stuffing his mouth. Kyrie got up and got a cup of coffee for herself and one for Old Joe. She took a sip from her cup while she waited for him to answer.

"Like," he said, at last, "like when the king is dead someone becomes king; so like, the king is dead, long live the king?"

"Oh. The new Great Sky Dragon gets...knowledge? What knowledge?"

"The knowledge of all the sky dragons before. The dragon egg it's called." He frowned. "Or was called when the curr—the last Great Sky Dragon inherited." He reached across and patted her hand, as if he thought she needed reassurance. "A long, long time ago. More time ago than I can count. The other Sky Dragon. Before dragon boy."

Perhaps Kyrie had known it all along. Surely she had known it was a danger since she'd heard Bea's story, but the idea was so preposterous that Kyrie had been keeping it at bay. "I...you mean Tom is the Great Sky Dragon?"

Old Joe nodded. "At least...there seems to be...Something is not right, but he is, at least, in the place of the Great Sky Dragon right now"—he clacked his teeth together in the way that, in alligator form, always gave the impression that he was laughing—"acting Great Sky Dragon."

"But Tom would never accept it," Kyrie protested. "Tom would never want to be...they're a criminal organization. He'd never—"

"No," Old Joe said. "You don't understand. No choice. No choice for dragon boy. It's in the blood. The memories follow the blood. It was...built that way when we came to this world."

"When we came to this world?" Kyrie repeated, as she suddenly had a disturbing vision of Old Joe as a UFO cultist. Besides, she was absolutely sure she hadn't come to this world, she had been born here.

"When our kind came to this world," Old Joe said, and again patted her reassuringly.

"We were built so some people would...remember for everyone. And the Great Sky Dragon might be the only line that still goes on that remembers. Part because they keep to themselves, dragons do..." He frowned. "The rest of us have forgotten. Even I have forgotten, and I was supposed to remember. I was...But dragon boy has the inheritance in the blood, he has the dragon's egg, and if he has the Pearl..." An odd sound as he put his tongue up between his two widely spaced front teeth and sucked air. "If he figures out how to use the Pearl...then he could remember all that he needs to remember."

Kyrie's head reeled. "Built? No, forget that. Just tell me...Why would Tom need to remember anything?"

"Well," Old Joe's eyes had a look of faraway remembering, as though looking upon unheard-of vistas. "Our people were hounded from world to world, weren't they? We came here for refuge, didn't we? But we must remember, because I can sense their agent among us...Whatever happened to the old dragon was their doing and unless dragon boy is ready to stand up to them..."

"Yes?"

"Even if he's ready to stand up to them, but doesn't know how to...we'll die in this Earth too, and we'll be gone forever."

Two tears ran down the dirt embedded in Old Joe's face while Kyrie tried to make sense of all of this. Only thing she could know for sure was that Tom was in danger. Tom had been thrust into a position of prominence he didn't want and he was now in danger because of it.

She fixed Old Joe with a stern gaze. She didn't know if it would work on him, though she had, in the past, managed to stop him from eating cats and dogs by convincing him that she could see everything he did and that she was not amused. But her gaze and her voice of command worked on the strangest people, even Rafiel. So she stared at Old Joe and said, sternly, "Don't you dare wander away and disappear. You must talk to Tom about all this. We must go and find him, so you can talk to him."

"Why would I disappear?" Old Joe asked, in a puzzled tone. "I was coming to talk to dragon boy and you. I got myself clothes for that. And I know where you'll find him. He'll be in the place of dragons, of course."

The dragons vanished much too quickly, and Tom, almost dropping from tiredness, found himself shifting back and being alone in the parking lot, except for two middle-aged Chinese gentlemen behind him, Conan to his right side and...He frowned at the girl at the other end of the parking lot. She looked eerily familiar. "Bea," he said.

"Bea Bao Ryu," Conan said. "We spent years investigating her family...back when I was...that is, when..."

Tom understood Conan was suddenly afraid of saying that this had happened when he was working for the Great Sky Dragon, because now Tom was the Great Sky Dragon, and so Conan must be working for the triad again. Tom sighed and looked sidelong at Conan, "You know you're free, right? To do whatever you please, and pursue your bliss with that damned guitar and that ridiculous ten-gallon-hat of yours?"

Conan gave him a smile, but then the corners of his mouth shook and he looked even more tired than Tom felt. "It's not that... simple... uh... sire?"

Tom laughed at that, impossible not to. "If you call me your reverence or something like that, I swear I'll hurt you."

Conan's eyes went out to the two corpses on the parking lot. "Like you did them?"

"No." Tom had almost forgotten what he'd done, but now he shuddered at it, a shudder made worse by his being covered in blood. "No. Conan, I had to do it. Do you think I had a choice?"

"No. I know you didn't. And I think I know more about this than you do," Conan said, his voice low, steady, but filled with an odd vibrating tone. "And if I'm right, all of us are going to find ourselves rather short on choices."

Tom was going to ask Conan what he meant, but at that moment one of the middle-aged Chinese men behind him said, "Sir, if you would."

Tom turned around. He vaguely remembered meeting the one who spoke, at a get-together of owners of local eateries when they'd planned the last "Eat Goldport" weekend, at which people could buy a coupon book then sample several eateries at discounted prices during the weekend. The speaker was the owner of record of the Three Luck Dragon. A careful search of his memory disclosed the first name Kevin and the family name Jao. Tom said, "Mr. Jao," and raised his eyebrows.

The man bowed again. "We have quarters prepared for you... and your bride, and we will tell you the whole situation as we know it. What happened to... to your revered ancestor and..." He looked at Conan. "If you trust him, he can join our councils. We gather you trust him, since he's long been your henchman."

Tom looked at Conan. "I trust him. But I have no bride. At least no bride here."

The man beside Mr. Jao cleared his throat, and looked intently at the other side of the parking lot. "Miss Ryu will more than adequately provide dragon—"

"No," Tom said, with near-horror. Not that he had anything against Bea Ryu, of course. She seemed okay. But she suffered from the terrible handicap of not being Kyrie, and that was insurmountable in his view.

"Uh," Mr. Jao said. He spoke perfectly unaccented English, which Tom found fascinating, since at the dinner of restaurant owners he's spoken like a stereotypical Chinese immigrant. Wheels within wheels. He supposed the man would now tell him to whom he was lying and for whom. Maybe. But he didn't want to know. He had a strong feeling the triad was into far more shady business than drug running, murder for hire or even hunting down innocent dragon shifters. He had a feeling the business of the triad was far bigger and more dangerous and dirtier than anything he could have imagined. That feeling was partly from his gathered impressions, while he was in everyone's mind for that brief moment after...

After what? After the Great Sky Dragon had died? He didn't know. Instead, what he knew with absolute certainty was that he wanted no part of any of this.

Jao raised his voice and called, "Miss Ryu."

She came. She was good to look at naked. Tom could think that, even while being aware that he'd rather die a thousand deaths than marry her or anyone but Kyrie.

Bea was slim and shapely, but she walked towards them like a beaten dog. He suddenly remembered she'd just come back from death, and wondered what had managed to make her change and come here. What could have been a strong enough impulse?

Then he thought that, of course, the call had been that strong. But she must be famished and half dead. He was famished and half dead. He needed protein to recover from his shift. So would all of them. He turned to look at the men. Well, they'd have to get help from them. And he supposed listening to them wouldn't hurt either, since he wanted to know what had got him in this predicament, to figure out how to get out of it. "Meat," he said. "We'll need protein. We all shifted."

"Of course. If you come to your apartments with your bride and your...assistant, we'll provide food and clothes." He looked up and must have read Tom's resistance to the whole bride thing in Tom's eyes, because he said, "We'll explain why it is your duty to all dragons to do what you must do."

✧　　✧　　✧

"Tom," Kyrie said, as she slammed the brakes on, and ran out of the car. She was hugging him before she realized he was smeared in blood, and stepped back and said, "Ew" at the smears of blood on her clothes. Tom looked whole, so the blood...

"Whose blood?" she asked.

Tom looked tired, so tired. He turned to one of the older men in the group and said, "Would you see to the Liu brothers, and put them somewhere until they... recover."

The man looked like he was going to say something, then sighed. "The one who is... limbless will..."

"Take longer, yes." Now in addition to tired, Tom looked vaguely embarrassed. "But I'm sure his brother will be back before that and can look after him."

Again the man looked like he was going to speak, but only nodded. And looked disapprovingly at Kyrie. But Kyrie had possessed herself of Tom's hand, and even though the man glared at their hands, together, he said nothing.

However, as Old Joe, whom Kyrie had decided to bring along, also shambled out of the car and walked towards them, clacking his teeth, the man looked at him, and then at Tom and said, "That, no."

Tom looked puzzled for a moment, then smiled a tired smile at Old Joe. "He's a friend," he told the man, his voice full of sudden hauteur and command.

"He can't be a friend. He is—"

"A friend," Tom insisted.

The man looked like he was on his last nerve. How someone could look that disapproving while completely naked, and showing off a little middle-age belly and a lot of white chest hair, Kyrie didn't know. But he did.

"Very well. It is always as the Great One wishes, of course. Though we're not used to that rapid a change in policy without knowing all that lies behind it." He bowed to Tom and led them into the restaurant. It was closed of course. It must be...

Kyrie could not remember, but she knew it was well past midnight. The restaurant had that look the diner only had once a year, when they closed the day after New Year's and things got really cleaned. It always spooked Kyrie a little. It was like entering a place that had been alive and full of people and finding a silent tomb.

The Three Luck Dragon had the same empty feeling, like eye sockets devoid of eyes, like a house with all the curtains closed, and the rooms dimly lit. The dim lighting was true. There were what appeared to be nightlights burning along the restaurant, here and there, enough to allow them to avoid tables and furniture while following Jao.

He took them to a small room across from the kitchen. In it were a table and two chairs, as though disposed for an interview. He walked past the furniture to the opposite wall and lifted up a picture of several fat children playing on a dragon. Behind the picture was a lever which he pulled.

The entire wall slid away, revealing a sliding door designed to look like wallboard.

Tom stopped just ahead of Kyrie and said, "Whoa." Which was about what she was thinking. It was something like what a hotel casino called the Forbidden City might look like, in the center of Vegas, or at least what its honeymoon suite might look like.

For one, there was entirely too much red. Red dripped in tassels from elaborate chandeliers painted with more scenes of dragons and children. It made Kyrie wonder if it was a desire for fertility or a meal setting. Red draped the bed in the middle of the room, red was the color of the silk carpet that covered the floor and the walls were lacquered red, gold and black, in a shiny, polished look. Was it possible to sleep in this room and not dream of blood? Was that a plus?

Kyrie blinked at it. Fortunately the light was somewhat dimmed to mood lighting. Then again, perhaps that was not fortunate. The bed was large enough to accommodate ten people who didn't need to be really close friends, either. What had the Great Sky Dragon done for amusement? She glared at the pictures of happy dragons and happy children, one of which was in a mural, occupying most of the wall.

"Cozy," Tom said, in a definitely dry tone.

Jao didn't seem to catch the irony. Instead, he said, "It is not your primary residence, but only the place where you—where he—where Himself stayed when he was in town. Lately that was, of course, often, because he wished—" He gave a look towards Tom and another at Bea and seemed to run out of steam. In a rather less fluent way, he led Tom to the closet and showed him clothes, in his size.

Kyrie noted most of them were exactly the sort of thing Tom wore most of the time: T-shirts, jeans, though there appeared to be a tux at the back, and there was definitely a suit. But on the extreme right of the closet were what appeared to be traditional Chinese attire from before the revolution. The sort of thing one expected to see in movies about China in the nineteenth century. She quirked her mouth slightly, wondering what Tom would look like in those, and knowing there was no chance in hell of ever finding out.

When Jao opened a door to the side of the closet, which like everything else around here seemed to be a trick door hidden in paneling, she could barely glimpse a bathroom within. But Tom turned around and said, "Bea, if you wish to wash first?"

Jao gave Tom a wounded look. "Sire," he said. Then turned to Bea, "I'll show the lady her bathing room." It apparently came with a closet of its own, filled with rather a greater variety of clothes than Tom's side.

How nice, Kyrie thought. *His and hers.* And felt rather dizzy and a bit nauseated. She had an impression that the expectations of the triad would be more difficult to defeat than she expected.

Servers swarmed in, setting up little tables with bowls of food on them. It did not improve her mood.

Tom leaned back under the water, feeling it soothe him, deriving great comfort from its immediacy, its warmth. He didn't look down until he was reasonably sure no blood would be running down.

He should be used to blood by now. It wasn't the first time he'd been covered in blood. Many times, it was even his. But he wasn't used to it. Didn't want to be used to it. He wanted blood to remain something alien, as it was to most people. As it hadn't been to him since the night he'd been kicked out of the house. He still remembered the bloodstains on the sidewalk, blood sprays staining the walls and the elderly orangutan shifter telling him that, really, he didn't want to know. He still had nightmares about that night sometimes, but whatever had happened remained locked in his memory and inaccessible.

When he was sure that the water was running clear, he washed his hair and body. They had exactly what he used, including Mane and Tail shampoo, and he thought that it was impossible

the Great Sky Dragon had used the same products he had. So
they must have stocked for him, and they knew him far better
than he was comfortable with.

He came out of the shower, still not sure what to do. He had
a strong feeling that he should—if he wanted to keep power in
the triad—marry Bea. But he didn't want power in the triad. Of
course, the question was if he could give up power in the triad
and stay alive. As in despotic government systems, the alternative
to being the heir to the throne was not being allowed to go your
merry way—it was being dead, so that whoever took the throne
didn't feel threatened by you.

There was a white terry robe behind the door to the bathroom,
and he could have wrapped himself in it, but that seemed a little
too intimate. He was going to have to go out there and have a
conversation with all those people, including Jao and Old Joe. Any
gathering in which Old Joe seemed to be the sanest noninvolved
participant was enough to give a man cold sweats.

So, instead, he dried himself, then dressed in the clothes he'd
brought in with him: jeans, a clean T-shirt that he only realized afterwards had the saying DRAGONS ARE FIERY LOVERS. He
wondered who'd picked it. In normal life, it was the sort of sly
humor that might have appealed to him, but just now it didn't
seem nearly as funny.

He tied his hair back with a ribbon provided, and made a
face at himself in the mirror. Where had those dark circles come
from? He knew Kyrie had thought he was having a stroke in the
storage room. Perhaps he'd had one. Perhaps he was now lying
in a coma and all this was a hallucination. It made as much
sense as anything else.

When he came out of the bathroom, things made even less
sense. Apparently the war council was going to take place at the
foot of the bed, with everyone sitting on cushions on the floor and
partaking from the food on tables around the room, using little
bowls and porcelain spoons also distributed around the room.
The only person who looked...well, not *right*, because he never
looked right, but moderately natural in that situation, was Old Joe
who was merrily eating with his hands out of a little bowl, while
clacking his teeth and clutching something—was it an extremely
dirty trench coat?—to him like some sort of security blanket.

Kyrie and Bea were sitting side by side and seemed to have

formed some sort of united front. Part of it, Tom noted, was that Kyrie was wearing a dress, which had to have come from Bea's closet. The disapproval of this action was written in Jao's face as he glared at Kyrie, and the mulish stubbornness of Bea's look told him she wasn't about to take much of this.

Which at least was good, right? It meant he had an ally, right?

Tom took a clean bowl, wishing it were much bigger, and piled it high with meat from a nearby serving bowl.

Jao and his counterpart sat opposite Kyrie and Bea. Old Joe sat facing the bed. The only spot open was with his back to the bed, but Tom decided it had been a long time since kindergarten, and he was not going to sit on a cushion on the floor. Besides, if he settled himself above the others, on a physical plane as well, perhaps he'd have more command over the outcome of this.

Bea's doubts about Tom got worse, as he came in, walked straight past them, got food—how could he eat food after tearing people to shreds?—and sat on the bed, staring down at them as if they were unruly children and eating with scrupulous manners.

Yeah, okay, so the idea of taking pillows off the bed, and sitting on them on the floor might have been stupid, but this room didn't have any chairs for people meeting here, and she'd be damned if she was going to sit on the bed with all these people, or if she was going to stand while the two Chinese guys sat on the bed and glared at her.

It was bad enough that they'd thrown a fit when she'd lent a dress to Kyrie. Yeah, okay, so that dress was probably never going to be usable by Bea after this. It only fit Kyrie at all because it was stretchy material, but the points at which their figures differed were likely to be stretched out of shape forever. On the other hand...

On the other hand, Kyrie had been blood-smeared from hugging Tom, and she wanted to change, and Bea didn't understand why she shouldn't lend Kyrie clothes. It wasn't as though Bea had chosen, paid for, or had any interest in the clothes in the closet, even if their mimicking of her taste had been deadly accurate.

But they clearly thought this was Bea's room and Kyrie was an intruder. Bea shivered. Out there, in the cabin in the forest, she'd been getting used to the idea that there might have been a man for her. Oh, it wasn't love yet, not even a crush, but being with Rafiel felt right. She liked spending time with him, and was more comfortable with him after a day's acquaintance than she'd ever felt with a man.

For one, she didn't need to make excuses for her shifting. And yet, he wasn't a dragon, or part of the dragon hierarchy, and she didn't need to worry he belonged to a whole mysterious world she'd never understand.

Which, beyond the fact that this man was taken, and that she wasn't sure she liked him all that much, was the big problem with Tom. He walked in, sure of himself, as though he knew rules she didn't, between the people sitting on the floor, and plopped himself down on the edge of the bed.

He looked over them, with an amused glance, then said, in a dry voice, "Who cares to start telling me what this is all about?"

Jao started first, hesitatingly, "Your revered ancestor . . . That is, for some time now, he's been aware that he's been in danger, grave danger of the sort that— That is, he knew there was a good chance he might die, and therefore he . . . made preparations, so that if you stayed behind you'd have dragon descendants who might follow your footsteps, and the line that came all the way from the stars wouldn't die with you."

"The stars?" Tom asked, with a lifting of the eyebrows. "I take it you don't mean Hollywood."

Jao scowled but hesitated. "It is not *stars* stars, though that's what we've always called them. I mean, our legends do not talk of traveling through space in the sense that you might understand it, though there are legends of sailing the ocean of time, we're not sure that's time travel, either. It's just that . . . Worlds Dragons might be more accurate, as we think they came from other worlds."

Tom raised his eyebrows further. Was he trying to put them off making him their leader by acting as arrogant as possible? Bea had a feeling that wouldn't work. These people struck her as the sort of people who would positively enjoy being stepped on and made to behave like underlings.

Jao seemed to be trying to gather himself together. "Your esteemed ancestor, I said, knew there was a threat, there was something coming, and therefore he faced up to it, to protect us—"

The old man Kyrie had brought with her, and who had a truly disturbing habit of clacking his teeth together, found an even more distracting way to interrupt the conversation. He laughed, a high, discordant laugh and slapped his thighs while doing it.

Tom knew there was going to be trouble when Old Joe laughed. "He did not face it. He was dragged. From the parking lot he was dragged, before he could shift. He was killed and...taken away."

"He knew what the threat was," Jao said, trying to overpower the old man's voice. "He knew the threat was coming near, and he bravely defended against it and—"

"Dragged," Old Joe said, and clacked his teeth with enormous satisfaction, while his eyes looked merrily over the people around him. "And now kept somewhere, though I don't know where."

"He's dead," Jao said. He looked sour. His mouth set in a straight line. "Which is why it's so important for the new Great Sky Dragon to—"

"Oh, you want to say that," Joe said. "And it might even be true. For now. But *truth* is something different. Yes, daddy dragon is dead. Impossible to pretend otherwise and have dragon egg pass to dragon boy. When dragon dies, dragon egg passes. And it did. But death is not permanent for our kind. Or it need not be. And dragon egg does not distinguish, because even temporary death is rare for daddy dragon. And it could always turn permanent."

Jao opened his mouth, then closed it. "The Venerable One is dead. We must find his assassins and—"

"Yes, he is dead, but was his head separated from the body? Do you *want* him to be dead, Jao? Is that the game? Do you want him to be dead forever?" Old Joe asked. He clacked his teeth together, while his gaze played, in amusement, over the assembled people. "I wonder why. Are you afraid whoever killed him will activate dragon egg and get knowledge from him?"

"We—" Jao looked at Tom as though for help, though Tom had absolutely no idea what he could have done to help at that point. "We are sure he's dead," he said. "The power wouldn't have passed to the son of the dragon's son otherwise."

"Sure, sure?" Old Joe asked. "You have body and are preparing to send him to his ancestors in style?"

Jao opened his mouth, and this time Tom thought he had to intervene. Not to save Jao. It was quite possible nothing could. Old Joe was having his fun, making fun and mocking, jabbing and withdrawing, but Tom was starting to see a shape through the fog of amusement the old shifter projected, and the shape he saw was making the whole thing seem like a nightmare... but also, perhaps, offering him an opportunity of escape.

He did not want to be the Great Sky Dragon. He didn't want to preside over the shady activities of the triad, or to be the leader of a criminal organization. And he didn't want to marry anyone but Kyrie.

He looked at Kyrie and their eyes met, and he recognized in hers the same thought that had been in his. No. They didn't want to marry anyone else. And perhaps, Tom thought, it was about time they married each other, if nothing else to keep crazy people from planning marriages for them.

He smiled at her and hoped she realized what he was thinking, but then he turned to Jao and said, "It bears asking. Do you have the Great Sky Dragon's corpse?"

A dark blush tinged Jao's cheeks. "Well, no, but we are sure he's dead. If this were just the long sleep, the temporary death, then the power and the knowledge would not have passed to you." Pause. "Sire."

"No. Drop the sire and tell me straight why not. If the mechanism is set for the knowledge to pass at death, why would it not? The long sleep, you call it? Temporary death? Nice words, but if you remember it happened to me and when it happened to me, the doctors said it was death in every way. I was in the morgue, before I came back by some means no one can determine. And when I came back, it was almost instantly. So—do you care to explain what it is that makes you sure that the power won't pass on the long sleep? Has it not passed before?"

Jao plucked at his bottom lip with thumb and forefinger. "I am not old enough to have experience of the long sleep ever happening to the Great Sky Dragon, and if it happened before you were born, sire, it would not matter anyway, because who could say what had happened? The dragon didn't have a son's son who could shift, so the power wouldn't pass. It would be lost as it was to other lines."

Tom took a deep breath. So, that question was tabled as a qualified "no" as in "no, they had no idea if the power passed on temporary death or not." He glanced at Joe, who was looking very smug and happy with himself, which, frankly, in Tom's experience was not really a good thing. "Do you care to explain to me," Tom said softly, to no one in particular, "what all this stuff about passing the knowledge or the power is? I've experienced," he said, lifting his hand, as he guessed what Jao had opened his lips to explain. "I've experienced it as having file upon file in my head, which will open if I touch them so I can look within. I know there's some mechanism to integrate it, I can feel that, but I don't know what the mechanism is. They seem to be the memories of the Great Sky Dragon, or perhaps of many Great Sky Dragons."

"Many," Jao said. He looked grave. "All of them, since . . . since the beginning."

"Since we came to Earth, he means," Old Joe said. "And it might be all of their minds you have in you, dragon boy, but you can't use them all nor know what it all means without—"

"We don't know how it passes," Jao cut in, with every appearance of a man intercepting a dangerous pass. "We just know by tradition that when the Great Sky Dragon dies, his oldest male descendant on the unbroken male line, receives all these memories. They help guide him in the difficult times ahead and they—"

"You said if the Great Sky Dragon had experienced even the temporary death before I was born, no one would have known because it would only mean it had been lost, like the other lines. What other lines?"

"The lines . . ." Jao said. "Other shifter lines."

"There were fifteen when they came to Earth. Fifteen different lines," Old Joe said. "The cats and the flyers and . . . many others. But only the son's son can inherit and not all lines produced that. Only the dragons are left."

Tom took a deep breath. He looked at Kyrie. "And for all I care it too can go."

Instantly, shocked, he found himself in between Old Joe and Jao, both of them yelling at him that he didn't know what he was saying, and that it must not happen. He ignored Jao. He looked at Old Joe. "Why? Why should I care about keeping that knowledge?"

"Because that knowledge is the only thing that will allow us to survive, dragon boy. They've found us now, and only that will allow us to stay alive here. We have nowhere else to go."

Tom blinked at Old Joe. "What? Who are *they*? What is this all about?"

"You don't know, and you can't know until the knowledge in you is activated. I don't know either, only what I heard over many centuries, gossip and legends."

"What do you mean until the knowledge is activated?"

"He means," Jao said. Then appeared to think about it. "He means nonsense. He's clearly insane. There are legends that—"

Old Joe cackled unpleasantly. "I'm clearly insane? So, when your Great Sky Dragon went missing, they didn't also get the artifact? You have the artifact?"

"The artifact?" Tom asked, feeling like he had been dumped in the middle of a family argument referring to events he'd never even guessed at.

Jao looked like he had a headache. He put two fingers in the middle of his forehead, as though to contain it, or perhaps to prevent a third eye from popping open. Right then, Tom wouldn't put that past him, either. "He means the Pearl of Heaven."

"What? You lost that?" Tom asked, remembering the two-hand-size pearl, smooth and shining in his hands. "Again?"

And Kyrie stood up. Tom could easily see she meant to take over.

Kyrie hadn't meant to speak, but it seemed to her that Tom, Jao and Old Joe were all talking at cross-purposes and she wanted to know for sure what was happening.

Part of her rebelled at the mystical implications of knowledge that passed at the death of someone onto someone whose relation with the possessor of knowledge was that possessor's long-distant siring of a remote ancestor. But how could someone who shifted into a panther whenever she wanted, and sometimes when she didn't, doubt the existence of strange, nonmaterial things?

However, one way or another, she was sure this discussion was too strange, too diffuse, and not at all rational. She stood up. "Now, both of you have said that we came from elsewhere, we shifters. From which I understand you to mean our really distant ancestors, since at least I don't think I've come from anywhere, and I'm fairly sure that none of you has either." She wasn't sure, of course, when it came to Old Joe. And she didn't know if he was sure, either. But she glared at one and then the other of them, doing her best "grown-up among children" expression, until Jao sighed.

"This is legend, and we can't be sure, but our ancestors said, and passed among us, from generation to generation, the idea that our ancestors came from other worlds to this one, the last refuge of our kind who were..." He made a face. "You could call it rebels of some form of empire or kingdom."

"But almost every culture on Earth has such legends," Tom said, then closed his lips hard, as though he hadn't meant to speak at all.

"Yes," Jao said, and then, as though remembering that Tom was supposed to be in charge. "Yes, sire, but perhaps those legends come from us."

Old Joe put both hands in the air. He had backed up from Tom, after his outburst where he'd yelled at him that no, no, he couldn't so blithely put an end to dragonkind of the sort that could inherit the dragon egg. Old Joe wiggled his fingers, food-greasy, and spoke in a tone that betrayed that this was something he had learned early in childhood, "Twice many times many thousands years ago," he wiggled his fingers as though to symbolize all the time that had passed, "our ancestors came from the stars, running from vile oppression from..." he struggled as if for words. "From the others with no body, and they ran to Earth which was then..." Another hesitation, and Kyrie got the impression that what he was saying had been learned in some other language, probably one so ancient that he could barely remember it himself, one so ancient that she was sure no one else on Earth would know it. She also had a feeling that in that language the words rhymed. "Which was then verdant and luscious but had yet few animals. And our people, the people from other worlds mingled their... their essence with other people from this world so they would have variable bodies, because they thought that they would be able to..." he paused and looked like he was doing some complex calculation in his head. "They thought they would be able to hide should the others come looking for them, which they thought would happen in no time at all. But the locks on the portals of the world held and for many, many hundreds of thousands"—again he wiggled his fingers as if to signify that many—"of father son and father son, the story passed on. To be aware of the others. And in the lines, the knowledge passed father son, father son, but it will not pass through daughter, and when sons not born, the great lines died out." He shook his head, in an impression of perfect sadness. Then shrugged, shambled back to where he'd been and sat down.

Kyrie wondered if this meeting, with people squatting around was like meetings that Old Joe must have sat around when he was young. But none of this made sense. "But our people...people like us can't have come to the world before there were humans," she said, in a tone that betrayed that her last nerve was about to fray. She felt it was. This was important and real, and involved Tom's mental health, and she did not wish to sit around and listen to Neolithic legends. "Because we can mate with humans. And...we're humans."

There was a long silence. Jao opened his mouth, then closed it, and Tom shrugged, as if to indicate none of it mattered, but if it had something to do with how they'd got into the here-now mess, it very well did matter.

"I don't know," Bea said at last, after clearing her throat. "But perhaps the reason there are humans is us?"

Everyone stared at her.

She shrugged. "Look, I studied comparative myth in college last year, and there is this Indian sect that believes the idea-form of animals and humans first came to the Earth and that this created humans and...and other animals. Kind of an intelligent design on turbo and without necessarily a god as such." She lifted her hands. "I'm not saying that's true. My parents are religious and I think I am too. I haven't been alive long enough to know better than my parents. But the thing is, even if life on Earth didn't involve—or human life on Earth didn't involve a creator, that doesn't mean that life or human life didn't have a creator, wherever it came from. It just means that here it was our people...

"Don't look at me like that. There were other life-forms on Earth. We should have suspected that from the existence of primitive shifters." Bea lifted her chin, as though braving their scorn. "But I know evolutionarily we keep thinking we have the date of the emergence of modern humans pinned, and then we find another one, older. And we now think that humans pretty much merged with every hominid life-form on Earth, except perhaps the Flores hobbits. Perhaps that's not just because our species is really randy." She blushed. "Perhaps it is that we were designed with bits and pieces of the DNA of every humanoid species on Earth, and other life-forms too, including some that were extinct

at the time, but whose DNA might still be available. It's clear
that the designing of shifters took science that we can't begin to
comprehend, so why not? If the purpose was to hide, we should
be able to hide among the hominids in our human form. I just
wonder why the human form..."

Jao cleared his throat. "They say...the legends say that we
look like...like people did before they went incorporeal, so...
The form they were pursuing might be the form they originally
had, or as close to this as the available material could bear." He
cleared his throat again. "The legends said that leaving bodies
behind would lead to evil. I don't know. I understood though
that our people were escaping sure death, and this was the last
of many worlds they ran to. And that they somehow crossed
through...through doors between worlds."

"Makes sense," Tom said. "Sorry, I've read a lot of science
fiction. I used to crash at shelters for runaway teens, and they
had that stuff. Portals between parallel worlds, and we somehow
closed them from this side, if what Old Joe says is true."

As though awakened by reference to his name, Old Joe lifted
his head. "Yes, but they have found us, after all the many, the
thousand thousand years, they have found us, and they are trying
to open the door. Someone..." He shrugged. "An enemy mind
is on this side and...and trying to open it. That...being has
taken the Great Sky Dragon and killed him. I think the long
sleep, not real death."

Jao sighed. "Why would you think so? What would the long
sleep do for them that real life won't."

"Easy. When you wake from death," he looked thoughtfully at
Bea, "you're helpless. Can't shift. Can't fight. And the Great Sky
Dragon is an old man, not strong and combative like dragon boy.
He's been alive many thousand years, and he is aging. If someone
takes him, waits for him to come back from the long sleep, then
it will be easy to hurt him, to...make him use the artifact and
make him remember how to open the gates, then force him to."

There was a long silence. Whether it was caused by Old Joe's
sudden eloquence, or by the thought that the Great Sky Dragon
might be held hostage in temporary death, until—

"The time to return from death is around three days?" Tom asked.

"Three days is usually the shortest," Jao said. "Might take as long
as two weeks. The median is about five days."

The silence returned, then Jao said, "But I don't think the person... That is, whoever killed the Great Sky Dragon, your venerable ancestor, even if they took the body, can't be counting on using the Pearl of Heaven on him, because the Pearl of Heaven disappeared a week earlier."

Before silence could return, Conan groaned. "I wanted to have a singing career," he said, as though out of deep and unavailing grief.

"You'll have a music career," Tom said, getting up from the foot of the bed. He set the empty bowl on a nearby table, walked to where Conan sat on the cushion, and touched Conan's shoulder in reassurance. "Hell, Conan, given your voice, I don't think we could stop you. I think once that video on Facebook went viral, all we could do was keep your fans from tearing us limb from limb if we tried to keep you from them. By the end of this year, you'll have to hire concert halls to fit all your local fans, and if you're not selling like crazy with whatever label or on your own, I'd be shocked."

Conan looked up, his eyes dark with something like fear. "But I can't, don't you see? It's just not possible. You'll have to be the Great Sky Dragon, and I might as well guard you, because no one else has the kind of loyalty—"

"No," Tom said. It was absolute. Decisive. "I'm not going to be the Great Sky Dragon. Oh, for a while at least, if I have to. And clearly someone has to, because someone has to direct the search for the real Great Sky Dragon before he gives away our secrets and lets these baddies from other worlds in here." He looked at Jao and grinned, though he could feel as though his face would crack with the effort. "But mind you, when the Great Sky Dragon comes back, your goal is to get him to have another son. Or perhaps you can find a nice dragon girl for my father. Hell, he might even like it. Myself, as much as I like Bea here, I can't marry her. You see, I'm already engaged to Kyrie Grace Smith." He looked at Kyrie, begging her with his eyes not to blow his cover, and not to protest at being proposed to in this very odd way. If he was right, and he thought he was, the upside of the triad's traditional ways was that they were all about family and dependents and the promises made to those around you.

Jao looked at him, then at Bea. He licked his lips. "I don't suppose you'd consider marrying one and keeping the other as your second wife? It is why our line has survived, I think, while the other shifter lines have been lost. The Great Sky Dragon always had more than one wife."

"No, I wouldn't consider it," Tom said and smiled, this time a genuine but tight smile. "You might think that would be a survival-enhancing trait, but not after Kyrie separated my head from my body."

Kyrie shook her head slightly, but smiled at him.

"So," Tom said, "I thank you for your hospitality here, and the great honor you've tried to do me. But I can't be your leader. And now, if you'll excuse me, we need to go. We have a diner to run."

"You can't go." Jao looked like he was about to have a heart attack. He actually grabbed Tom's arm. "Don't you understand? Whatever is out there will try to kill you or capture you."

Tom hadn't understood. He hadn't thought about it. And he still didn't know why any enemy would want to kill or capture him, except that of course they might think he would interest himself in the affairs of the Great Sky Dragon and try to find him. But if that was the case . . . He looked at Jao . . . If that was the case, then the fact that he wasn't living here would keep him safe. "I think they're less likely to come after me," he said, "if they think I'm not interested in being the Great Sky Dragon. They'll think that because of that I'm not interested in finding the Great Sky Dragon. I'll be safer in the diner than here. And you can set up someone here in my place, and pretend he is the Great Sky Dragon."

"But what will we do?" Jao asked. "Suppose you're right, or he"—a meaningful glare at Old Joe—"is right. What do we do? How do we find him and rescue him? How can you help us if you're not even here?"

"Think in my direction really loudly," Tom said. "I seem to have the same facility the Great Sky Dragon has for getting inside other dragons' heads. But I won't. However, if you think in my direction, I will hear you. Just find someone to play the part of the Great Sky Dragon while I'm left free to look."

Seeing Jao look at Conan, Tom extended an arm and pulled Conan to his feet. "Not him. He's going to be a singing star. And he's coming with me." He put his other arm around Kyrie. "She is, too. And so is he." He refused to embrace Old Joe, but he gave the old man a meaningful look.

Old Joe got up and shambled towards them. "We all leave," he said.

Bea got up and dusted herself. "I do, too," she said. "If you tell me where my truck is, I left a gentleman alone who will be wondering where I went."

Jao looked at her. "You can't leave. What if you're not safe?"

"I'll be safe. And what he said, about getting the old dragon or his father to marry a female dragon shifter? Find another one, it won't be me."

"Sir!" Jao said.

"You heard the lady," Tom said, amused. "It won't be her. Now, where is her truck, please?"

"In the back. In the employee parking," Jao said, looking at Tom. And for the first time Tom understood the power he had. Jao was afraid of him. Not just in the normal way people could be afraid of Tom when he'd forgotten to shave and was wearing his black leather jacket, not even afraid of Tom's dragon and what Tom's dragon had done to the brothers Liu out there. No. He was afraid of Tom in the way everyone had been afraid of the Great Sky Dragon. As if Tom could do horrible things to him without even trying.

As soon as he had a quiet minute to himself, Tom was going to go through those files in his mind and find out what in them could make a member of the triads so scared.

But for now, with his friends around him, he left the secret room of the Three Luck Dragon and walked through the deserted restaurant to the door.

There were two very large dragon shifters at the door. Tom could see they were dragon shifters, though they were in their human form—both taller and bulkier than Tom.

They were blocking the door.

For a moment Tom thought that he would have to fight. Then he remembered the dragon egg, as Old Joe called it, which he had received from the Great Sky Dragon.

He reached into his mind and found the link to the minds of those two particular dragons. *Now*, he said mentally. *You want to move. I don't want to have to take over your bodies and make you. I've never done anything like that, and I might accidentally hurt you.*

He touched their minds in just the way that betrayed that, yes, he could make them do what he wanted.

They moved. They moved out of the way very fast, and Tom and his friends emerged onto the parking lot, and to the breaking light of a new day.

⊰ CHAPTER 16 ⊱

Bea couldn't believe she had the keys in her hand and her purse too, which she supposed the Great Sky Dragon must have taken from her when he—her mind still flinched from it—killed her.

She'd gone over the purse and found her driver's license, her cell phone, everything as it had been. It was perfectly normal stuff for her to be carrying in her purse, including the little charcoal drawing kit in a folding pouch that her father had given her for Christmas, but now all of it felt like artifacts from a lost civilization. Or at least like artifacts from a lost Bea.

Was it only three or four days ago that she'd arrived in Goldport determined to make the dragon triad stop picking on her dad? It seemed like it had happened centuries ago, or perhaps in another life.

She adjusted the seat and the mirrors. Someone taller than her had been driving the truck. Then she turned the engine on, and looked at the gas gauge. Well. She'd have to grab some gas on the way out of Goldport, too. Not a problem, as her credit cards appeared to be intact.

A deep breath, as she realized that she could probably go home to her mom and dad. With Tom in charge of the dragon triad, she didn't think anyone would come after her.

But would Tom *stay* in charge? And if he didn't, who would take over?

She had a strong suspicion that Tom would be very careful and that the threat of marriage to Tom—or his father, though she wasn't so sure about the old Great Sky Dragon—was gone. On the other hand...

On the other hand it seemed to her that Tom and every other shifter here in town was in trouble. She didn't want to admit it, and it took her some small struggle with herself, but after a while the thought dawned on her that of all the shifters in town, the welfare of one mattered the most to her.

No, she wasn't in love with Rafiel, but she liked him an awful lot, and something about him appealed to her. Perhaps his devotion to duty as a policeman, as strong as his devotion to his kind as shifters. Perhaps just the way he understood her position with her parents—he was also too protected by his.

She would call her parents, she decided, and talk to them. She could do that much. But for now she would stay out here and figure out how this would end up, and make sure her father wouldn't be blackmailed in exchange for her obeying the Great Sky Dragon ever again.

With the truck in gear, she headed out of the parking lot. She could just barely, she thought, remember the way to the cabin. She would make it there before noon.

When Tom got back to the diner, it was largely empty. Anthony had gone home. Rya and Jason—who looked like he was sleep-punchy—were the only servers there. This was very good, Tom thought, because he could see the problem right away.

Standing at the counter, in a lab coat and dark pants was... a very large rat.

What puzzled Tom was not how often Dr. Tedd Roberts, the professor at the Colorado University of Goldport medical school who was one of the foremost researchers into brain processes in the country, showed up at the diner in his shifted form. No, what puzzled Tom was how he'd managed never to be spotted. Possibly the fact that both his forms were roughly the same size, combined with the fact that he kept unusual hours.

Seeing Dr. Roberts, however, made Tom think of the whole thing with the dragon egg and memories and heredity. No sane dragon would pick him for an heir, so it had to be something genetic.

The scientist was standing between two counter stools, reaching for a cup of coffee as Tom approached and cleared his throat. Dr. Roberts turned around and looked at Tom out of inquisitive rat eyes.

"Uh, Doctor. You're..."

Dr. Roberts' nose twitched, and he glanced quickly down at the general area of his fly.

"No, I mean you're—"

"Squeak?" Dr. Roberts asked, puzzled. Then he lifted the cup of coffee with his paw and took it to his mouth. Coffee dribbled out the sides of the rat's mouth onto the lab coat.

A very short, confused time passed, after which Dr. Roberts stood where the rat had been, looking at Tom in some irritation. "Damn it. Another lab coat to wash. Couldn't you tell me I was shifted?"

Tom refrained from saying he had tried. The absent-minded professor's annoyance was more at himself than at Tom, anyway. "I need to talk to you," he said instead. "At least, I think you can help me."

Dr. Roberts raised his eyebrows at Tom while taking another swallow of the coffee.

"It's...biological and brain stuff, I think. Otherwise, it's magic, and I refuse to think it's magic." Dr. Roberts' eyebrows rose higher and Tom sighed. "Look, can we go to the corner booth and talk?"

"Sure. I don't have to be at the lab for another hour," Dr. Roberts said. "I just thought I'd come in and have some breakfast and do some thinking, and I suppose you can help with that."

He sat down in the corner booth, while Tom surveyed what there was to eat. Then he realized that Laura had been at work in the back addition which they'd put in to attend to baking. She called good morning to him and pushed a plate of pastries towards him, "These are experimental. You guys might want to try them out. Aren't you early?"

"A little," Tom said. "We'll probably go home later."

"Tough night?" the diner's baker asked.

Tom shrugged. He never knew exactly if Laura was a shifter or not. She smelled like a shifter, but they'd never seen her shift, and she always seemed to strategically have her eyes turned when someone shifted nearby. Kyrie and Tom had a running bet on which form she changed into, the most popular being a deadly animal.

The plate of pastries she pushed into his hand were warm. "Kyrie might want some also," he said.

She said, "Already gave her a plate. You look like you need some food."

Tom took the plate to the booth and a cup of coffee for himself, plus a carafe to refill the coffee. Dr. Roberts looked up at his approach. He'd been drawing something in one of his notebooks. "So, what's puzzling you, Tom?" he asked.

"It's . . ." Tom looked over his shoulder. No one was sitting near the corner booth, which was normally left unoccupied by all but the diner regulars anyway. Kyrie's theory was that the blood-soaked painting of St. George killing the dragon that hung right over the booth kept all but the most devoted away. Possibly. But Tom also knew that, given a chance, when he was trying to have a talk with another shifter, Kyrie would move people away from them.

Then he sensed Kyrie behind him, and looked up and scooted a little sideways. "Not needed?" he asked her.

"Nah, Jason says he's good, and Conan is backing Rya up. And I'd like to hear this. Are you going to ask him about the dragon egg and the Pearl of Heaven?"

"Dragon egg?" Dr. Roberts looked from one to the other. "Does this mean you two are expecting a happy event?"

Tom chuckled and shook his head. "No. That would be way too easy. Or not, but you know what I mean. No. I want to know . . . That is . . ." He spilled the whole story about only male descendants of the Great Sky Dragon being able to inherit; about the packet of knowledge, with all its encrypted files, which seemingly passed to the oldest living male relative (or was it the oldest? Tom didn't even know that) upon the Great Sky Dragon's death; about what that packet felt like; and about the Pearl of Heaven, which was supposed to activate the whole thing.

When he finished, the scientist was biting his lower lip. Tom slid the plate of pastries marginally closer to the man, because he was starting to see the doctor's face acquire a certain . . . ratty look, and he knew the scientist shifted when he became too immersed in his own thoughts.

He focused on the plate as Tom moved it, then picked up one of the pastries. "These look new."

"Yeah, I don't know what they are yet," Tom said. "Laura wants us to try them out."

Dr. Roberts bit into one, and said, "Ooh. Hazelnut cream."

Tom grabbed one of the pastries and bit into it. Hazelnut cream indeed, still warm and squishy in the center. It was like a cross between a bear claw and a really good truffle. He took another bite before saying, "So, the thing is, you know, it can't be magic."

Dr. Roberts shook his head. "No, for sure not magic, though I can't quite explain all of it. Our science isn't there yet. I assume... from what you said, whatever it was, these life-forms who came through those portals or gateways or whatever were very sophisticated gene splicers indeed. Because they clearly spliced their own genes with Earth life-forms, or we wouldn't be the same as the rest of Earth."

Kyrie, sitting next to Tom, scooted closer. "Unless of course they seeded the Earth to begin with."

"True, but irrelevant for our purposes," Dr. Roberts said. "Or, as we like to put it around the lab, that's a fascinating conclusion but totally irrelevant to our question." He shrugged. "You see, in either case, it's a civilization much older than ours, and much, much better at the biological stuff." He got another of the pastries. "You could get addicted to these," he said. "But look, we are sort of on the same stairway of biological knowledge, only we're on the bottom landing contemplating putting our feet on the first step and they're on the second floor landing or something." He looked up with what Tom knew was his utterly blank expression. A look at Kyrie showed her looking utterly puzzled.

"What I mean," Dr. Roberts said, "is that we have some knowledge that indicates this could be possible. We've known for some months that we can encode memory in chromosomes, the same way we encode it into computer drives. So if you use the Y chromosome—there might be reasons this was easiest or best—it completely explains why only males could inherit. If on top of that, to activate it, it takes something that is inherent to the shifter genes, you require shifter males descended from the Great Sky Dragon on an unbroken male line. What is not clear is the whole other stuff... Why you'd only become aware of that memory when the Great Sky Dragon died, if you also have his memories, up to the moment he died. And of course, what is in the Pearl of Heaven that can make you—I say in computer terms, I suppose—uncompress and integrate the whole thing..." He shook his head. "I can make some educated guesses, but only guesses. First, I'm going to guess whatever the beings were that first came to Earth and became...embodied had some kind of powers inherent in them: mind communication, mind control, perhaps a whole host of other things we associate with magic.

"If they were beings that could at will, or without will, leave bodies behind and go on living, they clearly had abilities we don't have. So, yeah. Okay, we'll establish that."

"The Great Sky Dragon said the reason he knew I was his descendant is that he couldn't read my mind. And, also, he couldn't control me. He could communicate with me," Tom said, adding ruefully. "That's how we ended up with the bathroom in a total mess when I shifted in it last year."

"Yes, of course. That even makes some sense. Something about the transmitters being alike, so he could not communicate with you directly. Again, this is so far beyond our science I feel like someone who's never seen a radio speculating about radio trans-mission, but I can sort of guess at the shapes of things and what they're supposed to do. So, do you have the Great Sky Dragon's memory up to his death?"

"I don't know," Tom said. "The actual...personalities and life experiences of the other Great Sky Dragons are not accessible to me. The...files with the knowledge I need at any moment pop up, and I can peek in them, but not open them fully. If I inherited personal memories, too, they would not be obvious."

"Yes," Dr. Roberts said. "And you think you need those."

"I need them if I'm going to prevent the Great Sky Dragon from being...activated by the Pearl of Heaven and then made to open a portal to Earth for these creatures from other worlds. Mind you, I only have one side of the situation and it comes from the triads. For all I know these creatures from the stars are fine and dandy and would be the best thing that ever happened to us, but I don't know that, and it seems best to me not to—"

"Yes, of course. For now, we'll keep to the devil we know," Dr. Roberts said. "But here's what I don't understand: if the triad knows there is something, some packet of knowledge, this... dragon egg, which could be activated with the Pearl of Heaven, why haven't they done it before? I'm going to assume they have, right? So the Great Sky Dragon would already know how to open these portals, right? So, why would someone else need to ... activate him and make him open the way to Earth? Why not just make him open the way to Earth?"

"This," Kyrie said, in a tragic tone, "is what comes from a really busy night with no downtime, not to mention all the excitement. We should have thought about it."

"Yes, we should," Tom admitted. "The thing is, it was Old Joe who linked the missing Pearl of Heaven to whatever is going on with the Great Sky Dragon. And of course," he said, as he looked around the diner, "he's nowhere to be found. But the dragons didn't argue with him. You're right, that makes no sense at all, which means there must be something I don't know."

"I'd suspect if half of the story is true," Dr. Roberts said, "there are whole territories of things you don't know. Worlds of things you don't know, in fact."

After the doctor left, Kyrie and Tom sat in the corner booth, talking, sipping coffee. "We should go home and sleep," Kyrie said, but as she looked at Tom, who sat sideways in the booth, chewing the corner of his lip as if it had done him personal harm, she knew that would never happen. Not a chance. He was thinking of something.

"I believe," he said at last, "it's something to do with the Pearl of Heaven. Something has changed about it, or something can be changed about it, and once it has, then ..."

"Then?"

"Then you access all these memories and you get ... well, in game terms, you level up. All the Great Sky Dragon capabilities get increased."

"You must be sleepier than I thought," Kyrie said, taking a sip of her coffee.

"Why?"

"Because you didn't shudder when you said that."

"And I should have?"

"Do you hear yourself?" Kyrie said. "A leveled-up Great Sky Bastard, now with even more power, should make you tremble in your boots."

He looked at her. His eyes were within dark, hollowed circles, and his face looked . . . older somehow. Tom had always looked younger than his twenty-one years, a condition Kyrie attributed to the fact that he was, well . . . no one would call him that to his face, but Tom was frankly *pretty*: features that were perfectly regular, big enamel-blue eyes, and those dark curls framing his face. If he'd been a girl he'd have been beautiful. Because he was a man and one who looked like he didn't like to start fights but could finish any fight started around him, people called him "handsome" but that wasn't quite right. Handsome called for a more sharply cut chin, for rougher features.

Because of his features, Tom usually got carded everywhere he went, and if he shaved, people often assumed he was still in high school. But now his features looked graver, older. He looked his age until you peered directly into his eyes, and then he appeared an age that no human being could *be*, thousands and thousands of years old.

Still, as Tom looked at her, his lips twisted up in a smile, and his eyes softened. "Right now, my dear, I'm the Great Sky Dragon, and though many people have called me a bastard in the past, I don't think my dad would like to hear it."

"Speaking of your dad . . ." Kyrie said. "Isn't he supposed to visit sometime soon?"

"Not until the weekend," Tom said. "When we'll either be done with this or—"

"Or?"

Tom shrugged, then his look changed, and the eyes again had that impossibly old look, "Listen, if something happens—if I should not . . . well, if I don't survive this . . . Would you tell my dad the whole story? I don't know what he might make of it otherwise and . . . I'd like him to think well of me."

She felt her features harden, her mouth draw into a straight line, as she employed her strongest voice-of-command. "Tom Ormson," she said. "You are not going to die."

He chuckled, standing up, and kissed her on top of her head. "Even you can't order me not to die. I don't want to, of course, and I'll try not to. But—"

She grabbed at his arm. "But nothing. You're not going to die."

"I'll do my best not to. Meanwhile, if you go on home, I'll try to see about paying Jason and sending him home to sleep a bit, then wait till he comes back, and then I'll come home to sleep."

Kyrie looked up at him. She didn't need to be an expert in Tom Ormson to see trouble brewing. And she *was* an expert in Tom Ormson. "You're going to do something stupid," she said.

"Nah," he said. "Just gonna look out back and see if I can find Old Joe."

Bea stopped at, of all places, a Chinese restaurant—a small one, tucked into the side of a mountain, probably the only ethnic restaurant in a hundred miles. She was starving, and she thought Rafiel might or might not have cooked.

The restaurant didn't have the look of a triad outpost. It was small, with maybe ten tables, and what appeared to be a married couple working behind the counter, while a baby in a playpen slept in front of it. They were just opening to clean and set up for lunch, she guessed. She was three hours early for their advertised lunchtime. But they didn't make any trouble about it. Instead, they worked down the menu with her, explaining what could be made quickly enough and what couldn't. She ended up with some general or other's chicken and beef with orange flavoring, as well as two tubs of rice in a takeout bag. They offered egg drop soup and she took it, too, before paying and taking her leave.

Rafiel might very well think she was nuts showing up at ten in the morning with a bagful of Chinese takeout but she guessed he wouldn't. Shifters ate when they had shifted, and she hadn't eaten enough at that very odd conference. She felt too weak, anyway, and it was no good at all to be starved. She kept being afraid she'd shift into a dragon and go hunting rabbits or deer.

Her first thought on seeing the cabin was that something was terribly wrong. The door stood open to the outside, and when she walked in and called Rafiel, no one answered. She thought perhaps it was the habit, this far away from civilization, to leave everything unlocked while they went out. Perhaps he'd just gone hiking. But she had a very bad feeling.

She walked to the kitchen, set the food on the counter. And then she heard the water running. In one of the bathrooms, water was running continuously. Okay, so he wasn't out, he was taking a shower.

Following the sound of the water to the bedroom he'd taken, she knocked at the door to the bathroom. "Rafiel!" she called. "Rafiel."

No one answered. She cleared her throat and tried again, louder. Still no answer.

Something in her told her that there was a problem, that things had gone very, very wrong, that she should...What? Burst in on a near stranger while he showered?

But what if he'd passed out? What if—

She took a deep breath, opened the door a crack and called into it, "Rafiel." There was no answer, though it seemed to her she heard a sound like gasping.

Then she realized what was really wrong. When you opened the door of a bathroom where someone was showering, you expected to have a blast of steam hit you. Not in this case. Right. That was it. If he'd had a heart attack in the shower, he might have run out all the hot water.

And what if he just liked cold showers?

Into the cold bathroom, she called again, "Rafiel."

That sound like a gasp once more, but no words. Right. Bea opened the door completely and walked in. For a moment she thought the bathroom was empty. It was smaller than the one upstairs, and it only had space for a vanity, toilet and shower enclosure.

The enclosure was glass on two sides, and one of those premolded plastic things on the other two. The water was on and running freely, but no one stood in the enclosure. Then she looked down.

Rafiel was huddled in the corner, under the streaming water, his knees pulled up, his face resting between them, his hair soaked, his shoulders shaking, not as if he were crying, but as if he were struggling to breathe.

"Rafiel," Bea said, alarmed. She pulled the door open. He looked up. He stared at her, his eyes wild and uncomprehending.

It wasn't as if he'd gone animal, though. She'd seen animal eyes. She'd also seen the eyes of people coming off a high around campus, and that wasn't it either. It wasn't even as if he'd gone mad.

No. The expression in his eyes was one she'd seen once before when her father had found one of the dogs he'd treated for many years and who was one of his favorites dead by the side of the road.

She didn't know why Rafiel was in shock, but she knew he was. And shock she could deal with.

She opened the shower door further, reached in, turned off the water. It was freezing cold as it splashed her arm, and it couldn't have been doing the poor man any good. She reached for a towel from the bar next to her, and she spoke to him reasonably, "Get up, come on. We need to get you warm."

Bea had absolutely no idea what she'd do if he refused to obey her. After all, she probably weighed a third of what he did, and that would be with lead in her pockets.

But he dragged himself up. She noted there were five, parallel, deep cuts across his face, which she'd have sworn weren't there before, or had healed, because if his eye had healed, his face would have too, right?

She tentatively dried his shoulders and was more relieved than she ever wanted to admit when he took the towel from her hands and started rubbing himself. She had been trying not to look at what her mind had classified as *his fiddly bits* because he was clearly out of his right mind. She had seen him naked before, but now it seemed like she'd be taking advantage of him. She really didn't want to think of helping him dry there. For heaven's sake, she'd never even had a boyfriend. She'd seen Rafiel naked more than any other male outside of an art class, as it was.

As he was drying himself, she went back into the room to find him clothes, and was relieved to see a thick terry robe hanging from a peg beside the closet door. When she brought it back to the bathroom, Rafiel was standing there, the towel in his hands. He let her dress him in the robe and tie it around him. He was still shivering. "Come on," she said. "You need to eat something warm."

He let her lead him to the kitchen, but didn't actually make Bea spoon feed him the egg drop soup. Instead he ate it, slowly, with measured calm. She refilled his bowl, and made hot tea, which she poured for him. Sometime while eating, he stopped shivering and a frown settled on his face, as if he were trying very hard to remember something.

When she filled a bowl with cooked beef, he looked up at her and blinked, "You...went out? You...shifted?"

She filled her own bowl and plowed into it, ignoring the chopsticks and using instead the plastic fork also provided. Looking up, she nodded at him, "Yes," she said. And because she figured that talking to him might help him calm down, and would certainly take his mind off of whatever had made him go into shock long enough for his mind to get past it, she told him about the call, the strong impulse to go and respond to whatever the call was, the crawling out of the skylight, flying to Goldport.

As she described what had happened in the parking lot, Rafiel stared at her. "Tom did what? Tom does not—"

She shook her head. "I was shocked too. I don't know him like you do, but I formed an impression of him...but then afterwards I got to thinking. I think whatever information he got when the Great Sky Dragon died that...well..." She paused. "I think that whatever the information was, it told him that he couldn't simply refuse the position, not without asserting his supremacy first. I think the triad works by primitive rules. The heir can't simply be allowed to slide off and be an anonymous someone. He either rules or gets killed."

Something about talking of primitive rules made him stare at her a long time. He finally nodded a little. Then he said, "When you left...I heard the chair fall."

"Sorry. I was afraid of shifting before I could get out. You know what—"

He inclined his head, and held up a hand. "Doesn't matter, but I thought you might be in trouble, and I—" He paused and looked past her, as he spoke. "I went outside and I was hit... Have you ever had blood lust? That is...did you ever...?"

"Want to eat something alive?" she said.

"People. Want to eat people."

Bea blinked. "No. I've wanted to beat them to death with a weighted sock on occasion, but not to eat them."

"Oh. Well...when you're really tired and hungry and..."

A monstrous idea crossed Bea's mind. "You ate someone?" She wasn't sure that was something she could forgive, or something she could even start to understand.

He shook his head. "No, but...it was the same thing."

Bea stared, confused about how anything could be the same as eating someone. "You killed someone?"

He shook his head again. "No, but...when I stepped outside, there was this smell, like...like...I can't describe it. I shifted and...and...when I came to, when I got control over the lion's mind again, I found that...that is...The creature who attacked me before? She...I was...We were having sex in shifted form. I tried to pull away and she..." He touched the deep gauges on his face.

Bea didn't know what to say or how to say it. Part of her, having contemplated the possibility of his having eaten a human being, now wanted to laugh with relief, but she realized the experience had shocked Rafiel to his core. And looking at him, she slowly understood why. "How long..." she asked. "How long has it been since you lost control so completely, and weren't aware of what you were doing?"

He frowned at her. "Not since I was very young and in college," he said. "Not since..." He shook his head. "It was...I feel no attraction to...I don't even know what the woman looks like in person...It was like..." He shook his head again, as though to clear it. "It was as though something or someone had taken over my mind. It's a very disquieting, scary feeling. I wanted to...I want to know why, how. I want to make sure it won't happen again. If she can make me do that, what else can she make me do?"

Bea looked at him. "I expect," she said. It was a slow word, drawn out. "I expect the next time, you'll have more control. We learn to control the beast by being the beast. This...mating in lion form... it was the first time?"

He made a face and smiled a little. Red flooded like a tide into his cheeks. "At the risk of alarming you, it was the first time in either form." He lifted his hand, as though to defend himself from an accusation she hadn't made. "You have to understand," he said. "I can't be sure...I've always been afraid of losing control and shifting. Tom...Tom says it doesn't happen, and anyway, you know, he's not afraid of that with Kyrie, because she knows he shifts, though I don't think his bedroom is big enough to— Never mind."

"To hold a dragon? No. Particularly now. He's...he's grown. There seems to be something—beyond. I mean, it's like magic. The Great Sky Dragon died, and it's like his death activated something that changed Tom from a juvenile dragon into a full adult. Oh, that's not right. It made him into a full adult Great Sky Dragon, not just a dragon."

Rafiel looked at her for a long while, then sighed. "He's going to need our help, isn't he?"

Bea opened her mouth, then realized he'd said "our." He thought of them as a unit. She should have been horrified, particularly in view of the fact the man had been mating in lion form with some prehistoric horror. But then...but then he was even more shocked by it than she was. And she meant what she'd told him.

In the future, knowing it was possible, knowing what it felt like, he'd know how to resist it—how to keep his head. And if he didn't...well, if he didn't, he'd *really* need her.

She took a deep breath, understanding that this was right, that, somehow, they were supposed to be a team, and that he understood it too. "Yeah. I think so," she said.

She shouldn't go home without him. Kyrie wasn't stupid enough to go home without Tom and think he would keep out of trouble till she came back. But unfortunately she was tired enough to *have* to go home. She must sleep.

In the parking lot of The George, getting into her car, she looked back at the diner. It was full of people having breakfast and, on the addition side, where it was all enclosed in glass and you could see everything, Tom was talking to a table of regulars, Rafiel's colleagues in the police force.

She frowned a little, wondering how Rafiel was healing, and if there was any relation between his troubles and the Great Sky Dragon. It seemed too big a stretch to connect a feral juvenile shifter and the byzantine hierarchy of the triad organization. No. It was just their luck that right now they had two loads of trouble in town, both of them related to shifters. Because they were just that exceptionally lucky.

"It never rains but it pours," she said under her breath, feeling somehow comforted at the trite phrase. When you're knee-deep in shifters and threats from the stars, you want to be reassured today really *is* the first day of the rest of your life. Of course, she would prefer being reassured that life would last more than a few days. Particularly for Tom, since Tom seemed to have one of his ideas, and that was never a good thing.

Kyrie toyed with staying on and following Tom in whatever he intended to do, but then she thought through what he told her: he was going to let Jason go home, then have him come back, *then* Tom would do something. Kyrie yawned. She would take a quick nap and return in more than enough time to figure out what Tom was up to, particularly since it involved finding Old Joe, a task that was often, at best, hazardous.

She drove the short distance home through the narrow neighborhood streets. Since most of the small homes in the area were occupied by older couples, the only signs of life were people watering their lawns or walking their dogs. She pulled up the inclined driveway and parked. At the back door, she started to turn the handle and froze.

Something was wrong. Seriously wrong. She could feel it not quite as anything rational, nor as anything she could have put into words, but as a creeping feeling up the back of her spine, something that made her pause and feel . . . wrongness.

She couldn't put it any better than that.

The house was closed, as she and Tom had left it. The neighborhood looked perfectly normal for this time of morning. There were no strange cars parked near their yard. There were no unfamiliar cars at all. She could name all the cars around. Mr. and Mrs. Jones' brown, ancient station wagon next door. And the other way the Phillson's van. And across the street, the red truck that was always parked there.

But there was still the feeling that somewhere, somehow, doom lurked. She tried to push away the uneasiness, tried to put her keys in the lock, but the desire to get back in the car and drive away was almost overpowering.

Now, Kyrie thought. *Now. It can't be. There can't be anything around here that would hurt me. I'm imagining things. I've had too many shocks in succession.*

But one thing she was quite sure of. She could not get in the house and go to sleep. Would never happen. And that denied the whole point of coming home. Might as well go back and go search for Old Joe with Tom when he went.

She sighed, and turned around to get in the car.

There—movement in the bushes, in the almost nonexistent space between the back of the house and the fence that enclosed the backyard. Her first thought was squirrel, but then she realized there was *someone* there, with a mask and some sort of weapon. She turned to face the threat as her body tensed with the precursor of shifting.

And then—

And then something hit her upper arm really hard, and she looked down, unbelieving. *I was* not *shot with a tranquilizer dart,* she thought.

Even as she thought it, her legs folded under her, and her vision faded to dark. Before she hit the cement of the driveway, she wondered what Tom would think.

— CHAPTER 17 —

The breakfast rush over, Tom realized how exhausted he was. He'd sent Jason home at the beginning of it, and didn't expect him back till lunch, but for all that, he felt like he could fall asleep in his tracks. It had been much too long a night, since they'd woken with Rafiel's phone call. Under normal circumstances—like those ever happened around here—just the rush of people for Conan's maiden show would have been enough to leave Tom feeling battered, but there had been so much on top of that.

He stared out the back window at the parking lot, and squinted at the burned-out ruin of the bed-and-breakfast. He wondered if Louise would be able to rebuild, if she had the money. Though the operation had always kept up a good front of seeming classy and well stocked—which he supposed was essential in the boutique hospitality industry—he felt that it had been run very close to the bone.

Perhaps it's a reflection of how we run the diner, he thought, and rubbed his hand pensively on his chin, shocked to hear and feel the grating of half-grown beard. Vague, disconnected thoughts ran through his mind. With a quirk of the lips, he wondered about Rafiel and Bea and how they were getting along. Rafiel could be forbidding and patriarchal. Part of being the policeman in charge of anything involving shifters in this area, Tom thought—unofficially in charge, of course, which made it worse. Also possibly something to do with the fact that he was a third generation policemen. Such families tended to raise boy children in the expectation of serving and protecting.

And Tom wasn't, of course, absolutely sure about Bea. He'd barely met her, even if he'd seen her twice so far, but he got the impression you could tell her what to do all you wanted to—you just couldn't get her to obey. A young woman who would tell the Great Sky Dragon where to put it and with how much force, even if he suspected she'd been more polite than that about it, was not the sort of young woman that Rafiel could intimidate. He grinned at the idea that she and Rafiel would probably hate each other the more time they spent together. It didn't matter, of course, provided they both were safe.

Then he thought of Conan and that voice. Who would have thought it? Certainly neither his parents nor the triad to whom Conan had been handed over at puberty when his shifting started. But Conan had dreamed of a career, and Tom meant to make sure his dreams came true. Which, even taking into account that Conan was dating Rya and that Rya was the more practical of the two, probably meant Tom would have to keep a very close eye on everything. Dreamers could be good artists, but most of them were terrible businessmen. And being a businessman, it turned out, required training and thought—a fact Tom was learning, slowly, through his mistakes. He'd not at all been prepared to run anything, by his drifting existence as a young man, moving from place to place, always afraid someone would notice that he was a dragon shifter.

On the other hand, he thought, *at least it prepared me to survive by my wits, and figure out how to live. Conan didn't even have that. He was handed over as a slave, his every thought controlled.*

Thinking of that brought the memory and feel of the . . . thing in his mind. The intrusion of all the—for lack of a better word—files of Great Sky Dragon memory, the hidden knowledge of the members of the triad, all those shifters he could control. He felt around in there. If he focused, he could sense this or that dragon shifter, here and there, all over the world.

He didn't want to be aware of them; he didn't want to focus on them; he didn't want to know what they were doing. If he did, he'd find himself an unwitting accomplice to hundreds or thousands of illegal activities. It wasn't like the triads were benevolent social clubs, after all. He could neither denounce their illegal dealings—which police department would buy "I know it through telepathy"?—nor did he want to know about them.

So he skimmed lightly over them, and felt the mass back there, his dragon self. No, the Great Sky Dragon's self, even if it wasn't the same Great Sky Dragon that was external to Tom. Tom chewed on his lip.

What it came to was that he had to find out what was going on with the Pearl of Heaven and he had to figure out where the Great Sky Dragon might be. Tom would be damned if he was going to get stuck with this job.

In fact, it had better all be over with by the time his father came to visit, because what his father might make of it gave Tom cold sweats.

A touch on his shoulder made him turn. For a second he thought it would be Kyrie, but it was one of the shifters who often helped around the diner, and who, in fact, had helped last night during Conan's thing. He smelled like a shifter, and he called himself a half-horse, but Tom had never asked what his form was. A horse, he assumed, of course. Maybe. Well, none of his business anyway.

In his human form, James was a dark-haired young man who worked as some sort of nursing aide at the local hospital. He had a habit of always glowering, which, at first, had made Tom think he hated the diner, and Tom couldn't figure out why he kept showing up there so often. But it turned out—as they got to know the man better—the glowering was protection for social awkwardness. Which was good, because the tone in which he asked, "Do you need help?" might have sounded pretty aggressive otherwise.

"Yeah," Tom said. "How did you know?"

"Other than the fact you look dead on your feet?"

Tom rubbed his chin again. "Yeah, I've been up . . . very long. Yeah, I could use some help." Remembering the man worked nights, though, he said, "But shouldn't you go home and sleep or something?"

"Nah. Could use some more money anyway." A small smile. "Horse feed, you know? Got to keep the ponies happy."

Tom nodded sagely, refusing to ask if the fodder was for himself or for actual horses, then said, "Yeah. If you can take over, Jason—the new guy—should come back before lunch, and Anthony too. And then Conan and Rya can go home," he said, looking behind the counter where the two were jointly manning the cooking. He thought they looked very happy but neither of them was particularly competent. *Only me,* he thought. *I train a greasy spoon cook and waiter and end up with a musician.*

James had gone behind the counter and got his apron and signed in. He did this often enough, if irregularly, that the procedure was familiar to him. He brought his eyebrows down low over his eyes, as he touched Tom on the shoulder. "Go on then," he said. "Go home and get some sleep."

"Yeah." Tom thought about doing just that. About going back home to Kyrie, about climbing in bed with her, asleep and peaceful. About Not Dinner curled up on their feet—

But he didn't know how long he had. If Old Joe was right, then at any moment the Great Sky Dragon—depending on the extent of his injuries—could wake up and be forced to activate the Pearl of Heaven, whatever that meant. If it meant something bad...

He sighed. "I'll do some stuff first."

He took off his apron, stowed it in the place under the counter, ran his hand through his hair. He felt naked without his black leather jacket, but it was too warm to wear it. And his beard, the way it looked, half-grown, if he wore a leather jacket with this, people would run from him on the street.

He rapped on the counter to get Conan's attention and told him to man the fort till Anthony came in. Both Conan and Rya smiled and nodded, and Tom wondered if they'd heard a single word he'd said.

The parking lot was half-empty, the breakfast rush ended. Tom stood for a moment wondering where to find Old Joe, then thought that the alligator shifter was, after all, worried about Tom himself, and therefore would be somewhere around.

He checked near the dumpster, which Old Joe often mined for food. Tom didn't understand why the man preferred his food discarded and half-rotted, when he could simply come in and ask for some. Perhaps he just didn't like asking. He seemed to be almost pathologically independent. Except for a soft spot where Tom was concerned—and not very soft, he just appeared to not want Tom to get killed—Old Joe didn't seem to like any Earthly attachments.

The dumpster was not full, and there were no alligators near it. Tom walked to the alley, and that's when he caught a glimpse of someone in the ruins of the bed-and-breakfast. It was a person and he was looking for an alligator, so it took him a moment to realize it was Old Joe. Particularly since the old man, asleep in the ruins, was fully dressed.

"Joe?" he said.

Instantly, the old vagrant was awake, and sitting up, his eyes wide. "Dragon boy?" he said.

"Ah—I'd like to talk to you," Tom said.

Old Joe nodded. "I thought you might. So I didn't go. And I didn't shift." He sounded almost virtuous. "I stayed here and waited for you."

"Good," Tom said. "Come inside. I'll get you some breakfast and we can talk."

"I feel like I should let you sleep," Rafiel said, "before making you drive all the way to Goldport again."

"You're not *making* me," Bea said. She'd showered and dressed, and come out to find that Rafiel had cleaned the kitchen and dressed too. She assumed that he had showered enough the day before. "I also think we should go back." She tied her hair back with a scrunchy. She was wearing her comfy jeans and a large man's shirt she'd liberated from her father's drawer some months ago. She was aware that on her it looked cute and made her seem like a little kid pretending to be grown up, without distracting from her obviously feminine figure. She was also aware that most men would think she was being careless and casual, Rafiel likely included. Sometimes she thought it was unfair to let men think such things—they were in many ways curiously innocent creatures.

Rafiel made a face, then smiled. He had changed into khakis and a dark blue, short sleeve shirt. And he looked good. Really good, despite the healing scars across his face. "Yes, but I'm not sure we shouldn't rest first and—"

Bea shook her head. "I'm fine, really. I drove down all the way from Georgia by myself, you know. Yeah, I'd like to actually sleep tonight, but come on, it won't be the first time I skip sleep for one night. I'll be fine." She hesitated. "Unless you'd rather drive, because—" She almost said "because you don't trust me," but stopped herself in time, realizing that would seem manipulative, and it wasn't what she'd meant to do. "Or you want to drive the van and follow me?"

He shrugged, and this time his smile was open. "It's your truck. It would be a little odd for me to drive your truck. And besides," he said, and his smile clouded a little, "it's not like I slept much longer than you did last night. We'd best pick up the van later. One . . . the dragons can always fly out and get it, if it's needed."

Which she guessed was true. And she guessed he didn't want to think about what he'd been doing instead—*much of it standing under a freezing cold shower*, she thought and realized he didn't want to be alone, even in a van right behind her truck—and so she smiled and said instead, "I closed the skylight in the bedroom."

"Oh, good," he said. "I meant to ask you." He sighed. "I wish we could stay longer. It's really nice up here."

"Yes," she said. "I figured that it would be really nice to point that telescope up and . . ." She trailed off and blushed, as she realized she sounded like she was inviting herself back here, which she supposed she was. But all the same . . . she didn't want Rafiel to think that she didn't care for the place that was clearly his pride and joy.

He didn't seem to notice any awkwardness. He picked up the suitcase she'd brought in to get her clothes and which was now closed and resting in the front hall. He escorted Bea out and locked the door. "I have an astronomy manual somewhere, from when I was little," he said. "And when we come back, if it's nice, we'll look up, and I'll try to figure out names and constellations." He grinned, as he put the suitcase back behind the seats. "My dad used to do that with me when I was little, but I never memorized any. I just liked the shiny lights and the blue in the back. I guess I never thought of something like being an astronomer or anything. I always wanted to be a cop, like my dad and granddad."

She got into the driver's seat and waited till Rafiel climbed in and secured himself, before starting the truck. "You never thought of being anything else?"

He lifted an eyebrow at her. "Should I have?"

"I don't know," she said. "I guess because part of my background is Asian and they always, you know, expect you to follow family footsteps, I . . . perhaps I rebelled against it a bit. I wanted to do my own thing. I wanted to be myself. Dad is a vet, and when I was little, he and Mom talked a lot about how good I was with injured animals, and maybe I wanted to grow up and be a doctor."

"But you didn't?"

She smiled. Shook her head. "No. I never really wanted to do anything but draw."

"Well," Rafiel said. "In my case, it wasn't so much following family tradition, you know. It was just what I wanted to do. I heard Dad talk around the kitchen table about his cases, and it seemed to me like it was really important work, and really fascinating too. He and Mom said, once or twice, that I could be a lawyer or . . . or anything I wanted, but that wasn't what I wanted to be. I wanted to—" He sighed and leaned back. "I wanted to be in the streets, protecting people. I only had doubts after . . . after I found out I was a shifter. I thought I might not be safe around people. I've worked . . . very hard, at being safe around people."

"Which is why yesterday shocked you so much," she said.

"Yes. You understand. It wasn't . . . the act itself, though it felt odd, I mean, in lion form—" He stopped short, and took a deep breath. "It wasn't that, though. It was that I was out of control, that I couldn't stop myself."

"Now that you know what it is like," she said, "you'll be able to. Now you'll be able to control it, like you control the blood lust or the need to change when you shouldn't."

"You sound very sure," he said. "Did you ever—"

She laughed. "No. But I know how the process works, if it makes sense. I don't like to do things I don't mean to do, so it's really important for me to control this sort of thing."

"I can't imagine anyone making you do something you don't want to," Rafiel said.

"Oh, I can," Bea said, thinking of how close she had come to considering the Great Sky Dragon's idea, if it meant they would leave her dad alone. If Tom hadn't had a girlfriend. If he hadn't been a total stranger. She might at least have considered pretending to go along with it. "But it's not easy. This is probably fortunate for your friend, Tom Ormson."

She laughed, but he didn't, just nodded solemnly. "For all of us, really," he said.

✧   ✧   ✧

Old Joe ate bacon and eggs with the relish of someone who had been years without food. Tom knew for a fact that this wasn't true, because he'd fed Old Joe several times in the more recent years, and he was sure Kyrie had too, not even counting the fact that he'd watched the old shifter put away food at the back of the Three Luck Dragon.

But no one watching the old shifter push strip after strip of bacon into his face could believe anything other than that he was starving. Tom kept his cup of coffee filled, and thought that at the very least, it did a man good to see someone eat with that much gusto. It gave the impression that some things were worth doing full tilt. And when a man had been alive and eating for thousands of years, to still find that much enjoyment in mere food was amazing.

Tom's mind leaned briefly over vistas of thousands of years, of seeing all his friends who weren't shifters grow old and die. It wasn't just a matter of seeing Anthony grow old and die, but Anthony's son and grandson, and great-grandson, until—if Anthony's descendants survived to that time—everyone on Earth was descended from Anthony. He blinked, thinking that Old Joe, probably looking much as he did now, had seen the era come and go when it was cutting edge to domesticate horses. He'd seen the time when the ax was the most cool and awesome of weapons give way to the nuclear era.

How did you stay sane through such shifts? How did you stay human? He didn't want to know. He had no more desire to die than any other human did, but he also didn't want to outlast the entire world he knew. It was one thing for the world to change around you and along with you. It was another matter entirely to find that you were alone and your world dead and buried and the subject of archeological excavations.

And yet, Old Joe managed it and seemed to still enjoy life. He looked up, his brown eyes seeming to laugh at Tom. "So, dragon boy?" he said. "Worried?"

"Yes," Tom said. He had found long ago that Old Joe was not nearly as simple as he seemed, and he was certainly not simple-minded. After several thousand years of watching people dissemble and change, the old shifter knew very well when he was being lied to. Stood to reason, you would. Practice made perfect and one thing that Old Joe had lots of practice with was humans.

Old Joe laughed, a rattling sound in his throat, and opened his mouth, displaying sparse teeth. He clucked his tongue behind those teeth. "I thought you'd be. You're not stupid, you. And dragon egg would worry anyone that isn't stupid." He sobered up, but his eyes narrowed, as though studying Tom. "You know, stupid people would think dragon egg is power."

"Yes," Tom said. Then he tried to put into words what he felt about what he was being offered. "It is knowledge. Perhaps more knowledge than anyone has in the world today? And they say knowledge is power. But it comes with . . . obligations. It might, because of the way dragons are, allow you to control several thousands of people all over the world. But that kind of power over people . . ." He tried to make sense of it enough to put into words. "That kind of power over people means that they have power over you, too. Like . . . You know Rafiel, my policeman friend?"

Old Joe nodded. "Cat boy," he said, and shoved three strips of bacon into his mouth.

"Yes, well. He's a police officer, which means he has a certain amount of power. He can charge people, and he can arrest them, and if nothing else, he can make people's lives very uncomfortable. But at the same time, that means he has a duty. Particularly since he is the only shifter member of the police force, it means he must be involved in every shifter-related crime, and keep people from finding out what and who we are. It comes with a duty. He can't just shrug off . . . well, like the young feral shifter killing people out at the amusement park."

The moment the words were out of his lips, he realized he was giving Old Joe information the alligator shifter hadn't had before. The man sat up, and his eyes opened wide. "Feral shifter? Like Joe? Free of clans? Free of associations?"

"No," Tom said. He felt his voice was dryer than he meant it to be. "Feral as in doesn't speak. Not human. He's a skinny kid. Teenager. And he's feral."

"Skinny kid? Boy? Yea tall?" Joe got up and indicated a height above himself.

"Uh. Yeah. About that."

Joe fell back on the seat so bonelessly that the sound of his sitting down made people turn to look at him. His mouth dropped open. He closed it with an effort. "Her son," he said. "Where her son is, she is."

"She?"

"She...Maduh. When I knew her, Maduh. She. You know..." Looking up he was faced with the fact that Tom didn't, in fact, know. "You know, Dante, the...the sabertooth. She's his mate, his..." He lifted a hand with two fingers together. "She's his half, his other."

"His wife?" Tom asked. He seemed to remember that the sabertooth who'd come to town determined to kill them all, the sabertooth that had tried to seduce Kyrie, had seemed remarkably single.

Old Joe bit at his lower lip. "Well...In a way, maybe, but not...No. It's different. It was...a long, long time ago. They're one. They stayed together..." He shook his head as if trying to go beyond where words could go. "I don't know how to explain, but she and him, could sense each other and..."

"You mean, she's come to avenge him?" This seemed to lose Old Joe, but Tom was thinking of the female who had attacked Rafiel. "And that the young one is her son?"

Old Joe nodded. He made a gesture with his fingers, waggling them as if to indicate something. "He—boy—was born in other form. Beast form. He—"

"You mean, he's a human shifter? He shifts into human? Like others shift into animals?"

Old Joe gave a grunt of assent, and Tom tried to think. What did that *mean* exactly? What was the difference? Except perhaps that he hadn't spent much time in human form. He looked over his shoulder, but the entire area around the corner booth was empty. "This is what Kyrie and I are afraid of and why we decided we shall never have children."

Suddenly, unexpectedly, Old Joe erupted into laughter. He laughed so hard that Tom thought he'd gone mad. There was something a little repulsive in that unbridled guffawing, and all Tom could do was stare. Trying to talk to Old Joe would fall on deaf ears just then. Perhaps the old man had gone mad? He had reason enough. Besides, it could be argued he was always, at best, on the short end of sanity.

But the laugh died down, and he wiped at his eyes with the back of his hands, and then with the paper napkin. Looking at Tom caused him to jiggle with amusement still. "Dragon boy," he said, in the indulgent tone someone might talk to a small child, "you can't have shifter babies with cat girl. Not happen. Different seed, that. Not pass on. That is why daddy dragon's people are so upset. No kitty dragons. Not exist."

Tom opened his mouth, closed it. "You're saying any children Kyrie and I have will either be cats or dragons? Or that they won't be shifters?"

Old Joe shook his head. "No shifters. Human only. Seed in blood. Might come out in time, if they find nice dragon or cat girl or boy, but they won't change. Human only."

"Oh," Tom said, and filed it away to talk to Dr. Roberts about. Seemed . . . possible, if not plausible. It was entirely possible that the genetics that created either cat or dragon shifters could not possibly create a mix. "But what about those who are born shifted?" he asked. "Beast side."

"Not yours," Old Joe said. "Not with cat girl."

"Okay, not with Kyrie. But, if Kyrie were to run off with Rafiel—" He saw Old Joe's eyes acquire a mutinous look and said, "I know, not possible, but suppose it was. Could they have a child who was a lion and only changed to human now and then?"

Old Joe inclined his head. "Only if they made child while beast. Can't shift while . . . Female can't shift while carrying."

This too made a grim biological kind of sense. "So you're saying Dante and . . . Maduh had . . . that they made the child while shifted, and so the poor bast— The kid can only shift to human when a teen . . ."

"Yeah. I think. Used to happen. Sometimes. Most don't live . . . long. But Maduh defends her cub."

Tom really didn't like the sound of this, but he tried to wrench his thoughts back to what he'd meant to ask Old Joe. He knew the reason his mind kept straying to things like *Kyrie and I could have children,* was that he was too tired to think straight. Right now he needed to know how to deal with the triads, which would allow him to then think of these other matters, to plan his life. "What I meant to ask you," Tom said, "has nothing to do with this. What I wanted to ask was about the dragon egg and the Pearl—"

Old Joe nodded, as though he'd been expecting this all along. "The artifact," he said. "You're supposed to use the artifact to unlock the dragon egg." He looked up at Tom, and said, as though it should clear everything, "Like key. The artifact allows you to control it."

"But how?" Tom said.

Old Joe shrugged. "How do you unlock dragon egg? Don't know."

"But..." Tom frowned. "If they have Great Sky Dragon, if they can make him open the gates, why would they need the Pearl too..."

Old Joe looked at Tom a long time, as though studying him. He made a face, with his mouth slightly open, his tongue lolling out, which made Tom think very much of the alligator, with its mouth half open, waiting for prey. "I don't know," he said. "Can't tell you. Not dragon. But—"

"But?" Tom said.

"But I think the dragons don't know how to use the artifact anymore. I think it got passed one time, and the knowledge of how to use it didn't. Like...something like now, but with the final death. A son son of a dragon's son, one not raised as dragon, inherited, and he didn't know how to use the Pearl, and he thought it was just mystical, uh stuff, like crown, and he never unlocked dragon egg, because he couldn't so he never found better. He only had little bit, like what you have. Locked dragon egg lets you see bits, and living he learned the rest, but he could never open it. I don't think..." He clacked his teeth together in the way the gator did. "I think last two dragon daddies didn't know how to, maybe more. The dragon clan has not been as powerful as it was."

"I see," Tom said. He narrowed his eyes again. "So, you're saying that the Great Sky Dragon..." And in response to Old Joe's look, he specified, "The *other* Great Sky Dragon never learned how to open interworld gates, never learned how to do any of the things that the Pearl should allow him to do, and because of that, someone had to take both him and the Pearl? But that would mean that whoever took him—"

"Knows how to unlock dragon egg?" Old Joe said. "I think so. I think that whoever took daddy dragon has been talking to star people. People from other worlds. I think they know everything they need to do." He looked at Tom, his eyes suddenly tragic. "And unless you find out where daddy dragon is, and stop it, or unless daddy dragon returns stronger than people do from death, they're going to open the world gates and invite the people of the stars over."

"Are they bad?" Tom asked. "I mean, really bad? I know the dragons—"

"Not the dragons," Old Joe said. "All our people say they're bad. My grandfather's grandfather's grandfather said they're bad. They don't like..." He made the sound of hitting his teeth together again, thinking. "They don't like people in flesh. They think people in flesh bad. They think..."

Tom didn't say anything. He could see in Old Joe's eyes the remembered terror of a child who had heard about this unspeakable enemy. Was it true? Or was it the legend passed by descendants of a persecuted people? Who knew? And could he risk it? If you're not sure if the man outside your home is a robber or not, the best thing to do is keep that door closed, not throw it open and ask him in and offer him the best chair.

Tom would prefer to determine who these people were before he considered whether to let them in. Besides, he thought, if this person or persons, whoever this was, had attacked the Great Sky Dragon and intended to make him open the world gates by force, it wasn't the work of honorable people. Though, of course, the Great Sky Dragon was, in many ways, despicable, at least by Tom's lights.

But then Tom had a strong feeling that his morals and his views on the world were quite different from those of people who lived thousands of years. He'd still believe his morals and his sense of the world over theirs, but he could see how that might change if he lived several thousand years. He didn't have the same sense of morals as his father, and though... well, he wasn't sure his father had *any* sense of morals. This didn't mean Tom didn't love him, no matter how strange things could get. After all, it probably wasn't his father's fault he was a lawyer.

How much more different would be the morals and the minds of those people from other worlds? It wasn't that he believed the nonsense that people kept spouting about all cultures being equally valid. Tom was fairly sure that cultures where your wife was a possession and your neighbor's possessions yours for the taking if you could muster enough firepower were inferior to American culture. But other cultures existed. It was no use denying that different places and times shaped people differently. As nice as Old Joe was most of the time, he had tried to eat Not Dinner, and had probably eaten a lot of cats and dogs over the centuries. Which just went to show—

And that was Earth, and someone who had lived at least some time in Western civilization. Invaders from the stars... well... The question was not if Old Joe was right or if they were good or bad. They were probably so different that they'd be bad news in either case.

Besides, he thought, the whole New Age idea that no one would travel across space to start a fight was the purest nonsense. In fact, starting a fight was the only reason people were ever likely to travel that far. Why else do it? If you didn't want to steal something or take over the space, why make the effort to open a locked door? Tom kept coming to that. People rarely broke into a house in order to clean the floor and leave a nice set of matched cutlery behind.

"Right," he said. "And how can I figure out where they took the Great Sky Dragon?"

Old Joe shrugged. "Don't know. You should have... When he came into your mind? When you got dragon egg? There should be a feeling with it? A... perhaps words?"

"Not that I can—" Tom started. At that moment, his cell phone rang. He fished it out of his jean pocket. Earlier, Conan had rescued it from his clothes in the alley.

The window of the phone showed Kyrie's number.

Tom pressed answer, and said, "Hi. Are you coming in?"

Kyrie was in the dark. There was an overpoweringly sweet smell in her nostrils, something like perfume, but not, something that made her stomach clench and turn. She had a vague idea it was something that had made her lose consciousness, or perhaps that kept her unconscious.

She remembered the dart in her arm. Who would use a tranquilizer dart to kidnap her? Why? Unless they knew she was a shifter and likely to change shapes.

Okay, so people who knew that were likely to use a tranquilizer dart to kidnap her. But why would they kidnap her at all? And where was she?

After a while her eyes adjusted, and she could see that she was in a room of some sort.

Not that she'd been absolutely sure what to expect, but in her mind when people kidnapped you, they were supposed to put you in some kind of cell, or hole. This was a small room. The floor felt like carpet. There was a single bed against the wall, and Kyrie was lying on it. She was not tied or confined. She thought there was a table against the wall, or at least it looked like that, from the contours of deeper shadow in that area.

Kyrie got up and felt around the walls. There was a door. She tried it. It was closed. Going the other way, she came to a board on the wall, which she would bet was a boarded-up window. She could feel the corners where the board was nailed to the wall. A small window. From the way it was high up on the wall, she guessed it was a basement window.

Another careful inspection both of the wall and the objects in the room—yes, a bed and a table, as she'd thought—revealed that there was no lamp on the small table—though there was a chair—and no light switch in the wall. Interesting. Did they intend to keep her in the dark forever?

Kyrie briefly considered shifting into the panther, which had better night vision. But then the panther had truly horrible standing-still vision. It worked much better with things that were moving. And besides, she thought, the panther was not something she needed to unleash in this closed space. If anything, she should congratulate herself on not panic-shifting at finding herself imprisoned. Yes, it was quite possible that the panther would be able to rip through the door or that board over the window in a moment, but the problem was doing it quietly. Kyrie suspected any great amount of noise, any great display of aggression would bring about a tranquilizer dart.

No. She must think how to get out of here, and she must do it carefully. Whoever had kidnapped her—she had no idea who it might be, though she could formulate suspicions as well as the next person—had waited in ambush for her, and had been provided with a tranquilizer dart. Since these weren't normally used on women, this must mean that they thought she might shift.

Which meant they'd be ready for the panther. And they'd taken care to enclose her in a place where, unless she guessed wrong, the window would be very hard for the panther to get out of. But not the woman. Not if Kyrie had felt the dimensions right. They wanted her to shift...

She sat on the bed and drew her knees up, encircling them demurely with her arms. Then, on second thought, she checked her pockets. She'd transferred her phone and keys to the dress she borrowed from Bea. Well, from what the Chinese had meant for Bea.

The keys were still there, but the phone was gone. Right, so it wasn't going to be that easy. But she had her keys.

⇥ CHAPTER 18 ⇤

For a moment no one answered Tom's question, but then a voice came on, and it was definitely not Kyrie's but a man's. It was a whisper but still identifiably male.

"Mr. Ormson?" the man said.

"Who is this?" Tom asked. He was aware that he'd spoken too loudly. Though this part of the diner was mostly empty, he could feel Conan turning around to stare at him.

"That is unimportant, Mr. Ormson. What you want to know, rather, is who we have, and what you must do to get her back, right?"

Tom bit back a cry of "Kyrie." It was quite clear this wasn't Kyrie at the other end of the phone, and calling her would do nothing more than to tell whoever was on the other end that she was important to him, or that they'd scored a hit. No. They would know she was important to him. But the fact was that he didn't even know they had her. Maybe they didn't. All he knew was that they had her phone. "Who is this?" he repeated. "I don't know what you're talking about."

This seemed to disconcert his interlocutor. There was a moment of silence and a distinct, noisy throat clearing, and then, "We have Kyrie Smith. If you want to see her alive again, you will step up to your duties as the leader of the dragon people. That is all. As soon as you do what is required of you, and secure descendants for the dragon with your chosen and suitable bride, we will let her go. But not before."

The phone clicked off. Tom dialed back immediately, instinctively, but no one answered. He then dialed home. Kyrie had probably dropped her phone back at the Three Luck Dragon. That was probably all that had happened. He'd call home and wake her and—

The phone rang and rang, and Tom could visualize it, hanging in the kitchen, ringing loudly, forlornly, startling Not Dinner who would be sleeping in his favorite perch by the bedroom window. The idea of the empty house and the phone ringing made him feel vaguely sick.

A rough hand grasped his wrist. He looked up into the unexpectedly understanding eyes of Old Joe. "They got cat girl?" he asked.

And Tom became aware that Conan stood by the table, looking down at him.

Tom set the cell phone on the table, very carefully. The thing was, as the Great Sky Dragon, he could reach into the minds of the men under his command. He extended a tentative tendril of consciousness towards Jao. Jao was sitting behind the reception desk at the Three Luck Dragon. He was staring unseeing at the TV screen which showed some sport or other. Tom probed deeper. There. There was a node of secrecy they were trying to hide from him.

Surely the triads wouldn't be stupid enough to try to force him to marry Bea by kidnapping Kyrie? Surely they would know he could reach into their minds and control them? Surely...

"You didn't scare them enough," Conan said. "You didn't make them take you seriously. You didn't make them realize that *you* were serious."

Tom looked up at him. He wanted to say that he'd taken two dragon shifters apart limb by limb. He wanted to say he'd rained blood and destruction on them.

Conan pushed Old Joe further into the booth and sat next to Old Joe, looking intently at Tom. "No, listen, I know you think you were very cruel and terrible, but Tom, you don't know what these people are used to. You don't know what they expect."

Tom didn't know whether to feel grateful that Conan had called him Tom and not something like "sir," or be worried about Conan's intent look.

"Yes, you temporarily killed some people but not permanently. Listen, the Great Sky Dragon would set tests that people were supposed to fail, and then kill them for failing. The entire hunt for . . . for you, when you had the Pearl of Heaven, was a made-up quest, to try to corral you and figure out what you were made of. But he killed those who failed all the same."

"You can't expect me to kill people just to prove I'm serious," Tom said. His voice seemed to come from a long way away.

"No? *They* do. They kill people without a second thought. Most people in the triad aren't very important, unless the Great Sky Dragon needs them for some reason, like he needed you. They expect you to be the same. For millennia, they've thought of themselves as nothing but possessions, nothing but an extension of the triad, nothing but . . . a piece of the Great Sky Dragon's mind. Nothing. They expect that sort of mind at the top. You didn't take over. You didn't show them the same ruthlessness. So, no, they think of you not as the Great Sky Dragon, but as his heir, who is not obeying his will. They're trying to bend you to his will."

Tom looked up, suddenly suspicious. "How do you know? You can't have heard what—"

"No," Conan said. "But I heard you answer expecting Kyrie. I know it wasn't Kyrie who answered you. And I could feel your mind probe looking . . . for someone harboring guilty knowledge. You're not very good yet at not broadcasting these things. Don't feel bad. He had thousands of years of practice, and sometimes he wasn't very good. But he was ruthless."

Tom looked up at Conan's anxious face. Conan looked like hell, tired and sleepless, but also pale and scared. More scared than he'd looked in the Three Luck Dragon parking lot.

Old Joe was still grasping Tom's wrist between two calloused and greasy fingers. "Listen to the young man, dragon boy. He's right. You weren't harsh enough. The dragon clan always, always expects their leader to be strong and demanding. They don't know the difference between cruelty and strength. You're not cruel, they think you weak. They took cat girl, didn't they?"

"Yes. They said they'll free her if I marry . . . whom they want me to marry."

"You know it's not even true, right?" Conan said. "Oh, it might be true, in a way, or they might think it is. But if they find they can control you that way, no one connected to you will ever be safe, nor will you ever be able to do anything at all you want. You will always have to do what they want you to. You won't have a will of your own."

Tom felt his lips curling upward, which was strange, because he wasn't in the least amused. "No fear there," he said. "I have not the slightest intention of marrying Bea. At any rate, I don't think she has the slightest interest in marrying me."

He looked up and realized that Old Joe and Conan were staring at him with a half-expectant, half-apprehensive look.

"So?" Old Joe asked.

"So," Tom said, "if it's ruthlessness they want, it's ruthlessness they get."

Rafiel and Bea drove into Goldport as the sun was setting. Though saying they drove in was not the right idiom, insofar as Rafiel was fairly sure he had slept half the way into town. Bea hadn't complained of driving while he slept, and when he'd awakened, he'd found she was listening to music very low.

"We're almost at Goldport," she said. "You know, I have absolutely no idea where to stay. I remember looking it up beforehand, because I figured I would have to stop somewhere overnight after talking to the triad, and I found a hotel and a bed-and-breakfast..." She paused for a moment. "I guess the bed-and-breakfast is gone now, but at any rate, I thought that they were both too expensive for me—and then there were a bunch of motels, but I wasn't sure which ones were safe. I guess you can tell me which are safe?"

Rafiel bit back his instinctive *Of course you'll stay with me,* just in time, so that instead of saying anything, he growled low in his throat, which he turned into a cough as he sat up. But truly, the motels around Goldport were fairly dismal, as he should know. They'd been tourist motels in the fifties, when it was fashionable for families of mom, dad and kids to drive around the country sightseeing.

Many still retained the folksy appearance and even names from that time. There were motels called after Old West heroes, like the Kit Carson out on Ore Road. And there were others named after exotic locales which had absolutely nothing to do with the American

West, but which might very well have provided incitement to the would-be travelers of a bygone era. He remembered how the Mecca Motel had hung up a sign saying AMERICAN OWNED AND OPERATED right after 9/11, lest anyone would suspect the dismal collection of whitewashed buildings on the road out of town towards the mountains of being owned and operated by petro dollars or Saudi princes.

But the fact was that the type of tourist that stayed overnight at that kind of low-rent motel had gone the way of the dodo. Most of the motels around Goldport were now occupied by people whose credit was so bad that they couldn't even get a rental contract and must instead rent week to week, often paying with the aid of government assistance. There were also some, like the one on Sierra Street downtown, which had convenient arrangements with ladies who only needed the bed for a night or two, and the one up on the west side that was often used by sex offenders as a temporary place to live after release.

For a city with as low a crime rate as Goldport, the motels still managed to be a focus of bad things happening and bad people hanging out. In fact, Rafiel often felt that if they could just get rid of all the flea-bag motels, the rest of the city would be very little trouble. This thought was countered by his colleague Cas Wolfe, though, who insisted that the motels worked as collectors of people prone to undesirable behavior, so that if they weren't absolutely sure there was anything wrong in town, they just had to go knock at one or two doors at the nearest hotel to find something illegal. He maintained this was the best way for them to show work and keep their jobs.

"You are very quiet," Bea said.

"Look, none of the motels are safe," Rafiel said.

"Are you sure? There was this one as I was getting into town, with a big neon, er . . . Native American in traditional headdress, and the cabins were shaped like log houses, and I thought—" Something must have made her look at him, and he knew what his face would be showing. "No?"

"Well, they're not used to renting the rooms for the whole night," Rafiel said. "And I've never checked that they change sheets between—"

"For the whol— Oh no. Really?"

Rafiel shrugged. "Most of the time we can't prove anything, and they have lookouts, and if we tried to raid it, we'd just end up coming up dry, but yeah. I mean, it's well known. People make jokes about Tomahawk Motel. Like, you know, school kids in my day said things like 'Your sister has her own room at the Tomahawk Motel.'"

"Oh, how sad. It looked cute."

"People fly nowadays. And people who come to town on business want to stay at a hotel or, at most, a nice bed-and-breakfast with a family atmosphere, but between the horror movies giving the impression that roadside motels are psycho magnets, and the fact that, well . . . most of them were designed for people with kids making their leisurely way across the land, their clientele has just vanished. I suspect most of the people who used to stay at those now stay at the campgrounds on the east side of town."

"Maybe you can lend me a tent," Bea said. "I don't think I can stay at the hotel, really. I looked at the rates. And I probably shouldn't ask your friends if they'll put me up, right?"

Rafiel had been trying to figure out how to phrase it, and now he thought he had it. "No. Of course not. You can stay with my parents."

From the way his offer fell, heavy, between them, he guessed he'd been misunderstood. "Listen, it's like this: I know I theoretically live with them, but I don't really. When I came back from college, they had the basement converted into an apartment, and I have my own entrance . . . You can have my place as long as you need, and I'll stay upstairs in the guest room, or you can stay upstairs. In either case you'll be perfectly safe. I wasn't making an untoward—"

She got very red, but laughed at that. "No. Really. We were alone in a cabin in the woods. I'm aware if you were of a mind to ravish me, you could have done it there. It's just that I feel I shouldn't put you and your family through this kind of trouble. My problems are not your fault. I came to town to deal with the dragon triad. It's nothing you've done."

Rafiel could feel his lips compressing. You can't, he realized, tell a girl you've met just over twenty-four hours ago that it is your duty and right to look after her, not even if you feel in your heart that this is absolutely true. Correction. You don't tell her that, particularly if you feel in your heart that this is absolutely true. Because any girl—particularly a girl who has had a particularly insane arranged marriage pushed on her—is likely to run for the hills at that type of thing.

The only time he'd tried to seriously court a woman since his high school days—beyond the constrained first dates, in which he tried to be pleasant but not so pleasant that they were heartbroken when he failed to call—had been his attempt at telling Kyrie that they were meant for each other. The spectacular failure of the technique in that case did not encourage him to attempt it again.

But, he realized, there was a way he could tell Bea he felt responsible without telling her he'd spent the last twenty-four hours feverishly dreaming of her as his wife, and of the cute kids they'd have. At least the part of the twenty-four hours when he wasn't having wild animal sex with some creature whose human form he wouldn't even recognize. He was very grateful that Bea had taken that particular revelation with absolute calm, but he didn't need to *remind* her of it, either. Or make her think he was more unstable than he was.

So, instead he said, slowly and reasonably, "Listen, I know it's stupid, but I do feel responsible for your safety, because, you see, I am the only shifter in the police force. My duty to protect the public and keep criminal activity down is particularly strong when it comes to crimes committed by and against shifters. With my knowledge, and without my being able to do much to curb it, a criminal organization run by foreign gangsters set up in Goldport, and I ignored it because they weren't even selling drugs in the area. But I should have known they were up to something, and if I had investigated and pursued their ties, they might not have been able to bother your father, and you wouldn't have come all the way up here. So the fact that you're here is my fault, and it's up to me to keep you safe while you're in the area."

She was quiet a long while. Then she gave him an evaluating look, just as they passed the sign that said, WELCOME TO GOLDPORT COLORADO. "You're right," she said. "It is stupid. If you had managed to stop them from doing stuff in Goldport, they'd just have conducted operations elsewhere. It's not like you could, singlehandedly, stop a dragon triad that spans the globe. And if I hadn't come to Goldport on this business, I'd have gone elsewhere, Denver or somewhere. And you wouldn't be able to protect me there."

"Then it is fortunate I *can* protect you here," he said, with his best smile, and hoped that his face had healed enough that it didn't look creepy.

It must have, because she laughed. "You're a lunatic."

"Oh, yes. Guilty as charged. Now, if you don't mind, I presume my car will still be outside Riverside Amusement Park. If you don't mind taking me there to pick it up, I think we can get it before dark. And then you can follow me home." He realized belatedly that he'd called his house home, but she didn't say anything, and he dug in his pocket for his cell phone. "I'll call Mom and ask her if there's enough dinner for two more. If she's not cooking, or there's something that can't be stretched to four, I'll take you out to dinner."

"Oh, really," Bea said. The blush was back. "I wouldn't want to put your mom to any trouble."

"No trouble at all." He didn't want to tell Bea his mother would think that her prayers were finally answered. Even less did he want to tell her that he very much hoped they were. Instead, he said, "Turn left at Madison, then right at Mariposa Street." And he dialed his parents' number.

"You can't just go to the Three Luck Dragon and set fire to it," Conan said. He spoke in the sort of urgent whisper he might use to calm down a dangerous mental patient.

The whispering part was because Anthony had come in to take a late shift in response to Tom's call begging him to come in. They must have trained Anthony well, because he barely looked askance at Tom sitting in the corner booth with Conan and one of the more disreputable vagrants around.

"You know I'm only supposed to work days not nights, right?" was all Anthony had said.

Tom nodded and said, "That's why we pay you double for nights. Look, I just want you to take over and stay as long as needed. I have . . . some stuff to do and I don't know when it will be done."

And then Anthony had muttered something or other about a diaper service and gone behind the counter. Moments later, Rya had been sent home, and now Anthony was running the area behind the counter with Laura's help, acting as though this were perfectly normal and also as though Tom weren't there at all. Jason was waiting tables. James had left a while back, probably for his night shift at the hospital. Tom fleetingly wondered if the man ever slept, but it wasn't any of his business.

The war council in the corner booth continued. Or rather, Old Joe and Conan were doing their best to convince Tom that he couldn't—he simply couldn't—fly over to the Three Luck Dragon and set fire to the building.

"I fail to see why not," Tom said.

"Mostly because ashes are really hard to interrogate."

"Fine," Tom said. "I'll only burn them a little. They can recover."

It was the recoil in Conan's eyes that reminded him that Conan had been burned nearly to the point of no return and had come back over excruciating months, and that he really, really, really would have preferred to die than endure that. "I'm sorry," Tom said immediately. "See, I'm not very good at being ruthless. I hate... but I want Kyrie back. I'm very afraid of what they might be doing to her."

"My guess is that they'll keep her quite safe until they see what you do," Conan said, "and that the worse thing you could do for her safety is give in to their demands. Since I don't think you intend to do that—"

"No, but—"

"There is time to think of what you can do. You can control Jao and the others, right?"

Tom paused, then nodded. "Yes, but— I mean, I can control them, but I can feel there's this area in Jao's mind that is closed to me, and I'm not sure—how do I put this? I'm afraid that if I push on, it I might destroy his mind or at least his sanity... such as it is."

"Oh, he's sane. Very well adapted to the culture he grew up in. I see. I know the old bas— the Old Great Sky Dragon could reach into our minds and make us do things, and find information, and... well, he used me as a spying device for a while."

"Yes," Tom said. "And I can do that for minutes at a time, but it's not very targeted. I end up going from triad member to triad member, more or less at random. I don't think... I mean, as you said, I'm still rather like a blunt instrument when it comes to using Great Sky Dragon powers. I expect it takes practice."

"It must," Conan said, deep in thought.

But Old Joe, who had ordered, and got another big plate of bacon, and was munching his way through it contentedly, said, "Then be blunt instrument."

"Beg your pardon?"

"No, no begging. Blunt instrument. You can have them do what you want? Have boss man of clan, man who ran things for daddy dragon, come here. Then you can interrogate him in your home territory."

Tom thought of bringing Jao here, but all he needed was to bring attention to the diner. More likely than not, Jao would arrive in dragon form. He sighed. "No. Better go to my home first and have them come there."

Going to his home, at any rate, gave him the chance to check and see how they'd got Kyrie, and whether they'd hurt her. Because if they hurt her, then ruthless might not begin to describe his behavior.

Kyrie wished she knew whether it was near dinnertime, and if they had any intention of feeding her, because if they were to bring her dinner and come in at an inconvenient time...

But after sitting there in the dark a while, she decided it was nonsense, anyway. If they came in and caught her while she was loosening the board, there was a good chance no one would notice. Even if they brought a flashlight or something, it was likely the light wouldn't be very strong. And if they came in after she'd loosened the board...she'd just leave.

The thing about keys and key holders—her key holder being a heavy, flat, steel rectangle with *Kyrie* engraved on it—was that they could make really handy levers. Particularly when you had as many keys as she had, between the keys to the various supply vans, her car, the diner, and the home keys, plus that old key she carried around, from her very first apartment, as a souvenir and a guarantee that she could survive on her own.

She could afford to bend or break a couple of keys and still pry the board off the window. Besides, as far as she had felt with her fingers, the board was not exactly very well fastened. If you wanted to fasten the board in a way that would be difficult to remove, you'd use screws in the corners, and her captors had not.

Perhaps they had never thought to use a bunch of keys as a tool, and therefore thought they were tossing her in there without any tools, in the dark, and therefore assumed she could never figure a way out.

Kyrie worked a long time, doggedly. To her relief, there was no knock at the door, nothing that foretold dinner. Sometimes she could hear steps above her, which confirmed the idea that she had guards, or people moving above her.

The nails came out of the first corner, and Kyrie felt them.

They were really long nails, but had been run into stucco, which is the sort of material that lets go, once you've pulled enough. Armed with this knowledge, she now knew to pry them a little loose, then pull at the corner of the board with her fingers. The process was considerably faster after that, though it made the tips of her fingers hurt.

Under the board, as she expected, there was glass. Kyrie felt it, cool against the fingers. It let light into her cell, too, which revealed itself as small but not particularly squalid. She noted the lack of a bathroom and wondered whether that meant they didn't intend to keep her long, or whether they were just stupid. She wouldn't bet against the second.

Outside, she could see ground level, and her idea that she was in the suburbs vanished. For one, the area immediately outside the window was all pebbles, then concrete. More importantly, she could see the reflected light of garish neon. And, with the wood out, and the window it had hidden consisting of a poorly insulated frame and thin glass, she could hear traffic nearby and, periodically, the sound of car radios that indicated considerable traffic stopped at a light.

Goldport wasn't that large a town. It had once been a mining town, left almost abandoned in the silver bust. Then the tech boom had come in, and a few firms had moved to town. And then CUG had opened, and its research facilities had brought in another batch of well-educated residents. So Goldport was a small town that, in summer, had a halved population, except for the influx of tourists, while during the school year it swelled with college students.

The only place that had that sort of sustained traffic was downtown. This meant she couldn't be very far from either The George or her place.

Right. By the scant light, she looked at the wood frame. She could break the window, of course, but there was simply no way, absent a glass cutter, to make window breaking noiseless. Kyrie might risk it when the traffic was at its loudest, but she doubted even the most obnoxious hip-hop beat sounded like breaking glass. She could also wait for the inevitable ambulance wail or police siren. But those weren't regularly spaced. That meant she could be waiting a long time, and if during that time someone came to bring her dinner . . . or something . . . and noticed the wood was off the window . . .

Kyrie bit her lower lip, thinking. The frame of the window looked like something from the mid-twentieth century, two parts, with the glass in some sort of recessed groove, and then with the interior frame nailed over it. It wasn't designed to open, and the frame might very well be held together mostly by paint.

She could probably use one of the slimmer keys to pry the frame away, then dislodge the glass. She shrugged to herself. It was, at least, worth a try.

She inserted the key for one of the cargo vans that belonged to The George—a slim, pointy, Ford key—into the side of the frame where she could feel the breeze coming through. It went in easily, and the wiggling of the key produced a groan of wood and nails, and a considerable loosening.

Right. But she couldn't trust that the builders of this place hadn't been stupid enough to put the groove that held the glass on the interior frame. Who knew? Perhaps they had mounted the whole thing as one piece. That meant by prying at the frame, she risked having the glass fall and shatter, which would be noise enough to bring her captors to check. Unless, of course, they were deaf.

Thoughtfully, Kyrie pushed her bed towards the window, as tight to the wall as it could be, and then, just in case, took the blankets and bunched them in a heavy roll between wall and bed, so if the glass fell, it was likely to make less noise.

Then, to ensure that the chance of the glass falling was smaller, she worked at the frame from the top.

To some extent, this was easier than removing the board. Doing so broke the key to the van, and then the key to the other van, but that was because she had to work through tighter portions, and the dried paint keeping the frame together was harder to break. But it finally gave.

She'd been right, she thought, sweaty and shaking, as she gently pulled the frame off from the top. Someone had been dumb enough to set the glass in the interior portion. So she had to pull it down, gently, gently, till it was horizontal, like a picture frame with the glass resting in it.

She stood a few minutes, taking deep breaths, holding the frame and the glass in it.

Then she stepped down from the bed and set frame and glass on the floor.

She climbed back on the bed, and put her head and shoulders

through the opening. There was enough room to pull herself through, though it was tight. Outside, as she'd expected, was a pebble bed with an ancient, weathered statue of a frog seeming to indicate that sometime, perhaps long ago, someone had cared enough to decorate the area.

Kyrie worked her arms through, so she could put her hands against the external wall and work her body out. Above her, she could see a lighted window, and hear the noise of people talking and—from the sound of it—some sort of computer game.

When she was up to her hips outside the room, a shadow fell on the window above. For a moment, Kyrie had a glimpse of a young man, around college age, with a can of some beverage in one hand, and she froze, hoping he wouldn't open the window and that he wouldn't look out.

Turning her head, she saw, to her right, a neon sign with a stereotypical cartoon Indian chief, the headdress blinking in garish green and blue, and a hand lighting and blinking to seem to wave up and down. Beneath it the words, only partly illuminated, in yellow, but still legible, read Tomahawk Motel.

As he turned back away and towards the inside, she pushed harder with her hands, to pull herself out.

This was a mistake. Something in the frame of the window caught at her dress and gave a groan like a spirit caught in eternal torment.

From inside, loudly, came a swear word followed by, "What was that?"

And Kyrie shoved for all she was worth and pulled free from the window, feeling the pocket of her dress tearing, and not caring. At the back of her mind, she quickly realized that if she ran towards the road she would be more likely to be caught. She could hear a door open on the other side of the motel cabin in whose basement she'd been captive. They'd come here, they'd see—

She was already running, hunched over, towards a dark area, past other cabins, out, and down, away from the road.

Although she'd never been here, she knew the area from driving past. Down there was a creek and an area full of brush and trees. She ran towards it, and crawled under the first clump of bushes she came through. She half expected to find condoms and needles under there, but clearly the people who frequented the Tomahawk were not the type to commune with nature by the creek.

She heard shouts and calls, and finally a couple of cars starting up. She wondered if those were her captors going in search of her, or thinking they were doing so, going towards the road, towards The George.

The George was south of here, two cross-streets away. Her house was the other way from this little wooded area, past a small maze of neighborhood streets. Which way did they think she'd be more likely to go?

She took deep breaths and tried to decide what to do.

It was when they got to his car, in the parking lot of Riverside, that Rafiel realized he was an idiot. Okay, so he probably had good indications before, including the fact that he was falling for a woman about whom he knew precious little, other than that she was an art student and could shift into a dragon.

He also knew that she had talked back to the Great Sky Dragon, that she wasn't put off by danger—in fact she'd volunteered to come into greater danger in order to help Tom—and that she viewed his relationship with his parents as he viewed it, which, now that he thought about it, was damn rare.

Maybe he wasn't totally stupid for starting to think he'd like to spend his whole life with Bea. Fine. But he was totally stupid for not having remembered that his car keys had been lost more than a day ago in that disastrous change into a lion.

Bea didn't make him feel any better either, when she said, "But why didn't you have it attached to your leg, with the phone?"

Rafiel sighed. "Normally," he said, "I just call my parents, or Tom, for the spare set of keys."

He'd called Tom first, but got no answer at home, and when he called the diner, he was told that Tom had left with Conan Lung and Old Joe. That sounded like official business, and weird official business at that, so he'd not called Tom's cell phone. The way things were, he might get Tom mid-transformation, or perhaps mid-conference with some triad guys, and Rafiel had a strong feeling that there was nothing worse for the image of a great leader than stopping in the middle of a conversation about the possible invasion of the world to go take a friend his car keys. He tried Kyrie's phone and no one answered.

He could call his parents, but he'd asked his mother if he could bring a friend for dinner, and maybe to stay a couple of days, and had barely escaped embarrassing questions which Bea would overhear. If he called again...

Then he thought of his colleagues in the police. He'd got his mom to call him in sick yesterday, and of course they wouldn't have his particular key, but it was a little known fact that there were a limited number of vehicle keys, per make, and that the police had copies of most of those. They had to, because when a car was discovered by the side of the road exuding a strange smell, not causing more damage than strictly needed was important, just in case it turned out to be a crime scene.

Rafiel wasn't absolutely sure that all police departments throughout the land did this. He thought perhaps the fancier and better equipped ones, in the bigger cities, had expert lockpickers or something, who could get into anything. But Goldport had exactly four officers in its serious crimes unit, and so they collected each variety of key that came into their hand.

He called the station and got Cas Wolfe.

"Yeah?" Cas said, followed by "I thought you were sick," when Rafiel explained his predicament. There was always a feeling of amusement when Cas talked about Rafiel missing work, and there was often great amusement when Cas noted that Rafiel had changed clothes in the middle of the day. The conceit around the police station seemed to be that Rafiel had a complex love life of the sort that involved changing clothes several times a day and, possibly, climbing out of windows just ahead of enraged husbands.

At least, Rafiel assumed that's what they thought, and Cas Wolfe and his cousin Nick, the newest addition to the serious crimes unit, were absolutely the worst. They had been raised as brothers, and acted like brothers a lot, and they were at least half Greek, or possibly all Greek, which brought with it a culture of machismo and an idea—Rafiel supposed—that all men were supposed to be philanderers. The fact that Cas was, so far as Rafiel could tell, absolutely faithful to his girlfriend, and that Nick was absolutely faithful to his boyfriend, didn't stop them from imagining that other men lived the lives of roving Casanovas. Sometimes the looks they traded when Rafiel returned to the station having changed clothes because of an unfortunate shifting accident, were just about as much as Rafiel could take without blowing up.

Cas' voice had that suggestion of amusement behind it that often infuriated Rafiel.

"Actually I was in an accident and got a bit bruised," Rafiel said, figuring that the scrapes that still showed on his face might make it clear. "But I'm better."

"You were in an accident but not your *car*?"

Was that skepticism in Cas' voice? He was junior to Rafiel in the department, and he really wasn't supposed to be checking Rafiel's movements. "Tom's car," Rafiel said drily.

"Oh, yeah. I see. And you lost your keys when you went to emergency?"

"I didn't go to the ER," Rafiel said. Cas wasn't supposed to be checking on his movements, but all the same, it wasn't out of consideration that he might, at some point, be at the emergency room and ask... Even though calling in a sick day when you weren't sick—and Rafiel had been sick—wasn't that serious, there was no point undermining the confidence of his colleagues in the department. "I have no idea what I did with the keys. Look, if you don't want to help..."

"Nah," Cas still sounded more amused than suspicious. "Nick and I were just about to leave and go grab some pizza. Our respectives are out shopping for Dyce's wedding dress again, so we're just the two of us this evening." Dyce was Cas' fiancée and their wedding was any day now. "We'll come out. Which car is this? Your Explorer? I'll grab the keys."

Rafiel hung up and met Bea's curious eyes. "It's just my coworkers," he said.

Her eyebrows arched, and he realized he was blushing. "They have written this entire life for me, you know, where I'm some guy who sleeps around a lot and keeps losing his clothes. I still don't understand how sleeping around a lot would cause me to lose my clothes, but never mind. They get juvenile, and wink at each other about it."

"Oh my," Bea said, but there was a tremor of a smile at the corner of her lips.

"Yeah," he said, and thinking of it belatedly, "I'm afraid they might get juvenile when they see I'm with a woman, too, but—"

"Eh. I'm a college student. Juvenile doesn't scare me."

"My colleagues can be far more juvenile than college students."

Bea smiled and turned off the engine. "I guess we'll wait a while."

"Yeah," Rafiel said. His mind was working. He wondered what

exactly might have happened with the investigation of the remains found in the hippodrome while they were at the cabin, and what his colleagues might have made of it. He'd have to ask Cas. He knew the culprit was the feral shifter, but other people wouldn't know that. The problem with the shifter cases was that Rafiel always had to run double books, so to put it—what was really happening and what he could afford to share with the public, even that part of the public who were law enforcement officers.

He didn't even know what he could do about the feral teen shifter. It was one thing to execute his private brand of justice on murderous adult shifters who had killed other shifters and other humans in full knowledge of what they were doing—with full intent and malice—but to go after a kid, particularly a shifter kid who might not know he was doing anything bad, seemed wrong. And yet he couldn't be allowed to run free, could he? The kid would just kill more people, and more shifters, and eat them, all unaware that he was doing evil.

In a society in which shifters were known—Rafiel snorted at the idea—the kid would simply be confined and not allowed to be destructive, but allowed to live, because it really wasn't his fault.

Rafiel remembered what he had seen in those eyes, the perfect lack of awareness not just of having broken any rules, but that there *were* any rules, or anything he should hold to. Rafiel couldn't think of it without shuddering. To destroy a kid for being that way was like taking a feral kitten and killing it for soiling the rug.

He put his head back and groaned.

"What is wrong?" Bea asked.

He looked at her, and slowly explained, leaving many of the details out, his dilemma. She blinked at him. "But why do you have to decide?" she asked. "I mean, why is it *your* responsibility?"

"Because I'm a policeman. And I'm a shifter. I have a duty to both the police and shifters. I have to keep people from knowing that there are shifters, lest, you know, horrible things happen to our kind. And I have to keep the law. I mean, I swore to protect innocent. I can't just say 'Well, never mind,' when the criminal turns out to be my kind."

Bea pursed her lips, then stretched them. She shook her head and sighed. "It doesn't seem right," she said. "The responsibility shouldn't rest on your shoulders."

"If you think I'm taking power I shouldn't be taking, I'd rather—"

"No, I don't think you view it as power at all," she said. "You view it as a chore. Which is good. But the thing is that there are no controls. Suppose the one shifter in the police force was power hungry and saw this as an opportunity to amass power? To start a group of shifters who'd terrorize the city, or—"

Rafiel suddenly felt very tired. "I know," he said. "I've thought about it. I've wondered what it would be like if another one of us joined the force, and then I realized it could either be helpful or very, very bad. Long ago, I figured someone in a position of power, who was inclined to build an army, is what resulted in things like the triads and the other organizations we've got trouble with. So I don't complain too much about the trouble, I don't complain too much about how much work it is for me. I just wish there was someone to help decide what to do with this particular kid. That's supposing I can catch him—"

Bea was still looking at him, her eyes wide open. He had a moment of fear that she would think he was a wimp, complaining like this, but she put her hand on his shoulder. "I'm sure you'll figure out something, and that it will be the best possible solution. Meanwhile, you can always talk to me, you know?"

And after a minimal pause, she continued, "Why is there so much activity in the park? Isn't it supposed to be closed?"

The shocks Tom felt as he pulled up his driveway started with seeing Kyrie's car in the driveway, the door still open. He looked inside. Her purse was on the floor of the passenger seat. Nothing else was disturbed. He didn't see or smell blood anywhere. There was no blood on the driveway either—Tom couldn't have sworn to what he'd have done if there had been blood.

The back door hadn't been opened. There were no signs of a scuffle. Maybe Kyrie hadn't been kidnapped, he thought, knowing he was being foolish and trying to console himself with a vain hope. Maybe all that had happened was that she'd dropped her phone and someone else had picked it up.

But she'd dropped her phone on the way to *what*? What would cause Kyrie to drop her phone and not find another way to communicate with Tom? What would cause Kyrie to leave the car open in the driveway? Not just unlocked. Open.

True, their neighborhood had almost no crime, but Kyrie had not grown up in this kind of neighborhood. Tom might forget to lock the car, but Kyrie never would, and she checked front and back door twice before going to bed, and had insisted on putting a cat door on the back porch window, rather than just leaving the window slightly ajar, so the cat could go in and out. That meant they would have to replace the entire pane of glass when they moved out, but Kyrie felt safer that way.

No, Kyrie would never leave the car door wide open and go somewhere. She wouldn't even leave it unlocked.

Tom sighed. Nothing for it but to deal with the fact that Kyrie was missing, that it was the doing of the triads—at least if what he felt in the secretive place in Jao's mind was accurate—and that he would have to punish them in a horrible way.

The problem was . . . No, not that he felt bad about visiting fire and blood on the dragon shifters. He didn't. Emotionally, the thought that they might have hurt Kyrie made him want to go on a rampage and kill them all, slowly and in interesting ways, but intellectually, he felt as though that would be a betrayal of everything he and his friends stood for.

Sure, they'd killed shifters before, but they'd done it only in self-defense. Well, most of them had done it only in self-defense.

Tom had, with malice aforethought, killed a sabertooth, Dante Dire. He wasn't sure that could be considered self-defense, exactly, since he'd found Dire, and killed him, and made sure body and head were well apart and hidden. He was sure if Rafiel ever found out about that he would be very conflicted on whether or not to punish Tom. But the truth was not that clear. Tom had known, with absolute certainty, that as long as Dante Dire lived, neither he nor Kyrie would be safe. Had he been alone, had he had no Kyrie, no friends, no one else affected, he'd probably have left town to avoid the confrontation, and kept moving ahead of Dire. But realizing that if he simply disappeared Dire could go after his friends made it all different. In Tom's mind the killilng was self-defense. He had had to slay Dire to keep himself and his own safe.

He only wished he were sure Rafiel would agree with him. And—this was important—Tom was almost absolutely sure that were he to kill half the triad to punish them for interfering with Kyrie, and to make them take his authority seriously, Rafiel would view that as a very bad thing.

While the world was full of shifters' organizations who killed normal mortals without a second thought, Tom and the others had decided early on that they were humans among humans. If they were different, and if they had to hide that difference, it didn't exempt them from the duties of common humanity.

But what did that mean when it came to his taking control of an ancient organization that behaved according to very different rules?

It meant Tom had an ache in the front of his head, right in the center of his forehead, and he didn't know what he could do. He knew he had to make an impression. And he had to get Kyrie back. Above all he *must* get Kyrie back.

As he opened the door to the kitchen, the big orange tomcat, Not Dinner, came sauntering up, then smelled Old Joe and arched, hissing. Tom reached down and petted him, almost absently, "Old Joe won't eat you, Notty," he said. Not Dinner still clung to Tom's ankles, weaving in and out. From habit, Tom got the bag of kibble, and filled Notty's bowl, then blocked that area with his arm, as he led Conan and Old Joe to the living room. He gestured for them to sit on the sofa, and noticed—approvingly—that Conan was keeping an eye on Old Joe.

Good. He didn't think the old shifter, with more important things on his mind, was going to shift into an alligator and eat Tom's cat, but you never knew. And if Old Joe ate Notty, Kyrie would . . . probably kill Tom. Maybe not permanently. If he was lucky.

He had to get Kyrie back.

Old Joe was making a *clack-clack* sound with his teeth. Conan was sitting at the edge of the sofa, leaning forward, looking at Tom intently. Tom had to do something. He had friends, and he had allies, but he was the one who had to do something.

Like it or not, for the time being—and he would make very sure it was for no more than the time being—he was the Great Sky Dragon and must make sure they feared him as such.

Conan was leaning forward on the sofa. He said, "Summon him."

"I wonder what they're doing in there," Bea said. With the motor turned off, sitting in the car beside Rafiel, she'd been looking around idly—anything but to think of Rafiel right there, next to her. She wasn't afraid that she'd suddenly feel a need to tear his clothes off or something, though she *did* spare a moment to imagine him with his clothes off when he wasn't out of his mind with shock. No, she was afraid of something far more material. She was afraid she'd start talking to him. Honestly, she couldn't seem to go a few minutes without some nonsensical thought coming up, like, "I wonder what our kids would look like?" or "What if he works too hard to have a proper family life?" or even, "Would it be a good idea, with both of us being shifters?" She was very much afraid if she started talking, one of those questions would come out.

So instead, she looked around, and after a while it hit her that though the parking lot was empty—the truck rocked a little under the impact of a warm wind—there seemed to be a lot of activity in the amusement park itself. At least, lights came on in there now and then, seemingly erratically, and twice, Bea saw something or someone slink in through the gate.

It was hard to know if it was something or someone, because it was little more than a shadow, very fast, then gone.

Rafiel responded to her question about the park casually, "It's probably just maintenance of something." But his features were anything but casual, locked in the sort of frown that brought his blond eyebrows low over his eyes. She didn't know him well, of course, and yet she thought that the expression was the one he wore when he was trying to tell his back brain not to worry about something he clearly did worry about.

He drummed his fingers under the window, then he lowered the window a little and—to Bea's surprise—sniffed the air. He made a face. The drumming fingers turned into a fist, rhythmically hitting the place under the window.

After a while, he turned to her, "Look . . . we found a bunch of mauled bodies in here." He told her the story of finding corpses and the feral teen shifter. "It was that feral shifter I was following when I—when you met me." The frown intensified, and she thought that it served to hide stronger emotions, in this case probably embarrassment. "So . . . so . . . I was . . . that is, he might be here again. I'd like to go take a look, but I . . . Promise me you'll lock the car, and put the windows up. And don't open for anyone but me or two guys who look Greek and who likely will be driving a restored convertible." To what must have been her look of sheer confusion: "Cas and Nick restore old cars in their free time, and at least one of them drives the car around for a year before selling it."

"Oh," she said.

"I don't remember what they're driving now, but it being summer, it's probably a convertible. Likely something from the fifties."

"Right," she said. Her mind seemed to be stuck on the idea that it wasn't fair for him to go and risk himself alone. On the other hand, he was a police officer and she wasn't, right? He was paid to take risks to protect people, while she wasn't paid for anything, frankly.

And what he was asking her, she realized, was that she not add to his worries by going into danger when she wasn't prepared to handle it.

She looked up at him, and arranged her features to the most compliant she could manage. "Sure," she said. "Just . . . be careful."

He looked over his shoulder, as he was about to open the door of the truck and then, unexpectedly, a smile broke out. With the scars across his face still visible—would they vanish?—he looked piratical.

She was quite unprepared for what he did, grabbing her hand and kissing it. His lips pressed against the back of her hand, hot and pliable, and somehow, indefinably, very intimate. "I will," he said, and his voice was oddly husky.

And then he was out of the truck, walking in long, easy strides towards the gate to the park. She locked the car and ran up the window, and then she watched intently as he slipped into the shadows near the gate and went in, melding with the darker shadow. Through the open gate, she could glimpse, in cool green shadow, a bunch of kiddy rides, including something that looked like a huge frog holding a basket.

She heard the sound of metal hitting metal, distant and forlorn like wind-driven noise can be. She leaned back with her head on the seat rest. Rafiel was a sensible man. He would go and see what was going on, and then he'd come back.

She'd just reached this point in her thoughts when she heard the scream. It was an animal scream—no human throat could make that noise—and it was loud and insane.

And before she knew what she meant to do, she was pulling the keys out of the car and sticking them in her pocket, then running towards the sound of trouble.

✧   ✧   ✧

Kyrie was hot and thirsty and tired. How weird it was that a distance she could cover in the car without noticing, seemed so long while on foot.

Of course, part of it was the fact that when you walked anywhere near the Tomahawk Motel you were assumed to be walking the streets for a living. Kyrie had come around the park and onto the sidewalk near the main street, on the assumption that if anyone tried to kidnap her from the public sidewalk, she could scream the place down, and there was at least some chance one or more people would stop and either come to help or pay attention to who was dragging her away.

Sierra Street, which ran parallel to Fairfax and about eight long blocks away, might not be the best area of town, but it was well traveled, which, in the circumstances, meant an abundance of witnesses to keep her more or less safe.

But in the meantime, and possibly because—damn it—she was wearing Bea's too-tight dress, she got cars slowing down next to her, and even guys calling hopefully, "Hey, hey," and in one case, with misguided courtesy, "Miss? Miss?"

She was tired enough to almost consider answering one of them and scaring him into taking her home. But scaring one of them took shifting, and once she shifted, as hot and hungry and thirsty as she was, there was no telling what she would do.

She had tried to shift, in fact, down by the river, on the idea that sightings of black cats weren't even rare, and, after all, the panther could run a heck of a lot faster than a human. But though she tried with all her might, the shift wouldn't come. She figured it was some sort of psychological block. She knew if she shifted she would be dangerous.

And so she walked on in the heat, breathing the fumes of cars.

Three blocks away from The George, she considered that perhaps she should just go there and bully someone into driving her home. Heck, Tom might very well still be there.

But she had a bad feeling about going there, about that empty parking lot where, not so long ago, she and Tom had discovered bodies. Besides, two of the blocks between Sierra and Fairfax, where The George sat, were lined with deserted warehouses. She didn't know who had kidnapped her or why—though she could make some guesses—but she knew they had hid near her house and used a tranquilizer dart on her. That meant they probably were organized and financed by someone, not street gangsters in a spur-of-the-moment thing. More, they'd locked her in a semi-secure room, which meant that they'd been planning to hand her over to someone.

It reeked of the triad, frankly, which meant they had more than enough people to have a group lurking in each of the warehouses. And though most of their foot soldiers were not what you'd call bright, they were all dragon shifters. Kyrie could hold her own against dragons. At least the panther could. She could fight one or two of them. But if there were more than that . . .

She walked along the sidewalk, footsore and hot, wishing that she'd thought to wear better shoes. You never think you're going to have to walk four miles suddenly. From now on, she'd wear walking shoes all the time. Even while naked in bed.

The idea made her smile despite herself, and she gritted her teeth and pushed on. If she had brought a phone or money . . . but those were in her purse. Maybe she should start following Rafiel's lead and strap gear to her thigh.

As she passed the intersection nearest The George, it seemed as though she heard the sound of wings unfurling above, the sound of dragons passing. It was a sound she knew all too well, from her time with Tom. She looked up, hoping it was Tom, hoping he was looking for her.

But the glimpse of wings above was a bright, iridescent blue, nothing like Tom. The body shape, too, seemed more sinuous, more Chinese dragon than Nordic one.

Were they looking for her? Quite likely, she thought. They had always been one of the contenders if not the main contender for who had kidnapped her.

She knit herself with the shadows of buildings, trying to look inconspicuous. It seemed to her that other dragons passed overhead. How many? And why? Was the entire triad out, looking for her?

⊰ CHAPTER 19 ⊱

Tom looked at Old Joe and Conan sitting at the edge of the sofa, waiting. He wondered if they knew how little of their expressions, how little of their body posture showed any sort of confidence that he could handle this challenge. He wondered if they knew how scared they looked.

He doubted it. But maybe they did. Conan licked his lips and said, "You should call him now."

Tom nodded. Things he could not explain to his friends—and to Old Joe, whom he refused to quite call a friend though he supposed the old alligator was somewhere between a mentor and an advisor—included how difficult it was to access the dragon knowledge.

Not difficult in the unlocking it and looking inside sense. That was easy enough. In fact, sometimes, he had to keep the…dragon egg, for lack of a better word, from prompting him with things he really did not need to know or wish to know.

But it was difficult to unlock just a little, to see just a little, and not to be prompted by the rest of this weight of knowledge in his mind. It was much like carrying a whole group of people in his mind, people who, objectively, were older and probably more knowledgeable than him. It wasn't easy to ignore their promptings, their ideas, the fact that they were there.

And now he had to reach in, to deliberately think how to reach for one of his subordinates, to open the locked knowledge in his mind. What if he couldn't close his mind to it again? What if he ... what if the power to summon his subordinates erupted, or became addictive, or—

Part of him thought he was being ridiculous. The other part of him could remember what had happened in the parking lot and under the Three Luck Dragon, where he'd reached into the guards' minds. There was a feeling that this sense of power, the sense of being able to command other people might very well become addictive.

Yet there was Kyrie, and no, he didn't think he could get Kyrie back by simply asking nicely. Those people who said that everything could be resolved with negotiation had never gone to kindergarten, or at least not to the same kindergarten Tom had gone. Things could be solved with negotiation between reasonable people, of course. But what that had to do with solving things with people who wanted to hog all the animal crackers, or with people who wanted you to marry a girl you'd never seen until yesterday, was beyond Tom.

In this case, what he was trying to do was not merely show two low-ranking dragons that he could reach into their minds and force them to move aside. No. What he had to do involved bending one of the higher ranking dragons—perhaps the highest ranking one, besides the Great Sky Dragon—to his will. To think it would be easy was nonsense. And to think that once having conquered the power he would be able to give it up easily was even sillier.

Yet, for Kyrie, Tom would do quite a lot more than risk becoming addicted to the power of the Great Sky Dragon to summon his people.

He went into his mind, into those same depths that had poured on him, like a submerging flood, when the Great Sky Dragon died. It felt much the same for a moment—as though he had many arms, many legs, as though he was many people in a variety of situations, and all he could do was hold on tight to the idea that there was still a Tom there—a person, immutable, at the heart of the storm.

Once he'd found himself, as the center and fulcrum of all the perceptions, all the knowledge coming at him from everywhere a dragon was, he found Jao.

For a disconcerting moment, he found his mind inside that of Jao, who was standing inside the Three Luck Dragon—in the little space behind the reception counter/bar, where the TV was always on some sports show that no one in his right mind could possibly be interested in: curling or synchronized banana peeling or extreme ironing.

In this case, the sport appeared to involve throwing something that looked like hedgehogs across a marked space. Tom didn't see it very well or for very long, because Jao had just looked over his shoulder at the screen, and then looked down at the papers on the little desk space behind the counter. The papers were written in Chinese, but in Jao's mind, somehow, Tom understood Chinese, and knew the papers were spreadsheets of figures and profit for the Three Luck Dragon.

He became aware of someone nearby, a young man—perhaps one of the guards Tom had scared—who said something in Chinese.

Jao answered, "No, we shouldn't need any more vegetables, because—" also in Chinese. And then he became aware of Tom in his mind.

Tom could feel Jao sensing him reaching into his own mind. And he could feel the surprise and irritation at it. He could feel Jao's body stiffening with opposition to the intrusion. There were no words exchanged, just Jao feeling Tom within his mind and registering his disapprobation, his distaste.

And then Tom said to Jao, within Jao's mind, *Come.*

It was more than that. It was more like pulling a tether; more like reeling in a fish. It was an unavoidable command. Tom knew it had the same force of the command that had, instinctively and unavoidably, called every dragon within wing reach to pay his respects to the new Great Sky Dragon.

Come, he said, and forced it. And behind it, he could hear Jao say "Come" as though relaying the command, or perhaps tasting it. He didn't know which.

But the dice were cast, and now all he could do was wait.

Halfway to the door of the amusement park, Bea heard a noise behind her, like something—it didn't sound like someone—running. She turned a little, looking over her shoulder just in time to see two dogs go by her. No, not dogs.

She'd never seen wolves like this before. All her experience with wolves came from nature specials and from visits to zoos, and in the first, wolves were never running full tilt, one on either side of her. And in the latter, wolves tended to lounge around, with the ease of predators who had been shown they'd get food three times a day, regardless of what they did.

But once this pair ran past her, and then ahead of her, side by side, in easy, long strides, she realized that they were in fact grey wolves, a matched pair, shiny and well-cared for. Not like wild wolves should be at all, something at the back of her mind said.

Which was silly, because she had no idea what wolves *should* be like.

It didn't stop her. She sped up and ran just as fast, behind the wolves, who disappeared into the park, running.

Part of her thought they had to be shifters, of course. And maybe they were, but didn't Colorado have a native population of wolves and coyotes and such?

The funny thing was that even though she thought all this, she didn't even slow down, running after the wolves into the darkened entrance of the park.

There was a stile of the sort that is supposed to count people as they go through and, in the normal way of things, it would have stopped her—at least if there were anyone in the tower next to it, with the window for paying and collecting tickets.

But Rafiel had gone this way and obviously hadn't stopped. The dog-wolves didn't stop either, running wildly one after the other under the stile. And she went after them, ducking. It was a good thing that she wasn't a very big woman, because she only just got under, nearly bent double, and almost touching the sides.

Once inside she found herself on a slope, and there really wasn't any way of knowing which way to run. To her left was the hippodrome, closed and boarded up, and now festooned all around the entrance with yellow tape proclaiming it a "crime scene."

She ran past it, thinking of what Rafiel had told her about human remains in there. Quite suddenly she found herself in front of a dry fountain—at least it looked like it had been a fountain, done in a quite daring style, for the seventies—and made up of jutting planes, bits of metal and a cement shelf.

From that point, she had a view of the whole park, which seemed to be filled with crisscrossing paths, lined with rides of various kinds, all of them looking like odd, silent shapes in the failing light. In fact, if she squinted, she could imagine she was in some kind of odd Jurassic party, where ancient creatures reached out, in glistening tones of green and black, extending arms that looked armored and bits that looked clawed.

She knew it was nonsense, but it made her feel very lost. The warm breeze, bringing with it a scent of decay, didn't help at all.

The problem was that she didn't know where to go. She didn't know where Rafiel was, or where that scream had come from. She didn't even know where the wolves had gone, in their trotting pant full of exuberant dogginess.

She squinted at the landscape, the long shadows, the odd shapes. She'd seen darker shapes come in here, shapes she couldn't tell were human or animal. Now, squinting, she seemed to see the same shapes. No. It was too much to call them shapes. They were more like . . . Yes, they were more like movement. She'd never have believed it, if anyone had told her that she could see movement without seeing whatever made it. But in this case, that was exactly what she was seeing: there was movement, but nothing behind it. Like . . . like wind was movement felt but not seen. If you squinted just right, you could see movement of leaves and grass as though something had passed, but you couldn't see *what*, you couldn't hear it, and you felt no breeze from that side.

The movements were stronger near an arching bridge that went over a concession stand, and then down towards the water. Squinting harder and moving sideways, she could see a dock in the water and moored boats. So the bridge probably led there. Well. And the movement was there. Whatever was happening, Rafiel had come here to investigate the shapes coming into the park, and the movement must be related to that. Which meant that Rafiel must be where the movement was. And—she remembered the animal scream she'd heard—he was in dire trouble.

She went trotting down the slope, taking the path to the bridge. The question was whether she could hide at all, while on that high arched bridge. But she hadn't seen any movement on the bridge itself, only around it. Fine.

As she got closer, she moderated her running, and studied the path. There were trees by the roadside, and they led pretty much to the place under the bridge where the movement was.

She plunged into the trees, and behind the first irregular row of them, which would screen her from view of whatever the

movement was. Oh, it was entirely possible that the movement
was not sentient nor capable of sight. But what if it were? No
reason risking it. And yes, in normal circumstances, she would
say it was impossible for invisible movement to be sentient. But
then *she* shifted into a dragon on demand. Perhaps other people
shifted into invisible forms.

What she knew was that she must save Rafiel.

She was walking as rapidly as she dared behind the row of
trees, when she found herself grabbed by strong arms. A large
hand covered the mouth she opened to scream.

The doorbell rang loudly, startling Tom and making Old Joe
and Conan jump. Before Tom could move to open the door, a
fist pounded on it, loudly.

By then Tom had recovered enough of his wits to know that
he should not open the door. So much about his dealings with
the triad was appearance and protocol. Or at least they'd expect
appearance and protocol. The fact that Tom couldn't care less for
either of those made remarkably little difference. He would have
to impress his authority upon them, in the way that the Great
Sky Dragon had. And that meant he didn't open doors, and he
didn't do the running around. He remembered the huge, gaudily
decorated room. He was supposed to be some sort of hereditary
royalty, and not merely a common man—or a common dragon,
for that matter.

He motioned for Conan to open the door, while he sat on the
chaise, to the side of the sofa. He wouldn't go so far as trying
to look regal, but he did try to look as though the pounding,
which had reached levels where he feared it would smash down
the door, didn't trouble him at all.

Conan rushed to open the door, then stood aside.

The oddness started with the fact that Jao was stark naked.
Perhaps that shouldn't have surprised Tom, since he had sent
a strong and absolute command to come, and he supposed in
dragons, or to dragons older than himself, that would translate
into "shift into dragon and fly there with all possible speed."

But it did surprise Tom all the same, partly because Jao looked
more stern and reserved in his nudity, standing there with his
arms crossed, than he would have if he'd been wearing a suit,
or for that matter a royal medieval outfit.

And partly because, behind Jao, were two other men, equally naked.

A delegation of dragons, Tom thought, and raised his eyebrows at them, saying nothing.

"You summoned us," Jao said, not making a step over the threshold.

"I summoned you," Tom said. "I wish to ask you some questions." He considered using again the summon to come, but he had a sudden and all-too-vivid image of Jao changing shape right there, at the threshold. It had been hard enough to pay for replacing the bathroom after Tom had shifted in it, breaking all the fixtures to bits, stripping the tile from the wall, and bending the piping in on itself. They had to fix it, of course, and improve it, and then make some excuse to the landlord about having wished to remodel. Nothing else would have explained that damage, except perhaps claiming a bomb had exploded in the bathroom.

Explaining that they wished to remodel the front door or, worse, the front wall of the house, would be somewhat harder. And besides, if Jao got stuck half-in, half-out, it was quite possible he would be too agitated to shift back, and what would the neighbors think?

So Tom refrained from saying *Come* with the same force he had before, but he reached for Jao's mind and said *I wish to speak to you about matters that shouldn't be discussed in front of strangers.*

Jao looked pointedly at Old Joe, sitting on the sofa, clacking his teeth, but he didn't say anything, and came into the house, step by step, his entrance having the air of both a royal procession and of his doing Tom an enormous favor. Tom remained sitting. It put him at the disadvantage of having to look up at Jao. On the other hand, it conveyed the idea that he was not some underling to get up at Jao's approach, and also that he was not in any way afraid of Jao or what Jao could do. Which was almost true. He was not afraid of what Jao might do to himself.

But he'd fallen in love with Kyrie and he couldn't bear the thought that Jao would do something to Kyrie because of the way Tom treated him.

Jao stood in the same stance he had adopted at the door, legs just slightly parted, as though balancing himself to receive a punch, arms crossed on the chest.

"I want to know what you did with Kyrie," Tom said.

Strangely, he caught Jao off guard. They hadn't expected Tom to know they were the ones who had taken Kyrie. Tom was sure of that. Jao was good at the bluffing game of power, and probably had played it since well before Tom was alive, and truth be told, since before Tom's father or grandfather were born. But he couldn't avoid a momentary start of surprise, and Tom saw that. He saw the minimal widening of the eyes, the head thrown back just a little, the bracing legs bracing harder. And the two men— dragons, almost for sure—behind Jao were even more transparent. Probably they were no older than their apparent age, which was about the same as Tom's.

Jao had recovered though, and said, "I don't know what you're talking about."

"Yes, you do," Tom said. He supposed he should be circuitous and ceremonial, but he didn't know how to be either, and he'd just about run out of patience. "I saw it in your mind."

Jao opened his mouth, then closed it, then opened it again. "You could not have."

Tom raised his eyebrows. "I could have," he said. "But you're right, you'd have known if I'd forced your secrets open and looked at the thoughts you try to hide from me. I didn't do that, but it was enough to know there was a secret place which you were guarding with the whole force of your personality, and also that it was somehow related to Kyrie, which I could sense quite well."

Jao compressed his lips, until they looked like one thin, twisted line. He might have posed for the part of villain in some panto- mime. Well, probably not naked. He glared at Tom. "I will not tell you anything."

"Oh, I think you will," Tom said, his voice steady and rea- sonable. Inside, he wished he felt that he was being steady and reasonable. "Because the alternative is to have me riffle through your mind to find the information, and I don't think you want me to do that."

Jao looked at him. He huffed a little. "You're not—" he started, then took a deep breath. "You wouldn't do that. He will come back. He would avenge me. You know that as well as I do."

"Avenge you?" Tom asked, and arched his eyebrows. "I do not intend to kill you. Just to find what you have done, against my express will, to force my hand in matters that do not concern you."

Jao was quiet a long time. When he spoke, his voice had an

unpleasant tone of an adult talking to a child. "I've served the Great Sky Dragon all my life," he said, "which is longer than yours, young man, and perhaps longer than you can conceive of." He paused, and Tom would very much have liked to know how a naked man could invest himself of so much dignity and power. He looked at Tom, not a glare, but worse, an evaluating appraising look, something he might give those vegetables he bought for the Three Luck Dragon, looking them over to see what might be made of them. "There is an honor in serving him. I know that I'm doing what my ancestors would want, what I was designed and created to do, carrying on traditions that are important and things that mere mortals never hear about." A haughty shrug of the shoulders. "The long life, the power to fly, all those are compensations, but hardly needed. Neither my father nor my mother were dragons, but when I was revealed to be one, they gave me over to the people of the dragon—at the time there was a whole city near the village of my birth—and the people of the dragon raised me to know what to do. I was nimble and smart, and in time, the Great Sky Dragon himself chose me as one of his wings, one of his close advisors." He frowned slightly. "He expects—expected immediate and complete obedience, of course, and he punishes with death the slightest deviation from his plans, or the slightest balking at his will. It would seem to someone like you, raised in this undisciplined time, as though I were little more than a slave. But there is a . . . mutual duty in my service. The Great Sky Dragon will not hesitate to kill me, if that's what it takes to make others see the price of disobeying him, and the price of substituting my judgment for his. On the other hand, he too is bound. He does not do what very well pleases me, but what is needed for the good of our people—for the good of all dragons. It is a duty he learned young, though he came to his post quite unprepared. His mind always dwells on what is good for the dragons. Do you think he wanted you for his successor, or was pleased that the only one to ascend to the throne of dragons was a young man from a quite alien background, on whom no one ever impressed his duty to serve?

"He did not. And though his testing of you showed you less unworthy than he feared, that only changed how he treated you. If you'd been as unworthy as he feared, a coward with no self-control and seeking only your own pleasure, he'd have forced you,

I think, or bribed you to create children for the dragon throne, and then disposed of you. But he thought there was in you a spark, a . . . something that might be made into a good Great Sky Dragon." Jao frowned slightly, and his shrug was less majestic this time. "At any rate, he feared that an emergency such as the one that happened would befall him and make you Great Sky Dragon long before any children of yours were able to do more than mewl and crawl. So he tried to preserve you, and he got us to swear that we'd protect you and serve you once he was gone.

"But he forgot something—he forgot that you can't and won't put dragonkind first. And so, we must do it for you. We'll protect you and we'll serve you because he told us to, but if you won't do what you must, then we'll do it for you. Bea Ryu was picked as your bride because she has the best chance of giving you dragon sons. But if you don't like her, we'll pick another. The thing is—"

"No," Tom said. "The thing is that I have absolutely no obligation to dragonkind, as you put it. I don't know what obligation you imagine I have, but no one of my family ever felt the need to look out for dragons in—"

"Not true. You are descended from dragons on both sides, from both kinds of dragons. If you think that neither of them carried about dragonkind—"

"I meant, of course, that no relative I knew ever changed into a dragon, and that I have no reason to be loyal to a group of people just because they do. My association with your charming group has involved threats and attempts to coerce me. Why should I?"

"Why?" Jao looked like he would like to take Tom over his knee, and as though, had Tom been ten years younger, he would do just that. "Does it not matter to you that you are *our kind*? Does like not call to like?"

Tom allowed his lip to curl upward in the disdain he felt. "Where I come from," he said, "racism is frowned upon, and to cleave to a group of people simply because they look like you or share a characteristic with you is considered both weak and a sign of bigger character problems."

"Pah. A young civilization, with nothing to recommend it." Jao made a gesture that seemed to signify something dissolving into thin air. "Who knows how long it will last? But the way of mankind is always for like to cleave to like, and if you don't cleave to us, of whom the rest of humanity is in dread, who'll protect you when *they* come for you?"

The thought did stab at Tom, now and then, in the dark of the night. Sometime, long ago, sometime between that night when his father had turned him out of the house in his robe and bare feet, and the Tom who had found Kyrie and a semblance of normal life, he'd become very aware of how different he was, how odd. If he were all alone— If people found out what he was—

The best prognosis he could think of was secret labs somewhere in the bowels of some military installation, but he suspected that was a dream of thriller—or perhaps comic book—writers. On the few occasions when normal people had seen him or one of the other shifters, Tom had become acquainted with the human tendency to ignore and deny what they couldn't accept. And people changing between humans and animals was something most people couldn't accept. Tom, as far as he'd been a normal human for over half of his life, and insofar as he still tried to think as one, would very much like to believe such a change was impossible, too.

What normal people tried to do with something impossible was to destroy it and bury it, so that they could then feel it had never happened and never existed.

And sometimes, still, Tom woke up in the middle of the night—or more likely, given his hours, early morning—beside the sleeping Kyrie, and stared at the ceiling and imagined what people who were truly terrified might do. To him. To them.

But that was something he'd lived with since he'd known he shifted, something he'd faced in those long lonely vigils while Kyrie and Not Dinner slept. It was not something that compelled him to orient his whole life around dragons and what Jao called "dragonkind." Tom had been alone before, he'd evaded danger before. He could do it much better now that he had friends. Even if his friends were not dragonkind.

Tom said, "Yes, yes, humanity came from families and tribes. Animals usually do. But we're better than animals, aren't we? At least we're supposed to be. Yes, I'm human. Yes, I'm a shifter. Do I owe particular loyalty to dragon shifters? I won't let you be destroyed, since I was left in charge of you, and therefore I owe you some kind of, er...Chinese obligation. And I will try to get your Great Sky Dragon back, or, if not that, find some-one else to fulfill those duties. But I will not betray myself and marry someone I don't love, or fail to marry someone I love just because of imagined duty to these people who happen to shift into forms close to mine. That is nonsensical."

Tom let a glare shine forth to go with the words, but the glare met Jao's own glare, and clearly Jao had been practicing that glare much longer than Tom could have in the time he'd been alive.

Worse, as Tom looked away, he saw poor Conan, standing just behind Jao and looking at Tom with something akin to horror. Had Conan also believed that Tom would be loyal to dragons simply because that was his other form? Insane. And if he did, had Tom just disappointed him horribly?

Jao clicked his tongue. He said something in Chinese which Tom failed to understand, except for the tone giving him the impression that it was something uncomplimentary about himself. Then he sighed, as though having to use English were a debasement of his principles. "What do you want of me?"

"I want Kyrie back," Tom said, "and I want you to make what efforts you can to find where the Great Sky Dragon is held. Then I'll do what I can to rescue him."

Jao narrowed his eyes. "I can't give you the panther girl—" He stopped Tom from opening his mouth with a hand held up. "I can't give you the panther girl back, because she has escaped her captivity sometime before you called me. There is no point at all asking me where she was held or how she escaped. I didn't know those things. It was all arranged on what we call the long hand, someone else being hired to arrange it. I couldn't have the details at the surface of my mind, where you could find them."

"Was she held in the city at least?" Tom asked, with a thought that he could always shift and fly over Goldport until he found her. By now, Kyrie would have shifted, and a very upset big black panther had a way of making its displeasure known.

Jao shrugged, and Tom bit his tongue to avoid screaming. All right. He would go into the dragon egg. He would use all his eyes-bodies, that confusing multitude of dragons to look for Kyrie. It was all their fault, after all.

"I don't know where the panther girl is," Jao said, "and we've made no progress in finding the Great Sky Dragon's remains. I hope they are still intact, I trust he will indeed come back to us." His lip curl matched Tom's. "I don't think you are worthy of the position." He lifted his head, and looked from beneath partly lowered lids at Tom, managing to convey someone looking from a moral height and a great distance away. "But whether the Great Sky Dragon comes back to us or not, we must fulfill his plans and get sons for the dragon clan, and like it or not you're our only chance. Your feelings and your vaunted individuality will not be allowed to stand in the way."

"Perhaps," Tom said. "But you won't secure my cooperation by kidnapping the woman I love."

Jao pushed his lips out, then said, "There are ways," in a manner that made Tom think of syringes and laboratories. Jao added, "If he comes back and finds I failed his wishes, he will kill me. What will you do?"

When she came within sight of the house, Kyrie couldn't—for a moment—believe the dragons in the yard. Oh, it wasn't that they were totally unexpected. Not after she'd seen them flying overhead. It was more that they were *so* unexpected, there in the tiny, sloping yard of their brick workingman Victorian. They crouched, one on each side of the front door, like outsized gargoyles. It wasn't even fully dark yet, and Kyrie wondered what her neighbors would think as they started coming home from work—which some of them would be doing about now. Or what her next-door neighbors, who happened to be a very nice retired couple, would think if they looked out of their enclosed front porch in the direction of her front lawn.

Perhaps, Kyrie thought, looking at the glistening red scales or one, the almost phosphorescent green scales of the other, *I can tell them these are inflatable yard decorations that I'm trying out for Christmas.*

She wasn't very coherent. Her feet hurt her even more than they managed to do after a double shift waiting tables at The George, and besides, she could kill for a glass of water.

That thought connected to the thought that though the dragons hadn't seen her yet, they *would* invariably notice her if she tried to run up to the—open? Why was the front door open? There was more than likely another dragon guarding the side door she normally entered through.

Which meant... which meant it would be very difficult to get into the house. And she wanted to get in the house and have a truly massive glass of water and, if she could, a shower, and put on her walking shoes, and call Tom and ask him for help.

The dragons couldn't fit in the house. Not only couldn't they go in in dragon form, but in the tiny rooms of a house that was all of six hundred square feet, they would do themselves severe injury while demolishing the building around them, were they to shift.

So . . . inside the house she would be safe from them, or about as safe as she was likely to be.

And that meant she had to get in the house, but how to do it when two large, glistening, Chinese dragons lay down on the front lawn staring at the front door with all the intent alertness of a cat watching a mousehole. To walk up the garden path would be the equivalent of a mouse walking into the cat's mouth.

Kyrie stood half-hidden by a parked car in front of her neighbors. The dragons had a slight heat distortion above them. The setting sun was clearly enough to warm them.

And then she saw, near her, the curled end of her neighbor's hose. She knew the family. They weren't home. They were a little older than Tom and Kyrie, and had two small children. Their interactions with Tom and Kyrie were friendly but somewhat forced, as though there must inherently be something wrong with a young couple not setting about having kids. Of course, in a way they were right in that there *was* something very different about Tom and Kyrie, had they but known.

But the other reason they weren't particularly close was that both couples worked long hours and were rarely at home at the same time. Right then, the couple who owned this house would be picking their kids up at daycare and swinging by the fast food place.

Kyrie closed her eyes and promised herself she would pay the Johnstons for the water she was about to waste. And then she leapt at the coiled hose, grabbed the end and, pulling it with her, went to the faucet on the side of the Johnstons' house. Before turning it on, she wedged the hose behind a bush, between two forked branches, held by two rocks. Aimed at the hot dragons.

Then in one long sprint, not stopping to draw breath, much less to think, she turned the faucet full on and started running madly towards her front door—betting that the startled dragons would lurch to where the hose was.

Bea shoved back with her elbow, but before it made contact, the man behind her had sidestepped, taking himself out of harm's way. "I've been trained, Bea," Rafiel's voice said in a whisper. "I expect the elbow to the ribs." And the relief that it was Rafiel made her legs go weak and her knees buckle.

"I only covered your mouth to keep you from screaming," he whispered. "What are you doing here? I thought I told you to stay in the car."

He removed his hand from over her mouth and let go of her. She turned around, relief turning to anger. Really. Couldn't he have approached her from a side she could see him, instead of playing games? She told him that in an angry whisper, and added, "You might as well have covered my eyes and told me to guess who you were."

His lips twitched. "No. You could still have screamed when you saw me suddenly."

She was fairly sure she hated that smile more than anything, except that she didn't hate it at all—instead it felt safe and right to have him here. Like things should be this way. "I had to come," she said, her whisper just as urgent as his. "I heard a scream. I thought you needed help. I couldn't let you be killed while I—"

He shook his head. "I wasn't being killed. I'm a trained police officer." She thought he was going to say that he didn't need the help of art students, but instead he said, oddly softly, "I didn't want you to be in danger." And his golden eyes were soft too.

"I don't think danger can be helped," she said. "And it was an animal scream of pain. It might have been a lion."

He nodded once, but said, "It wasn't this lion."

"And then there were the wolves."

This got her a very odd glance. "The—wolves?"

"I don't know where they came from, but two *wolves* went running by me, side by side, when I was halfway between the car and here. I thought they were shifters. Not sure why, even, but I thought so, the way they ran, side by side, the way they didn't even look at me, and the fact that they were...well fed."

"Did they smell shifter?" Rafiel ask.

"Smell?"

"Sort of metallic and spicy. You probably smell it, and I know I smell it. So do Tom and Kyrie. I was told...six months ago, that not all shifters have the smell. Some aquatic mammals don't. But I think it would take a special wolf to be aquatic."

"I didn't smell anything," she said. "But I wasn't—"

"You might not have noticed," Rafiel said. "Anyway, this whole place smells like it was drenched in shifter pheromones for a while. All of it. Probably the feral living in the hippodrome, but..."

Bea nodded. She could see he was worried. She could see he was scared. She was completely ready for what he would say next.

"I'll figure out what's going on." He ran his hand across his forehead, in a gesture that gave her the impression he was really tired. "You go back to the truck."

She shook her head.

His lips twitched. "Why not?"

"Because I won't be any safer out there. Didn't you hear what I said, about there were two werewolves—I'm sure they were werewolves—who went past me? Anything could happen to me out there in the parking lot all alone. And anything could happen to you, in here, all alone. If we're together, at least we can watch each other's back."

His eyes went really soft again, and crinkled a little at the corners, while his lips pulled into a smile. "Right." He pointed towards the place where she'd seen the movement. "There is something going on down there," he said.

"Yeah," she said. "I was headed there to figure it out."

He reached and took her hand. His own hand was much, much larger than hers, and very warm. It felt somehow protective, as it enveloped hers. She looked up at him and nodded.

Tom stood up involuntarily as Kyrie came running into the room. For a moment he didn't recognize her. She rarely wore a dress, and besides, she was soaking wet. But as he stood up, she came running into his arms, and clung to him, which was not something he thought of Kyrie doing She was panting slightly, as though she'd been in a race, and shuddering while she made disjointed remarks like, "Two of them," and "garden hose" and inexplicably "Tomahawk."

Tom was aware of the look of disgust Jao cast him, which frankly had the power to neither surprise nor worry him. He put both arms around Kyrie, and kissed her ear because it was the only place he could reach, and asked her why she was soaking wet, and—when he looked up—found that Jao had gone.

Old Joe was edging out the door after him, and Tom said, "Stay," just in time to have the old man turn around, looking resigned, and come back to sit on the sofa.

Conan made as if to shut the door, then said, "Why is there a jet of water across the yard?"

This was when Kyrie lifted her head from Tom's shoulder and said, "If you would, if there are no dragons around anymore, would you go turn off the water? In the house to the east."

Conan nodded and darted out the door. Tom wanted to tell him it might not be safe. Then he realized nowhere and nothing would be safe for his associates. At least not until he got the old Great Sky Dragon back, and perhaps not then. After all, the dragons would still want Tom to reproduce with the right woman, wouldn't they?

Kyrie was telling him the story of being tranquilized and finding herself in a basement, apparently in one of the cabins at the Tomahawk, and of walking back on sore feet.

"You should have stopped someone. A motorist or something," he said, "and asked to use a cell phone."

"On Sierra," she said, looking at him in disbelief. "They would have wanted to see me use the cell phone in a totally different way."

He inclined his head to the side, conceding the point, then said, "From now on—"

"I strap a disposable phone to my thigh? I was thinking the same," she said. "Rafiel has the right idea." She took a deep breath. "Tom, I could kill for a glass of water."

"I'd say you had plenty of water," Tom said, as he tracked Conan coming back into the house. "Conan, please lock." He took Kyrie's hand to lead her to the kitchen, while she told him about the two dragons in the yard, how she'd trained the hose on them, and how it had worked to distract them.

"I guess they thought someone hidden behind the bush was wetting them, or perhaps it was just the shock of being hit with cold water when they were steaming hot."

"Or both," Tom said.

"Well, then," she said. "I couldn't avoid running through the spray to get in."

He nodded and left her at the door to the kitchen, while he went to get her a glass of ice water. Old Joe and Conan trailed behind her, while Not Dinner rubbed at her ankles, despite being dripping wet.

Kyrie drank the water quickly. "Probably can't strap a glass of water to my leg, too," she said in a sad tone.

"Probably not," he said. "Maybe some cash to buy water. But you didn't shift to come home, did you?"

She frowned. "No. That's why I'm still dressed. Though..."

"Though?"

"Though I tried to shift. I thought the panther would make better time getting home, but it didn't seem to work. I guess I was too tired and hungry. Have you guys eaten?"

"No," Tom said. Something about not being able to shift wasn't right. He kept thinking that he'd heard something related to that recently, but he couldn't put his finger on what. "But that's not the important thing right now. I think we're all in terrible danger, Kyrie. You guys more than me, because they wouldn't dare kill me. Not without another heir. Well, at least not *this* set. Those two who challenged me might not mind. But now they've got the idea that by getting someone close to me, they can force me to do what they want—"

"Yeah," Conan said mournfully from behind Tom. "You *are* going to have to kill a few of them."

Rafiel and Bea walked hand in hand between the trees to the very end of the wooded area. All along the way, there was the sense of movement from the path. Rafiel wished he could have convinced Bea not to tag along. He didn't like this. He didn't like this at all.

He wasn't a superstitious man. He didn't buy crystals, he didn't believe anyone could tell you the future and he most certainly didn't believe in ghosts.

It wasn't just that they got their share of crazy people who said they had to beat the cashier and steal the game system because his aura was all wrong. That didn't bother Rafiel, because they got crazy people of all descriptions and types.

No, it was more as though the fact that he turned into a lion and was friends with people who turned into animals used up his full allowance of weird. After that, he had no more left to give, and anyone wanting to discuss his aura, or in general, talk of the uncanny, would have to meet with his hard and skeptical nature.

But the things out there were uncommonly like ghosts. He could sense them. He could see the results of their passage. But he couldn't see *them*, and it was unlikely they were there in any physical sense. Rafiel didn't like it, and he liked even less the feel that he couldn't protect Bea from whatever this was. Maybe he should have studied table-turning and exorcism?

As they came to the end of the little wooded area, they found themselves facing a play cottage. Bea looked at him with a question in her eyes, and he leaned in to whisper in her ear, "It's part of the train line that goes around the park. It still does, but now mostly at night, and they don't bother with this stuff. It's just the lights on the lake, and the lights of the rides that make it fun. But when I was little, the train went around all day, and they used to have these staged scenes of fairy tales, you know, cottages and Snow White and castles and Cinderella and all. The cottages used to do double duty as concession stands. But sometime in the nineties, the figures of Snow White and the dwarves started looking ratty and instead of painting them, they just carted them away. Some of the buildings are still concession stands, but these, in hard to reach places, were just left to rot. Maybe they were too expensive to demolish. Like the hippodrome."

The hippodrome and all the bones left behind there was a bad image to have and he watched—no, he sensed—*entities* slip into the half-open door of the cottage.

He and Bea couldn't go into the half-open door. In fact, he didn't want to go anywhere near the place where the things were converging and . . . seemingly being sucked into the cottage. The way they'd been slipping in, it must be chockablock with them in there.

The idea of having one of the things move through him made him shudder, which was stupid because he didn't even know that there was a way the things could go through a person. He thought it was more likely they'd go around. After all, the door was half-open to let them in.

But all the same, he could imagine one of the things going through him, all clammy and ethereal, made of cold energy like a wind that blew through a person, instead of around. He shivered, grabbed Bea's hand harder and pulled her around the cottage, away from the things, a way from the door. He remembered vaguely that there was a window on the other side. If it was a real window or just painted on the façade there was no way of knowing.

He hoped it was real. Otherwise it was going to be kind of hard to listen in through what looked like stucco.

✧   ✧   ✧

Tom was outside the bathroom, shouting through the door while Kyrie showered, telling her the story of his confrontation with Jao, trying to explain his dilemma. "It is not," he said, "that I don't think it's going to take a lot to keep everyone safe. And I'm perfectly aware that they act according to a different code, but it seems to me, if I kill him, I've already lost."

He heard a sigh behind him and guessed it was Conan, because Old Joe had ambled towards the kitchen. Other than making sure that Not Dinner had gone the other way towards the bedroom, Tom ignored Old Joe. He'd told him not to leave the house, and so far, he'd not heard the back door open. He did hear the sounds of someone rustling around in the fridge, and—leaving aside how much Old Joe might eat—he could imagine Kyrie declaring they'd have to disinfect the whole kitchen. But right now that was the least of his concerns.

He expected Kyrie to tell him to grow up or to grow a pair, or something, or maybe to make as exasperated a sound as Conan had just made, but as she opened the door and came out, wearing the jeans, T-shirt and shoes she'd taken in with her, and combing her hair, she said, "No, you're right."

"You don't understand," Conan said, in a tone of exasperation. He was leaning against the wall down the hallway. "If this is your idea for winning hearts and minds, or whatever, you're going about it entirely the wrong way. It won't work, Tom. They... dragons don't understand this."

Kyrie and Tom both looked at him, and Kyrie said, "You can't say dragons don't understand kindness. You—"

Conan shook his head. "No, that's not what I mean, though you should be aware, I, myself, am a very atypical dragon. Most are older than this country, let alone having been raised in it. They don't understand our codes, and they were raised in a pretty rigid code of their own." He sighed deeply. "It's like you're speaking in a language they never heard and hoping they understand you. And it's not kindness, exactly, to do that. What you're doing is confusing them and making them feel leaderless. No wonder they want to betray you, or at least to please the old Great Sky Dragon, whom they're hoping very much comes back. He will kill them for any reason or none. Individually, he doesn't value them very much, but at least they can understand him."

Tom did understand what Conan was saying. He had had that

exact feeling, while talking to Jao, as though they were speaking different languages. "Yes, Jao kept saying that it was my duty to look out for dragonkind or something like that. But I keep thinking that if...I mean, look, it's a lot like the Ancient Ones wanting to punish us for killing shifters, even though the shifters were killing other people. If it comes to that, if it comes to a choice..."

Conan nodded. "I'm not saying that you should do otherwise, Tom. I'm not sure what I would have done, and I was handed over to the Great Sky Dragon when I was a teenager. My parents would say I deserted him or something, the way I'm behaving." He looked up at Tom, and the way his eyes narrowed, Tom got the feeling Conan was getting a headache. "Look, they're going to try to get me to make you fall in line. You know that. You know what they've done to me before."

What they'd done to him included leaving him on his own, to come back from a severe burning all on his own. "And, Tom, I understand what you say—I left once, though I needed your help to leave—but...but they're going to keep pushing all of us until you do what they want."

Tom opened his hands in a show not so much of helplessness as of exasperation. "What do you want me to do?" he asked. "Do you want me to marry Bea, or, I suppose, any ten females, just to make sure I have a dragon son? Would you leave Rya to marry someone they picked for you?"

Conan made a face. "If it hadn't been for you," he said, "I wouldn't have had any choice. And I doubt I'd even have met Rya. But now? Now I can have Rya. Now I can...I know I can sing?" it was a statement, but it finished in a rising, interrogatory tone.

"You can sing," Tom said.

"Now I know I can sing, I couldn't leave Rya and...and music and go back, no."

"Well, I can't go back either," Tom said. "Particularly since I was never there."

"Tom, if it would be easier to pretend you and I have broken up, just pretend until, you know, we figure this out," Kyrie said. She bent to pick up Not Dinner and pet him. Tom couldn't see her expression, but he didn't need to see her expression. He knew how to answer that.

"Don't even joke," he said. "If they think they can make me

do what they want, there will never be an end to it. No. We will not give an inch. Frankly, I'm starting to wonder if the beings from the stars could be any worse."

There was a crashing sound from the kitchen. Old Joe appeared on the doorway holding an egg. There was raw egg on his lips, and raw egg smeared on a hole atop the egg. He seemed to have been sucking a raw egg. But the face, around and under the smeared egg yolk was white as a sheet, leaving his network of dark wrinkles looking like tattoos, and his eyes looking like black holes. "No, don't say. They are worse," he said.

⇥ CHAPTER 20 ⇤

There was a window in the cabin wall, and when they got near enough, Rafiel saw the wolves. He'd thought that Bea had been seeing things, or perhaps imagining things, but there were two matched grey wolves, side by side, just under the window. And from the way their heads were cocked, it was impossible not to imagine that they were human enough or sentient enough to be listening very carefully to what was going on inside.

As they got nearer, voices became more obvious, or rather one voice that Rafiel could call as such, and a swarm of odd buzzing that seemed to form words. It was like having words formed by the sort of static you get on radios between stations.

The voice was female and said, in an imperious tone, "But you have to show me how to do it. I don't think the old fool knows. Even when he comes back."

The buzzing back was less distinct, though Rafiel thought he caught the words "receptive" and "right."

Closer yet, he realized that there was a hole in the glass of the window, which was probably why the sound was so clear. The wolves, he noted, turned to look at him and then away. The moment they'd looked at him had been enough, though.

Something you got used to, as a shifter, was knowing that the eyes remained remarkably the same between human and shifter. Oh, you might lose the whites and the shape might change, but you usually retained the same color and, strangely, the same expression as you had in human form. The two pairs of eyes that turned to him were startlingly familiar.

His shock was not so much that Cas and Nick, his colleagues in the force, were werewolves—he supposed considering Cas' last name was Wolfe, he should have thought about this before—but the fact that he'd never smelled even a hint of shifter-scent around them. If it was going to be that way, then he couldn't be sure about anyone.

And then he felt a niggling prickle of anger at the two of them. How could they have let him shoulder the burden of solving all the shifter crimes in town, of thinking he was the only one holding the line of justice on shifters, when they could and should have been shouldering their share? How dared they?

But he said nothing, just squeezed Bea's hand and said, "It's all right," then guided her so they were positioned on either side of the small window, each with a wolf standing by their knees.

A first glimpse through the window shocked Rafiel, almost as much as the smell from inside that hit his nose.

First, the woman he'd heard, the woman who stood in the center of the cottage, could have been a Renaissance madonna in a painting by da Vinci. She had that broad forehead that they seemed to prize, and almost perfectly regular features, framed by golden-blond hair. Despite wearing jeans and what looked like a peasant blouse, she had a certain antique air—an impression of being not so much old or out of a time long ago, but of being ageless, someone who had always looked like this and would always look like this.

The effect was heightened by the soft silvery light reflecting on her face.

The cottage interior was dark. There seemed to be some broken furniture in a corner but if it had ever been used as a concession stand, and had been wired as such, it had been a long time ago. Now it was dark, filled with something shadowy and not quite visible, with this blond woman in the middle, holding in her hands—

Rafiel had seen it once, long ago, and he remembered it because immediately afterwards he'd watched the Great Sky Dragon punish someone in a way that had seemed at the time irrevocably fatal.

It was about the size of a grapefruit, perfectly round, and it had the softly white reflections of a pearl.

In fact, Rafiel knew what it was. It was what the dragons called the Pearl of Heaven, their special and carefully guarded object. Tom had stolen it once, because he had thought that it would help him get over his addiction. It hadn't, but it had seemed to have other effects on both him and the dragons. The dragons had chased him over half the country and exacted terrible punishments until he returned it.

Now, it didn't look exactly like a normal pearl. It seemed to be shining with an interior light, a silvery pale light, which shone up into the face of the woman, making her look ethereal and not quite real. Paradoxically, it bounced off the shapes around her. There were dozens of them, and they seemed to flow into each other. The light bouncing off them made them look exactly like shrouded humans and made the fact that some of them were partially inside the others or twined with the others seem as wrong as the more nightmarish drawings of Hieronymus Bosch.

Rafiel ignored the shapes and concentrated on the woman— partly because he could smell her, and he recognized the smell. He would lay very good odds she was the creature who had beat him after he followed the feral shifter, and the same creature who had seduced him in the woods.

He still couldn't think of that event without a vague nausea stealing over him and causing his stomach to plunge. He could imagine, all too well, Tom teasing him over it. Why be so upset at copulation? After all, though they'd all been afraid of it, it seemed to bring with it no bad side effects, despite their shifter nature.

But it was that he'd had sex with someone he didn't know, someone in animal form, and worse, that he'd had sex with her in a completely helpless way. Once he'd smelled her, he'd been gone. There had been absolutely nothing he could do to prevent himself from copulating with her, despite all his misgivings, despite his higher principles, despite the fact that he had always wanted to be sure he could trust anyone he did *that* with.

It felt, he thought, rather as it must feel to be raped. He'd heard rape victims—usually female—describe that feeling of not being in control, of not being able to say no, of being overpowered, of never again feeling safe, and he felt it echo in him. There was also the same guilt. Rape victims would go on and on, analyzing their clothes, the way they stood, and what they'd done, trying to figure out if they'd done something, anything to bring the ordeal on.

The analysis resulted badly for him, because he had betrayed himself. The woman—the female—might have put out heavy pheromones, but in the end, it was his own body that had reacted, his own body that had made him engage in sex in animal form.

Even now, feeling sick to his stomach at the thought, the smell of her, attenuated though it was in her human form, caused him to react. Part of him wanted to go through the window, part of him wanted to dive through and cavort with her right there, despite the scary immaterial creatures.

He felt as though a cold hand were drawing up his back at the thought, but then he looked over at Bea, and saw her gazing at him. Did she know? Did she guess? It didn't matter. She looked scared and worried, and her look made whatever arousal had started in him subside. Nothing was more important than keeping Bea safe, except perhaps earning her respect. And he was going to guess her respect hinged on his acting like a human being and not like a rutting animal.

He gave her a smile he was afraid was sickly, even as inside the shapes whispered in their buzzing words, "You can't activate it. You don't have what it takes. Only some of you can. The dragon boy, the new Sky Dragon can. I'm not sure the old dragon can, even if he knew how."

"I must know how," the woman said. "I'm sure the old dragon can, if he doesn't have any choice but do it. I got his measure when I felled him. I tasted his soul. He's weaker than I. Even if *I* can't activate the Pearl, if you tell me how to do it, I can make *him* do it."

"It's not tell," the things buzzed. "It's show. We can no more show you how to do it than you can show us what it's like to have such an abomination as a body. That thing was built for one like us, for one with the spirit—the soul—to be able to operate it. You don't have that soul. It's like...you don't have the right..." The buzzing stopped and Rafiel had the impression it was groping for words. "You don't have the right appendages," the last word was pronounced as if it were something distasteful, perhaps one of the grosser scatological words.

"But I can make it glow," the woman said, in a tone of peevishness, like a child that is being lied to or denied something it thinks essential.

"A child's trick," the voices buzzed. "Making it glow is easy. Making it fully operate, making it revive the knowledge of how to unlock the world gates is something else, and you can't do it. When you got locked in the fleshy self, you lost that. You lost the parts of you that would allow you to do it. Perhaps it wasn't such a good idea to rebel. Perhaps you shouldn't have been so headstrong."

The woman stomped her foot. She looked mutinous. She looked exactly like people do when told "I told you so" when they themselves had already figured it out. She glared at the immaterial beings. "Maybe you need more feeling," she said.

She reached out, while holding the Pearl in her right hand. Her left hand plunged behind the clutter of broken furniture and dragged out—pale and naked and trembling, his hands over his head—the feral shifter Rafiel had fought before. As they watched, the woman's nails, which seemed unusually large, tore a strip across his chest.

The creature screamed, a scream of pain and terror, and his eyes turned in trembling, uncomprehending terror towards the woman inflicting the pain. It seemed to be trying to snuggle to her, even as she ripped again, this time down the feral's arm. Blood flowed in the wake of her nails, and a sort of shiver went through the cottage. The invisible creatures, seen only by their reflection of pale light, moved in, one crowding into the other, compacting, through and into the feral who shivered and cried again, a high, animal sound.

Rafiel was running. He'd always thought he was a brave man. He'd never run from any physical threat: not from prehistoric shifters, nor from the more human threats that he'd confronted in the past. But he couldn't stop his recoiling horror, he couldn't stop himself from running.

Maybe it was in part the knowledge that he'd had sex with that creature who was hurting what seemed to be a defenseless young, perhaps her own. Maybe it was the dumb look in the feral's eyes, as it tried to snuggle up to the very person hurting him.

Most of all, though, he thought it was those mostly transparent creatures, silvery in the light of the Pearl, flowing into each other and crowding for what the woman had called the "feeling." They were worse than vampires. After all, at least blood was something physical. But they were crowding to something else, and Rafiel's stomach clenched at the thought of what that something might be.

He realized he was leaning on his car and throwing up, when he felt Bea's hand on his shoulder. He thought he'd now disgraced himself completely in her eyes, but all she said, in a concerned voice, was, "Are you all right?"

He wiped at his mouth with the back of his hand and nodded, trying to muster the ability to talk again through a throat that burned with bile. "Yes . . . I . . . I'm sorry."

"No," she was passing him something. He realized it was a bunch of folded-over Kleenex, and he wiped at his mouth and looked at her.

"I'm sorry. I don't even know why I ran, much less why it made me sick."

She gave him a small smile. "I know," she said. "Hungry ghosts. That's what I was thinking when I ran. I wasn't far behind you."

They'd cleaned up the mess that Old Joe had made in the kitchen, which was quite an epic mess, Kyrie had to admit, even by Old Joe standards. She'd known when she'd seen him with the half-eaten raw egg that there was a mess, and there was: yolk and eggs smeared all over, smashed shells on the floor. Normally she wouldn't have bothered beyond sweeping everything he might have touched into a trash can, but they needed to talk, so she'd started to wipe down counters, handing the leftover milk in the open carton to Old Joe and saying, "Finish it." Because there were no used glasses anywhere, she was fairly sure he'd drunk from the bottle.

Tom and Conan had squeezed into the kitchen, too, which meant the tiny room was rather more crowded than it ever was meant to be. They edged around the folding table and the two chairs, but Tom swept the floor, and Conan got spray cleaner and a paper towel and started wiping the fridge inside and out, leaving Kyrie to clean the counters and the stove and wipe at the finger marks on the window sill and the door.

They worked around Old Joe who moved like a sleepwalker and made sounds about how the people from other worlds were really, really bad, and how they didn't want to meet them in the flesh. "They send spirit forms over, sometimes, but not full spirit forms. No real energy. Even then, they can kill, they can—"

They walked around him, cleaning. Kyrie thought that all of them needed the sense of normalcy that came from cleaning and returning things to a mundane everyday appearance.

"We can't stay here," she said at last. "I mean...I know they can't come into the house as dragons, but it wouldn't be all that hard to lay siege to the place, then send someone in human form, one by one, to collect us. The house is not that secure, and while Not Dinner is fearsome, he's not exactly a guard dog."

"No," Tom said. "The thing is, I think they can sense me no matter where I am."

"Not if you turn it off," Conan said.

Tom gave him a worried look, then said, "Oh, I see."

"You see?" Kyrie said.

"Something like what Jao did, to keep me out of the part of his mind that knew whom he'd hired to kidnap you, so I didn't have a picture of them and couldn't find them. Only, of course, I'm much better at locking parts of my mind against him. I would be, right, I mean..."

"Yes, you're the Great Sky Dragon," she said.

There was a moment of hesitation, and Tom drew in breath. "I don't think I am," he said. "Worse, I don't think I can be, and that's why we must bring the old Great Sky Bastard back." He looked at Kyrie. "You know what I mean."

She was looking back at him, intently. "Yes, and yet, no." Tom looked perfectly blank and she had to smile. "Look," she said. "You look after everyone all the time, so it would seem logical that you should be in charge, but..." She shook her head. "I see what you mean on taking over the triad as it is. On the other hand, maybe as it is is merely a reflection of the Great Sky Dragon, not—"

Tom shrugged. "I really don't care what it is a reflection of— or not. I don't want to spend the rest of my life ruling over a bunch of people whose only resemblance to me is that they too can turn into dragons."

Kyrie almost said it, but she bit her tongue in time before the words he didn't want to hear came out. In her head, though, they sounded as loudly as though she'd spoken them. *But, Tom,* the words ran through her mind. *What if they need you? What if this is what you were born to do? Can you walk away? Do you even have a choice?*

✧   ✧   ✧

Bea sighed without meaning to, as she thought that apparently she was destined to see way more naked males than she ever meant to. She could only hope it encouraged her facility at life drawing.

She thought this as the two wolves, who'd come running sometime while Rafiel was throwing up and stood a little while away looking at them, now turned and writhed in the agony spasms of shifting. She looked away. She knew what it felt like when she was shifting forms, and she couldn't avoid the idea it was somehow indecent to watch other people do so.

When she looked back, there were two men there. It was undeniable, she thought, that they had considerable Mediterranean blood. It was there, in the dark curls, the olive skin, and the proportions that recalled Greece's statues.

It was also undeniable they were related, perhaps brothers. They had that look of family, even if one's eyes were grey and the other's dark, dark brown. And they were smiling at her in a way that recalled the way that dogs had of giving the impression they were laughing, with tongues half hanging out.

Rafiel, finishing wiping his mouth, glared at them. "Damn you," he said. "Damn you. Why didn't you tell me?"

The slightly taller grey-eyed one grinned, this time a very human grin. "I swear it never occurred to me that you didn't know, Rafiel. I mean, we knew."

"You don't *smell* shifter," Rafiel said. The other man, the one he wasn't talking to, went around Bea's truck, and she realized there was a convertible there, something beautiful and curved, clearly of fifties vintage, and painted hot pink. He came back carrying two bundles of clothes and handed one to his—brother? Friend?

"Oh, is that what you were going by?" the policeman said, grinning. "There is . . . well, there are certain herbs you can eat, which mask the smell. My mother told me about them when I started edging towards puberty. It keeps cats and dogs from reacting to you as though you were an animal, see? I think it must have kept many of our ancestors alive."

"Damn you," Rafiel said again. Bea wondered why he was so mad. There didn't seem to be any reason for it. True, the wolves hadn't helped them, but then really there had been nothing to help them with, had there? Just listening to that horrible scene in the cottage. She didn't think that if she and Rafiel had decided to attack queen bitch in there it would have made any difference.

The grey-eyed man looked obviously puzzled at Rafiel's anger. He arched his eyebrows. "I don't understand. Were we supposed to tell you? Report to you?"

Rafiel leaned against her truck, away from the place where he'd been sick. "You let me carry the burden all alone."

"The . . . burden?" the man said, and looked towards Bea as though for enlightenment, then gave a smile, as though noticing her for the first time, "Sorry, Miss, I'm Cas Wolfe, and this is my cousin Nick—Stravos Nikopolous, the last of which is his crazy dad's idea of what Americans can pronounce, and not a real name at all. He was wrong too. On the pronouncing. So my, er . . . *junior* serious crimes investigator cousin goes by Nick. You can also call him 'Hey, you,' but I'm the only one who can call him stupid."

The other man, almost fully dressed, shook his head. "Ignore Cas. He has a tendency to run off at the mouth around pretty women, but he's an almost-married man."

"Eh, so is Nick for all intents and purposes, though he doesn't tend to get enthusiastic around pretty women." This earned him an elbow to the ribs, making Bea think that if the men weren't brothers, they acted like it. "And you are?"

"Beatrice Ryu," she said. "Bea to my friends." Because it seemed only polite after she had seen them in their shifted form, she added, "Dragon shifter."

Cas opened his mouth, but before he could say anything, Rafiel cut in, "If you two are done with the music hall comedy routine, the reason I'm furious is that you let me think I was the only shifter in the department. You let me deal with crimes by shifters alone. You let me—"

"Oh, chill," Cas said. "We really didn't know you didn't know. I wondered about that shark thing. I smelled shifter all around there, but I—"

"Guys," Nick said. "It might not be the healthiest thing to sit around here, discussing this. Not to put too fine a point on it, but that . . . female, back there, did not strike me as the kind to let bygones be bygones, and it strikes me if she should find we saw her and overheard her—"

Cas turned pale. "I got the impression that was her cub, and she was hurting it just to . . . to feed the things."

"Yes, I got the impression they feed on pain and fear," Nick said. "And she's clearly not afraid to inflict both...and she spares no one."

"The poor dumb thing," Rafiel said. He sounded like he was going to throw up again, and Bea was very sure he was not talking about the woman back there. "That poor dumb thing."

Nick cleared his throat. "So, you see, it is a matter of...I mean...If she saw us leave. If one of the things sensed us—"

"Yeah," Cas said. "We should go somewhere."

Rafiel gave every impression of making a great effort to gather his wits. "That was the Pearl of Heaven she was holding," he said. "It's Great Sky Dragon business."

Bea could tell from the look the cousins traded that they had absolutely no idea what Rafiel was talking about. For a moment it occurred to her to wonder how it was possible for someone— some shifter—to live in a town with the power of the Great Sky Dragon and not to be aware of it.

Then she realized that the power was mostly over dragons. Clearly shifters not connected to or involved with dragons in some way could and did ignore the power. But she didn't feel like explaining it or what was happening with the dragon triad. Nor how the power seemed to have devolved to an outsider. No. She didn't want to explain any of it, and she'd give much not to tell anyone at all about the Great Sky Dragon's plans for her, either.

She didn't need to. Rafiel nodded gravely and said, "I'd better call Tom."

They'd gone to the diner, on the idea that they might as well. Not that it was more unlikely for the triad to find them there than at the house, but first, they did have a responsibility to the diner, and as Tom said, they'd left it oddly staffed, if not short-staffed, exactly. They couldn't ask Anthony to work around the clock. Also, it was harder for the triads to confront them there than at the house, because, well...after all, they had as much invested in keeping everything secret as Tom and Kyrie did. And having it all out at the diner was rather too public. Even if a lot of people at the diner were shifters, not all of them were, and the triad wouldn't risk others finding out, no more than the rest of them would.

Of course, they'd already gone too far, parking those two drag-ons on their front lawn, but Tom supposed having summoned them over in dragon form, he'd already done that damage, and they'd figured, Why not? *And that's why they think I'm really dangerous, too,* he thought. *Because I summoned them in dragon form, I risked discovery.* Jao's words came back to him, "You don't care for dragonkind."

Driving in the car, with Old Joe and Conan crammed in the back seat, he tried to make a joke of Jao's threats that they could too make him reproduce with the right woman.

Kyrie gave him a quizzical look, "I suppose they mean date rape drugs or something?"

He shook his head. "I'm not an expert, mind you, but I understand those don't work really well on men. We have to be, you know, active. Even alcohol can stop that. I had the most horrible thought of needles and stuff." But once he said it, he wondered if there were other ways. The problem with all this, he thought, was that he knew so little about the nature of shifting. And that was, of course, another reason to go to the diner. Dr. Roberts was as likely as not to go into the lab at night. Driven by his shifter nature, or perhaps not wanting to shift near his wife and children, he said that he liked to check on experiments when the lab was empty and quiet, and that might very well be true. At any rate, he would be by the diner for breakfast very early, and then Tom could question him. Hopefully. And maybe he could shed some light onto . . . everything. Though it was going to be a problem, since Tom didn't have a clue where to start asking questions.

When he got to the diner, the parking lot was full, which struck him as odd, because at near eight p.m., the dinner hour should have been on its way out and the diner starting to empty.

Coming in the door made him raise his eyebrows. The George was in a downtown area, and as such, even in a white-bread town like Goldport, it had plenty of ethnic variety. Not that Tom normally gave ethnicity or skin color much thought. He didn't have any clue what Kyrie might be, and it bothered him not at all. Kyrie was Kyrie, and he was himself. The fact that they shifted worried him far more considerably than any variation in human forms, because normally he thought about the regulars in the diner by smell: those who smelled like shifters and those who didn't. Anything else, as far as he was concerned, was ephemeral and unimportant variation.

But damn it, you couldn't come into the diner and find it half packed with Asian people and not wonder why. As large as the Asian population was in Goldport—relatively speaking—it wasn't that large in total. The George wasn't some sort of Asian restaurant that would be frequented by all the best Asian families, which was just as well, since the people at the tables weren't families, but mostly single men.

Tom suppressed a groan as he ducked behind the counter. He put on the bandana he used to confine his long black hair, to keep it from the cooking, and donned the apron with THE GEORGE and the image of the dragon flipping pancakes blazoned across the chest.

Anthony looked anxiously at him, and when Tom nodded, said, "Right. We're working very funny hours, aren't we? Are you going to tell me what is going on, or just send me home and tell me you'll call me again when you need me?"

Tom opened his mouth to tell Anthony it was the latter, but then saw that Anthony looked worried. Really worried. This wasn't the normal teasing and complaining he did about the long hours and Tom and Kyrie's habits.

"Why?" Tom said. "Why?" He couldn't get any closer to phrasing it clearly.

Anthony's head jerked towards the nearest tables packed with Asian men. They were eating, or at least they were ordering, judging by the profusion of plates stacked on their tables. Perhaps they thought they'd get thrown out if they didn't order every so often. Their incomprehensible conversation drifted back to Tom, together with their smell: shifter.

"So?" Tom said. He couldn't let Anthony know these people smelled of shifter, nor that there was anything threatening about their presence. For a moment, the mad thought of telling Anthony everything—all about the triads, all about becoming the Great Sky Dragon, all about shift and change and the weird forms of half the people in the diner—came to Tom. He wondered, even after all this time, how long it would take Anthony to grab a cell phone and call a psychiatrist to deal with Tom's illusions.

Better not try it. The problem is that though you could almost always be sure that people wouldn't take you seriously, you couldn't be *sure* sure. And never with someone like Anthony.

Anthony sighed and rolled his eyes, "I'm not stupid, you

know," he said in a whisper just loud enough to be heard above the fryer, but not loud enough to be heard by the people at the tables. "It's not normal for us to get these many Chinese people."

"Maybe there's a convention in town or something," Tom said.

"Appealing only to Chinese?" Anthony said. "Funny. And don't think I don't realize they're all men, all relatively young, and more than a few of them tatted up."

"Yeah, and...? Anthony, I just got here. I don't know what you're insinuating, but I didn't conjure these people up out of nowhere. I don't know who they are." Okay, that was a lie, because he could know who they were, and very easily too. All he had to do was concentrate and he could be in any of their heads, looking out through their eyes. Momentarily, without meaning to, he was in the head of a young man with a Chinese character tattooed on his forehead, and he saw himself, obviously upset, talking to the cook behind the counter. And Tom realized he'd put on his leather jacket before leaving the house, and forgotten to take it off when putting on his apron.

He now removed it, and Anthony's look said, "See? I can tell you're rattled." But what Anthony said aloud was, "You guys were helping Rafiel with something, and it's no use at all telling me this isn't blowback because I know about triads." He huffed. "I know there are triads in town. Some of my relatives...You know I have relatives everywhere, and some of them have talked about triads and Chinese drug dealers, and look, Tom, if Rafiel was undercover it had to have something to do with drug trafficking."

"Not that I know of," Tom said. He thought back on what they'd actually helped Rafiel with, and thought it would actually be nice if that had something to do with the triads, because it would give them only one problem to solve. Unfortunately he was fairly sure that was its own problem and something quite different.

"I don't think this is related to Rafiel at all," he said, putting conviction into the words.

Anthony's dark eyebrows went further up. "Whatever, Tom, I just want you to know...Well, I have a lot of family in town." He paused and looked slightly puzzled, as though he weren't absolutely sure if he was happy about it, as he repeated, "A lot of family. So, if things become ugly and you need help, you know my number. And I don't mean just help at waiting tables or manning the fryer."

"No problem," Tom said, and tried to say it casually and not show he was far more touched than he could show. Anthony didn't even know who or what Tom was. Not really. But he could sense something was wrong, and, despite the fact that, over the year that Anthony had worked for Tom, Tom had been a troublesome boss, irregular about the hours, and strange about changing equipment, Anthony was ready to come to Tom's rescue, in something that might involve a confrontation with criminals.

I don't deserve this, Tom thought, and it occurred to him that it applied just as well to the unfortunate fact of being the Great Sky Dragon's heir, as to Anthony's loyalty. He didn't deserve any of it, but he was glad he didn't have to have one without the other. He looked over at Anthony, "Thank you," he said. "Really."

Anthony flashed him a smile, and punched him on the upper arm, "Hey, what are friends for? If things get ugly, call me. My uncle Pete...Well, you'll see. Very resourceful man, with tons of descendants and employees."

And then he was gone, ducking under the pass-through and out. And Tom's cell phone rang in his pocket. He fished for it, saw Rafiel's number, and almost swore under his breath. Instead, he turned it on, took it to his ear and said, "Yeah."

"We're coming over," Rafiel said.

"We?"

"Bea and I, and...well, two of my colleagues appear to be shifters."

"Two of—"

"Cas and Nick. We should have known, considering they're regulars, but— Never mind. We have information you have to hear. We'll be there in twenty minutes or so." And then, as though belatedly wondering, "Where are you?"

"Diner. Me, Kyrie, Conan, Old Joe."

"Old Joe?"

"He's sticking close," Tom said. "He tried to leave once, but I told him no, and either he thinks the orders apply forever, or he thinks that..." Tom's voice trailed off at the thought that Old Joe might be in as much risk as the rest of them. Or at least as the rest of his associates. He'd be at risk that the triads would capture him and keep him to make Tom obey. They'd gone for Kyrie first, but they might think that Old Joe—or the hapless Conan—was a better choice.

Tom looked around, locating each of the people who were associated with him in the triads' mind. Old Joe had slipped into the back booth. Tom would have to take him a plate of meat. That would keep him still until Tom could figure out what to do to keep him safe. Conan was cleaning a table and taking the order of one of the women who worked in the warehouse down the street. She was built like a tank, but for some reason that Tom couldn't put his finger on, he'd always thought she turned into a raccoon. She smelled shifter, but he'd never had the chance to see her shifted. On the other hand, she was a motherly woman and took an unusual amount of interest in the relationships between what she called the young people in the diner.

Right then, part of what she was telling Conan floated up to Tom, "Quite an extraordinary voice, my dear. You should make something of it."

Conan smiled delightedly and said, "I'm going to try. And now? What will you have?"

"Oh, the usual. And bring me a pot of coffee. I just can't seem to get awake today."

Tom had waited on her enough that he knew what her usual was. Nothing that involved him. Pie from the freezer, or perhaps fresh, since Laura usually baked in the late afternoon and did the prep work for the next morning. If it was frozen, Conan knew well enough to warm it and put on a dollop of cream before giving it to the woman, so he didn't need Tom. And Kyrie—

For a moment Tom panicked, not seeing Kyrie at any of the tables. Then he realized that was because she was standing by the counter, handing him a sheaf of orders. "Well, at least it's good for business," she told him.

He made a face as he went over the orders. First he piled a plate with gyro meat and told her, "Take this to Old Joe; that will keep him still. I have a weird feeling we're going to need his expertise."

"Expertise?" Kyrie said.

"What he understands about the old stuff," Tom said, and by way of explanation, "Rafiel and Bea and two of Rafiel's colleagues he said are shifters are coming over. They say there is something I must know."

Kyrie sighed. "Tonight is about to get really eventful, even by comparison to today, isn't it?"

He laughed, kissed her, and said, "Yeah. Yeah. I think so."

He'd started preparing the other orders, when someone cleared his throat from one of the bar stools on the other side of the counter. Tom turned around. It was James Stephens, a man with frowning brows and the sort of forbidding expression that would make you shy away from him if you met him in a dark corner. Like Tom he favored heavy work boots and a black leather jacket, but Tom had an idea he worked at the hospital and not, as it looked, in contract killing. He also knew that James was one of those people who often offered to wait tables, and it came to Tom, like a sudden flash, that he'd need backup waiters. He could see Jason Cordova in the annex, attending to a table. How was it possible, Tom wondered, that in a diner full of Asian men, Jason had managed to find the one table packed chock-full of Colorado University at Goldport co-eds? Well, at least one of them was Asian, but the other five were a perfect rainbow of colors. And all were giggling at Jason. Tom envied him heartily, then turned to James Stephens, who'd said, "I was wondering—"

"Yeah," Tom said. "If you want to wait tables, for some spare money or—" He stopped. He knew the man wasn't exactly well-off, but he always paid his bills, and when he volunteered to help, he volunteered to help and didn't ask for pay. Tom was the one who offered to pay him. "I mean," Tom said, "we could use some help with the tables tonight."

The dark eyebrows came down harder over the dark eyes. Tom had a vague memory of one of the man's cronies who identified himself as coming from some bar or other greeting James Stephens as "Dark Horse." The name seemed to apply now, to that ferociously scowling face, the eyebrows like dark wings over his eyes.

"What I mean," Tom said, "is that we're really going to need help tonight. It's quite possible that Kyrie and I will have to go out, and maybe even Conan, too, and there will be only Jason, and I . . . Well, I'll turn the fryer off, if Anthony can't be here, but the dinner hour rush doesn't seem to be stopping, and I think we'll need someone to help with the tables. We'll gladly pay the usual rate."

James dismissed the rate and the working with a wave of the hand. "Yeah. It's my night off. If you need me . . . sure. I can always use the money for horse feed. But that's not what I wanted to tell you."

Tom looked at him. "Uh...what did you want to tell me?"

"There's trouble, right? I can feel it. I just wanted to tell you that if it comes to trouble, you can always call me. I will do what I can. This diner is my home away from home. Sometimes I think it's the only home I really have."

Tom blinked. "Are you related to Anthony?"

"Anthony?" James said. "The cook? I don't think so. Why?"

"Never mind. I don't think...I mean, what kind of trouble do you expect?"

To his surprise, James didn't point to the tables near them, or to the Asian men who seemed to have come in for the express purpose of glaring at Tom all through the night. Instead, he frowned harder. "I can't tell you, right? When— I just know I can feel it, right? They say that horses can sense when there's a big storm coming, or an earthquake, or something. Well, they say it about all animals, even cats, but I know it's true with horses. It's kind of like that. I feel this prickling, crackling energy in the air, and the horse sense has kicked in, and I know there's going to be trouble. Big trouble. So I wanted to tell you, if there's trouble, call on me, right?"

"You're...a horse...?" Tom asked.

The eyebrows went lower over the eyes, until it looked like they'd have to merge with them and disappear, but then unexpectedly they climbed again, and the eyes beneath them sparked with mischief. "Not exactly. You'll see." He grinned at what must have been Tom's puzzled expression. "Now, let me grab that apron and start busing tables. And do you mean to burn that hamburger? I hope the customer wants it well done."

"We know where the Pearl of Heaven is," Rafiel said. If he'd said that he'd just found convincing proof of the zombie apocalypse, he couldn't have surprised Tom more. He'd installed Bea and the other two guys at the corner table with Old Joe, and come behind the counter to talk to Tom, which was as good a way to do it as any, since the diner was way too full to speak comfortably even at the corner table.

Tom registered that Bea was looking around scared at the crowd. He didn't blame her. She had as much reason to fear them as he did. Maybe more. The syringes to extract her eggs would be far bigger than anything they might poke into him.

He looked at Rafiel, as he pulled a batch of fries out of the oil and put them in the draining basket. "Bea told you it was missing?"

Rafiel nodded. "She told me the whole story. But I wasn't looking for the Pearl." He told Tom about going to the parking lot of Riverside to get his car, having forgotten that he'd lost the keys in the shift. How he'd had to call Cas and Nick and how, while waiting for them, they'd seen the suspicious movement.

When Rafiel got to the story of what he'd actually seen in the little cottage at the park, his voice grew thick. And then he backed up his narrative and told Tom about what had happened earlier, in the woods, about the creature having followed him, about the mating, about— "Sorry," he said, as his voice got pasty and strange. "Sorry. I don't know why I let it affect me so much."

Tom clicked his tongue on the roof of his mouth. He couldn't help it. "Rape victims usually do get upset," he said. He arranged plates, put them on the counter, rang the bell for people to pick them up.

Rafiel looked shocked. "I wasn't raped. I mean, I lost all control, but—"

"I think," Tom said, "you were ambushed and that pheromones, possibly pheromones released at will, were employed to make you lose control and the ability to think. I fail to see," he said, his mind on Kyrie's idea they would use rape drugs, "what the difference is between that and rape drugs." And then he thought maybe that's what the triad meant to use. Some form of pheromones he couldn't resist. He wondered if there was one such for dragons, the same as for lions, and thought probably there was, and wondered if he'd also lose all control. That would be bad. Very bad.

Rafiel sighed. "Maybe you're right. But if she set out to look for me..." He paused. "I wonder why."

"Well, I wonder why too," Tom said. "And I'm very afraid we'll end up finding out. Now, about the Pearl of Heaven—"

They gathered in the storage room. Tom and Kyrie, Bea, the three policemen, Old Joe. Conan did not join them, because he said someone needed to stay out and keep an eye on things. "I'll man the fryer too," he told Tom, "but I don't feel quite comfortable with all of them out there." He ducked behind the counter, when Tom had called him, and spoke in the sort of loud whisper mostly drowned out by the sound of the fryer.

Tom said, "What if there's anything I need you to help us with?"

Conan looked up. Something in his expression gave Tom the idea that Conan didn't know what he could possibly help with. Tom wondered if all the loyalty had gone out of Conan on realizing that, no, Tom couldn't put dragon shifters before everyone else. Tom didn't think so. Surely Conan was the last person to think that you should follow your preordained path in life, just because you were born something or other. Surely. But there was no getting around that Conan seemed miserable.

He appeared to notice Tom's expression, because he smiled a little and shook his head. "It's just that I thought Rya would be here," he said. "I am not paying a lot of attention to her, what with—"

Tom almost laughed at the mundane concern. It seemed so sane, so reassuring. He patted Conan on the shoulder. "I don't think Rya is going to throw you over just because you're kind of busy and aren't fawning on her."

"No, that's not it," Conan said. "Something feels . . . off."

That Tom could agree with. Perhaps it was that sense of a storm gathering that James Stephens had mentioned. Perhaps it was the sense of something approaching. After all, they had many odd senses because of their condition. Why wouldn't this be one of them?

All he could say, as they all gathered in the storage room, was that something was very definitely off. Really, he and Kyrie should have chairs here, and maybe a sofa, or a sleeper. He thought of the inflatable mattresses they'd brought and put in the back of one of the vans, in case they needed to sleep somewhere they wouldn't be easily found by the triads. He had a crawling feeling at the back of his neck, a cold feeling in the pit of his stomach, a certainty that they would be sleeping very little if at all tonight. Because a storm was gathering.

And just as he reached that point in his thoughts, a thunderclap shook the whole diner.

Everyone jumped, and Tom thought maybe it was this electrical feel in the air. But somehow, he knew it wasn't. Somehow, even as the rain came crashing in waves upon the flat roof of the diner, he could feel the other, bigger storm still gathering and growing, like a wave climbing ever taller before it must fall.

"It needed only that," Rafiel said, looking up.

But Old Joe narrowed his eyes, and looked at Tom and said, "So, you can't fly, dragon boy, and you must drive, but you must go get Pearl of Heaven. Pearl of Heaven is yours, not Maduh. You must get Pearl from Maduh. Pearl is only artifact left. In the whole world, only artifact left. And if people from the stars are coming, someone must know how to lock gates." He thought about it a while. "You're our only hope."

Tom did a double take, then looked up at Rafiel, trying to silently ask if there was any way that Old Joe had ever watched the movie. All he got in response was a shrug.

"So this person is Maduh?" Tom asked. "And she's a shifter?"

"She's a sabertooth tiger. Like Dante. Dante's mate."

Tom, conscious of having killed Dante, wondered if Maduh knew this, if the whole thing was some kind of deranged revenge, and he felt a great wish that this revenge and counterrevenge would stop. How could they stop the killing among shifters, the killing of shifter by shifter, and the killing of humans by shifters, if all it did was start a chain of vendettas, because shifters were loyal to their own kind and only their own kind?

He didn't realize he had said anything aloud until he saw the two policemen, Nick and Cas exchange a look, and then Cas said soothingly, "It's just human tribalism. It's not even a characteristic of shifters. You just feel safer around your own kind, of course, and from there to caring only about them is a step. Peace. I'm not defending it, I'm only stating that it is a normal human characteristic. We're no more guilty of it than anyone else. And, truth be told, no more immune."

"Yes, but . . . It's going to kill us all, it's going to reveal us and destroy us, if we don't defeat it," Tom said.

Rafiel just inclined his head, but Old Joe said, "No, it's going to kill all humans. And everyone on Earth. They will come through, and they don't like fleshy bodies." He thought about it a moment, then said, "Not even plant bodies."

Tom groaned, and midgroan—even as, above, the rain redoubled in intensity, in the way that Colorado rains did, coming out of nowhere and turning into a deluge—he felt something.

It was . . . like the smell of ozone in the air after rain, like the foreshock of an earthquake, only what Tom felt was . . . something moving in his mind. Something . . .

He got a feeling it was a stirring of the Great Sky Dragon, as though the ancient creature were wakening or coming to life. And he remembered their conference at the Three Luck Dragon. If it was true that the Great Sky Dragon was wakening, that what Tom sensed in his mind was like the first grope of a sleeper towards awakening, then it was bad news. He remembered the idea that the killing of the Great Sky Dragon had hinged on bringing him back unable to shift, and then forcing him—somehow—to open the world gates using the Pearl of Heaven.

Almost in self-defense, against the hair rising on the nape of his neck, against the tightening of his muscles, Tom said, "But Maduh—if this is her—said that the Great Sky Dragon wouldn't be able to open the world gates, right?"

"No," Rafiel said. "The . . . things, told her that they couldn't show her how to activate the Pearl of Heaven and also that the . . . old dragon wouldn't be able to do what she wanted, that he had never managed to use the Pearl of Heaven to activate the deeper knowledge. We knew that."

Old Joe had been on the outskirts, but now pushed his way to the center of the circle, hands flailing in agitation, "Can still open world gates. Yes, we knew old dragon, daddy dragon never came into full power. I think he thinks he did, but the artifact working on his dragon egg only released dragon knowledge, not all knowledge. He's strong in dragon knowledge, but not . . . not what he could be. But"—the hands fluttered up and wavered in the air—"but still strong enough to open the world gates. And you can't let him open the world gates. He's wakening, dragon boy. He's wakening. How do you stop him opening the world gates?"

"I have to find him," Tom said.

"You have to get the Pearl," Old Joe said. "It will help you find the old one. It will."

Tom couldn't see how. He said, "I can feel him stirring, too. I can feel him wakening. Shouldn't I get to him first, while someone else gets the Pearl of Heaven?"

There was a short, ghastly silence, and then Bea said, "Like whom? I'm sorry, but you shouldn't volunteer if you haven't seen the creature, and if you've seen the creature . . . She has twice defeated Rafiel. She seems to have some sort of control—perhaps mind control—though it might be only pheromones—"

"Dante, her mate according to Old Joe," Kyrie said slowly, "could project illusions. He used them to entrap us."

"Against that, which of us can do anything?"

"I can," Tom said, "I think."

"Like hell you're going alone," Kyrie said.

And Tom felt both exasperation and gratitude, because when it came to that, he didn't want to go alone, but the last thing, the very last thing he wanted was to put Kyrie into danger.

"We could all go," Rafiel said.

At that moment someone knocked at the door. Tom called through it, aware that to just about anyone not in their curious fraternity, this gathering in the storage room would seem very weird, if not a reason for the police to search the room for illegal substances.

"It's Conan," the answer came, and it sounded like Conan, but not like Conan's normal voice.

Tom opened the door to a white-faced, trembling Conan. "It's Rya," he said. "Someone has taken Rya. Her father just called. She was supposed to be here. She left hours ago, but her father says..." Conan paused, and looked around at all their faces. "They called him, see? They told him that they took her, that unless I pressure you...they will kill her.".

Did the triad really think they could get what they wanted to happen by kidnapping first one, then another of Tom's associates? Rafiel shook his head. "This is crazy. I guess we'll have to talk to her father and figure out where she was taken. We don't know if it was the triad—"

"It *was* the triad," Tom said, and Rafiel looked at him, because Tom spoke with unusual authority and also in a tone of great distaste. "They hired common thugs to do it, but they are behind it, and it is absolutely certain that they can get me to do what they want. They warned me it would happen. And they packed the diner"—he shook his head—"to make sure I reacted properly. It seems insane, but it isn't, of course. It is an attempt to make me fall into line, to make me behave as a Great Sky Dragon that they can understand."

Rafiel could even see it. Sort of. "We still have to go talk to her father," he said "and figure out how—"

"Yes," Cas said.

"I'm coming with you," Conan said, and glared.

Cas looked at Rafiel and Rafiel sighed. He was the senior

officer in the department, and though that came with absolutely no authority, people still tended to consult him. The fact that he came from three generations of Goldport policemen also contributed to the effect. "It's a bad idea," he said gently to Conan. Unlike Cas and Nick, Rafiel knew something of Conan—together they'd been involved in a very big fight against a very scary threat before, and Rafiel was aware that convincing Conan to stay home and wait for his girlfriend to be returned to him was not very likely. The young singer's defining quality was loyalty, and after Tom, Rya was probably the person to whom Conan thought he owed the greatest duty.

But if it were possible at all to convince Conan to stay safe, gentleness and logic would work better than ordering him to stay out. "You'll get in the way of the trained professionals, Conan. Let us do this. We'll call you if we need you."

But Conan's lips went thin; his eyes went mutinous. "You can't keep me out. And besides, while I might not be trained, I am the only one among you who fully understands the triads. If Tom leaves, they might follow. No, they will probably follow. And they'll keep ahead of him, and move Rya accordingly. But if I go with you, they're not likely to think much. They don't think of me as a threat, or as someone who will act without Tom." He smiled wryly. It was a smile without any joy. "Particularly if you handcuff me, and I do a perp walk, and Tom leaks something in the diner about you suspecting me of kidnapping Rya. In fact, that will probably throw them. They'd never understand my agreeing to be shamed like that in front of everyone, so they'll think you really suspect me. They'll go into a panic, probably try to talk it out with Tom, thinking their plan failed. In the end, they'll be so confused that we can look for her without interference." He looked at Tom. "Can you give us details on what these... non-triad people look like? Any names?"

"I get the name Mike Miller," Tom said, "and the impression he is a tall, blond man. He might live in the general area around the Founder's Museum. By the way, I think they're the same people who kidnapped Kyrie—properly chastised—perhaps the triads don't know anyone else who'd do this? So, if you ask at the Tomahawk, someone should be able to give you directions."

"Got it," Rafiel said. "Nick, you go to the Tomahawk. I'll take Cas with me, since we're apparently pretending to arrest Conan."

Nick got up, snapped a mock salute.

Rafiel looked towards Tom, "If you come up with anything else, call me, or have Kyrie or Bea call me, right?"

"Hey," Bea said. "You're not going into this—"

Rafiel turned and smiled at her. She looked concerned, worried for him. Her green eyes showed something like what his mother used to look like when he was very small and tried to do something difficult. As much as it touched his heart, now was the time to stop this. A police officer who has his girlfriend following him around trying to protect him is already doomed. If she was going to be his girlfriend, she was going to have to learn that it was normal to be worried about him, and that she couldn't protect him.

Certainly, if she was going to be his wife, she would have to learn that. It might be difficult for a girl who could turn into a dragon to realize that she couldn't fly over him, hovering, keeping him from harm, like a scaly guardian angel. But in the end the situation wasn't much different from the dozens of officers' marriages that Rafiel had seen ruined by wives who didn't get that you can't be a policeman and stay perfectly safe. "Now, Bea," he said, softly, "I appreciate your concern, but it's really impossible for you to come with me. You know it is. You'd add absolutely nothing to our or Rya's safety. All you'd do is make me worry about you."

She opened her mouth. He put his finger on it. "Yes, you're a dragon and perfectly able to take care of yourself, and if I need help, you're the first person I'll call. But this should be relatively easy. You know I face danger whenever I go to work. If—if we're going to be together, you'll have to get used to this."

He expected her to say something like "we're not going to be together." He'd flung the words out hesitantly, afraid she would say he was presuming too much, but instead she looked at him, her gaze filled with confusion, somewhere between annoyance and worry, somewhere between irritation and love.

He grinned; then leaning down he kissed her lightly on the lips. "You stay here and help Kyrie, and I swear I'll call if I need you."

Cas was already cuffing the hands that Conan willingly held out. As they left the storage room, Rafiel heard Bea draw a sharp breath and say, "The most infuriating man." And Kyrie's answer, "Isn't he?"

At this moment, with a potential alien invasion in the works, what Bea felt for Rafiel should not matter—and yet it did, as much as ever.

Looking resolute, Tom turned to Kyrie, and she knew what he was going to say. She'd heard it in Rafiel telling Bea to stay with her. Did the two men think they could order her to stay when Tom was about to run his head into danger in the most spectacular of ways?

It wasn't that Kyrie had any interest in getting herself in danger. Her feet hurt, and she was still very tired from her adventures, and she'd give just about everything to be safe in her bed and asleep. But it didn't work like that.

She and Tom were partners in the diner, in the house, and in life. She was the first to admit whatever it was that had happened to him, with this Great Sky Dragon affair, had left her discomfited and more than a little confused. She knew that he had something in his mind, something that Old Joe called the dragon egg. But it didn't matter. He was still Tom—additions or not. He was still essential to her happiness and well-being.

"Tom," she said, urgently. "If something happened to you . . ."

"Nothing will happen to me," Tom said. And then his glance showed the kind of wavering it got when he was having second thoughts, or considering that perhaps what he'd said might not be perfectly true. He said, "If something happens to me, chances are the Earth as a whole won't last much longer."

"Only fleshy things on Earth," Old Joe said, and clacked his teeth. "And plants."

"Yes, of course," Tom said. He turned a sudden, dazzling smile on Kyrie. "You see where that is a great relief. There is no way that you'll know for very long that I'm gone."

Kyrie found that her hand had somehow twined itself into the material of Tom's T-shirt, forming sort of a handle by which to pull him to her. "Tom, don't be an idiot," she said. "You can't go alone. If you go alone, and something happens to you, one way or another . . ." She paused. "Tom, I have gone through this once, where I thought you were dead and gone forever. Don't do this to me again."

"I have no intention of doing that, Kyrie. But truly, I can't have you with me. And we can't call Anthony back just yet. Chances are he isn't even home yet. And you know how worried I'll be if you're not around to man the fryer. Conan likely left it set to explode."

"The fryer doesn't have a setting to explode," Kyrie said.

"That's what you say," Tom said. He kissed her on the forehead. "Please, Kyrie. I don't think I can think of recovering the Pearl and what to do with you there, while worrying about you."

"So," Kyrie said, before she could think. She crossed her arms on her chest. "The little ladies are to stay behind and safe. Have you spent too much time with Rafiel? You know better. We've fought side by side."

And then it happened. Tom's face changed. Okay, not in any way she could easily describe, but the weight of centuries seemed to descend on his gaze, like the knowledge of ages before humanity could speak, much less write.

It seemed to take him as much by surprise as it took Kyrie. He frowned, then shook his head. "Yes, we've fought side by side, and yes, Kyrie, I know how well you can fight. But this time—this time—if Rafiel didn't lie in his story, and I don't think he did, then what is at stake is so immense, that if I lose there is going to need to be someone here to pick up the pieces."

She must have looked startled, or perhaps scared. It wasn't a reaction to Tom, of course—she couldn't imagine being scared of Tom. It was an instinctive reaction to the way his eyes looked, deep and dark and troubled, the blue looking like the depths of a stormy sea, a sea old as time and concealing cold, dark secrets.

"Do you think," he said, and his voice fell into careful cadences and exact pronunciation that betrayed an emotion that mere screaming and raging wouldn't have. "Do you think I wouldn't prefer to be with the guys right now, with Rafiel and Conan, looking for Rya? Do you think I'm not worried? The triad is my bailiwick. My lookout. Whether I want to think of dragonkind or not, dragonkind thinks of me first, and the only reason that Rya is involved in all this, is because Conan is my friend. I want to be there—setting that right. But I can feel the old Sky Dragon— the real Great Sky Dragon—stirring, and Kyrie, if I don't get to him, we are going to have those . . . things here. We're going to have them on Earth, and we'll have to fight them here. I don't know what you think they are. I'm not sure what I think they are. But if these projections feed off fear and pain, I don't want to see what the real deal invading aliens will feed on. And Old Joe's reassuring repetition that they hate all fleshy life including plants doesn't fill me with warm fuzzies either. And that's why you must stay behind, Kyrie. That's why you must remain safe. As safe as you can be in this.

"I don't know if I will win or lose, and I'm very afraid I'll lose, because we're up against terrible odds, and I might never be able to activate the Pearl of Heaven—even if Old Joe tells me I can. And if I activate it, I don't know if it can also be activated by the Great Sky Dragon afterward. I don't know if these are one-use artifacts." His hand lifted with the same kind of precise deliberation in his pronunciation of words. He let it rest on Kyrie's shoulder, just rest, barely closed, a caress more than a grasp. "Kyrie, it's entirely possible that unless I can steal the Pearl, run with it"—he grinned, recalling that he'd done that once before—"and keep away from the creature, from Maduh, until the Great Sky Dragon is himself again, she can manage to make the Great Sky Dragon open the gates, whether I activate the Pearl or not. And if that happens, if the creatures come upon the Earth, I count on you to save us all." He leaned forward and kissed her lips very lightly.

"But," Kyrie said, "Tom!"

"Yes?"

"How can I save the world? I'm just the manager of a diner. I'm just—"

"You're the only person I trust to do it," he said. And now the fingers squeezed, very lightly. And then he let go and looked at Old Joe who, Kyrie thought, looked terribly embarrassed, as though they'd been involved in some lewd display. Perhaps it was, Kyrie thought. After all, how many shifters had relationships? Good relationships? Sane ones?

Tom had his hand on the handle of the door to leave the storage room when Kyrie said, "Tom?"

He turned around again.

She didn't know what she was going to say, but his eyes were Tom's again, and she spoke in a rush to the Tom she knew, to the man she'd first met when the old diner owner had hired him from the homeless shelter down the street. Tom had looked streetwise, and she'd known he was addicted to heroine. The old owner had known it, and had told Kyrie about it. And she'd spent months fighting her attraction to him, telling herself that he was bad, that he would turn on her.

But in the end she had to give in, because Tom was Tom. He was caring, responsible...good. Tom was good through and through. And that brought the words pouring out of her mouth. The thought of that something else, the dragon's egg in Tom's mind, the thought of that thing—cold, ancient—the thought of it unleashed, permeating everything, touching all that was Tom, made Kyrie's blood run cold. "Tom," she said, and her voice was small and helpless, helpless as she'd never felt, not even when she was a foster child, shuffled from home to home, at the mercy of strangers and bureaucrats. "Tom." She swallowed because there were tears in her voice, and she didn't want to shed them. "I don't want you to— I don't want you to change. I don't want you to go. I don't want you to do anything with the Pearl and... and the stuff the dragon put in your head. I'm afraid it won't be *you* anymore. I'm afraid it will be like that sentence when I came in, and you said...you said it was something about being buried under the dragon. I'm afraid you'll be buried under the dragon—that Tom will disappear under the dragon. That the man I love will stop existing, taken over by...the dragons."

Tom looked at her. It was a long, intent look, and his eyes were his own: worried, overshadowed, carefully controlled. For the first time, she realized what it must feel like to him, that alien thing in his mind.

"Tom," she said again in a strangled voice. "I just want you to come back. I mean, *as you*."

He blinked at her, and she had the odd idea he was trying not to cry. But there were no tears, no water in his eyes. His hand rose again and cupped her face. It was a tender gesture, intimate. "I'll come back," he said. His voice was husky. "If I come back at all, Kyrie, I'll come back as me. For you."

And then he was gone, followed by Old Joe, who somehow gave the impression of an alligator's reptilian crawl, even while walking on two legs. Then the door closed behind Old Joe. She wondered if Tom would manage to get out of the diner unseen. She wondered if he really would come back.

A clap of thunder shook the building, like a bad omen, and she thought she'd best go and help make sure the fryer didn't explode.

Some people went out to fight ancient horrors. To others it was given to stay behind and make sure that fryers didn't blow up. "However small," she told herself, "I have my part to do." But it didn't feel small. Nor did the confidence Tom reposed in her—that she could save the world or some of the world if all else were lost—seem small. It seemed like he expected her, Atlaslike, to raise the weight of the world on her shoulders. And she wasn't sure she had the strength to even lift herself.

But she meant to try.

Rafiel walked out of the diner, and into pouring rain so close and heavy that all he could do was reach out and grab Conan's shoulder, to make sure he didn't lose him in the storm.

It wasn't, he thought, that he was afraid that Conan would run away, but he was afraid that the small Asian man would get lost in this mess and . . . And what? Drown?

But immediately after the facetious word, it came to Rafiel it wouldn't be that impossible. In the way of Colorado rains, sudden and violent, if it went on for more than a couple of hours, it would overwhelm the storm water system that was designed for no more than a trickle.

Rafiel remembered being five and going to school at a time when it had rained for a week, and the entire road had become a raging river. The school hadn't closed, but Rafiel's mom had held onto his hand very tightly, as they walked on the sidewalk, a few inches above the roaring water.

For just a moment, this cold torrent made him wonder if just maybe, it was an omen, if they were going to be fighting blind. Well, it wasn't going to be helpful. They couldn't have Conan fly above and find any landmarks.

They got inside the car by touch, Rafiel pushing Conan through the door he'd heard open. Inside, they sat in the car, streaming water.

"Take the handcuffs off," Conan said.

Rafiel looked at the diner. He was sure people were straining to see them, but the chances of their seeing inside his car, in this, were next to none. He reached across and removed the handcuffs. Both he and Conan looked like they'd stepped out of a shower.

He saw headlights come out, and from the flash of a white top, thought that Cas and Nick had put their top up, at least. That car must be good and soggy.

Conan pulled back at his streaming hair, and looked up at Rafiel. "We can't fly above and..."

"I can't anyway," Rafiel said. "At any time."

"No. But I can't either. Not in this. Once, Tom flew to Denver to see his father in the middle of a storm, and said he was almost at Pueblo before he realized he'd gone wrong. It's not...easy."

"So, we don't go above. Our challenge right now," Rafiel said, "is to stay on the road and find the motel."

They took off from the parking lot, the white SUV almost hydroplaning in the water already accumulated, and fishtailing madly as they hit the minor river that Pride Street had become. Rafiel was aware of the headlights of Cas and Nick's convertible ahead of him, and just hoped he wouldn't accidentally hit them.

"Well, no flying," Old Joe said, as they stood just outside the back door to the diner, under the tiny cantilevered overhang there. "Not in this. Not that I could, of course."

Tom's mind had gone instead to how convenient this downpour was. In the blind sheets of rain falling—something rarer in Colorado than a diamond in a sandbox—no one inside the diner would be able to see them leave. Even if they weren't distracted with the drama of Conan being dragged through the diner in handcuffs, which Tom was sure they were because Rafiel, Conan and the other two officers had waited outside the storage room door for Tom and Old Joe to come out. When they'd come out and turned towards the back, the officers walked Conan to the entrance to the corridor from the diner, very effectively blocking both sight and the chance of anyone coming back there and seeing Tom leave. They'd been reciting Conan's Miranda rights loudly as Tom and Old Joe got out the door.

But even with all this, Tom thought, even with the distraction, even with most diners—or all of them—concentrating on the Conan drama and not on what Tom was up to, it would be useless to get out stealthily if there had been good weather. Tom was not so stupid—nor did he imagine Jao was—that he wouldn't have a lookout flying above the diner.

Tom looked up, towards the slate-grey sky that lent its color to the upper layers of the deluge. It wouldn't last. It couldn't last. It rarely did. Colorado rains normally came in boring drizzles that went on for weeks or in sudden terrifying torrents that let floods down the canyons, but which did not last.

But for now, it gave them a hiding space. "It's a good thing," he said. "No one can see us leave."

"You don't want dragons in the way, as you find the . . . artifact?" Old Joe asked, as he and Tom stepped out into the sheets of rain. "You might need their help, dragon boy."

Tom nodded. "But not their interference with doing whatever needs to be done with the Pearl of Heaven, whatever you think I should do."

Old Joe clacked his teeth, in that laugh thing he did. "Yeah," he said. "I think you think right, dragon boy. We'll call them if we need them, but afterward. The problem with dragons is that they're stupid."

"Present company excepted," Tom said pleasantly. He'd been edging towards the white van in which they picked up supplies from the farmers' markets in the spring and summer, and Old Joe paused, looking at Tom, so close that Tom could see his face, greeny-brown eyes seemingly shining in the rain.

The eyes filled with mischief, and the teeth clacked. "I don't understand," he said, then grinned, a ghastly, broken-toothed grin, and said, "Just pulling your leg, dragon boy. I would not try to save you if you were stupid. But most dragons are. Reptile brain."

Tom refrained from telling Old Joe that alligators are reptiles, too, but as the old man started moving, weaving under the rain in a fair imitation of an alligator, Tom said, "Hey. We'll use this van."

Old Joe turned and clacked his teeth. "We will? Why not walk?"

"Not enough time," Tom said. "I can feel the Great Sky Dragon stirring. We must get to him before he's somehow forced to activate the gates."

Old Joe hesitated, then nodded.

But as he took the passenger seat in the van and let Tom buckle him in, he sighed, regretfully. "It's such lovely water," he said. "Not much water here anymore."

Tom wondered briefly about that "anymore." Had Old Joe come from warmer, wetter climes? Or had he been here since Colorado had been a warmer, wetter—and lower—clime?

There was no use asking. You got roundabout answers like "Before horses" and "When it was different." Tom had tried before.

It occurred to him, with a shiver, that if the spirit creatures truly were the ancestors of shifters, or perhaps of everything on Earth, and if they'd taken flesh on Earth and then shaped everything around them, then it was quite possible that when Old Joe was visiting Dinosaur Ridge, he was remembering old friends. It would be like normal old people visiting cemeteries.

Once more Tom felt as though he were leaning over the unfathomable possibility that he, himself, would live so close to forever as made no difference. It was rather like leaning over an abyss and finding out it was, in fact, bottomless.

He started the van and backed carefully out of the parking lot and into the alley. If anyone *were* following from above, they would be less likely to catch a glimpse of movement, of white, if the van followed the alley to the next major intersection. The alley was so narrow, looking down into it was difficult due to the buildings on either side and the occasional overhanging tree.

Once at the major intersection, their lights, their movement would get lost in the stream of other lights and movement.

"I guess," Tom told Old Joe, "you've been alive a long time?"

Old Joe was staring ahead. "You lose track," he said, "after a while. And anyway..." He stopped a long time and sighed. "Numbers. I never liked numbers."

"Did you come from the stars?" Tom asked.

This caused a chuckle, a clacking of teeth together, a shake of the head. "No. Not me. Earth-born me." Another long silence followed, and Tom looked to Old Joe, as they stopped at the end of the alley, waiting for a break to get into the flow of traffic again.

Old Joe had narrowed his eyes, as though he were trying to see something through the rain. But since he was looking at the buildings across the street—shuttered warehouses with blank brick facades—Tom guessed that he wasn't actually looking at much of anything but the past, or his own thoughts. Old Joe sighed, again. "It was a long time ago, but I knew some of the came-from-the-stars people." Another silence. "There was lovely girl, but she—"

A long break and another sigh. "It's all the same, you know, born from the stars, born wrong, Earth-born human. Shifter and human and all. We all learn to be human."

He pronounced human "hooman," which gave Tom a brief vision of Old Joe as a LOL-alligator, as he turned into the stream of traffic and tried to decide whether it would be easier or more difficult to take the highway up to the amusement park. "We are human," Tom said.

"Yes, that's what I said. Human nonshifters need to learn to be human too, like star-born, like wrong-born."

"Wrong-born?"

"When your mother and your father..." He sighed. "Like Maduh's child. When you mate in...not-human form. Then child born not-human form. Live longer. Spend more time animal. Take longer to learn to be human. But in the end must learn to be human. There is nothing else."

"There is animal," Tom said, genuinely puzzled, because he knew Old Joe spent a lot more time as an alligator than as a human, and seemed to enjoy it far more, possibly because alligators didn't have to wear clothes, wash or use silverware. Though once when he'd asked, Old Joe had told him that the problem was that human itched. Which Tom wasn't even about to parse.

In the silence, he saw, through the corner of his eye, Old Joe shake his head violently. "Animal is fun for shifter. It's like... playing. But you're always a little human, even in animal, when you learn to be human. You stay. And you enjoy being animal, but is playing. Being animal without being human is not... really being alive. It's...it's nothing. It's one day and another and another; it's doing wrong without knowing is wrong. It's not living."

"You're saying animals are not sentient?" Tom said. Then, realizing he might have outstripped Old Joe's English vocabulary—he often got the impression he should be having these discussions with the old man in ancient Egyptian or something—he said, "I mean, animals are not aware they're alive."

Old Joe shrugged, a movement Tom glimpsed as he started up the ramp onto the highway. "Don't know. Your cat boy, the Not Dinner one, might know he's alive. Don't know. Their brain is different. But shifter-born animal isn't right until he learns to be human."

"You mean, like the little feral, Maduh's son? The one who killed a lot of people around the amusement park?" It came to Tom that whether the young creature was pathetic or not, whether innocent or not in the sense that he didn't know he'd done anything wrong, Tom was heading towards his lair. He wondered if the creature would be a problem. What if Mom had left the feral cub guarding the Pearl of Heaven? What if she was guarding the Pearl of Heaven herself? What did Tom intend to do about that?

"Yeah," Old Joe said, though it had the feeling of repressing some other thought, some other words he was not going to say. "I worry a lot about him. I don't know what become of him." The sudden cackle and the clacking of teeth. "And I don't know what become of us, when we go up against him. He's likely to be guarding the Pearl. I don't want to kill innocent cub, but we might have to give him the sleep-death." He clacked teeth. "Because stupid doesn't mean not dangerous, and those in animal form who don't know human often are cunning, fast. Lethal."

"I was thinking the same," Tom said. The highway was relatively clear of water, at least most of its length, though a bit collected in the shallow bottom of hills. At least highways were built to shed water, even if old city streets and alleys seemed sometimes to be built to collect it. "I was thinking that we'd have to find a way to get him out of the way without hurting him."

"Without hurting?" Old Joe said. "I didn't say that. I don't think that is possible. We all hurt, dragon boy. Life is hurt. You know you're still alive because you still hurt. You're too soft. You're too kind. You've never had to face real. But real is there, and real hurts."

Tom started to open his mouth, to tell Old Joe that he knew *real* plenty. He had lived the life of a big city runaway, and even if, by shying away from most humans, by reason of his shifting, he'd never experienced most of this personally, he had seen all the varieties of what could go wrong, and how bad things could get.

But then he thought of the time since Old Joe had been young, the time since . . . Since dinosaurs? Since Colorado had been a subtropical wonderland?

He didn't want to know. There were things that he didn't want to know, even if he could. But he knew even without pinpointing the details, that Old Joe had to have seen more *real* than Tom could ever see. In a way, the life of modern man wasn't and couldn't be real. People had shelters from the rain, and antibiotics, and soft furniture. Even before one got to the internet, and cell phones and modern conveniences, even the most wretched of the big-city homeless would seem to someone—even a chieftain—of the Paleolithic as living so far in the lap of luxury as to be in paradise.

Old Joe cackled, as though realizing where Tom's mind had got him. A grubby hand reached out and patted Tom's arm. "Don't worry, dragon boy. Real comes to all of us, sooner or later. And until you find the courage to face it, you got me."

The rain was slackening a little as Tom saw the exit sign for Riverside. He looked to the sky, but saw no sign of dragons.

Rafiel saw the sign for the Tomahawk Motel, the cartoon Indian chief, bending forward under the rain, then straightening again, in a weird war dance, as now this, now that neon tube lit.

It had been one of the fun memories of Rafiel's childhood, a landmark on his way home from school in winter, past the early Rocky Mountains nightfall, or on his summer trips to the zoo with his parents, when they drove home after dark, with Rafiel tired and happy in the back seat. Seeing the Indian meant that his parents' house wasn't that far off and, early on, Rafiel had been enchanted by what seemed to be images made of pure light. Even getting older and being able to see the dull neon tubes that lit off and on hadn't killed the magic.

He turned, just past the Indian and up the graveled drive. Fortunately, he didn't need to see well to be able to drive to the cabin that housed the check-in and office. It wasn't as if every other day there wasn't some complaint that required the police to come here and talk to the manager. In fact, the night manager, whom they would be seeing right now, was almost an old friend, in the sense that friends are people you don't arrest even when you know that you really, really should. Also in the sense that friends are people whose character defects you have to put up with, because you can't change them. And the fact that they now and then sell a little blow on the side doesn't mean your relationship changes.

He gave a motion of the head to Conan, as he parked in front of the building. "You stay here," he said. "The window glass is bulletproof, so you'll be—"

"No. I'm coming." Conan looked stubborn. "I can take care of myself, Rafiel. For heaven's sakes, I can change into a dragon."

As if that were protection from anything, Rafiel thought. But he guessed before he embarked on that line of reasoning that it would be useless. Conan was worried about his girlfriend, and even if Rafiel could convince him that he would be less than useless in a fight, what would that do, other than make Conan even more desperate to prove he was not useless? Which in the end would probably only get him in greater danger.

He said, instead, "Fine, you can come out." And realized Nick was knocking at the window. Rafiel lowered it, and Nick's hand emerged from his sleeve, holding a smart phone, which he handed to Rafiel. "I looked up the description Tom gave us in the list of usual suspects, and this guy came up. Harry Rivers."

Rafiel looked at the picture of an unprepossessing young man with close-set eyes and a pimply face. "I see," he said. Very young. The story of Kyrie's escape from her captors came to him. Perhaps these were the only non-dragon thugs the dragons knew. Minor drug suppliers, he guessed, people the triad dealt with.

Perhaps their youth and stupid look meant that Rya wasn't in danger at all. Or perhaps she was in more danger. When it came to incompetent thugs, you never could tell.

Kyrie taught Bea to handle the fryer, to the extent of calling Kyrie when something went wrong. Jason and James seemed to have the waiting at tables under control. Particularly since half the triad members had left. Kyrie wondered if they'd left to follow Tom, and wondered why they would. She wondered what their cluttering the diner tables had meant, anyway. Did they really think that Tom was that easy to force into line? Or was there some other reason? Were they perhaps protecting him from something? Was that why half of them remained behind? But what could they be doing?

She couldn't answer any of the questions, and it would have looked like a perfectly normal day, except that everyone—the dragons and Jason, and James, and everyone in the place that she knew for sure were shifters, and Laura, who might be one— looked like they were tense.

It was, Kyrie thought, like when you were waiting for the phone to ring.

Which, of course, is when the phone rang. She picked it up and said, "The George, how may I—"

"We have the fox girl," a voice said, "and we will kill her, unless the Great Sky Dragon marries Bea Ryu and provides children for the dragon."

She opened her mouth to tell them that this was no way to get what they wanted out of Tom, that they were more likely to get what they wanted with a sob story, but they weren't likely to manage this even with the saddest story ever, because— But they had hung up.

She looked at the phone a few seconds. Then she looked around the diner and noted the feeling of tension in every back, the odd posture of everyone. No, this was not going to end well. As much as she wished to imagine that nothing bad could possibly happen, as much as she wished to believe that tonight would be like all other nights, she knew better.

She grabbed the phone again, dialed Anthony's number.

"Can you come in?" she asked.

He didn't even ask who it was. Doubtless he recognized her voice. And he didn't put in the token resistance he normally did, or say his wife would kill him. Instead, he said, his voice tight and full of feeling, "I knew it. I knew I'd be needed. I'll be right there."

The motel manager looked fifty, though Rafiel knew, from having had cause to look at the man's license in the past that he was only thirty-five. He was shorter than Rafiel—almost as short as Conan—with a ferrety face and untidy red hair that was going white in the way red hair sometimes did, by fading all over, like aluminum siding in the sun.

He stood behind a pale green counter that looked like a plastic structure with a Formica top trying to pretend to be marble. The only lamp still working was a fluorescent light in the ceiling, its fellows on either side completely dead, which was good, Rafiel thought. The lack of light prevented their seeing just how dirty the grey carpet was, and how the smudges on the wall might be blood or even more unsavory substances. Rafiel had been in there during the day, and he remembered how very difficult it was to avoid staring at those stains and trying to figure them out.

The manager looked at Rafiel out of strained eyes underlined by bruised, puffy skin. "There was no reason for me to stop them," he said. "Two guys with money, and well, they paid for a night, and what was I to do? Follow them to see if they had a woman with them?" A sudden unpleasant grin. "Think about it, that could be much better than the alternative! Not that I want to know. People pay for the cabins, and they're entitled to their cabins and I—"

Cas rushed in, telling the man that for once they didn't think he had done anything wrong, but did he remember this guy, and did he have his name and driver's license noted down anywhere?

Rafiel thought the chances were very high that it was a fake license, but what the heck, they had to at least try.

The manager came up with a name: Harry Rivers. After some deliberation and apparent trouble interpreting his own handwriting, he came up with an address on Sierra Avenue, about eight blocks away.

They jotted it down and left. Outside, they all clambered into the white SUV, out of the rain. In the back seat, Nick brought up the app that allowed them to look up addresses from the license number.

"What was that address again, Rafiel?"

"4530 Sierra, Building 5, Apartment 30b."

"What do you know?" Nick said.

"The same one?" Rafiel said.

"Maybe it's the true one," Cas said, leaning forward, his hand on the back of Conan's seat. Conan looked pale and terrified, and hadn't said a word. Rafiel hoped he wasn't working himself up to do something heroic or something stupid. He was fully aware that for Conan, the two would probably be one and the same.

"The guy is very young," Cas said. "Probably under twenty. I don't think it has occurred to him to use a fake license, not since he needed it to buy liquor. What's his record, Nick?"

Nick looked at his phone, then rapidly punched a few buttons. "Minor stuff," he said. "Really minor stuff. Shoplifting, some pot selling. No time served. Everything plea-bargained for fines and probation and rehabilitation programs."

"So kidnapping is new to him?" Rafiel asked, hoping it was so, hoping that for a change this would be an easy case, an easy rescue. "I wonder why he decided to try it?"

"I suspect," Nick said, "those dragons can be pretty convincing. One hears things."

"So, do we go there?" Conan asked. "Do we try it?"

Rafiel thought it would be a fool's errand. Even the dumber of henchmen wouldn't take a kidnapped wench home, right? Unless he was intending to kill her before she could be rescued and rat him out, and they really didn't seem the type.

On the one hand, all criminals were small criminals till one day they snapped and went big. On the other hand, where else could they start? If Harry wasn't home, perhaps someone at the place would give them another lead.

"Yeah," he said. "We might as well try it."

✧   ✧   ✧

Riverside Park looked even worse at night and under the pouring rain than it looked midafternoon in the merciless glare of the sun. No, Tom thought. That wasn't quite true. It didn't look bad exactly. You couldn't see the worn-out paint or the chipped walls, or the shabby appearance of many of the rides.

Mostly, though, it looked dark. There were some lights on. Tom thought they were the lights on the trees that lined the walkways. They were white and sparse, and seemed drowned under the downpour, like the lights in ships that have sunk, shining back at you out of the water. A wind had started up, or perhaps there was always a wind around here. There were places like that. Perhaps the wind gathered speed over the water. At any rate, it shook the lights, making them seem even smaller and more forlorn.

There were lights outlining the entrance tower, too, but it was empty, as it had been when Bea and Rafiel had gone in. Old Joe, just beside Tom, clacked his teeth at it, as though happy at this, but Tom thought that the park looked dark and forbidding and more like a house of horrors than a place of amusement.

Then he though that he only felt that way because of Bea and Rafiel's story, and, after ducking under the stile, he turned back to Old Joe, and whispered, "Maybe the Pearl is no longer where they saw it."

"Maybe not," Old Joe said. He grinned one of his ghastly grins, all broken teeth. "Maybe it is now where the Great Sky Bastard is. Daddy dragon," he added self-consciously, as though he were afraid of offending Tom. "Can you feel him?"

Tom started to shake his head, then his eyes opened wide. "Not exactly, but I can tell he is very close. How odd."

"Not odd at all," Old Joe said. "I'd say the park was where Maduh hides out, with her cub. Easy to have only one place to guard, yes?"

Tom didn't know. He'd never had any place to guard. Well, except The George and his greatest danger there was someone forgetting to turn off the fryer and causing it to explode. He concentrated on following the path to the cottage, as Bea and Rafiel had described.

When it appeared in front of him, looming dark and smelling funny, he looked at Old Joe, but the old alligator gave him a challenging look, as though asking if he didn't have the courage, then grinned. "We should shift, dragon boy. There will be a battle."

"Maduh?"

"More likely her cub, but all the same. You say he's eaten shifters before..."

Tom tried to remember the doglike creature, running with Rafiel after him. No match for a dragon.

Self-conscious and feeling more than a little strange at undressing before going into danger, Tom took his clothes off and folded them carefully. He'd gotten killed in his good leather jacket before, and he had no intention of letting it happen again.

He told his body to shift, even if it was difficult under the rain and with no moonlight to help, but he forced it, forced his body to twist and writhe, ignoring the pain as he shifted into his dragon form.

At the same time, he sensed into the cottage. Not feeling for anyone in particular, but for that thing—the warm glow he'd once stolen for its calming influence—the Pearl of Heaven. And he could feel it, he realized. It was in the cottage. That meant...

A scruffy dog-bear creature came screaming out of the cottage, making a sound like baying and growling combined. Tom felt his impact midbody, sharp claws tearing at his sensitive left wing. He reacted by instinct and backhanded the creature with a powerful paw.

The little feral—Tom's human side knew it—went flying through the air, and even before he hit the wall of the cottage with a sickening crunch, Tom was shifting—willfully shifting himself back to human, putting his clothes on quickly. A dragon was much too conspicuous a form. If the creature's mother came— If that baying had been an alarm—

"I didn't kill him!" he told Old Joe, more in hope than in any certainty. "Surely I didn't kill him?"

Old Joe in human form was bending over the kid, feeling the side of the neck. "No," he said. Then, "We should kill him now. Maduh will smell his distress or feel his mind. If we kill him—"

Tom remembered the young creature. He remembered what Old Joe had said about being born in another form. You wouldn't know good from evil, then. You'd barely know good. He couldn't kill the kid. It was a kid, even though it might very well be older than Tom. "No," he said. "No. Don't kill it."

He went into the dark cottage, and looked around. It was dark, but not so dark he couldn't distinguish a pile of what looked like broken stuff—a counter and a bunch of chairs. But his feeling of the Pearl guided him unerringly.

It called to him, as concrete and clear as if it were smell or sight or another of his senses. He scrabbled at the floorboard in the middle of the structure. It was loose and came up easily.

Beneath it, the Pearl of Heaven glowed. It glowed as though sensing him. It glowed with a soft, white light, very gentle, like a mother's kiss, like...like peace, like the promise of perfection.

Tom smiled, remembering the first time he'd seen it, and how he was sure it would be able to save him from himself. Was this personal? Was it responding to him? Or was it something it did for everyone? He remembered Rafiel saying something about making it glow being the easy part.

He started to reach down for it, then thought that he would have no more clue what to do with it than he had more than a year ago. But Old Joe knew what to do. And also, if Tom left Old Joe out there much longer with that feral kid...Well, sometimes he thought Old Joe wasn't very far from feral himself. He might very well decide the kid was a snack. Or, more likely and ruthlessly, that he was less trouble dead than alive. He'd tell Tom it had all been a horrible accident, and that it didn't matter. Even with the kid's blood around his mouth.

So Tom found a piece of rope. It was sitting on the floor, and it was very thick, if somewhat ratty. It looked like the type of rope used to tie down boats, and it had probably been used for just that, with the little pleasure row-and-pedal boats for rent in the lake in the summer.

Tom took it out to Old Joe, who was looking at the unconscious feral shifter with the sort of speculative look someone might give a burger. Tom noted that the feral shifter remained in animal form, which was odd, since when you lost consciousness and control, you defaulted to your natural form. Then he remembered what Old Joe had said about being born shifted, if you were conceived shifted, and he felt slightly ill.

They bound the creature's paws in the style commonly referred to as "hogtie."

All the while, Tom could feel the Pearl of Heaven calling him.

The apartment building turned out to be one of a series, set within something that might, once upon a time, have been a park. The first thought Rafiel had was that even on Sierra Avenue, which had its rough patches, you didn't normally see true squalor this close to a main thoroughfare. Up the street, restaurants were open, and across the street an old theater converted into a bar did a brisk business.

But here . . .

From outside, you shouldn't have been able to tell there was something very wrong with the apartment complex. They were just buildings made of brick, tall, rambling-looking.

But there were unsettling details. Like the door being open, light spilling out, and the number of people walking by with barely-contained large dogs on leashes—even under the pouring rain.

Closer up, it was weird to note that there were no numbers on the buildings. And that the door frame and the doors themselves looked worm-eaten battered. They looked like they'd been standing for centuries—an impossibility—without a coat of paint or any maintenance.

Getting out of the cars, they noted that several of the people with dogs looked extremely interested. Nick grimaced, visible in the light of door. "Damn, we should have known better than to bring the convertible."

"I'm surprised we never made an arrest here," Rafiel said.

"You haven't?" Cas said. "Gee, they must send us juniors here. Battered children on the right, domestic disputes on the left, and straight ahead what I presume is the largest meth ring in the country, spread over nineteen apartments. What was the address again?"

Rafiel told him. "Right. That's on the left, fifth floor."

They walked past three open dumpsters exuding an unpleasant smell of rot, and past an incongruous group of children playing outside in the pouring rain, jumping into puddles and shrieking. At night? Where were their mothers?

The door stood open, as it had stood on the other building, and inside it looked like a normal apartment building that had come seriously down in the world. Though from the design and the way things looked, Rafiel guessed it had been built in the seventies, the building managed to convey the impression of sagging under its own age. The floor shook and creaked under their steps. The walls looked like they'd been mended many times, with whatever was at hand. Most of it was still plaster, or at least wallboard, but there were patches of mildewy molding and bits of fake tileboard nailed up, and further on, something that looked like Victorian wallpaper, slapped in a vast, irregular patch on the wall where, underneath, a long vertical crack was still visible.

"I don't think we should go in this way," Conan said.

"What do you mean?" Rafiel asked.

Conan started shaking lightly. "It's on the fifth floor. I'll fly." He made a gesture towards the outside of the building and up.

Rafiel looked around, at a man edging down the hallway, with a large—bulldog? part dragon?—on a leash, and thought that he'd better get Conan out of a place where he might be overheard. He said, "Uh, okay."

"If we go in this way," Conan said, very sure of himself, "they'll take her out the window."

At that, he might have a point. Rafiel made a head gesture to Nick and Cas, signaling they should go on up. "Don't knock. Just wait till they try to come out."

Outside, the rain had stopped, and Conan undressed, then started to writhe and cough, in shape-shifting mode.

At the last moment, Rafiel thought of something and said, "How will you know which window is the right one?"

Conan, his mouth already an odd shape, spoke indistinctly, "I'll look at all the windows," he said, "on the fifth floor."

Rafiel wished he could tell him not to do that, but from the numbers he'd seen on doors on the bottom floor, there was no rhyme or reason to the numbering scheme and the window could be anywhere. He groaned and said, "Try not to be seen."

Conan, already a red dragon, nodded.

Rafiel hoped the people inside were tripping so hard that they didn't figure out that, for once, the dragon was real.

"Reach in, like so," Old Joe said.

Tom couldn't see anything. He couldn't even see the gesture Old Joe made. He was holding the Pearl of Heaven in his hands, its glow brighter than ever in his eyes. But he felt as though Old Joe had reached into Tom's mind. No, not quite that. But as though Old Joe had touched Tom's mind and was now guiding it, like an adult with his hand over the child's hand, guiding a pen across the paper. Only what he was guiding was Tom's *mind* to feel—to explore—the entire surface of the Pearl. Odd, to Tom it seemed like this surface wasn't smooth at all, but a network of patches and places that looked like buttons or perhaps hot spots.

"How do you know how to do this?" Tom asked.

"My mother," Old Joe said. "Great one of alligators. Great one of all reptiles not dragons. She had something like it. Jade. I saw her activate it. I could feel what she did. I couldn't do it, but I could feel." He made a sound like an admission of failure. "I might slip. I don't know precisely."

His mind was firm in orienting Tom's as Tom's awareness explored the patches. It was much like, he thought, running your mouse across active content on the screen, and seeing the label pop up. Not that a text label popped up. But he could feel what *this* area did, what that one affected. And there, in the center he found the area that throbbed like a migraine, and which felt like it somehow reached into him, even as he reached into it.

He pushed. It was like pushing the surface of the Pearl open, causing it to peel away and then . . . And then it engulfed him.

Tom would never be able to fully explain the sensation, but it was like falling, headfirst, into rushing water, or like entering a completely different world, or perhaps like changing completely, inside and out. The light of the Pearl seemed to shine inside him, taking him over. It was more than an illusion. He could see his hands glowing pearly-white as they rested on the Pearl of Heaven. Old Joe gasped an "Ah, yes."

And then the thing that Old Joe called "dragon egg" within Tom exploded. It exploded outward—knowledge, thoughts, language, all running through Tom's mind, uncontrolled.

He thought, *I promised Kyrie that I would come back unchanged.*

And then he collapsed under a torrent of ideas and feelings too strange to endure.

As far as Rafiel was concerned, the night became a cacophony of screams. There were female screams, male screams, and the shrill screams of children, all preceded and followed by the barking of dogs and high wailing of cats.

Apparently there were people in this horrible place sober enough to recognize when a dragon looked in their windows. Fortunately, as the windows began to be thrown open, Conan found his mark. He kicked a window in. There was a different kind of scream.

Just as Rafiel had changed his internal pleading to *Please let him not bite anyone to death*, Conan exploded out the window with a girl held in his forepaws. Rya, Rafiel supposed, though it was hard to tell as she appeared to be unconscious. *Please let her not be dead. At least not permanently.*

Behind Conan, orange flames shone inside the room, and then—seconds later—billows of smoke.

Oh hell, he set fire to the room. This whole place will go like tinder. Rafiel dialed 9-1-1 reflexively. Minutes later, he saw two very odd-looking young thugs come running out of the building. Very odd, as most of their hair appeared to have burned away, and so had most of their clothes. They were followed by the casually strolling Cas and Nick.

In the distance, sirens started up.

Conan landed next to Rafiel. Men with dogs started approaching, then looked uncertainly at the dragon and stopped.

Conan handed the girl to Rafiel. It was Rya, and she was unconscious, which, Rafiel reminded himself, was better than dead. Rafiel picked her up, reflecting on how light people could feel heavy when entirely unconscious, and lay her on the back of the car. By that time, Conan had managed to return both shifted into human and dressed. He climbed into the passenger seat, looking exhausted, and said, "Let's get out of here before the firemen... Let's go to someone's house."

Nick was on the driver's side, as Rafiel got in. "My house. Follow me. We didn't prevent the perps from running, so much as we made them stop, drop and roll." He grinned. "No lasting damage, I think, but they'll learn not to mess with dragons' girlfriends. Hell, they might go honest from now on."

Rafiel hesitated as he started his car. "We should be reporting the kidnapping. I know how tricky it is, but—"

"No," Nick said. "Are you mad? You straights aren't very good with hiding things, are you? Do you want to explain the whole thing? Including the dragon?"

"No."

"Good, then follow me."

They made it out of the parking lot just ahead of the fire trucks entering it.

Tom woke up. For a long and strange moment, he wasn't sure who he was, or even where he was. He certainly couldn't remember going to sleep, and from the way his head throbbed, he wasn't sure he had.

He could smell blood, and his wrists hurt, and he felt vaguely queasy.

Then he remembered that he and Old Joe had been...in Riverside Park, with the Pearl of Heaven. He remembered the Pearl of Heaven suffusing and permeating his being. He thought—

"Joe?" he said. No one answered. There was an odd smell of blood in the air. With great effort, Tom opened his eyes. The first thing facing him was the baleful eye of an alligator. He thought *Old Joe* and that Joe didn't look right. Then he managed to bring his eyes fully open and stared.

He closed them. It had to be a nightmare. It couldn't be true. No one—*no one*—would want to kill Old Joe, certainly not by ripping him apart limb from limb. Not by splitting his skull and removing his brain.

But when Tom opened his eyes, the alligator was still there. There was no lying to himself that this wasn't Old Joe, either. He'd known the old shifter long enough to know which teeth were broken, and the exact pattern of the scales. Even in the dim light, he knew it was Old Joe's corpse he was looking at.

Grief and horror caught in his mind, paralyzing it, mingling with the throbbing pain at the back of his head. He wanted to throw up, he wanted to cry, and he wanted to be elsewhere, where Old Joe was still alive, and where he'd make that teeth-clacking sound and call Tom "dragon boy."

And then Tom realized that overlaying all of this was the feel of the Great Sky Dragon nearby, very awake. And then, closer at hand, someone breathing.

He saw feet in shoes, beyond Old Joe's corpse, by a piece of Joe's mutilated foot. He swallowed, hard. He looked up.

She was blond and beautiful and—he remembered Rafiel's description—had the sort of widely separated eyes and broad, clear forehead that the Renaissance had praised.

She was looking at him with unblinking eyes, somewhere between gloating and anger. "You were very clever, coming in here while I was busy with your ancestor. But your luck is at an end. Stand."

Tom wouldn't have been able to obey, but the feral shifter was near him, naked and filthy and with completely inhuman eyes, reaching for Tom, helping him up, then tugging on his hands—his hands were tied together behind his back—and leading him, dumbly stumbling and dragging after the woman. Was this Maduh? It had to be Maduh. She'd killed Old Joe, or perhaps let her son kill him. What they'd done to him... They really didn't want Old Joe coming back.

She'd stunned Tom with a blow, while he was concentrating on the Pearl. She—

It was then he realized that Old Joe's corpse was an alligator. You always reverted to your true form when you died.

No wonder the old man had had trouble with his human form and with living indoors. And yet—

Tom remembered Old Joe talking about how everyone had to learn to be human anyway. And he'd learned. Old Joe, whatever he'd been born, had been human.

A lump caught at Tom's throat, and he felt tears run down his cheeks and wished he could wipe them away.

Nick's place was half of a duplex in what had been a suburb of Goldport back in the fifties. Now it was close enough to downtown to be considered a walking neighborhood, with easy access to museums and restaurants.

Nick opened the door, turned on the light, and turned to admit them: Rafiel, Cas and Conan, who had insisted on carrying Rya, despite staggering under her weight.

Inside, the house had clearly been modified to accommodate more modern living. They entered a vast space that comprised a living room, dining room and an open kitchen at the end. The walls were a cream color that seemed weirdly rich. There were curtains and two dark leather sofas.

Nick directed Conan to one of them, and Conan laid Rya down on it.

"Is she hurt?" Rafiel asked, and felt stupid for asking. Of course, she was hurt. But Conan shook his head. "No. Tranquilizer dart. Still in her arm when I picked her up."

"Oh. Same thing they did to Kyrie," Rafiel said.

"Yeah. She'll probably be fine. We heal fast." He still looked very upset. He gave Rafiel a shaky smile. "I don't think of myself as a fighter. I...I like to sing. But...they upset me very much. I thought I was going to eat them."

"I thought you were going to eat them too," Rafiel confessed, sitting on the sofa in front of Rya. He was relieved that Conan hadn't.

"Coffee, whiskey, beer, eggs, bacon?" Nick asked.

Conan opened his mouth. Rafiel could see him considering saying that he was fine, really, but what came out was a small moan. "I'm so hungry I could eat someone."

"I figured," Nick said. "Just remember it's bad manners to eat your friends, and if you eat your girlfriend... Well, that's between you and her."

"Huh?"

Rafiel bit his lip. Nick would have to be pulled aside at some point and told that Conan wasn't likely to understand most racy jokes. While he hadn't been raised in a monastery, he'd been raised in the Great Sky Dragon's service, and that might be similar in its way.

Nick disappeared into the kitchen. Doors opened and closed, and shortly there was the smell of eggs and bacon and then the smell of coffee.

Moments later, Rya sighed and opened her eyes. She looked around, bewildered, then looked at Conan.

Someday, Rafiel wanted to have some girl look at him that way. Her eyes widened and filled with joy, as though Conan were the best and most wonderful sight she could behold. Rafiel realized it was Bea that he wanted to look at him that way.

"You saved me from those— They shot me... But you..." Rya said. And Conan seemed to grow at least a foot, as he hurried to her side.

Just before they reached the dragon ride—a sort of roller coaster with covered carts, whose designers had counted on the sense of disorientation of the passengers to make the ride seem far more exciting than a circular, up-and-down track (for in the dark everything seemed longer and more convoluted)—Tom realized that this was where the Great Sky Dragon was, and knew a full measure of regret and shame. He'd known the ride was here. He'd heard of it, even if he and Kyrie didn't have much time for amusement parks and had never actually come to the park for the rides.

But what else could "I am buried beneath the dragon" be? Tom had been an idiot. A blind idiot, at that. He should have known.

He should have guessed. He should have, long ago, stolen the Great Sky Dragon back and—

But he probably would have been captured trying to rescue the Great Sky Dragon, just as he'd been captured activating the Pearl of Heaven. And it hadn't even done anything. All that knowledge, the dragon egg with its carefully nestled, compacted files, had been allowed to open, to pour out, but it had poured out of his head altogether. He no longer had the knowledge, or the feel. Perhaps it was the result of the Great Sky Dragon waking? Perhaps all it meant was that Tom was no longer the Great Sky Dragon.

It should have been a relief but it wasn't. The real Great Sky Dragon was recovering from being . . . dead, which meant he couldn't shift for a day or more. And in that time, he was human, and all too vulnerable.

Numbly, Tom watched the blond woman open the trap door to the side of the ride. He saw stairs, but he wasn't given a chance to descend them normally. Instead, he was pushed, and landed in a heap at the bottom of the stairs.

He was in a small, circular chamber. There were gears and things above. This must be how the maintenance crews accessed the ride to fix it.

The Great Sky Dragon lay trussed in a corner of the chamber.

But Tom wasn't as completely bound. All that was tied were his hands, behind his back. In a hundred shows watched in his childhood, in a hundred books read, even in games he'd played, Tom had seen the bad guys tie the good guy's hands behind his back, and then, the good guy would slowly work his hands free.

While being walked here, Tom had already tested the tightness of the ropes, and that beloved standby of adventure writers—the loosely tied rope—was not present. However from what he could feel of this, the rope was the same with which Tom and Old Joe—

He stopped and flinched before that thought. No. But he remembered the rope, all the more clearly because he was trying not to remember the baleful alligator eye, fixed in death, and the split cranium, with the brain missing.

The rope, he thought desperately, had been frayed, old, probably water-corroded, dropped there after service as a mooring rope.

Tom could probably—given the slightest protuberance in the walls, the slightest irregularity upon the walls—work his hands up and down and split the rope strand by strand. As tightly as it was tied, it was going to require him to rub his skin raw, too, but that could be endured, while this captivity had only one end.

They would either force him or the Great Sky Dragon to open the world gates. Tom had no idea how that worked—even if his mind insisted he did.

"Why did you let them capture you?" the Great Sky Dragon asked. He looked greenish, like someone who has been seriously ill and is not yet fully recovered.

Tom bit his tongue before saying, "Because I didn't have anything better to do just then," and instead said, "I believe they can hear every word we say, sir."

The Great Sky Dragon closed his eyes and groaned. He said something in Chinese. Tom heard it, and knew it had been Chinese, but he also knew what the words were, which surprised him a little. It surprised him even more when his words found the answer, and he said, his tongue tripping on the unaccustomed sounds, "I believe there is no language we can speak they cannot understand." He didn't know why, but he had a feeling it was so, a certainty that they wouldn't have put him and the old man together unless they meant to listen in, unless they meant to use what they heard. He was going to guess that the creature—Maduh?—hadn't been successful with the Great Sky Dragon, or not as successful as she hoped to be.

He remembered Rafiel's description of how Maduh had tortured her own cub to get the star beings' attention and cooperation. She would probably be ready to do worse to the Great Sky Dragon, and to Tom himself. But the problem was that her torturing the Great Sky Dragon ran the risk of killing him. Tom could see that in the greenish skin, the strange pallor, the look which proclaimed the old dragon was barely back from the dead, and might go back into the shadows at a touch.

And she didn't want to kill Tom, for the same reason. She meant to force one or the other of them to perform what she couldn't.

"She is afraid," the Great Sky Dragon said slowly, "that if she doesn't hurry, someone else will find a way to open the world gates. I gather the . . . star beings have other agents on Earth, and that she's afraid . . . You see, she's repented ever wanting to be enfleshed, ever rebelling against the ruling ones of her people. And she wants to make sure she recovers her rank among the bodiless ones. Which I gather was very high indeed."

For a moment Tom was alarmed, afraid the Great Sky Dragon had somehow read his mind, but as the Great Sky Dragon went on, Tom looked at him, and realized he was only talking because he didn't feel well and he had to talk to someone—to confide in someone.

"I inherited by accident. The three Great Sky Dragons before me died suddenly. It was a time of great turmoil on the banks of the Yalu River, long before recorded history. I— I had just started shifting. I was thirteen. I hadn't even been given over to the dragon people when I got all of my ancestors' knowledge. Only I never figured out how to unlock it. The separate . . . the two ways of doing it . . ." He shrugged. "Maduh—oh, yes, I've known of her a long time. She was one of the ones who came from the stars, the first ones. But not, interestingly, one they trusted with the codes to the world gate. Not a clan leader. Maduh says that my knowledge, what I received from my ancestors, the scrolls in my mind, are too old, too . . . too set in their pattern to unfold. The Pearl of Heaven can no longer open them. She says the bodiless ones told her they could open yours."

"Well, that would be nice," Tom said pleasantly. He'd gathered himself up with difficulty, because it proved to be quite difficult to get up with your hands tied behind your back. But he managed it, and stood, and looked around. The place where the Great Sky Dragon was, the wall seemed a little rougher. Not that any of it was very smooth. It was the sort of place you'd create, on the base of something that needed a sturdy foundation. Cement blocks, held together by poured cement, none of it neatened up—what Tom had found craftsmen doing work around the diner called "making good"—because no one was expected to come down here except repairmen. He found a particularly rough area, and stumbled to a sitting position against it, casually rubbing the rope binding his wrists down the whole length as he sat very close to the Great Sky Dragon, where he could talk to the old man in a quieter voice. Not that he thought this would prevent their being heard, of course. "That would be very nice, sir, but I no longer have what a friend very happily nicknamed the dragon egg." He felt a prickle at his eyes at hearing, in his mind, just how Old Joe had said it, but he kept his voice steady. "You see, when you woke up fully, it seemed to be gone."

The old dragon lifted his eyebrow at Tom. "Indeed?" Tom could tell that somehow this made the old man very relieved. He could imagine why. The old Great Sky Dragon wouldn't want a rival. And Tom thought in the unlikely event that they both survived this, he wouldn't want to be the man that the Great Sky Dragon viewed as a rival.

But he wondered if the dragon egg was truly gone. Perhaps it was. Tom didn't know. He didn't feel the connection he'd once felt to every dragon. He'd tested. That sense was gone. He might be able to reach them with effort. He hadn't made the effort.

Yet, he'd understood Chinese. And he felt...like he knew *more* than he'd known, that he now thought differently. He couldn't put his finger on the feeling, and frankly, he was afraid to. It must be that they—whoever *they* were—could read his thoughts, and use them against him.

As though to make things worse, the Great Sky Dragon said, "She got in my mind. Riffled about in there. I don't know exactly what she can see of my thoughts." He paused. "That's why I'm not sure she'd put you in here so she could listen to us. Not if she can see my thoughts."

Not unless, Tom thought, *she* can't *see mine.*

All the same, he positioned himself so that neither the Great Sky Dragon nor anyone looking at him from above—those boards on the floor of the dragon ride didn't seem to be too close together—could detect the gentle up and down movement of his hands behind his back, rubbing the rope against the rough wall.

He had some vague idea that if he shifted, he could get right out through the floor boards of the dragon ride, up, away, into the sky, away from this damnable trap. But to shift, his hands must be untied, or else, if the rope weren't completely rotted—and it wasn't—he risked cutting the dragon paws right off. It was thick rope; he could do that.

So he rubbed away at the wall, while his wrists, too, became rubbed raw. At any rate, he might end up without wrists in one form or another.

He could smell his own blood, sharp in the air, and the Great Sky Dragon was giving him the look a shifter gives someone who smells tasty. The Great Sky Dragon opened his mouth, but before he spoke, the door opened, and Maduh came down the stairs.

"How cozy," she said. Then she grinned at Tom. "But you're lying. I know you're lying, cub, because the star people say you're lying. They say you are full of the old knowledge, and that you know how to unlock the world gate."

Through Tom's mind, unwilling, went a list of places, a glimpse of certain places where the division between worlds was thin, and a vision of how it had been sealed. Symbols and mental tricks that would flip the areas right open flitted through his mind. It didn't shock him that the amusement park was one of those places, but he felt a sudden stab of fear. Had he just given away the secret?

But Maduh looked like sweet reason, as she sat down and said, "Now, are you going to cooperate, or will I have to turn your nearest and dearest against you? I can, you know." She looked indulgently at the Great Sky Dragon who looked paler than ever. "I can. Anyone who can turn into a dragon is mine to call. I got it from his mind. I can call your friend Conan. How would you like to fight him to the death? I'm sure you could kill him easily. From his mind"—she grinned at the old dragon with malice—"I gathered that the red dragon is made of poor stuff. But all the same, I'm going to guess you, soft and young as you are—" Tom thought she pronounced it as though it were culinary specifications. "You don't wish to have to kill your friend. Or do you?"

Tom didn't. Fortunately at that moment, he felt the rope part behind him. He had to change fast, and he wasn't even sure that he could. He didn't know if the blow to the head that they'd given him might not have killed him—however briefly.

He willed the change upon himself and felt, with relief, the horrible pain that came with shifting, and the cough that caused his body to twist.

Taking advantage of Maduh's momentary surprise, he ran past her and to the stairs. He was sure that she had locked the door behind her. But it would be nothing to the force of the shifting dragon, whose very mass, as it increased, would pop the door out like the cork of a champagne bottle.

Either that, or Tom would die crushed, from trying to shift in the narrow stairway.

⊶ CHAPTER 21 ⊷

Tom felt the door give before him, and he exploded upward, like a popcorn kennel leaving its envelope.

He had practice now thinking as Tom even in the dragon's body, and he was thinking that he needed to get away from here, fast. He needed to get reinforcements.

His wings felt abraded and bruised. His paws felt raw, and he could see spots rubbed clear of scales near his front paws. But he must fly. He spread his wings, to the blessedly cool breeze from the lake, thinking that it had stopped raining.

And then he realized he couldn't fly away. He must kill Maduh. If he didn't kill Maduh, she would hold the Great Sky Dragon hostage. Even if she couldn't make Tom come to heel, she knew that he could open the world gate. Her semitransparent friends from other worlds had told her so. And while she was alive, she would keep him on the spot. She would kill or hurt everyone he cared for. If she truly could control dragons through the Great Sky Dragon, she would bring them, one at a time or all together, against him. And if she couldn't, she would blackmail the triads to do it.

No, he had to fight her now or—

He heard her laugh from down in the hole in the ground. He

heard her say, "You can run away, dragon boy, but you can't get me, unless you come back in. And if you run away, I will find you. Sooner or later I will get you to do my bidding. I have been alive much longer. I am more cunning. I am smarter."

Tom realized he couldn't just flame down into the subbasement and make the whole structure catch fire, because then the Great Sky Dragon would die also. Which would mean Tom would have to step into the old dragon's shoes. And he had no intention of doing that.

And then he understood that he didn't need to flame Maduh directly. All he needed to do was make it so hot that Maduh, who was free to move, would have to come out. Oh, yes, it might also temporarily kill the Great Sky Dragon again, but it wouldn't incinerate him, which meant he could come back from that death.

And then, very carefully, Tom leaned into the underground chamber and aimed his flame at the cement wall. The idea was to heat the chamber. And if he could flame Maduh as she ran out, all the better.

He heard her scream. And then he felt something in his mind and knew she hadn't been bluffing. She had called the dragons.

Nick served bacon and eggs at the granite-topped isle in his kitchen. Conan fell upon them as if he hadn't eaten in ages. Rafiel hadn't shifted since the last time he'd eaten, and contented himself with a cup of coffee. Cas didn't seem to let his lack of shifting stand between him and a meal and neither did Nick. Rafiel found himself wondering if wolves burned an unusual amount of calories, because he couldn't understand how those two could eat like that and remain less than completely spherical.

At some point, Nick had gotten up and gone to the window. He'd mumbled something about Ben, whom Rafiel guessed must be his partner.

But what he'd said, when he'd twitched the curtain was, "What the hell?"

And when Rafiel went to take a look, he saw them—a lot of men, all of them Asian, dressed in a variety of styles, up front. On the lawn.

It looked like something out of a horror movie, and Rafiel thought, *It Came from the Chinese Restaurant*, then felt guilty about it. Aloud, he said, "The triads. Okay. Conan, get ready to take Rya—"

He never got any further. The guys up front all jumped as though they'd been poked. Without transition, they went into the coughing, writhing fits of shifting.

As Rafiel watched, his mouth dropping open, they grew wings. One took to the sky. Then another. A car driving down the street stopped suddenly, as the driver, no doubt, questioned his own sobriety and pulled over.

A plate clattered to the tile floor. Nick and Rafiel turned as one. Conan was writhing, coughing, his body contorted in agony.

Rya shouted, "Conan!" and started towards him, but he made a gesture to keep away, and yelled indistinctly, "I've been called. Not Tom."

He flung the door open, ran out. Rafiel ran to the window, and saw Conan shift and fly out with the other dragons.

Before they could say anything, a tall man, with reddish hair and impeccable shirt and tie, stood in the door. He was holding onto the door frame and looked...bug-eyed. He stared at them, found Nick and said, "Nick." And then, "I saw...there were... dragons?"

Nick rushed forward, "Darling. You were out too late. Dyce took you somewhere funny. Too much coffee? Come in. I'll get you a drink."

Kyrie saw Bea step back from the grill and bend in two. She looked at the other woman, alarmed. "Are you okay?"

Bea turned towards her with a face that was already less than human, elongating into the shape of a dragon muzzle, the eyes slanting oddly, the pupils vertical. "No," Bea said. "Shifting."

"What? Why?"

"Being called. Great Sky Dragon. Not Tom. Must...answer."

Without removing the apron or her clothes, Bea ran out back. When Kyrie followed, she found Anthony standing over a pile of rags, the torn George apron conspicuous among them.

Anthony looked into Kyrie's eyes. He didn't look shocked, or even curious. For a moment she wondered what he shifted into. Then he looked at Kyrie and said, "So, that's what's been going on, is it? Good to know. I thought I was imagining things."

"I—" Kyrie said.

"No, not now. I'm going to guess there's some big emergency afoot? That dragon-girl took off out of here like an express train.

Come and show me what's what and what orders are started, before you too take off on the wing."

"I don't—" Kyrie started, then decided there was no point. Either Anthony was a shifter, Anthony knew about shifters, or they'd driven Anthony nuts. Now was not the time to figure out which. "Okay," she said. "Come on."

Tom saw the dragons rushing towards him. The sky was blue and green and, here and there, golden and red with them. He thought he must take to the sky. He couldn't allow himself to be trapped down here. True, Maduh didn't want to kill him, but she would have no objections to having his wings burned off, or his feet bitten off, or both, so he couldn't escape.

He flapped his wings, to take to the sky, but too late realized he was surrounded by dragons. Dragons above him too.

He landed awkwardly on the nearest perch, the top of the wooden roller coaster—famed throughout the world, the part of him that was still Tom remembered. It creaked and swayed with his weight.

The other dragons clustered, flying around and around, making Tom dizzy. None of them landed on the roller coaster, though, and none of them got too close, because if they did, Tom flamed them.

Unable to get into flaming range, they started flaming the structure itself, trying to make it catch fire. Fortunately the wood was still too wet from the storm, but it would eventually catch.

Tom felt panic rise somewhere within him. He could choose to land, and allow the other dragons to capture him. He could try to fly, and allow the other dragons to pile on him and bring him down. Or he could become dragon flambé, on a bed of roller coaster.

Somewhere in his mind, something gave, something whispered, "Call the other shifters." And he felt in that direction blindly, like a man who gropes in the dark for a weapon with which to fend off sure death.

And he found that though his connection with the dragons was cut off—not by the Great Sky Dragon's wakening, but by whatever Maduh had done to the Great Sky Dragon—there was, still inside, a connection to other beings. Somehow, whatever the Pearl had done—was it because it, the artifact, was the last and he the last of such leaders?—had linked him to every shifter on

Earth. Every one of them. Including Kyrie, standing by the grill at The George. He could feel her, talking to Anthony. Anthony wasn't one of them, but most of the diner clientele, over twenty of them, were.

Tom reached out to every shifter within flying, galloping and loping reach. *Come,* he said, mentally. He knew the call was irresistible. *Come to me.*

Rafiel felt the call. He knew it was Tom. He could even see the scene. Tom, in dragon form, on a roller coaster track—what the hell was Tom doing on a roller coaster?—fending off masses of dragons, most of which were trying to set fire to the roller coaster. Tom needed help. Tom was asking for help.

There was a moment of Rafiel's body starting to twist and change. Around him, Nick and Cas and Rya were writhing in transformation.

But Rafiel had fought shifting before. And won. And had shifted before in response to a blind imperative and—

The scene of the mating in that glade came back to him, in shades of nausea, and helped steady him, helped his human mind take control. He would not shift.

Yes, Tom needed him. But the horrible blind call and the horrible need to shift weren't right and reminded him too much of the mating.

If he was right, Tom was at Riverside. Even a lion couldn't run there fast enough. The thing to do was get in the car and drive like hell, then shift—if it warranted it—and help Tom.

"Don't shift," he yelled to the other three. "We'll go by car and we—"

The other three were already shifted, but the canines did stop on the way out the door, and look at him. He sighed. "To the car," he said. "You guys can ride in the back. We'll get there faster that way."

He ran out the door, past Nick's partner, who had paled and was looking like he would either throw up or pass out. Nick was going to have great fun explaining this one. Rafiel wanted tickets.

But right then, he knew—knew with incontrovertible certainty—that Tom needed him desperately.

Fortunately, policemen could exceed the speed limit in an

emergency, he thought, as he opened the back door to his companions. Even if his police car was full of dogs.

Kyrie had just told Anthony that they'd need to put another batch of fries in, when she heard the call, loud in her mind. *Come,* it said. *Come to me.*

She could see Tom, in her mind, atop a roller coaster, surrounded by hostile dragons, even Conan. It couldn't be Conan. She refused to believe it was Conan.

Kyrie reached for the apron, started to remove it. It was the middle of the night. There were about twenty people at various tables, but only because people from the nearby warehouse district often stopped by before going to their shift. Jason and James were tending the tables, but had enough time to stop and talking to people.

She could go and—

"Oh, my God," Anthony said. "Mary, Mother of Jesus."

He was looking out towards the diner, and now Kyrie looked too. Everyone in the diner—or everyone she could see—was writhing and coughing, twisting and changing and shifting.

Jason, already in bear form, rushed to the door and hit it full with his body impact, before running, on ursine four down the street.

James ran out the door before shifting, to suddenly explode into the form of a majestic black Pegasus out on the sidewalk, under the corner light, and take to the sky. A car's brakes shrieked outside, and there was a sound of metal on metal, but Kyrie didn't even look.

There were wings, feathers, and fur... all of it moving in the same direction, out of the diner and northward.

When it was all over, there was only one old man in the corner, so absorbed in the crossword puzzle in his newspaper that he had seemingly seen nothing.

Perhaps he's deaf? Kyrie thought. *And dumb. And blind,* her mind added.

The call was still insistent in her mind, but her body wasn't shifting.

"Aren't you one of them?" Anthony asked, as he bent to pick up the plate he'd dropped.

"I..." she said. "I thought I was. I'm... I'm a panther, normally."

"Uh."

"I haven't been able to change. I think it's broken."

"Uh."

"But," she said urgently, "I can feel Tom is in bad trouble. At Riverside Amusement Park. And I must go help him!" The last was almost a wail.

Anthony looked confused. "Well... do you need to shift for that? Why don't you take a car and go? Seems to me a car would be faster than—"

Kyrie was already running towards the parking lot, but before she went out the door it occurred to her that either way at the end of this, there would be a lot of reverted-to-human-form shifters in need of clothes.

She went back to the storeroom. Once Anthony realized what she was doing—since he only had one customer left to mind—he helped her take the four bins full of used clothes they kept in there for emergencies and put them in the back of the remaining supply van.

She drove out from the parking lot carefully, because she had to avoid a couple of crashes. Fortunately there wasn't much traffic at this time of night, so there had been only one head-on collision on Pride Street, drivers stunned by the grotesquerie of animal bodies rushing out of the diner.

She drove carefully till she reached the highway to avoid the occasional latecomer—bear, badger, raccoon, harrassed-looking rat in a lab coat, and a very large and glossy bat flying low—crossing the street in front of her.

Tom was trying to pray the rosary, something that would have been much easier had he spent more time in his long-ago Catholic education days paying attention, and less time figuring out how to scam more treats from the elderly nun who ran the class.

The dragon portion of Tom was so panicked that his human mind couldn't get a fix on anything. The dragon was just flaming in every possible direction, trying to keep the dragons at bay. They wouldn't dare land, he figured.

But then he heard a creak up the track, and turning, realized that Maduh, in sabertooth form, was loping along the track towards him. And behind him, a smaller form of her, one that also bore some resemblance to the dreaded Dante Dire was zeroing in on him as well. They had him boxed in, and the dragons were above. He'd have to fly down, and then they could burn him at leisure. And then—

And then there were Pegasi. A whole herd of them, in every color a horse could possess. Tom, keeping an eye in front and one behind, could only see them peripherally, grey and pinto, brown and sable, swooping in.

For a moment he was confused about what these newcomers could do exactly, because, after all, the dragons could flame them, and then they would be roast horsemeat.

But the flying equines proved incredibly agile, moving with the ease of smaller things, and—seemingly—always out of reach of the flames, while managing to aim deft kicks at the dragons' heads. They worked together as though they'd trained at this, cornering the dragons, getting them down.

Which left Tom free to concentrate on Maduh.

She leapt through the air at his throat. He knew, without turning, that her cub would be leaping also. He flapped his wings, and felt the cub's claws just catch his back leg, while Maduh's teeth closed on air, and she fell down. For a moment, it seemed she would fall all the way to the ground, but she twisted at the last minute and fell onto the track, turning as Tom flew down to claw at her, and meeting his onslaught with claws that caught his foreleg and teeth that closed on his foot.

He screamed. He wanted to flame. But if he flamed, he was going to set the coaster structure on fire. And if he did that, then Maduh's cub would die also.

Tom shouldn't worry about the cub, of course. Even as he thought this, he felt the cub leap and catch his wing, rending it. Beneath them, on the ground, more and more animal shifters came and joined battle with the triad dragons.

Tom had to finish Maduh. He had to. The more he delayed and allowed her to control the dragons, the more casualties there would be.

Even from up here, he could smell the blood and hear the screams of pain. He could kill Maduh now, or risk massive casualties on both sides.

And he had friends on both sides.

Maduh was writhing. She was trying to shift. He thought she judged that Tom couldn't kill something that looked human. She would have been right—before.

Maybe I'll make an exception, he thought, as Maduh's face contorted, and her human-looking eyes stared back at him in challenge.

He thought of Old Joe who, really, had only wanted to continue dumpster diving and walking down memory lane at Dinosaur Ridge.

He thought of the baleful sad eye looking back at him, of the teeth that would no longer clack together with amusement.

He lowered his head and bit through Maduh's neck.

Her head fell down through the lattices of the roller coaster, completing its transformation from sabertooth to woman as it fell, the long blond hair fluttering in the wind like a flag.

Behind Tom, the cub screamed. Tom turned, just in time, to pin him with a claw across the belly, careful not to pierce the skin, to prevent him from diving down after his dam.

Below, the fighting still went on. Tom found that his connection to dragons had been restored and, realizing that he might have to make up a truly spectacular explanation for the Great Sky Dragon later, nonetheless chose to reach down and into the mind of the combatants on both sides. *Stand down*, he sent as a command. *Stand down.*

As the fighting stopped, and the two sides backed away from each other, he could see that there were some corpses on the ground. He hoped it wasn't permanent death for those.

He also could see, among the combatants, dark shadows, cowl-wearing beings, and he thought, *The creatures from the stars.* And then, *They feed on pain.*

He found he had shifted and was sitting atop the roller coaster, his arm across the feral shifter cub, who had also shifted, and who was lying on the tracks, looking up at Tom in pure terror.

Tom looked into his eyes, found total fear, then reached into his mind, into preverbal, confused thought, and commanded, *Stand down.* And also, *Hurt no one. No one in human form. And don't shift unless instructed.*

The creature made a pitiful sound of protest. He was no more used to orders than he was to instruction. But Tom had the force of the old shifters behind him, the first to come to Earth and to set order upon the chaos of the primeval world.

The young shifter looked up at him, and made a sound again,

one of submission, the sound of a confused young creature with no defenses.

Tom removed his arm carefully, and the young man—he looked all of maybe fourteen—pulled up his legs, shivering, to wrap his arms around them.

Tom stood shakily. One of his legs was torn from thigh to calf and pouring blood, but not fast enough for it to be the femoral artery. There was also a laceration across his chest, and the bite on his hand would probably make it impossible for him to cook for a day or two.

He offered his other hand to the young shifter. "Come on," he said, and put authority and images behind his words. He showed the shifter the stairs, and the way down them, then helped guide him.

The boy's hand felt calloused and rough and very, very sweaty in his, as Tom—limping—led him to the stairs and down. If he didn't have to bring the boy down, Tom thought he might just lay up there, on top of the roller coaster, and fall asleep.

But he *had* to get the boy down.

At the bottom of the stairs, he saw the big black Pegasus, the stallion who had led the pack, shift back into the form of James Stephens.

"Dark Horse?" Tom rasped at him.

James lowered his dark eyebrows defensively. "Yeah. And?"

"Thanks." Then, as he observed the group of men and women around James, "You know when you talked about the ponies, I always thought they were just...horses. You know, pets?"

James' face split in a smile. "Oh, there are those too. I own some at a friend's farm. But these are— We fly on weekends. We..."

"Yeah," Tom said, and walked past, leading the feral teen.

He walked past Jao, half of whose face was raw flesh, and who had a bite mark out of his shoulder. A bite mark from something big. He stopped. "The Great Sky Dragon is there," he pointed to the entrance to the space under the dragon ride. "I don't think he's very well."

And then, suddenly, Kyrie was running towards him, hugging him, not caring that he was naked and hurt and covered in blood. He put his free arm awkwardly around her, and she said, "Tom. Oh, damn it, Tom. You were in trouble and I couldn't change, and—"

"Shh," he said. "Shh. It's all right now."

✧   ✧   ✧

A call to Anthony on Kyrie's phone, told Tom that everything was all right at The George, kind of slow, though people were straggling in by twos and threes, some of them with big injuries.

"But *you're* all right?" Anthony asked Tom.

"Yeah."

"You sure? Kyrie was awful worried about you and she couldn't, you know, become whatever it is, cougar or whatnot, and go out to help you."

"She got here," Tom said. And up from his memory came the only reason a female shifter suddenly stopped shifting.

Most of the winged shifters took to the sky. Kyrie found clothes for most of the others, even if some of the women had to do with just one large T-shirt. A few of the shifters besides Kyrie and Rafiel had cars. The owner of the park, who turned out to be an elk shifter, dug up an ancient bus from somewhere, and some of the remaining shifters got into it.

"We'll need to come back," Rafiel said, looking exhausted, and holding onto Bea's hand, as though he feared she'd disappear. Bea and Conan were the only winged shifters who'd stayed around, probably because they were with people who couldn't fly. "I mean, sooner or later someone will find her corpse and call the police."

"I'll call," the owner said. "Later." Then hesitated. "Can we *not* have publicity? Look, this is my only income, and I—"

"Sure," Rafiel said. "We'll make up some story. Some animal. Komodo dragon has served us in the past. Not murder. Horrible accident."

"Before I go," Tom said, "there is a corpse, in the hut, under the bridge. It's an alligator. Can you wrap it in a sheet and bring it—" He paused confused. "Rafiel, how do we get an alligator cremated?"

"An— Old Joe? Damn."

"Yeah. He stayed in alligator form, after death."

"Oh. He shifted to human?"

Tom had nodded and looked at Maduh's cub, still clinging to him. "Like him," he said. "It happens when you're conceived in animal form."

"Damn," Rafiel said again.

"Yeah, but I don't want his corpse merely thrown away."

"No," Rafiel said. He looked pensive. "Look, it's probably

breaking all sorts of laws, but my cousin is an undertaker and has a crematorium. I'll talk to him."

"Oh, good," Tom said. "I figured we'd take the ashes to Dinosaur Ridge and let them go."

Rafiel nodded.

Rya came forward, with Conan and her father. Half of her father's scalp seemed to be missing, and there was a bloodstain on the T-shirt Kyrie had given him, but he looked at the young shifter and told Tom, "Conan says you made the young man there safe to be around. Conan says he could hear the orders. I couldn't because, well, I'm not that close to you, but if it's true, and if you can get him to obey me..." He looked at the young shifter attentively. "Can he learn?"

"I think so," Tom said. "If he were human it would be too late, but he isn't. Or not just human. He's a shifter. It's just she never tried to teach him. He followed her around, usually in animal form. I think it will be like teaching someone who is impaired, but he has a long time and I think he'll learn."

"Would you...do you think you could set it on him to obey me? The condo is awfully large, and I'm retired, and Rya is getting married and moving out, and...what the hell else am I going to do with myself?"

"I thought you were writing a novel?" Tom asked.

The man they had for years called the Poet shrugged. "It can wait. The thing is...shifters live a long time, right?"

"Yeah."

"So, there's time. And meanwhile, you know, I kind of ran out on raising Rya. My ex convinced me it was better if I left and...didn't embarrass them. So...this is my chance to raise a kid. It think I'll name him Mowgli."

Tom opened his mouth to protest, then thought it was no worse than Conan.

Before they left the park, Tom used a very old technique, yet a technique now quite within his abilities, to assemble all the shadow beings and send them back through a thin spot in the veil between worlds, a spot which he then sealed very firmly. But even as he did so, he could tell that it wouldn't stay sealed, that the Great Sky Dragon had been right. Now the star beings had found them, they were bound to try to get in again. And they had other ready and willing agents among humans. Yet Tom had the power to call all shifters. Which meant . . .

He swore softly.

Kyrie, who had watched him attentively while he made strange passes midair and did even odder things with his mind as the shadows from other worlds rushed backward through a greater shadow, now said, "How much are you still *you*?"

"I'm all me. I just know some very odd things. Let's go home, Kyrie."

Kyrie didn't want Tom to drive home but he did. She was surprised when he stopped by the drugstore two blocks from their house. They'd found his wallet in the space beneath the dragon ride, but all the same, she was puzzled, when he said, "I'll be right back," and dove out of the van.

He came back minutes later, carrying a bag. He took a small velvet box out of the bag and said, "I'll buy you a better one later, but right now, I want you to have this." He opened the box to show her an engagement ring in gold-painted plastic, with a cubic zirconia on top.

"What? Why?"

"Because you're marrying me."

If she weren't so tired, she'd have put more force into the outraged, "Thomas Edward Ormson, you—"

"No." His voice was very tired and very firm. "We own a diner together. We live together. You're my other half. I can't imagine living without you. We're going to get married."

"You're supposed to *ask*," she said querulously.

"It's not open to discussion. We're going to make legal what is already true."

"Damn it, if it's true, why bother?"

"Because," he said, and looked at her, very seriously. "Because I can't stand that you are not legally my wife. I want everyone to know—triads, clients, suppliers—that we belong together. That I belong to you."

She wanted to be mad at him, but she couldn't. She sighed. "You could still *ask*."

"Kyrie Grace Smith, will you marry me?"

"Can I say no?"

"No."

"Okay, fine. Then *yes*."

He laughed and kissed her and slid the cheap ring on her finger. Then he looked solemn and handed her the plastic bag. "When we get home, I want you to use that."

She looked in the bag. It was a pregnancy test.

The amazing thing, Rafiel thought, was not that the diner patrons looked very sheepish at nine a.m. the next day. The amazing thing was that neither the local paper nor the local TV stations, nor even one of the local blogs made any mention of the cavalcade of animals that had trooped through downtown.

True, one of the local morning DJs said something about almost getting run down by a bear headed for a bar dumpster, but that happened, anyway, now and then, in the Front Range.

He brought Bea to breakfast at the diner, and noted that Jason looked hungover when he took their order.

"So," Rafiel told Bea. "I'd like to continue seeing you..."

She looked hesitant. "It's very far away," she said. "Long distance relationships..."

"How many years do you have left?" he asked. "In college?"

"One," she said. "I'm in my senior year."

"We could get married," he said. "And I could visit. I have some savings. I can fly up every other weekend." Hell, judging from how happy his mother had been when he'd brought home a female guest last night, his parents would probably pay for it. He'd seen the glimmer of the hope of grandchildren in his mother's eye. It was a powerful force.

"We've only known each other a couple of days. How can you know—"

"I know," Rafiel said, and looked into her eyes, and found an echo there. "And so do you."

"Yes," she said. And sighed. "But it's so strange."

He shrugged. "When it's right, it's right. Don't worry about strange. You can come up here a few times, too. We should look for a place. We can't live in my parents' basement."

He became aware of a shadow over their table and, looking up, became aware of a middle-aged, vaguely Asian but much too tall and green-eyed man glaring down at them. "Bea," the man said. "Bea, what in hell do you think you're doing? I had to trace you out here, and I—"

"It's okay, Daddy," she said. "This is Rafiel. We're going to get married."

"Oh you are, are you?" The man reached down and grabbed the front of Rafiel's shirt hauling him to his feet. "I suppose this is the price required to leave me alone. Well, you can think again. I'm not going to have my daughter marry some triad member dragon shifter."

"I should hope not," Rafiel said primly, looking down at the hand on his shirt as though he were confused about why it was there at all. He looked up and into his future father-in-law's eyes. "I'm a lion shifter. And a police officer."

It was the sound that made Tom look up—or at least the lack of sound. The entire diner had suddenly fallen silent, and Tom turned to look and saw a middle-aged Chinese man enter. He was bruised, and he looked exhausted, but his glare had clearly caused the silence in the diner—his glare and the larger-than-life impression he made, even now when, logically, Tom knew he wouldn't be able to shift.

Tom stared, unmoving, while the Great Sky Dragon pulled himself up onto a stool. The man stayed quiet long enough that the noise in the diner started up again, a babble of voices just a trifle too loud.

He narrowed his eyes at Tom. Tom looked back. He deliberately did not sense the older dragon, did not use any of his new knowledge or his new powers. Internally he was trying to figure out how things would go. He came up with—and discarded—the idea of pretending he had lost all his powers and that the Pearl of Heaven had done nothing. But the Great Sky Dragon would have seen and sensed the call to the fight of every other shifter. And he was not a stupid man.

"How may I help you?" Tom said.

"You may tell me," the Great Sky Dragon said, "how we stand. Am I still the father of all dragons or—"

For just a second, Tom caught a glimmer of fear in the older dragon's eyes. *Oh,* he thought. Aloud, he said, "You are indeed the father of all dragons. I want no power of yours. I went a long way not to have it."

Dark eyes looked unblinkingly into his. "Why?"

Tom shrugged. "It is not part of my life plan to tell thousands of people how to live. I'd rather live...and be myself."

The Great Sky Dragon's mouth twisted to a wry smile. "You might not get to," he said. "The threat from the stars...that is, from other worlds—"

"Will be dealt with, if it becomes serious again. I understand the people from the stars think in a very long scale. It could be centuries."

The Great Sky Dragon inclined his head. "So you intend to let power go."

No, Tom thought. *I intend to let it stay. Stay untouched and unclaimed, until I need to claim it. Till then it can abide and let me be Kyrie's husband and a father.* But he just inclined his head in a half affirmative.

"Then," the Great Sky Dragon said, "we will not interfere with each other."

Oh, good. A noninterference pact, Tom thought wondering how long it would last. "That suits me."

"Very well then," the Great Sky Dragon said. He slid off the stool, heading out the door at a faster pace than his age and recent death should permit.

Tom cleared his throat and saw that Anthony was close by, looking at him with concern. He smiled reassuringly at Anthony and glanced over the diner. "So," Tom said, "I think that's Bea's father." He nodded towards the man sitting in animated discussion with Rafiel and Bea at a corner table. "I went over to bus the table next to it, and I heard him say something about his moving his vet practice to town."

"How good that would be," Anthony said. "It's not like this lot doesn't need a vet." His phone rang, and he fished in his pants. Then he pulled off his apron. "I'm taking three days off. My wife has started contractions."

"Right," Tom said, picking up the apron and putting it on. "Good luck."

He took Anthony's place at the grill and prepared several platters, then rang the little bell on the counter. Kyrie came to pick up the orders, and Tom smiled at her, "You're not doing too much, right?"

She glared at him. "I'm pregnant, not sick."

Tom opened his mouth to say morning sickness might come later, but before he could, a voice from near the counter said, "She's pregnant?"

Tom looked up and into the stunned face of his father. "Oh. Hi, Dad. Yeah. Kyrie is pregnant, but we were going to get married anyway, so..."

His father sat on one of the bar stools. He was frowning slightly, as though trying to solve a puzzle. "Is that dragon kitties?" he said. "Or kitty dragons? Will it be a litter?"

Tom looked up and down the counter. All three people at it were shifters. He sighed. "No. They'll be human. Children whose parents are different types of shifters aren't shifters at all."

"Oh." Edward Ormson looked ridiculously disappointed. He sighed. "No wings?"

"No," Tom said, repressively. "What will you have, Dad?"

His father looked at the menu. "Bowl of red," he said, following his custom of ordering in old diner lingo.

"Tomato soup? This early in the morning?"

"It's almost eleven," Edward Ormson said. "And can I have a grilled cheese sandwich on the side?"

exact feeling, while talking to Jao, as though they were speaking different languages. "Yes, Jao kept saying that it was my duty to look out for dragonkind or something like that. But I keep thinking that if... I mean, look, it's a lot like the Ancient Ones wanting to punish us for killing shifters, even though the shifters were killing other people. If it comes to that, if it comes to a choice..."

Conan nodded. "I'm not saying that you should do otherwise, Tom. I'm not sure what I would have done, and I was handed over to the Great Sky Dragon when I was a teenager. My parents would say I deserted him or something, the way I'm behaving." He looked up at Tom, and the way his eyes narrowed, Tom got the feeling Conan was getting a headache. "Look, they're going to try to get me to make you fall in line. You know that. You know what they've done to me before."

What they'd done to him included leaving him on his own, to come back from a severe burning all on his own. "And, Tom, I understand what you say—I left once, though I needed your help to leave—but...but they're going to keep pushing all of us until you do what they want."

Tom opened his hands in a show not so much of helplessness as of exasperation. "What do you want me to do?" he asked. "Do you want me to marry Bea, or, I suppose, any ten females, just to make sure I have a dragon son? Would you leave Rya to marry someone they picked for you?"

Conan made a face. "If it hadn't been for you," he said, "I wouldn't have had any choice. And I doubt I'd even have met Rya. But now? Now I can have Rya. Now I can... I know I can sing?" it was a statement, but it finished in a rising, interrogatory tone.

"You can sing," Tom said.

"Now I know I can sing, I couldn't leave Rya and... and music and go back, no."

"Well, I can't go back either," Tom said. "Particularly since I was never there."

"Tom, if it would be easier to pretend you and I have broken up, just pretend until, you know, we figure this out," Kyrie said. She bent to pick up Not Dinner and pet him. Tom couldn't see her expression, but he didn't need to see her expression. He knew how to answer that.

"Don't even joke," he said. "If they think they can make me